Hoss

Rebel Wayfarers MC
Book #7

MariaLisa deMora

Edited by Hot Tree Editing

Front cover image by Michael Meadows Studios

Model: Benjamin J. McKee

Cover design: Melissa Gill @ MGBookcovers and Designs

First Published 2015

ISBN 13: 978-0-9904473-8-2

DEDICATION

The truth is, everyone is going to hurt you. You just got to find the ones worth suffering for. — Bob Marley

For the mothers and fathers who hold their children first in their hearts. Your babies are truly blessed. They will never wonder if they are loved, and that is the greatest gift of all.

Contents

ACKNOWLEDGMENTS

So many folks have asked where the ideas about the characters come from. The way Mason and Mica invaded my dreams should be a known component by now, but for this book, the idea for the characters began as short descriptive notes in my phone. I wasn't certain where we were going, and the jotted bits and pieces were more tentative ideas than a story, or even an outline. Then, one night, I was attending a local professional hockey game in Fort Wayne and found my Hope.

During the first period of the game, just before intermission, the good folks in the media room flashed a picture up on the overhead scoreboard screens. It was the 'Oblivious Cam,' where they target someone who's not paying attention, and then put a timer on them until either they look up and see they're on the big screen, or someone around them brings it to their attention. Laughter and embarrassed blushes typically follow as they wave at the camera before the next hapless victim splashes across the wide screens.

This time it was a chick, a younger yet mature woman. Definitely not a kid, this gal was studiously bent over her phone, which isn't an uncommon sight when you're out and about, or hell, at some family dinners these days...but this was a public display of what looked to be a troubling moment in her life. The lines her body drew in the stadium seat were taut, stressed, and when she finally glanced up into the camera, her features were pale and she appeared deeply shaken. Something profound was going on with her; we were witness to a moment that might define her life, and it struck a chord inside me.

For the next fifteen minutes, in my mind, she became Hope, Mercy's sister. From what I saw with the chick on the screen, I knew Hope had to have a secondary reason to show up in Fort Wayne. She wouldn't uproot her little family just to find Mercy and introduce herself. Now, I just had to find out what that reason was.

Frantic tapping on my phone ensued and I wrote the opening for the first scene from the book sitting in my seat behind the home bench, patiently waiting for play to resume. In my head, I was sitting rinkside at hockey practice alongside a single mom and her beloved son, their lives teetering on the edge of disaster.

My Hope and Sammy edged their way into life that night, winding their way into my heart, and eventually finding their way into Hoss' as well. So there you go, now you are in the know! That, my friends, is how Hope and Sammy came to be.

I want to throw out a loud 'thank you' to photographer Michael Meadows for helping me find the perfect image for the cover. I believe Benjamin McKee, the model you see in the picture, makes an absolutely phenomenal Hoss, and meeting the man was such a pleasant surprise! So sweet and kind, he was quite patient with the starstruck author taking up so much time in the middle of an event in Nashville. Thank you, Ben. Mattered more than you know.

To my alpha readers: Thank you for not killing me. I thought I needed to just throw that out there. I know I'm demanding and hard to please, but with every story I nervously hand off, the connection we build is more resilient, stronger, and you help make me better. Hollie, Kristen, LeeAnn, Kay, Kori, Shay, and my own MirandaPanda – thank you for this, too.

Dyana, for the late night (or early morning, however you look at it) chats about all the important bits, you have my endless thanks. It helps to have a skilled and compassionate nurse in my back pocket, yeah?

Becky, Kayla, and the HTE betas, thank you for your work and feedback, and to Melissa Gill for helping bring my cover idea to life.

As ever, I want to thank my personal motorcycle men, members of MC, RC, and LE clubs in Michigan, Indiana, Ohio, Texas, Nevada, New Mexico, and Chihuahua. As much as a woman and a citizen can, I get it. That brotherhood piece that you all hold so close. The way you are brothers underneath the patch, and even when you disagree, it is with the knowledge that every man who put in prospect time has your back. Never alone, even if life ain't no fairytale. I hope I did that bond justice with this story. I'm sure you'll let me know if I messed up, just be patient with me, yeah? Love you all so hard. You can always count on my affection erection! Muuwah. <3

~ML

1. Crashing

Hope

Distracted, Hope noted Sammy's coach shouting at the kids and how his tone registered as encouraging rather than derogatory, which was good. It hadn't been long since she pulled Sam from his old coach, because he did nothing but scream at the kids about how bad they were. Evidently, the man hadn't gotten the memo that negative reinforcement went out of favor decades ago because it simply didn't work with eight-year-olds. Or twenty-eight-year-olds. Plus, his brother had been a total douchecanoe. Her fingers plucked nervously at the fraying seam of her hoodie, and she scrunched up her nose when she saw she had unthreaded another four inches. One more thing to repair. She checked her phone again, nearly six o'clock. Surely, it would be there by six.

There was a thud on the Plexiglas barrier in front of her and she looked up, startled out of her thoughts. Sammy stood there by the boards, frowning at her, and then reached down below the level she could see to help his teammate up from the ice and they skated away, side-by-side. He had evidently gotten in a good hit and she had missed it. Again.

Back to the phone. Three minutes after six. Unlocking the screen, with now-shaking fingers, she tapped the app for her bank, quickly logged in and then felt her shoulders sag. Still a negative balance. If her deposit didn't hit the account soon, overdraft fees would eat up most of it, and she would have reentered the destructive cycle she had vowed never to have to deal with again. When the local college semester had ended, as usual, students scooped up most of her part-time and cash-paying jobs. That left her with only her single primary job as receptionist for the trucking company, which meant digging out of the money hole would be nearly impossible this time, and if her rent check bounced again, she knew they were toast.

If only Gibson hadn't been such a jackhole, she thought, flicking her gaze up in time to see Sam deke around a slower kid, driving towards the goal. She tensed, waiting and ready to burst to her feet in applause, when the goalie shifted to the side of the crease and blocked his shot. Around the curve of the rink, she heard another mother applauding her own son and briefly smiled at the support the small pad-covered goalie enjoyed. Easing back into her seat, she looked down at her phone again and tapped the update button. No change.

Gibson had been Sammy's and her roommate, but moved out last week with his share of the back-rent still in his checking account. "Why would I pay for something when I'm not even going to be here?" had been his answer when she dared to ask for the money. Even when she pointed out he had lived there during the rent portion she was asking for, from that moment on, he studiously ignored her. Arrogantly walking around and past her, he loaded his car and was driving away within two hours of their non-conversation.

Why does my life have to suck so hard? she wondered, locking the phone and shoving it deep into the pocket of her jeans. Bleakly, she watched Sammy as he skated up and down the sheet of ice, executing all the drill demands of the coach. No apartment would mean they would be back in the car for a minimum of two months while she saved for the deposits needed to rent again. *He deserves better,* she thought, looking at the grimly determined expression on his face as he bent over for a quick breather, head up, eyes on the coach, absorbing every word about this game he loved.

He was the one thing in her life she would never wish to change, the only good decision she ever made. She smiled and gave him an exaggerated thumbs-up when he looked her way, and this time, she saw a glint of a smile behind the faceguard on his helmet. She watched as he set his hands, enclosed in those ridiculously oversized, stinky gloves, even more doggedly on the stick, waiting for the puck to drop in the faceoff. *God, I love him so much.*

Pulling her phone out, she went through the routine of unlocking and logging in and found her balance had fallen further into the negative range. Clicking on the notice for more details, her mouth dropped open in shock. The bank had taken out twenty more dollars, and the information said her deposit—her paycheck—had been returned as Insufficient Funds. Her paycheck had bounced.

Scrambling to dial her boss, she found herself squeezing her eyes shut tightly, muttering under her breath, "Please, please, please, please." Hearing tones instead of ringing, while not entirely unexpected, still shattered her remaining composure. "No. No. No no, *nono, nonono,*" she panted. "This can't be happening." She hadn't worked for the trucking company long, but they seemed solvent. In funds. In the black. Seemed to know what they were doing. She disconnected and dialed the other number she had for the office. After waiting for what seemed an interminable amount of time, she again heard the tones. "We're sorry, but the number you have dialed is no longer in service."

The barrier in front of her boomed again and she looked up to see Sammy, head down, elbows flying as he dug for the puck at his feet, trying to keep the other two boys from getting it. His face was rounded, and he wore glasses, but in his case, looks were entirely deceiving, because he was the toughest kid she knew. Sure enough, he came out

3

of the scrum with the puck, agilely dodging around the net and neatly tucking it underneath the goalie's leg pads.

He glanced her way and she knew the disaster in the works must have shown on her face, because his gaze stuck on her. Instead of celebrating his goal, the grin faded from his face and he frowned, his chin slowly tucking down into his chest. He glanced up at the clock by the press box and mouthed, *Ten minutes?* She nodded and he skated towards the coach, leaving her chewing on her lip as she waited for practice to be over so she could let her son down. Again.

She stood and walked to the entryway, waiting for him so they could walk out to the car together, heading to what was still home. For now.

"What are we going to do, Mom?" Seven words. All it took to break her heart. Those words uttered in her sweet boy's voice, asking her if she could make this right, if she could fix it, keep them together. She knew it was his greatest fear, because they had seen it happen to families. Kids got farmed out to grandparents or aunts and uncles as parents traveled out of state for work, and before you knew it, all ties were broken.

Even in the shelters, she and Sammy worried that somehow, through some unknown rule or law, they would be separated, because they didn't have the safety net of family. She had worked hard as heck over the past eight years to make sure it never happened. Yet here they were, standing right back at the mouth of the drain, watching the slow, inevitable failure come closer.

"I got this," she said with a grin, wrinkling her nose at him. In the apartment, they were sitting in their regular places for dinner, side-by-side on the floor, plates on the coffee table, faces turned towards the dark TV. After dinner, she would put in a DVD for him, but during the meal, she insisted on conversation, even if Gibson—*the jackhole*—had sold their dining room table.

"But if your paycheck was bad, it means there's no money. Are we gonna hafta move?" His voice didn't quaver, didn't give any sign of the distress she knew he must've been feeling. *He is way too old for his years*, she thought, leaning over to pat his knee reassuringly.

"It's probably just a mistake. I'll drive over tomorrow while you're at the library for story time and talk to my bossman. He'll get it all straightened out," she said, but he didn't look convinced.

"You could call Dad." He offered this solution quietly, gaze fixed firmly on his bowl.

She knew his belief that his dad would be willing to save them was her fault. She had determined long ago to never be the kind of woman who laid the entire blame at the feet of the absent parent, especially since, while he was also a jackhole, it wasn't entirely voluntary. That meant she bit her tongue more often than not when Sammy brought up his paternal parental unit, as she referred to him in her head. Although, sometimes that reference was sperm donor, whichever fit her mood at the time.

Only a few years ago, Calhoun Suiter had seemed to be the answer to her prayers. After an entire childhood spent in a stifling religious household, she had simply wanted to escape her hometown, find her way out from under her mother's thumb and away from her father's influence. She was fresh out of high school while Cal was several years older, and he promised her everything.

She had watched out the window of the car as the curtains in her parents' bedroom twitched only once as she drove away with him, a suitcase of her clothes in the trunk. A few weeks later that promised 'everything' fell apart when his hands sent her to the ER.

Flowers and fresh promises bought her trust again, but when it happened a second time, and then a third, she knew she couldn't stay with him. Especially not when she found out the news. Not once she knew she was pregnant. She and Cal didn't have a relationship worth saving, not at the expense of a child's welfare.

Out of options on that front, she did what she felt she had to do. Sharing with her parents about the child was the hardest thing she had ever done. Far harder than telling them she was going to live in sin with Cal. A baby was...permanent. Life-altering. A life-long commitment to love and cherish a little being. Seated on a stool in front of their fireplace, she had watched her mother's face crumple into tears, saw her father's grow rigid and foreign as he sat in his chair, looking at her.

That was the first time she learned she had a sister. A half-sister, it seemed, but still a sibling she had never heard a single word about. Her father didn't want to discuss the details, but as best she could discern, he and Mom had broken up and he had a one-night fling. Her parents patched things up the next day, and were married and happily pregnant within two months, but his single night of fun had far-reaching ramifications in the form of a daughter.

Her name was Mercy Harris, raised in Birmingham, not twenty miles from her own family home in Gadsden. Mercy and Hope, one daughter acknowledged, one ignored. It seemed babies didn't have to be a commitment after all, not in his book. Her respect for her father took a nosedive that day, learning about this side of him. She wondered at his callous attitude, because after hearing him preach over and over about how precious babies were, she couldn't understand how he could have turned his back on an innocent child.

When she asked him about Mercy, he sneered and told her, "You should look her up. You evidently have a lot in common." By that point in the conversation, she had been crying hard, and through her tears, she stupidly asked, "What?" thinking, *Other than the obvious, Daddy?* He retorted with the harshest words he had ever spoken to her, "You're both whores, aren't you?"

She hadn't responded, hadn't been able to, as if from far away, hearing his ultimatum and shaking her head vehemently. Packing her things had not taken long, and within thirty minutes, the entire scene had played out and she was in her car, tears rolling down her face as she drove aimlessly around, trying to escape the memory of his words.

Stopping at a friendly-looking diner in Birmingham, she sat in a booth alongside the big window in the front. Nursing a glass of sweet tea, she embarrassedly shook her head and turned away every time the waitress approached her. After a couple hours, the owner came out and gently offered to let her clean in exchange for a meal of scrambled eggs and toast, and with trembling lips, she accepted.

"Call me Mac," he told her gently when he placed the plate of hot food in front of her.

She looked up at him through tear-clumped lashes and said, "Hope." Mac had laughed and told her it was a fitting name for a beautiful young lady. His kindness pulled the first smile from her that she had felt on her face for days.

That had been the first of many nights spent in her car. Nervously not sleeping, she parked in a shopping plaza lot until about three in the morning, when security ran her off. Crying, she drove around until she found what looked like another likely spot to sit until dawn.

Over the next days and weeks, she fell into a comfortable routine for an uncomfortable situation, arriving at the diner in the evening after most of the customers had finished their meals and left, making their way to their homes and families. In those quiet hours, working alongside Mac she helped him clean and prepare for the next day's menu, eagerly taking up all the time he could spare for the human connection and conversation she found herself as hungry for as the the simple fare she felt was deserved for the work. She would never let Mac do as much as he wanted, nor his wife Nelly, the waitress with whom she became friends. She rotated parking spots, learning the schedules for the patrols, finding the dark corners most often overlooked, where she could get a couple hours of uninterrupted rest.

One job led to another, and she did what she had to do to get by. She cleaned the offices at a hotel in exchange for the use of a shower twice a week in one of the unoccupied rooms. Learned how to wash truckers' laundry to earn a few dollars in cash, and straightened shelves in a small grocery store for spoiling fruit and day-old pastries. And, with the passing of time, with the natural demands of life ignoring the numbness in her heart, her belly grew.

She often thought it didn't seem possible this had become her life. Only six months ago, things were so different. Back then, she had a warm bed with a frilly, ruffled comforter and a door she could lock to keep her parents from snooping. So many snacks in the refrigerator she could stand with the door open and look for five minutes, deciding what to eat. Expensive, scented shampoo to soften and tame her wild, curly hair.

Now, with the season churning deep into winter, she often wore all the clothing she owned in an effort to stay warm. These days, she was happy if she had a meal at all, much less a hot one, and she had stolen baggies filled with liquid soap from gas station bathrooms to wash her hair.

Then, Cal found her.

She hadn't seen him in months. He looked shocked when he located her, sleeping in the backseat of her car, waking her with a steady tap-tap-tap on the window over her head. When she saw who it was, she screamed and scrambled to the other side of the car in terror, staring at his face peering curiously at her through the glass. "Hope?" His voice came through muffled and distant, but no less frightening now than the last time she had heard him, shouting right beside her ear as he choked her unconscious.

"Oh, my God. You are. You're pregnant." His incredulity seemed absurd in the moment. He evidently found it more surprising she was a viable, reproducing female than that she was a girl who had been semi-affluent a few months ago, now resorting to eating handouts and sleeping in her car. "Your father told me, but I didn't believe him." Tap-tap-tap. "Open up, Hope."

She shook her head, gaze flicking to the front seat, where the keys hung on a hook under the ignition. Tap-tap-tap. Headshake. "Hope." Headshake. Tap-tap-tap. "Hope, open up." Headshake.

She climbed over the console between the front seats, arranging her limbs into the driver's seat behind the wheel, head down, hair curtaining her face and narrowing her focus to her next move. Clinically, she examined her hand as she reached out, trembling fingers clasping the keys. She had barely begun to push them into the ignition when the glass beside her head exploded inward. She didn't even have time to scream as he pulled her through the window, jagged corners of safety glass gouging routes through the flesh of her back.

It was one of the dreaded security patrols who saw him, saw her on the ground in front of him, saw his feet swinging forward and back, fists falling heavily as he bent over to reach her.

He had determinedly tried to kill the baby cradled in her womb. The child she birthed alone only days after the attack, their sole hospital visitors Mac and Nelly. Samuel, the child she loved more than life itself.

The judge had made Cal sign over all his rights, even before she had the baby. Done in lieu of a paternity test, to be conducted at a time of her choosing after the infant was live birthed, the results of which would not void the writ and decree of attempted manslaughter nor restore his rights. The legal language was straightforward, his lack of authority over the baby clear, which was good, because it meant he would never be able to take Sammy from her. Not even now, when she knew things were about to go to crap. Again.

If she had her way, Sammy would never know what a jackhole his father—*the sperm donor*—was. For eight years, she had given him two birthday presents each year, one with a bright, fancy homemade card saying 'From Mommy.' And one with a small folded piece of paper, with a pencil-written 'Dad.' Christmas time was treated the same, and even though he was older now, she still refused to let Sammy learn everything came from her. So now, in his mind, of course his oh-so generous father could become their savior.

"I got this, baby boy," she said with a smile she knew he would never believe. "I *so* got this."

"But what are we going to do?" He stirred the rings of noodles in his bowl, pushing them under the tomato sauce with his spoon, waiting for them to bob back to the surface and forcing another round of peek-a-boo pasta. "If we have to leave then we're in the car, right? Dad wouldn't want that."

She heard the unplanned words coming out of her mouth, as surprised as he was when she told him, "We're going to go find my sister, your Aunt Mercy, and see if we can stay with her."

Sam twisted in place, looking at her to see what the joke was, the skin around his eyes tight in a way that caused her stomach to twist painfully. "I don't...I didn't know I had an aunt."

She reached out, smoothing his thick, blond hair back off his forehead. She licked her thumb and grinned, saying, "Hang on. You got a little something—" wiping the dab of tomato sauce from the corner of his mouth. "You do have an aunt. We'll meet her together, okay?"

***

Hoss

He stood in the noise and chaos of a huge family backyard barbecue, a tolerant expression on his face. Looking around, he smiled to see the expansive space bursting with people he knew and trusted. Loved. The air filled with the cries and shouts of children, their toned limbs poetry in motion as they ran back and forth, sunshine bright and gentle on their faces. He saw the scene in splashes of color: the brilliant yellow of a little girl's dress imposed against the dark green bushes near the house, the radiant red lounge chair set with the faded brown fence.

As long as Isaiah Rogers could remember, he had always been this way, seeing split seconds as frozen windows into each experience, ways he could hold onto the moment beyond the instant as it happened. It was a frustrating trait for his father, because he would get lost in the scenes in his head for hours, instead of finishing whatever chore had been his assignment for the day.

Growing up, their family farm had supported them comfortably enough, and while they weren't rich by any stretch of the imagination, he never felt second-class or poor. When they took the drive into town, there were always folks who would walk out of their way to visit with Pop in the diner or store. They sought out his wisdom, friends and neighbors alike. Then, come Christmastime, their family would chip in with the rest of the community to help the church put together baskets for those 'less fortunate.'

That's always how his mother would term it, not that the ones needing assistance were poor, or destitute, or lazy, but that they were less fortunate. "There, but for the grace of God," she would say as she packed a box full of home-canned goods, handing him the blessing and bounty from their garden with a charge to deliver it safely.

Now, Isaiah was privileged enough to stand in the midst of a group of people with the biggest hearts of anyone he had ever met. Everywhere he looked in this big yard, he found friends he knew without a doubt would die for him. Emotional riches such as he had never seen, swirling around him everywhere.

"Hoss." He heard his road name called and turned his head, smiling to see Bingo seated in a recliner perched in the middle of the yard, kids ebbing and flowing around that firmly placed promontory. In his mind, he mixed pigments, using a palette knife to spread it thickly on the canvas. He knew when he returned home tonight he would be sketching out the idea of yet another lighthouse of a particular shade of gray to match the bushy beard the man wore proudly on his face.

"Yeah, brother?" he responded, walking across the grass, the heat of the sun beginning to soak through the black leather of his vest. Hoss was the vice president for the Fort Wayne chapter of the Rebel Wayfarers motorcycle club. He had come many miles since leaving Alabama behind in his rearview mirror. Now, with these men, he finally felt the strongest sense of home and family he had since leaving the farm and deciding to make his own way.

Reaching down, he grasped Bingo's hand, careful of the wounds from the recent IVs. "How you feelin', old man?" he asked.

"Good enough...for a tired old bastard who just had half his lung yanked out his motherfucking back." Bingo grimaced and shifted in the chair, which had been brought out to the yard from the house in the hope he could rest comfortably while still being part of the party. "Kane," he called with a frown, "get your sister off that slide."

"I'll get her," Hoss said, walking over to scoop Gilda up before she fell headfirst off the ladder. Without having to think twice about it, when Bingo's younger sister died a few years ago, the man had taken responsibility for her children. All nine of them. The club jokingly called them Bingo's tribe. Now with the diagnosis of, and resulting treatment for lung cancer, he and the kids had moved in with another member and his old lady, Jase and DeeDee. Hoss grinned, thinking if Jase got his way, soon he would be more official than just her old man. "Got you," he said, tickling Gilda and smiling to hear her sweet squeals. Setting her feet on the ground, he watched with a smile as she ran off towards the women, prattling about "Hoth."

"You like kids." He heard the voice and frowned, not having expected to see her today.

"That a question, woman?" He turned around, gaze sweeping up and down Mercy's small frame. He was glad to see she had toned down her usual wardrobe, in a concession to the setting. "Deke ain't supposed to be here, hon."

She wrinkled her nose, looking down for a moment. "I didn't come here looking for him."

"Bullshit." He laughed. "That want is written all over your face. Prez needed him to take care of something, but he might be by later." Looking around, it didn't pass unnoticed by him that, out of all the women present at the party, she was the only one standing near the men, not clustered into hens' groups chattering about kids and schools, neighborhoods and family. Shaking his head, he slipped his arm around her. "Darlin', you didn't expect any different, did you?"

She scoffed, and then looked down at the grass again. "Not really. I hoped some, because DeeDee's usually cool." She shrugged, leaning into his side. "It's okay. I know my place."

He sighed again, frustrated at the hurt she kept heaping onto her own plate. "You need to decide what you want, woman. Two years ago, you wanted to fuck every member you could, regardless of them having family or an old lady. I told you then it would come back around and bite you in the ass, but you didn't want to hear it. Not ten months ago, you set your sights on dancing at the strip joint. You're doing that, staying out of the clubhouse, finally doing right by yourself. Now, what, you looking for a rag and an old man?"

Before she could answer, there was a disturbance from near the house, and as soon as Hoss saw who had arrived, he winced. She unwrapped her arm from around his waist and smiled up at him, her expression fragile and sad. "Looks like that's my cue." Rising on her tiptoes, she gently kissed his cheek. "Night, Hossman. Shiny side up."

Wordlessly, he watched her walk away, edging around the groups to the side gate in the fence. With a quickly lifted hand, she waved goodbye, her gaze pausing for a moment on the tall man who had walked in, his arm wrapped around a thin blonde woman. Hoss shook his head again as he saw Mercy swallow hard then pull the gate closed, cutting off her view of Deke standing with his latest club whore.

***

"Nope, she ain't here," he said again, frowning at Deke. "Already asked and answered, fucker. You lookin' for a different reply?" It was the third time he had asked, and with each negative response, his brother became a little more agitated.

Slurring his words, Deke shook his head and said, "Saw her fuckin' car in the fuckin' goddamned street. I know she's here." He lifted his face, raising his voice to a shout as he yelled, "Where the fuck's Mercy? Bring out the whore." Raising the beer in his hand to take a drink, he gulped open-mouthed at the liquid, pouring half the bottle down his throat before digging into his back pocket and pulling out a flask, taking a healthy swig from that, too. Grimacing at the bite of the liquor, he offered some to Hoss, shrugging and mumbling when it was turned down.

Hoss looked over to Slate for help, but the Fort Wayne chapter president looked away, shrugging and shoving his hands in his pockets. "Shit," Hoss muttered, turning back to face Deke. "Like I told you, brother, she ain't here. She was here, but she left."

"Why the hell'd you let her go, man? She's a fun time." He shoved at the blonde who had been plastered to him since arriving at the party. "She never tells the brothers no." He staggered and Hoss reached out, pushing him against the house so he wouldn't fall. "Tells me no, but she's a pretty pussy. Always gets me hard. Just lookin' at her makes me hard. Not like this bitch."

He pulled out the flask again and drank deeply then followed it by another long drink of his beer. Hoss watched with a frown as the blonde rolled her eyes and walked away, pulling out a phone, probably to call for a ride from a friend.

Deke didn't even notice she had left; he was still looking around the backyard. "Always tells me no. Mercy me, she's pretty. You sure she's gone?"

"Yeah, brother. She left soon as you got here." He heard a brittle laugh and looked over, seeing the blonde had already latched onto the arm of one of their prospects. Maybe if Hurley were interested, she wouldn't need that ride after all.

"Whadaya mean?" His slurring more pronounced, Deke fumbled at his beer bottle, nearly dropping it on the patio.

"I mean she saw you show up with Rapunzel there and left." Hoss shrugged, and then regretted his bluntness when he saw first hurt then anger cross Deke's features.

"Well fuck 'er, then. Jus' fuck 'er." He listed sideways and Hoss stepped to stand beside him, pulling one of Deke's arms over his shoulders.

"You wanna fall down, or sit down, you useless piece of meat?" Hoss winced when he heard the voice, half-turning with Deke.

"Prez," Deke said with a wide grin. "I din know you 'er here. Yer a goo man. I like you."

Hoss gave the man approaching them a chin lift in greeting, for about the hundredth time critically cataloging the features of Davis Mason, national president of the Rebels. He was a hard man, and it showed in his face with a firm, chiseled chin and sharp cheekbones. The man's eyes were one of the most fascinating things about him. Hoss had spent hours trying and failing to reproduce the exact shade of grey,

15

mostly because it changed depending on the man's emotions and attitude. Light grey when he was laughing, with only a small, dark ring around the pupil, darker grey when things were more serious, and a stark, steely, brilliance showed in them when things were intense. Right now, they were on the lighter side, and Hoss sighed.

"Yet, here I am," Mason said. "Hoss, need some help?"

"I was thinking of just letting the bastard slide down the wall. Maybe take bets to see how long it'd take him, see if he left a snail trail." Hoss grinned and nodded. Mason gripped Deke's other arm, and together they guided him into the living room of the house, positioning him at the end of a couch and letting him drop backwards onto the cushions.

"Snail trail." Mason snorted. "We should call Marko, get a patch made quick, and tell Deke it's his new club name."

Hoss grinned at the thought and then laughed. "Yeah, but then I'd have to listen to him bitch about it for a long-ass time, so...yeah, naw."

"What set him off?" Mason rolled his shoulders. "I know he's been volatile for a while, ever since shit went down with Gunny, but he looked okay when he got here."

"Found out Mercy wasn't here." Hoss shrugged again, thinking he had done a lot of that tonight.

"She is here, man. I talked to her, wanted to find out how she was handling things after all the shit abuse she took from Birdy." Mason looked around the room, leading the way back to the kitchen and the sliding doors that opened into the backyard. "Where the hell did she go?"

"Whores and old ladies, you know about how well they mix, Prez." Hoss accepted a beer from Jase, waiting to see if Mason wanted to continue the conversation.

"Not at all, is what you mean." Mason shook his head ruefully. "She seems a decent enough gal, just took her a while to find herself." Looking around, he called Jase back over with a chin lift and asked him, "Hey, Captain, did DeeDee mention she was unhappy Mercy was here, man?"

Jase, road name of Captain, hadn't been patched into the Rebels for a long time, but he had been around the club for a couple years. Through that association, he had been exposed to the life. It also meant he met DeeDee, Mason's cousin and manager of Slinky's, the club's strip joint here in Fort Wayne. Jase shook his head at Mason's question, walking back to the grill and flipping a row of burgers. "No, she made sure Mercy knew the invite was for real. We thought it would be a good way to make her feel comfortable around us again. After what went down with Birdy, you know? On the plus side, DeeDee thought it also might help put Sharon a little more at ease having Mercy here."

Hoss shook his head. Things in the Rebel family were always complicated, but over the past year, life had twisted in strange and unusual ways. Mason was their national president, and DeeDee was Mason's cousin. Jase had a sister named Sharon. Jase and DeeDee were together, and Sharon worked at Slinky's, as did Mercy. A Rebel named Gunny had fallen in love with Sharon, binding the Spencer family even more tightly to the club. *Round and round the wheels go*, he thought.

The abuse he referred to was a bad beating Mercy took at the hands of a rogue member. It had required weeks for her to heal enough to go back to work, and the club had taken care of her during that time. *Fucking Birdy*, Hoss thought, looking down at the grass along the edge of the patio, the bright green now tattered, ground into the dirt, individual blades bruised from the men who carelessly strode over them.

"Why?" Jase asked idly, flipping another row of burgers.

"No reason." Hoss hurried to fill the gap, waiting for Mason to call him on the little lie. He didn't want this first club event in Jase and

DeeDee's new home to be marred by any sense of regret or remorse on DeeDee's part. He knew how serious she took her role at Slinky's and she would be devastated if one of her 'girls' had been compelled to leave because she felt unwelcome. "Deke's piled up on your couch sleepin' some shit off, man. Heads up, he is one ugly hangover. Might want to start coffee strong and early tomorrow."

Jase laughed and lifted his head, frowning when he saw Mason's face. Zeroing back in on the topic, he asked Mason, "Did she feel like DeeDee didn't want her to come? She's here; I gave her a hotdog not an hour ago." He started looking around the backyard, and Hoss snorted at the repeat of the scene with Mason.

"She left a little bit ago." Hoss shifted the leather of his cut on his shoulders and asked, "Why we talking about pussy when we need to discuss Bingo?" As one, their heads all swung to look at the old man. He was speaking to a group of members, his arms sweeping in grand gestures, and in a moment, they all heard the laughter accompanying the end of whatever story he was relating. "He gonna keep staying here, Captain?" He used Jase's club name deliberately, ensuring both sets of ears understood this conversation had definitely turned to club business.

Standing straight, Jase looked him in the eye and said, "He's my brother, welcome here for as long as is needed...whatever is needed. He and the kids, they're family."

He reached out and cuffed Jase's shoulder fondly. "That's what I like to fucking hear, brother." Yawning, he said, "I think I'm gonna make some of that coffee I was talking about. Beer's good, but damn this sun is warm. I need some wakeup sauce."

Without waiting for a response, Hoss turned to walk inside, finding his way around in the kitchen and starting a pot of coffee. Leaning a hip against the counter, he pulled out his phone and tapped a quick message, pressed send, and then waited. Before the coffee was ready, he had received the response he wanted. Mercy had gotten home safely, and from the picture was seated on her couch, secure behind a closed and locked door. The smile on her face in the image was as sad and strained as each forced expression he had seen from her for weeks.

"Fucking Birdy," he muttered, pulling down a mug and filling it with the hot liquid.

2. Tripping and not falling

"How much longer, Mom?" Sammy asked, gaze directed out the window, avidly watching as she passed a slower moving tractor-trailer on her right.

"About twenty miles less than the last time you asked, baby." She reached up and paused her audio book, pulling the earbud from her ear. This book was about some gorgeous town in Nevada, where all the men were hotter than hot and all the women were stupid, but everyone got a happily ever after in the end. She snorted at the direction her thoughts had gone. *My life sure isn't a fairytale.* "Next town is Indianapolis, which is the biggest city in the state. After that, it's about two hours on to Fort Wayne. Did you see the last sign for Indy?"

"Fifteen miles," he said absently. She watched in the mirror as he turned his whole body to angle his head and look up at the truck driver, his arm pumping furiously. "Got him," he crowed as the driver briefly blew his air horn, tooting at the small boy. Sammy waved in thanks and twisted back in his seat, looking forward and pointing. "There's another truck right up there, Mom."

"Yep, see it." She shook her head. He was a good traveler and had managed to keep himself amused for most of the drive. She glanced down at the gas gauge again, wrinkling her nose. Mentally, she riffled through her wallet, counting the remaining bills. Enough to fill the car up another time, with probably forty bucks left over, plus the two hundred she had tucked back for emergencies. She had known she wouldn't have a lot of wiggle room for the expenses of this trip—*move,* her brain supplied—but she hadn't expected to cut things quite so fine. Thank God, her boss had made her last paycheck right, and even been willing to give it to her in cash, so she wouldn't have to watch it be whittled away by those darn fees.

Glancing at him again, she watched as he focused on the truck, trying to catch the driver's gaze in the semi's mirrors. Looking forward, she saw the truck driver had noted them, but he wasn't looking at Sammy, he was looking at her. Distracted—*surely he wouldn't do it on purpose*, she thought—his truck and the big trailer with DRT in black letters began drifting over into her lane until he moved it back with a jerk. Once he saw she had noted his attention, he licked his lips elaborately and she wrinkled her nose in disgust.

Staring straight ahead, she ignored him as best she could, reinserting her earbud and starting her audio book again. If only real life were like her favorite stories, where good-looking alpha men would swoop in and save you without asking for anything except hot sex in return. The sex was only if you were willing, of course, and they always took care of you first. She scoffed at her fantasy and then from his stillness realized Sammy hadn't done his normal toot-request movements, so she looked at him quizzically. "Sam, did you see the truck?"

"Yes." That was all he said, but now his arms were crossed tightly over his chest.

"No horn? He didn't see you?" She stuck her bottom lip out in sympathy.

"I didn't like him." He turned his head to look out the window. As she continued to watch him for another moment, she saw movement behind the car; the truck had sped up, the driver pulling over into her lane and rapidly catching up to them.

"Crap," she muttered, turning on her blinker and moving into the other lane, slipping between two other trucks. "Why didn't you like him?" she asked, keeping watch on the truck now pulling even with the semi behind her.

"He looked at you weird. I didn't like him." He shrugged, keeping his gaze out the window.

"Well, duh. I'm kinda dorky lookin'. He was probably amazed at the geekdom sitting behind the wheel." She smiled, because her goofy tone had pulled a grin to his face. Focusing on driving, out of the corner of her eye, she saw her gas light blink on then off, and then on as she stared down at it, burning a steady amber. "Double crap," she whispered, peering around the big truck in front of her to find they were nearly at an exit that had signs indicating gas stations.

"Need to make a pit stop, bud. Gotta get some go-juice for the buggy," she said, flipping on her blinker and moving over for the exit. She was sitting at the bottom of the ramp, waiting for the light to change and trying to decide which gas station to choose, when the car lurched forward with a crunching sound, her head hitting the side window hard. If felt like something had—

"Mom, he hit us! He hit our car!" Sam yelled, twisting in his seat to look back.

Eyes fixed to the rearview mirror, she saw it was the DRT truck. He had evidently come off the exit after she had and smashed into the back of her car. He was currently backing up to move out of the roadway, but she could clearly see the driver, sunglasses and low-tugged hat hiding the top half of his face. "It's okay; let me just pull over. I'll check it out. It was scarcely a bump, baby." She took a breath, trying to calm herself. "Stay in the car, baby. Okay?" Contrary to her verbal coolness, inside she was shaking with anger. He had. The jackhole had hit her car and, given his behavior back on the highway, she immediately wondered if it was intentional.

She pulled to the shoulder and climbed out of the car, with a final firm reminder to Sammy to stay put. Hope was dismayed when she rounded the back corner and saw crumpled metal and broken plastic, which was all that remained of her trunk lid and one tail light. Even though it looked bad, she knew the car was only lightly damaged, still drivable.

Looking up at the truck again, she shivered, filled with a sudden, intense desire to *not* have a conversation with this trucker on the side of an off-ramp, out of sight from the nearest business. She jumped back into the car, rolled down her window a couple of inches, and waited, locking the doors as an afterthought. After maneuvering the semi to the side, he exited the truck and was sauntering up the shoulder towards her car. She called out the window, "I'm going to pull over to the gas station; you can follow me over there to give me your insurance information."

She was already rolling up the window when he bent down, placed his mouth near the opening, and asked, "Hey there, honey. Are you and the little man okay?"

She nodded, pointing at the station, and saw a look of something she didn't like pass across his face. Frustration? Evil? Ill intent? Her heartbeat doubled in response and she slammed the car into gear, spitting gravel from under the tires as she pulled onto the service road. She had nearly made it to the gas station when she glanced in the mirror in time to see the truck idle across the road. It gained speed as it pulled back out onto the highway, leaving shattered pieces of red and white plastic scattered across the road. *Just perfect.*

After five hours in a tiny, very local repair shop, the trunk lid replaced and light fixed, they were ready to roll again. So what if her car now looked like a skunk with a white trunk on the black vehicle? It would keep their stuff dry and safe.

She looked down at her phone again, trying to decide and then, in a rush, dialed the number she had. The only number she ever had for Mercy. She had tried looking it up online, but it simply said unlisted. The only thing she knew was the listing was for Fort Wayne, which is why they were headed there now. *What if she doesn't even live there anymore?* The thought passed through her head quickly, but she shut it out with a panicked push, mentally slamming a door against the possibility.

A man answered, and she hesitantly asked, "Is Mercy there?"

There was a laugh she could only have described as dark and angry, and the man said, "Fucking bitch making us her answering service now? I'll play along, baby. No, I'm sorry. Mercy is unable to come to the fucking phone. Can I take a motherfucking message?"

She had drawn in a shocked breath when he first answered, and the longer he talked, the less good she felt about this trip—*move*—even as her mouth moved to answer him. "Can you tell her Hope called? I'm her sister. I'm on my way to visit and wanted to let her know I was on my way."

"Hope, huh?" His voice deepened, developing a raspy quality that made her shiver. "You as pretty as you sound, baby?"

She didn't know how to respond, so after a moment, she asked, "Can you...will you tell her?"

He had lost the pleasant tone, his voice sneering when he said, "Fucking tell her yourself, bitch. I ain't schleppin' for the whore. She's working Slinky's tonight. You can find her there." And with that, he hung up.

Before she could second-guess her decision, she looked up the name of the business he had given her, mapping the address while calling across the shop to where Sammy was chatting with the mechanic. "Gotta go, bud. Tell the nice man thank you."

***

"Thank you," Sam said politely, backing up so he could watch the man. Sure enough, he got an ugly look on his face as soon as Mom turned for the door, his eyes duckwalking up across her bottom. Hearing the door slide shut behind her, he leaned forward, got the man's attention, and then hissed, "That's my mom."

Turning to follow her, he heard the man say, "Good for you, little man. We gotta protect the ones we love. Good job."

Sam lifted a hand like he did in practice to let Coach know he heard him, and walked out the door.

3. Our complicated story

"Mercy," Tequila called from the bar, and Hoss turned to look at him, wondering what he needed. She walked over and took the phone from him, putting it to her ear slowly, eyes squeezed tightly closed. They all knew it was a call that lured her to where Birdy had been waiting, one of the reasons why she much preferred to text now, instead of talking on the phone.

Her head jerked back, then she nodded and quietly said, "Thanks."

She handed the phone back, turned, and walked to the door leading to the back of the club, and he saw her shoulders slump miserably as she went out of sight. Frowning, he moved to the bar and asked, "What was that about?"

"Dunno. Deke said he had a message for her." Tequila laughed. "Ten guesses what he wanted, and the first nine don't count."

"Man, I wish that brother would get his head out of his fucking ass. He needs to wise up and take care of shit." Hoss shook his head, glancing back at the stage before he walked to the office, going inside and closing the door.

A couple of hours later, Hoss stood behind the bar, watching Mercy dance as he had done a hundred times before. He frowned. She seemed off tonight, her dancing suffering, because instead of focusing on the set, she kept looking over at the door. He glanced to where Gunny stood and noted he was watching her with a frown, too. Walking over, he leaned against the wall next to the big man.

"What's up with Mercy?" Gunny asked before he could, and he laughed.

"Came over to ask you the same question. I don't know what's up, but she's steadily eyeballing the door like it's the only thing between her and a monster."

There was a noise outside, the slamming of a car door, and Gunny grunted, "Cage on the lot." Hoss nodded and they listened again. Thirty seconds later, another car door slammed and he glanced up at the dancers, seeing Mercy's gaze firmly trained on the outside entrance.

"I'm going to take a peek and see exactly what kind of trouble she's expecting," Hoss said and walked over to the club's entrance. Before he could touch the door, it swung open, light from inside the building spilling through the opening into the darkness of the parking lot and illuminating a young woman standing there, holding a boy by the hand. She glanced up at him and froze in place.

Beautiful, her expression was fragile and haunted, and for the barest moment, he thought she looked familiar. Then she tore her eyes from him, peering around him and into the room, her gaze catching on Mercy, who was mid-pole in a spin. She still had most of her costume on, but the woman in the door clapped her hand over the child's face, blood fleeing her features, which had frozen in an expression of loss so profound he nearly couldn't breathe.

Without a word, she turned on her heel in retreat. Even as he heard Mercy call out, "Hope, *wait!*" he felt an odd sense of melancholy that she was leaving and would not be part of his life. She was beautiful, sure enough, blonde curls flying untamed around her head and eyes blue enough to pierce straight through him. Not petite and not tall, she was just the right height with curves aplenty; a man could get lost for days exploring her. Just right, like the bear from that children's story. She was all of that, but there was something deeper than the surface, something that immediately made him want to shelter her, keep her...make her life easier.

He broke his stare from the woman and glanced over at Gunny, who shrugged, then Mercy was barreling past him, shoving him out of the way, having slowed only to slip on a robe over her skimpy costume. She stopped a few feet away from the woman and child and asked a question, too softly for him to catch her words.

At a nod from the woman, Mercy stepped forward and wrapped her arms around them both. Seeing them side-by-side like that, pressed so close you couldn't slip a breath between them, with a start, he realized why he had the feeling he knew her. She and Mercy looked similar. Even with the difference in coloration and hair, they were too alike to be anything other than sisters.

***

"I'm so sorry." Pulling back, Hope apologized softly, looking up at the big man standing in the doorway and then back to Mercy, trying to find a graceful way to retreat as quickly as possible. She stepped back, Sammy tucked firmly to her side, moving them farther away from her sister. This had been a mistake. Huge. Epic. *Stupid*. "The man on the phone mentioned this was your work, but I didn't think it through. We'll just—" Before she could finish the thought, the dark-haired woman—*Mercy, my sister*—was shaking her head vehemently back and forth.

"No, don't leave. Please. I can...give me a minute to talk to my boss. I can be ready to go in like five minutes." She laid her hand hesitantly on Hope's arm. "I got the message, but couldn't believe it. I thought Deke was messing with me, so I didn't dare...Hope, I'm overjoyed you're here." That touch meant everything, pulling her back from the immediate flight she had been headed towards. Because if Mercy still wanted to meet them after she crashed her place of work like this, then maybe the desire to know about their connection ran both ways.

The door thumped shut, the noise startling Sam and he jerked under her hand. Glancing down at him, she saw he was staring at something and followed his gaze to the big man. That man was so solid, so there, standing and watching them with a tolerant and interested look in place on his face. She suspected once you knew him, once he let you in, he could make you feel safe by no more than being near him. His beard color matched his hair, and looked just as soft, dark and thick, the right consistency for running your fingers through. Still looking at the man, distracted by her unruly thoughts she softly told Mercy, "Okay." Dragging her gaze away with some effort, she gestured towards their car and said, "We'll just wait here."

"You can't wait in the lot. Come inside." Mercy dropped her hand and turned, walking back to the doorway, pulling to a stop in front of the man with her hands on her hips. He was shaking his head, and she seemed perplexed when he didn't step aside. "Hoss, they can wait in the office."

"Think for a minute, honey. He's a tad bit underage, and, although you seem comfortable with her, I don't know your chickie. ATC would not look kindly to findin' him even on the premises, but they would definitely highly frown on findin' him inside the walls, and you know all that. No one in there can afford to lose their liquor license or pay fines." He shook his head. "They wait in their car."

When he spoke, his soft drawl sounded so familiar and welcome, the sound sending a warm feeling through her as it curled into the air around her, and Hope was surprised to find herself smiling to hear it. In her confusion, she glanced down at Sammy again and pitched her voice to carry when she said, "It's really okay, Mercy. Sammy and me, we can wait out here. It's no problem at all." Mercy had called the big man a name, but she had missed it. When he laughed, Hope looked up, and her question must have been evident on her face, because he responded.

"You were pretty much laughin' at me, weren't you? I wondered why, and now I know. We're a matched set of southern transplants, ain't we?" He was smiling at her, and she couldn't help but return the expression, liking how his warm smile spread to his eyes.

"For a moment there, you sounded like home," she said quietly, reaching out to ruffle Sammy's hair. He ducked his head out from under her hand, still staring at the man. "Take your time, Mercy. We'll be fine out here."

The man said, "Yeah, you will be. I'm gonna be waiting out here with you. Go on inside, Mercy. DeeDee ain't here, so you'll have to talk to Tequila, but it shouldn't be a problem. I got this, sweetie. Don't worry about a thing."

She watched as her sister—*my sister*—went up on her toes to gently kiss the big man's cheek. Turning to glance at her and Sammy, still standing in the lights of the parking lot, Mercy instructed, "Don't go anywhere."

The door closed and she realized Sammy hadn't said a thing since they first exited the car. Squatting down beside him, she asked, "You okay, bud? We'll wait right here for Aunt Mercy."

"Why didn't I know about her, Mom?" He asked the question quietly, his chin tucked tightly to his chest, gaze fixed on the pavement. "How could you have a big sister you never met?"

"It's a long story, Sam." She sighed, resting one knee on the hard asphalt covering the parking lot.

"You've said that the entire trip, but never told me anything. You never tell me anything, Mom. I'm not a little kid." It sounded like he was struggling with tears, and she reached out, wrapping her arms around him and tugging him close, holding him tight, even when he halfheartedly tried to pull away. "I'm not."

"I know, bud. But it's complicated." She shook him. "It's a complicated story. Like a banana split."

As she had intended, he snorted softly and then giggled as he asked her, "Why is it like a banana split?"

"Because the story runs cold and hot, like ice cream and hot fudge. It's a little sweet and sticky, like strawberries, and can give you a headache if you try to understand it all at once, like utter frozen goodness." Pulling back, she looked him in the face, using one palm to smooth his hair back from his temples. "Love you, bud."

"Love you too, Mom," he said, snuggling in for a real hug for a minute. Then, laughing loudly, he said, "You made a joke."

"Nuh-uh, I never joke," she said, squeezing him tight.

"Yeah-huh, you said it was utter frozen goodness. Ice cream is made from milk. Cow's milk. Udder frozen goodness? You crack me up, Mom." He giggled again, his bright child's voice lighting up every corner inside her. This was worth everything, being able to hold him, to love him...to hear him point out her terrible, unintentional pun. She grinned and kissed the top of his head, and he sighed and relaxed into her for a moment then stiffened and pulled away when a noise came from right behind her.

Twisting to look, she instinctively pushed Sammy behind her to position herself between him and whatever the new threat was. She saw the big man had moved beside them and was looking over the top of her head into the darkness. She heard a rumble, and over the rapidly growing noise, she heard him say, "Why don't y'all go and get inside the car, sweetheart." He glanced down at her and frowned when she didn't move right away, the tone in his voice harsher when he told her again, "Hope, get your boy and get into the car. Now."

Reaching out, she picked up Sam and stood, hurrying to the car. She struggled for a moment, fumbling with the keys, then opened the door and pushed behind the wheel, telling Sam, "Climb over, bud. Get on the floor. Like when we sleep, okay?" Without a word, her son obeyed, reaching up to pull the blanket from the top of the boxes down and over himself, hiding his form from casual view. "Get all tucked in, baby. Stay there; you know the drill." She pulled the door shut and locked it, inserting her keys in the ignition in case she needed to start the car in a hurry.

She watched as the big man stood in front of her car, feet spread wide, arms folded across his chest. With a start, she realized that just as she had done a moment ago with Sammy, he had put himself between them and whatever was approaching. Between her and danger, it felt like. His back was to her, and she had a moment to appreciate just how big he was, broad through the shoulders; she could see his bare biceps bulging as he shifted slightly from foot to foot, waiting. The leather vest he wore over his sleeveless shirt had an emblem on it, and several pieces of fabric with words. Patches with sayings like *Rebel Wayfarers*. The emblem itself was a frightening looking skull, grinning around something held in its teeth.

A group of motorcycles pulled into the parking lot and she cautiously eyed the men who parked and dismounted the bikes. They were all dressed similar to her self-appointed protector, and he greeted them in a friendly manner. Then he put a restraining hand on the chest of one rider who approached closer than the others, speaking quietly to him. The rider said something in return then leaned over and pounded on the hood of her car with one closed fist. He seemed to be barely in control of himself, his eyes showing whites all around the dark irises. Not quite as big as the man who had spoken so kindly to her, he was still big...and seriously scary. She jerked a little with each hard hit on the metal, feeling her shoulders pulling in tightly. "It's okay, Sammy," she whispered, not even sure if he could hear her, but needing to say the words. Reassuring herself. "It's all right, baby."

The big man pushed him back, and she heard him say in an angry tone, "Brother, knock it the fuck off. That's Mercy's sister, man. She's got a kid in the car."

"Pussy works, who fucking cares?" the other man told him, eyes glaring at her through the windshield. His attitude was callused and arrogant, and he kinda pissed her off with his crude language, even as he scared the pants off of her. "Lookie there at the honeypot. You are just as pretty as you sounded on the phone. Come on out here. Let's play, pretty baby."

"Deke, knock it the fuck off." The command in the man's voice was unmistakable, and Deke reacted, immediately backing up and moving away, holding his hands up in surrender. She watched their interaction intently and shuddered, because she thought without the big man here, things might be ending in a very different way. Her fingers had wrapped themselves so tightly around the steering wheel that the tips were tingling and she shook out first one hand and then the other absently, focus still on the two men standing in front of her car.

"I'll go nail my usual piece of ass, Hoss. No problem, you want to throw some kind of claim or patch on the bitch, you go straight on ahead. Ain't no skin off my ass, brother. I got no problem." Deke turned and nodded at the rest of the men, who had stood by silently during the entire exchange. Together, they all walked inside, and it seemed only a moment later when she saw the door open slightly, a small figure slipping through the opening.

"Everything okay?" Mercy asked Hoss as she walked over. *Could that honestly be his name?* Hope wondered, shaking her head.

"Deke bein' a dickhead. Ain't nothin' new about his level of asshatness," Hoss said. He turned and looked through the glass at Hope. "You okay, sweetheart?"

She nodded, not trusting herself to speak, knowing her voice would be quavering and fractured, exposing her fear.

He stared at her for a second then shook his head. "Nope, you ain't. I can see that. It's all right, honey. I had you. He's harmless most of the time. Just had a burr on his ass tonight." He smiled and for a moment, she felt…lighter. She smiled back and he grinned more broadly. "Now that's a pretty sight to see. I'd deal with dickheads any day of the week to pull that kinda smile outta you. We'll make sure you're okay. You take care, and I'll see you around, sweetheart." He took a step backwards and lifted one hand in farewell, holding it until she matched his motion, waving goodbye. Then he turned and strode to the building, pulling the door open forcefully as he went inside.

Twisting to bend over the seat into the back, she wiped the tears from her face and then told Sam, "You can climb up and buckle in, baby. You did really well."

Mercy leaned down and Hope lowered the window, taking the piece of paper offered. "Follow me, it's not far. I wrote down the address for you, in case we get separated." She reached out, cupping Hope's chin in her palm. "I'm so glad you're here, Hope. Let's get home, and we'll sort things out."

***

Hoss stalked across the room to where Deke was leaning against the bar. Reaching out, he gripped the collar of the man's tee where it showed over the top of his cut, twisting and pulling it tight around his hand, the fabric constricting around Deke's throat and causing him to arch back. "Fucktard. What the hell were you playing at with Hope?"

"Shit, Hoss. Fuck. Let me the fuck go, man." Deke struggled, moving from side to side, but Hoss persisted, taking a wrap in the tee's collar with his fist. Choking and pulling him to his toes, Hoss bent him backwards a bit farther. Voice strained, Deke said, "She called the clubhouse, wanted me to take a message for the stupid bitch. Shit, man, get the fuck off me." He slapped ineffectually over his head at Hoss' hands, yelling, "Club whore, using the clubhouse as a fucking answering service. Pissed me off."

"Mercy's not a whore anymore." Hoss shook his head, giving Deke a final hard shake. "She's dancing and isn't fucking brothers anymore. You would know if you fucking paid attention, man."

"Once a whore, always a whore." Deke shrugged, tugging his shirt back into place as Hoss released his hold. "What the fuck do I care?"

"Ain't you got sisters, brother? I know I do, and that's how I try and treat the girls, how I'd want my own sister treated." Hoss shook his head and stepped back. "You got some kind of a stick up your ass where Mercy's concerned, and you need to fix that shit, or it sure as hell is gonna come back around and bite you."

Deke looked at him from the corner of one eye, and then glanced down at the bar. "Mercy left, then?"

Hoss nodded, flipping a hand at the bartender. "Delia, gimme a beer." She indicated she heard him and he turned back to Deke. "Yeah, she went home." He watched as Deke's mouth twisted, lips pressed tightly together. "What's goin' on, man? Something's eatin' at you. Gonna share?"

Glancing around, Deke turned to face Hoss. "She say anything about anything?"

"The fuck is that supposed to mean? You mean about you? Did she say anything about you? Why, brother? What does she have to say that you would be worried about?" Hoss couldn't figure out what was going on with the man. He was running hot and cold, swapping sides so fast it was nearly impossible to keep up with him.

"I just wondered if she had said anything. You know, about anything." He shrugged and picked up his beer, taking a long pull from the bottle. "Like me, or like Birdy."

Slowly shaking his head, Hoss said, "Nope. She didn't say anything, not even when you called." He stared at Deke for a minute. "She doesn't talk about Birdy, man. You know that."

"I know. I shouldn't have said what I did," Deke muttered.

Narrowing his eyes, Hoss looked at the man, taking in the repentant look on his face. "What did you say to her on the phone?" He remembered the look on her face, the way she had flinched away from the handset. "Deke, brother. What did you say?"

"Just another thing for me to apologize to that gash for, man." Rapping his knuckles on the bar, he drew Delia's attention and, waving, ordered another beer. "Seems like I'm always apologizing to her."

"Then stop bein' a stupid, thickheaded fool," Hoss said with a shake of his head, turning to prop his elbows on the bar.

With a snort, Deke nodded, accepting the condensation-beaded bottle from the bartender. Tipping it up, he took a long drink then said, "Like that's gonna happen, brother."

4. Proud of you

"How much farther, Mom?" Sam asked, and she glanced at him in the mirror, seeing him twisting familiarly in his seat.

"Gotta go, bud?" Wrinkling her nose when he nodded, she asked, "You okay for another five?" Tucking his chin, he nodded again, and she said, "Okay. First thing, I'll ask where the bathroom is, so you don't have to find a houseplant."

He didn't grin as she expected, instead asking, "You think she's got a dog? I'd like it if she had a dog." He was looking out the window and didn't see her shake her head. "Why were you scared back there, Mom?" Now his head swiveled, so he could see her eyes in the mirror.

Dangit, she thought, studiously looking at the road in front of her, keeping her eyes trained on the taillights of Mercy's car. "I don't know if she has a dog or any pets. Maybe where she lives won't let her, like our place in Birmingham."

"Maybe," he agreed, his eyes locked on her face in the mirror. "You were really scared."

"Maybe," she echoed his word, and he made a face. "Yeah, a little. There were a bunch of men standing outside the car for a minute. The big guy sent them on their way, though. He seemed nice, yeah?" *Actually*, she thought, *Hoss seemed more than nice. He is just so...comfortable.* She shook her head, because he was about as opposite from Sammy's father—*sperm donor*—as someone could be. *I evidently don't have a type.* At that thought, she snorted at herself, because in order to have a type, you would need to have a sample size greater than one. In all the years since leaving home she had never met anyone who made her breath catch, who made her eyes involuntarily lock on them like the man tonight had. Made her want to take a chance again.

"Maybe," he said again, and she grinned, repeating it back to him to draw a smile from him.

"Mooooom," he complained, and then struggled to keep a straight face. "His name was weird."

"Hoss," she said, trying the fit of the sounds in her mouth, reminding herself to ask Mercy about his name. Hoss, Deke, Tequila—they were all odd names. She slowed when she saw Mercy's blinker come on, and turned to follow her into the parking lot of what looked like a nice apartment complex. Slowly, she drove through the gate and up the winding drive, stopping behind Mercy when she parked. Rolling down her window, she looked at the space her sister indicated and nodded, maneuvering the car and deftly backing into it. One of the things you learned when living in your car was to always park in a way that facilitated a quick exit, and backing in was now second nature. "Here we are, bud. Grab your little bag and bring it in for tonight, okay?"

"Are we not staying then? We came all this way and we're not staying?" He paused in releasing his seat belt buckle, and she twisted in the seat to look him in the face. This was one of those times where she needed to invoke their pact.

"No lies," she said, and he stiffened. Those words meant this suddenly was a serious conversation and she had his full focus. "I told you I don't know her, and that means I don't know how this is going to go. Not for sure. We might not want to stay here beyond a single night, or at all, bud. She might be okay, but the situation might not be. Right now, we're in what you could call the feeling-things-out stage." She swallowed the lump of fear in her throat, knowing if this didn't work out, she didn't have any idea what they would do. "I have a good feeling about this, but I didn't call ahead, so she might not even have room for us. What if she has a big husband and fourteen kids?"

"Oh, okay," he said quietly, grabbing his backpack and easing across the seat towards the door. "I really gotta go, Mom."

"Alrighty, then." She opened her door, looking across to see Mercy standing in the doorway of a downstairs apartment, the light silhouetting her to create a radiant glow around her frame. "I have a really good feeling about this, bud."

***

Gunny cut his gaze over to Hoss, watching as he settled his shoulders against the wall. The announcer came on, sound system speakers crackling and the faint hiss of static bleeding through the air before she led the audience into the next set.

"What was that shit with Deke?" Hoss shrugged; he knew Gunny and Deke were tight, and the last thing he wanted to do tonight was get sideways with the man, especially when he had worked so hard to get on the right side of him. Gunny asked, "He fucking his head up about Mercy again?" The question startled him, and he glanced over with a slow nod. Gunny shook his head, tipping his chin down. "Don't know why the dickhead won't just admit he wants her on his bike."

Hoss asked, "You thinking he's looking for some patched ass?" *That would surprise everybody in the club*, he thought.

"Man's wanted her as long as she's been around. Used to make him crazy when she would hang around the clubhouse, rubbin' up on brothers. He would go tearing off on his scoot when she would head upstairs with someone. At least now she's only stripping, not fucking anything that moves and is wrapped in leather." There was a noise in the room, and Gunny's entire attitude changed, immediately on point and ready to react to whatever danger presented itself.

Gunny had been like this for as long as Hoss had known him, wound as tightly as an overtorqued engine. Over time, he had learned the man was a dependable brother and officer, and he was now a good friend. After a few seconds, he eased back and settled against the wall again. Hoss smiled as he looked at him. The man was a study in intensity, and Hoss had often tried to capture him on canvas. The best he could do was graphite pencil, harsh strokes softened by the application of a smoothing fingertip, the Slavic cheekbones strong and prominent, overshadowed by those penetrating eyes. He had heard Gunny's woman call him beautiful not long ago, and found himself agreeing with her.

Hope, on the other hand, was a dynamic package of softness and light. He had watched while her face relaxed when she looked at her son, love written there in huge, sweeping emotions for anyone interested enough to notice. He would bet good money she had been beautiful beyond belief when carrying her child. Face rounded by pregnancy, gentle hands crossed over her curved and abundant belly, filled with the promise of life. He would have loved to capture her in those moments.

She had hugged the boy, embracing him tight, and the emotions awakened at the way their bodies molded together were important to remember. He wanted to retain the feeling brought to mind by the tender gesture. Mother chickadee on a branch, wings spread over her chicks, tucking them close to her body. Shielding feathers fluffed to provide them a soft place to lean into, holding them there against the chance of danger, or fear of falling. The night and lights creating soft shadows around and on the mother and son, but her hold on the boy unshakable, protective, and secure. A magical type of mother, full of love for her child, a beautiful picture to put on canvas. That child a small but sturdy boy, with a scrappy feel to him at odds with the bespectacled look. Functional frames shielding slices of his face, giving him space to hide. Blond hair a touch too long, his love for his mother as evident and apparent as hers for him. A matched pair, happily dependent on the other tethered partner at this stage in their lives.

He wouldn't want to paint her face as she had looked after Deke pulled his shit, though. Seen through the windshield of her box- and bag-filled car, stark fear drawing long lines of tension in her brow. Face wet with terrified tears, her fingers clutched tightly around the top of the wheel, positioned thumb-to-thumb, the lot's harsh light and dark shadows striping bars across her figure.

"Mercy's sister, huh?" Gunny didn't look at him when he asked the question, his eyes ever moving, gaze sweeping across the crowd in the club.

"Yeah, she's a pretty little golden girl. Pint-sized boy, too. He didn't seem to like me much, but maybe it's all men. I'd be hard pressed to say which it is. I hustled them into the car when I heard the bikes. Wasn't sure who would be rolling in, and when I saw they were club, thought I'd be able to save her the introduction. But then Deke, par for the course, was an asshole about her and Mercy." He shook his head. "She's headed over to Mercy's now."

"Deke's a dick; we all know that. Like I said, he's hung up on the woman. Won't be right until he admits it." Gunny stood, eyeballing a man near the stage. "Fucking patched pussies, man. Damn, some nights I really fucking hate this ain't a club bar." He stalked over, and Hoss watched as he slapped his palm on the table between two men stuck in postures of aggression and animosity. With some surprise, he recognized Tater, a patched brother from the Chicago chapter of the Rebels, as one of the men at the table. Hoss watched as Gunny deftly handled whatever it was, and he relaxed. Trailing his gaze across the men in the crowd, he cataloged the looks of lust and desire, trusting his brother to deal with whatever shit happened.

Pulling out his phone, he tapped out a message and then waited. In a few minutes, the device vibrated, and he looked down to see an image of Mercy on her couch, but this picture included Hope and Sam seated there with her. Wide smiles on the women's faces, Mercy's arm around Hope, and Hope's arms around both Mercy and Sam. Mama in the middle. Chickadee on a branch. *Here you go. We're home, Hossman*, her text said. His phone shook again a second later, and he looked down to read, *Thanks for...well, you know...everything.*

***

Hope stood in the kitchen next to Mercy, rinsing dishes and handing them to her to put in the dishwasher. "You're sure it won't get you in trouble if we stay here?" They had talked through the evening, light conversation over pizza for supper, and then slightly harder topics after Sammy had bathed and been tucked into the double bed in the spare room. She was embarrassed her need was so apparent, but having her sister tell her family looked out for family went a long way to making things better.

"Not a bit of it," Mercy said with an easy grin, closing the front door of the dishwasher. She reached into the cabinet and brought down two tall glasses then opened the refrigerator and looked at Hope over her shoulder, asking, "White or pink?" Hope frowned and Mercy burst into laughter. "Wine. Do you want white or pink? I only buy the good stuff." She reached inside the refrigerator and turned with a box in each hand, tilting her head with a grin.

Hope laughed and shook her head. "Doesn't matter; it's all good." Shaking her head again, she picked up one of the glasses and held it out. Wine in hand, they walked back into the living room and sat facing the other on the couch. Staring at each other and sitting in silence for a minute, Hope laughed when they began to talk at the same time. She let the laughter die down and then asked, "How long have you known about me?"

"All my life." Mercy shrugged. "Mom was kind of bitter, so she was vocal about everything, especially after she had a couple glasses of this." She lifted her glass, half-full now. "I guess my mom was a little more than a month ahead of yours in the cooking process when she found him and informed him she was preggo. She always told the same story. She'd say, 'He looked me in the face and told me my body was mine to manage, and keeping the baby would be my decision.' Then she would look at me and shake her head."

Wrinkling her nose, Hope shook her head. "Ten years ago, I couldn't have believed it, but after what he said to me when I told my parents I was pregnant with Sammy, I can totally see him saying those words. I hate you had to deal with that, though. I feel like I should be apologizing for him and what he did to you and your mom."

"Nah," Mercy said. "Water under the bridge. Mom's still a twat, but I don't have to deal with her much, so we manage to get along for the couple days a year I see her." Her phone buzzed and she smiled. "Figured he would be checking in sooner or later," she said cryptically and tapped on her phone for a minute. "There, now he has a picture of you."

"Who?" Mercy had taken a selfie of the three of them earlier in the evening and made a big deal out of setting it as her home screen, her antics drawing a smile to Sammy's face. "Who in Fort Wayne could want a picture of me? I've been here all of five hours."

"Hoss," Mercy said with a smile. "Hossman. He's a good guy."

"Is that his last name?" Hope asked, tipping her head to one side.

"No." Mercy laughed. "His name is Isaiah Rogers, but everyone calls him Hoss. I call him Hossman, because one of the club members runs his words together and calls everyone 'man', so when he says the name, they sound like Hossman, or Slateman. Hoss is a decent guy; he's been there for me through a lot. Like a lot, a lot."

"Oh," Hope said, thinking the name Hoss suited him better than Isaiah. Isaiah made him sound like he should be a person her father would like, someone enamored of studious observation with lifelong rules. Hoss, now that was a name with a wild twist. Wild, but steady, like someone you could count on, someone to make you feel safe while still kicking up his heels at times. If he was as kind in truth as he seemed tonight, he was someone you would want in your corner. Someone she would like to have in her corner, but probably he was already taken. Nice guys usually were. She swallowed; she had seen him with Mercy and marked their casual, comfortable affection. "He seems really nice, was sweet to you. You make a cute couple."

With a shout of laughter, Mercy shook her head. "No, Hoss isn't the one for me. He's a loner, mostly. I don't think I've really ever seen him with anyone." Twirling her glass, she said, "He's single, Hope. But, he's a really good man. I trust him with my life."

"Oh," was all she could force out through her suddenly tight throat.

"So what's the plan, Stan?" Mercy glanced over, reaching out to twirl a finger in Hope's hair. "Staying here is easy. This place is a two-bedroom, and there's a ton of space. We can easily fit a single bed in the spare bedroom for Sammy. You guys would have to share the room, but that way he'll have his own bed. There are still a few weeks before school starts, and I have a friend who works in the school system. She can help us get things lined out for your little guy." She tugged at the curl, smiling as it bounced back into place when released. "I love your hair; it's such a pretty color."

Hope grimaced and looked down, reaching up to smooth her hair. "It's been a while since he was in formal school," she said quietly. "We spend a lot of time in the library, and he's smart. Really smart. He can read way above his grade level. But there won't be any recent records." Glancing up, she saw an unreadable expression on Mercy's face and looked down again to avoid the pity she assumed was coming next.

Speaking slowly, Mercy seemed to be thinking aloud. "Eddie can help. Her childhood wasn't...typical, either. She's not going to look down on you for what you had to do in order to keep the two of you together." She heard Mercy take a breath, and knew what was coming next. She waited for Mercy to say the 'but' part of the statement. *'But' you can't stay here. 'But' the state will want to know about him. 'But' what kind of mother are you?* Her eyes raised in surprise, gaze locking with Mercy's when she heard her say instead, "I'm so proud of you. Looks to me like you've done an excellent job with him. I'm in awe, Hope. You are so strong."

Scoffing, she shook her head. "I hate what I've done to him." Squeezing her eyes shut, she swallowed, forcing down a threatening sob. "He's never gone hungry, but he's lost a big part of his childhood that deserved to be normal. Ordinary. Instead, he had to grow up fast, and I *hate* it."

She was surprised when strong, warm arms enfolded her, tugging her head onto Mercy's shoulder. "You are an incredible mother, Hope. Just got handed a craptastic deal. Shit happens, and you made the best of it. You are so tough. I'm so proud of you."

They sat like that for a time, the awkwardness of newfound family fading away with the strength of the connection between the two sisters, whose backgrounds were so different. Releasing her slowly, Mercy sat back, ducking her head to look at Hope's tear-wet face underneath her bangs. "So let's make a plan. We'll sort out the sleeping arrangements first, and get Sammy a bed of his own. We'll make a list of things we need. I have friends. I'll introduce you, and we'll figure out what we have to do for school. Then, we'll find you a job, and you can get started making your way back onto your feet."

With a wry twist to her smile Hope didn't understand, Mercy said, "I got you. We'll figure this out and sort our shit."

5. What do you want?

Sam scowled at the woman standing in the kitchen across from where he sat at the table, and then quickly looked down, spooning cereal and milk into his mouth. While he was chewing, and in between mouthfuls, he used the bowl of the spoon to push the cereal underneath the surface of the milk, fixedly watching the yellow balls persistently pop back to the surface. His new aunt looked a lot like Mom, like they had to be sisters. That meant Mom wouldn't be going back to Mac and Nelly, because they weren't really family. Not like Aunt Mercy. He kept his gaze down and shook his head when she asked if he wanted juice.

What he wanted was for Mom to be happy again. He had crept into the hallway last night and listened to the two of them talking long after he was supposed to be asleep, and Sam had not liked what he heard. It sounded like he was the reason Mom was sad. He didn't want to make her sad, and didn't think she knew how much her keeping him with her meant. He had to figure out how to show her.

He was so focused on thoughts of what he had overheard that when Aunt Mercy spoke, it startled him, and the involuntary jerk caused a splash of milk to sail over the edge of the bowl and onto a newspaper lying on the table.

"I'm sorry!" he yelled, pushing his chair back too fast, the clatter of it falling over backwards adding to his confusion and dismay. *If I mess this up for us, if I make her mad*, he thought, *then Mom will be even more sadder than she is now*.

He was struggling, trying to tug his shirt over his head to blot the milk up, when he saw a kitchen towel sailing through the air towards him. Releasing his shirt, he reached up to pluck it from the air and swept it down onto the paper, careful to press straight down, not rubbing. Gibson had impressed the technique on him more than once when Sam had spilled on his things. "I'm sorry," he whispered to the towel, lifting the bowl with both hands and setting it carefully to one side. "I'm sorry. I never meant to ruin it."

Poop, he hated this feeling, like he had a huge chunk of something stuck in his throat. The one where the back of his neck got tight like he was gonna sick up. "Ain't no thang," he heard, and the comfort and warm care filling the voice effortlessly drew his tears from him. Within seconds, his shoulders were jerking and he was swallowing hard to keep the cries inside. He lifted the towel and squeezed his eyes tightly shut when he saw the smeared and ruffled spot on the paper. "I'm sorry," he repeated on a high-pitched whisper, and then there were soft hands on his shoulders, turning his body and pulling him into a hug.

"Sammy." He heard the concern in her voice and then felt fingers threading through his hair, cupping the back of his head and pulling him in tighter. "Oh, sweetie, it's no big deal." One hand scooped up under his butt and the arms lifted him. Eyes closed, he let himself be maneuvered, folded in half and seated on a lap, then his head tugged into place on a shoulder as he cried. And cried.

He wasn't aware of falling asleep, but he must have, because when he woke, he did it sluggishly, rising from dreamless darkness wrapped in warmth. There was a rumble in the room, and bit-by-bit, he recognized the voice of the big man from last night, the one who had been mean to Mom, telling her to put him in the car as if he were a dog or something. He remembered the way the man had looked at Mom at first, when he was still standing beside the big door that had let out the bright light, blinding him even before Mom covered his eyes. The expression on his face had looked like Mom was the last spoonful of sugar in the bowl, and he had his mouth set on sweet. Then he had yelled. *I don't like him*, Sam thought. His Aunt Mercy was talking, and he tried to piece together enough of what she was saying to make sense.

"She's had it tough, really tough, Hoss. On her own, totally on her own since she was not even an adult. Nine years, no one's been in her corner. On her own. I can't even imagine how she has held it together as long as she has. This little guy..." A hand stroked up his back and through his hair, and he turned his face into her shoulder a bit more, because it felt so good, like it did when Mommy held him, humming their song. She had continued speaking, and he heard, "...is a bundle of tough all on his own. They are both completely exhausted from trying to hold everything together. He's been sleeping on my lap for nearly three hours. The first thing he did this morning was cry himself to sleep."

"And Hope?" That was the rumble from Hoss again, making Sam scowl.

"She's still asleep. One glass of wine and she was down for the count last night." There was a noise in the room and Aunt Mercy moved, twisting a little. "Hossman, you don't have to do that. I'll clean the table, baby." More noise, and then the sound of running water. Sam sighed; no way could he go back to sleep with the man in the apartment. He picked up his head and opened his eyes to find his aunt looking at him. She smiled, her lips curling up at the corners and the edges of her eyes crinkling like Mom's did when she was really, really happy. He offered her a tentative smile back then glanced over her shoulder, where the big man was dumping his cereal into the sink.

"No!" he shouted and struggled, thrashing his limbs and trying to get off Aunt Mercy's lap. "Don't, I can still eat it. Don't pitch it. Don't. No." He slipped from her knees and gained his feet, quickly trotting around the corner of the couch in a half-run, pulling to a stop next to the table, his breath coming in soft gasps.

"Sam." Hoss shook his head at him. "Soggy cereal ain't good to eat." He finished dumping the nearly full bowl then ran water and flipped a switch, using the garbage disposal to grind the balls into cereal mush. Soggy, ruined cereal mush. One big finger reached out and tapped the switch again, turning it off, and Hoss gathered up the paper from the table, crumpling it to throw it away. *Poop.* Sam lifted his hand, straightened his glasses, and then covered his mouth. He had wasted a bowl of cereal and ruined a newspaper. Poop, poop, *poop.*

How can I make this right? he wondered, turning back to his aunt. That still sounded weird to him. He had an aunt. *I have an aunt.* He had two grandmothers and a grandfather, and now an aunt. "I'm sorry," he told her again, and was stunned by the smile she gave him.

She stood and took the two strides to get to him, and then lifted him and stunned him again when she turned him upside down, wrapping her arm around his legs. She suspended him like that with his head down, and used one hand to tickle him. The urge to laugh was immediate, but he was aware Mom was still asleep, and the man, Hoss, was in the room with them, so he tried to hold it inside. He remembered once when Mom took him to visit his grandmother and grandfather. They had goats, and one of the babies had gotten out of their pen.

His grandfather had captured the kid and carried it, struggling and bleating, back to the worried mommy goat by its back legs. The similarities didn't escape him, and even though he tried not to, he began to laugh. He blurted a giggle, then another, and another three or four, accompanied by a twisting jerk attempting to get away, even if it meant he fell on his noggin. *I'm a kid*, he thought and blurted a giggle again. She swooped him upside right and snuggled her face into his neck, blowing a wet raspberry on his skin and making him giggle again. "Stop," he yelled with a laugh, and was surprised when she immediately did, setting his feet firmly back on the floor.

"I'll stop doing this if you stop apologizing for things that aren't your fault." She squatted down, looking him in the face. "Cereal is cheap; we can buy more. As for the paper? Well, seems to me that I scared you with my crazy aunt voice, so if anyone's to blame, it's me. But, cereal is cheap, baby. Shoot, Hoss back there?" She pointed over his shoulder, and he twisted to look up at the man.

"Hossman can eat nearly a full box at one sitting." Hoss smiled and snorted a laugh, shaking his head negatively, still busy at the sink, and after looking at him for a long minute, Sam turned back to his aunt.

"Okay, maybe not a full box," she amended. "But he can eat a lot. And the paper? If I had a bird, and had a house, and kept that bird in a cage in that house, the paper would line the bottom of that cage in that house, so the bird in that cage could poop on the paper. That's how little I care for the paper."

He was staring at her, so he saw the shift in her expression, signaling she was serious. "I care about you. Not the paper, not the table, not the cereal, and not my raggedy old shirt." She smoothed out the wrinkles in her shirt from where he had been sleeping in her lap. "I care about you, Super Sammy."

"And Mom? Do you care for Mom?" He watched her face as he asked the question, and was amazed again by the transformation in her face. She went from happy-silly to crazy-happy, and he could *see* it. It shone from her, like a flashlight through thin covers after dark. *She loves Mommy,* he thought with joy, and could feel a smile on his face in response. Mac loved Mom like a daddy or a friend, and loved Sam like a granddad. But Aunt Mercy loved her without needing a reason, without anything other than love. No narrowing descriptions, no qualifications, just a whole passel of love.

"I love your Mom more than...ice cream." She nodded, her head moving up and down fast, and he giggled.

"More than vanilla shakes?" he asked, and she nodded enthusiastically. "More than...candy?" He grinned; he loved candy.

"Yep," she responded, "I love you and your mother more than candy, ice cream, vanilla shakes, chocolate, and bubble gum all rolled together into a big ball." Hoss made a noise, and Sam turned to look at him, steadily staring into Hoss' dark brown eyes, waiting.

"Just sayin', she means it. I can see she's sincere, Sam. She likes chocolate a lot, too. But I can see your pretty Aunt Mercy means what she says there." Hoss nodded seriously, and Sam turned back to look at Aunt Mercy.

"I like you, too." Sam rubbed the tips of his fingers with his thumb and then reached up to cup her face like Mom did with him when she wanted him to pay attention. His breath hitched when he invoked the words Mom used when she was super serious. "No lies." He waited for her nod and then continued, "Mommy needs you. She's tough and figures all kinds of things out all the time, but she hasn't had anyone who liked her since Mac." There was a noise behind him, and he turned to see an irritated scowl on Hoss' face, his lips twisting sideways, nearly hidden by his beard.

"Mac?" The man made the one word a question, and Sam frowned at him.

"Our friend in Birmingham." He offered, thinking even if Hoss was scary, at least Mac had to be safe from this man, because Birmingham was so far away he couldn't imagine going back. It was days away—wake-ups away.

"Not your Daddy?" Hoss asked in a gruffly fierce voice, and Sam frowned again.

"No, my Daddy is a good guy. We just try not to bother him very much." He nodded, repeating the words Mom had told him more than once. Now Aunt Mercy made a noise, and he turned back to see her lips twisted like she had licked something that tasted bad, like a deodorant stick. "Mac is a friend." He bent to look at Hoss again and saw he was grinding his teeth together. "Are you Mom's friend?"

Nodding slowly, Hoss looked at him. "I hope I am. I want to be."

Shaking his head, Sam felt his mouth twisting like Aunt Mercy's had. "I don't think so. You yelled at her. Friends don't yell."

"When?" Hoss seemed sincerely stumped by the statement, so Sam answered him.

"Last night. You yelled at her to get into the car. Then you yelled some more and hit the car a bunch of times. You scared her. She cried." Looking at Hoss, Sam saw the corners of his eyes get tight and knew he had made the man mad. Tucking his chin into his chest for a second, he pulled together all his courage and raised his head, meeting Hoss' gaze straight on, like Mac had taught him to do. *Big boys gotta watch out for our mommas and the ones we love.* He heard the scolding voice of Mac in his head and, ignoring the anger he thought he had seen, told Hoss, "She cried. That's not how friends act."

He leaned forward at the waist, making sure Hoss knew he was serious. "She's my mom, and you don't get to make her cry." He straightened and waited until Hoss gave him a single nod in response, and then he turned to look at Aunt Mercy, seeing a funny look on her face. Not sad, not happy, more like she was weighing his words against something. "I'm...I'm a little hungry."

"Then we need to fix that," she said immediately, standing. "Super Sammy, let's make an Egyptian eye."

"What's an Egyptian eye?" he asked, following her into the kitchen, stopping when Hoss didn't move, just stared down at him. Looking up, his voice funny because his neck was stretched so far, he said, "Maybe you could be friends as long as you don't scare her again. 'Kay?" Hoss squatted down, resting one knee on the floor. Sam tipped his face to follow him down and they looked at each other for a moment.

Sam thought he might like Hoss, but didn't want to, because of how he talked to Mom. If Hoss liked Mom, it would be good, since she would have a friend. That would be good, because Sam knew how lonely it was to be without friends. In a couple of the shelters, he had met kids his own age, and the freedom found in the give-and-take of playing pretend games with no rules, just for fun, was a giddy thing.

Mostly it was simply him and her. Their terrible twosome. She thought he had made friends in skate class, but skating was work. No playing there. The classes meant she was spending money on him—*on him*—so he couldn't let her down. Skate class was to get better, not joke around with the other kids. *So probably, Mom doesn't have many friends either*, he thought.

"I'll try not to, Sam. I really do hope I'm your momma's friend. I liked her last night, and I didn't mean to scare her. I was trying to keep her, and you, safe." He moved, and Sam looked down, seeing words on his black vest.

"What does that mean?" he asked, pointing to the small red-and-white patch. He read the words aloud, "I sa-san-snat-snatch kisses, and vice ves-ver-verses-us-versus? I snatch kisses and vice versus? What does that mean?"

"Oh, man." He heard Aunt Mercy behind him and twisted to look up. She had a carton of eggs and a loaf of bread in her hands and was standing stock still in the middle of the room with a broad grin on her face. With suppressed laughter in her voice, she said, "Man, oh, man.

We'll explain that one in a few years, Sammy. Now, let's make us some"—here she used a silly, creepy voice—"Egyptian eyes."

Five minutes later, he was again installed at the table, using the tines of a fork to smear the runny yolk of the egg over the toasted bread. Aunt Mercy had cut a diamond shape out of the middle of the bread, fried it in butter in a skillet, and then flipped it over and cracked an egg into the empty space. When it cooked through enough, she slid it onto the plate using her silly, creepy voice to say, "Breakfast is served, young master. Behold the beauty that is...an Egyptian eye."

Hoss had laughed at that, a big, booming, cheerful laugh filling up all the open space in the kitchen with happy, and Sam found himself smiling at him, even though he didn't want to. He thanked his aunt politely as she placed the plate in front of him, nodding this time when she offered him juice. As he was eating, he overheard Hoss ask her, "Hope in the guest room?"

His head popped up, looking at the two adults standing close in the kitchen. Hoss' hand was on her arm; he had stepped in close to her so he could speak quietly, and was looking down into her face. The look on Aunt Mercy's face told Sam a lot of things.

In the shelters and parks where he and Mom spent their time, in the back alleys and shopping center parking lots, in the backseats of cars parked next to theirs, he had seen lots of things. Some of it Mom knew about, but a lot of it was confusing, and he didn't have the words to ask. One thing he had gotten good at was being able to tell when people had spent important time around each other, when they were comfortable in a way that came from long association.

Hoss' face had gone soft, and his aunt's tipped up, chin lifted, her gaze to his. He could see Hoss and Aunt Mercy had an easy way between them, like Hoss liked her. Once he saw that, Sam knew it didn't matter anymore if he liked Hoss or not. Not now, because he would never be a friend of Mom's if he were already more than a friend of

Aunt Mercy's. "Yeah, she and Sam slept on the double in there last night. We're going to go today and buy a single to put in the room for Sam."

Hoss shook his head, stepping back, and the moment seemed to fracture, pull apart. Sam watched his face close down strangely when he asked, "Boy's gonna be sleeping in there with her?"

Aunt Mercy lifted an eyebrow when she looked back at Sam then to Hoss. "Yeah, he gets a bed of his own. I'm going to talk to Eddie today about school, too. We want to get everything lined out before the semester starts."

"Club has some furniture. Talk to Ruby. She'll know what we have and what's available." Hoss stepped backwards another stride, resting his bottom against the countertop.

"If she'll talk to me." Aunt Mercy shrugged. "Maybe I can get Eddie to call her."

"What the fu—hell, Mercy?" Sam hid a grin at this barely-caught correction, because Hoss nearly said one of the 'really bad words' Mom had forbidden him to ever utter. 'Pain of death,' she had said, then corrected it to be, 'pain of soap in your mouth' but he already knew she would never kill him just for cussin'. She could never kill him for anything. "You work for us; you're ours. That makes Hope ours, because she's yours. Ruby won't kick you to the curb, not that the woman would ever do that anyway. She ain't gonna give you any grief, Mercy. Pisses me off, the way you see problems where none exist sometimes."

"You know as well as I do club whor—girls don't mix with an old lady. The RWOLs are an exclusive club, even if their ranks have been growing lately." Aunt Mercy's voice was brittle and sad. She sounded like Mom did when she had to tell Sam something hard, something that had the potential to hurt.

"You ain't one anymore, and everybody knows it, Mercy." Hoss had a frustrated tone, and Sam looked up to see him scowling. Eyes on Hoss, he used the edge of the fork to cut another piece of toast, dipping it into the egg before putting it into his mouth.

He didn't often get to see grownups fight. Even when 'that jackhole' Gibson was moving out, Mom hadn't yelled, just got all frowny and tense.

"You are the only one who's still fu—hung up on what used to be, woman." He wasn't yelling, but the sharp-edged tone of his voice made Sam cringe, and he knew Hoss noticed it when he said, "Aww hell, now I'm scarin' the boy. Made him draw in on hisself like a turtle." Shaking his head, he turned and walked out of the kitchen towards the front door, calling over his shoulder, "Gonna get you in a three bedroom. I'll fuckin' call Myron and Ruby myself. Dammit, Mercy, you piss me right the fuck off."

Sam laid the fork on the plate and put his hands in his lap, bowing his head. Now he was the reason Hoss was mad and leaving. He was walking out, and Mom wasn't up yet, so he couldn't even tell if she wanted to be friends with him. He would have to wait to figure it out.

A warm hand caressed his shoulder, and Aunt Mercy quietly said, "He's fulla bluster and bother, but he's a real good man. You don't have to be afraid of our Hossman." Without looking up, Sam nodded, and her fingers squeezed the back of his neck. "Eat up, Sammy. I'm gonna go see if your mom managed to sleep through the drama."

***

"No, it's not a gang," Mercy told her in a testy tone of voice. "It's a club. It's a group of men, a bunch of guys who share a passion for motorcycles. They happen to want to live a certain kind of lifestyle most other people don't understand, and honestly most folks don't have any desire to learn. These men have mortgages, families, jobs...they are no more or less than regular people."

"Okay, okay. Clearly, I hit a nerve. Sorry. I don't know the terminology. I didn't mean anything derogatory by it." Hope backtracked quickly because she didn't want to offend, and could see these men meant a lot to her sister. "I want to understand what your role in their club is, where you fit, so I can find where Sam and I fit." Mercy tilted her head, a question on her face. Hope shrugged, and said, "Sammy told me Hoss said you were theirs, and it meant we were theirs by association. Sounds like something I need to understand. If for no other reason, so I don't do what I just did by putting my foot in it, and in doing so, offend someone important to you."

Sammy had been a little cautious with his responses when she questioned him, and she suspected there was more to the encounter between Hoss and Mercy this morning. At least Sam and Mercy seemed to have hit it off, and he had spoken without wariness about seeing Hoss, more interested in telling her about his exotic breakfast.

With a shake of her head, Mercy lifted one hand, raising her palm to Hope. "No, it's not that big a deal. Just don't use the word around the guys. What Hoss said was he's going to see if he can get us a bed from the club. They have some stuff in storage, and he's going to ask the chapter president's wife about it."

Hope frowned. "Just like that? They have furniture laying around, waiting for someone to need it?"

"Kinda." Mercy poured a mug of coffee and slid it across the counter to where Hope was standing. "The club owns a house here in town, and they furnish that and some apartments for members, or other folks, like me." She swung her hand out, indicating the apartment. "Like this place. The need fluctuates, so they store things in between times."

"What did he mean about you belonging to them?" Picking up the mug, she blew across the top of the liquid and then cautiously took a sip, walking alongside Mercy to the couch, the two women sitting on either end, facing each other.

"I know a bunch of the members. We're friends. I've been around the club for a long time, and now I work at Slinky's." Mercy shrugged, but a blush spread up her neck to her face.

"What does Slinky's have to do with it?" Hope sipped her coffee again, looking at Mercy intently.

"The club owns the place." Mercy set her cup down and twisted, glancing towards the back of the room. "Did you sleep okay?"

"Yeah, I did." She smiled, reaching up to rub the back of her neck. "I'm still crazy stiff from driving, but it was the best sleep I've had in a long time."

Turning back to her with a smile, Mercy said, "I'm glad. Means you felt safe here, and that makes me real happy, hon."

She took a breath, then said, "Next thing to do is for me to find a job, so I can help make ends meet around here."

"No rush on that," Mercy said, picking up her cup of coffee. "It was a long drive, Hope. You should take it easy a couple weeks, get yourself rested up and ready."

Hope snorted a laugh. "That's sweet, but not realistic. I'll start figuring out a job today. I can look online, and there's probably a temp service or two I can call. I...I have a little cash left, so you won't have to carry us, Mercy. I'm not at all afraid of working hard. Most of the time, I juggle two or three part-time jobs. It's about all I can do with no schooling, since I'm not qualified for anything that's full-time and pays enough to support Sammy and me."

She jumped and shrieked, nearly spilling her coffee when a low, growling voice came from directly behind her. "Working two or three jobs don't leave much time for motherin', sweetheart."

Twisting around on the sofa, she saw the big man from last night was standing in the doorway to the kitchen. From the other end of the couch, she heard Mercy's amused voice, "Hossman, you gotta start announcing yourself. Stop scaring my family."

"Sammy needs his momma." His eyes were boring into her and she felt her shoulders tighten, drawing in. *He thinks I'm a bad mother*, she thought, and was immediately near tears. She swallowed hard and opened her mouth to refute his words, when he shook his head, saying, "Like son, like mother, looks like, always thinkin' the worst. Relax, sweetheart. I didn't mean anything other than Sammy loves his momma and wants her around. Seein' you with him last night, it's clear you love him, too. Working two or three jobs means shuffling shifts and daycare. Let me help you find a job that can take care of you guys, without doin' you in." He walked across the room and leaned forward, placing his hands on the back of the couch and turning his head to look her in the face. "Now, relax those shoulders and take a breath. I was looking forward to seein' that little smile again."

Hope stared at him wordlessly. The man was gorgeous, and with his brown-eyed focus solely on her, she couldn't look away, couldn't speak, could only stare back at him. She watched as one corner of his mouth quirked upwards, pulling his lips sideways into a small, pleased smile. Without thought, she returned the expression back to him, which only caused his satisfied smile to widen. "Beautiful," he murmured and lifted a hand to cup her cheek. The feel of his hand on her face broke whatever spell he had woven around her and she jerked back, dropping her gaze to the cushion in front of her folded legs as soon as his tender smile faded into a scowl. He drew her eyes back to him when he asked, "Who's Mac?"

Frowning, she asked for clarification, "Mac? Mac Derringer?"

"Don't know about Derringer, but Sammy mentioned a Mac who liked you. He the reason you had to skedaddle out of Birmingham?" His eyes had narrowed, but his gaze was still fixed on her.

She was confused. How had they gone from talking about jobs, to discussing her friends? "No, Mac wanted us to stay, says he misses us when we're gone." She felt a smile curving her lips. "He's been really good to us and been Sammy's friend since before he was born. Likes to reinforce his claim to the longest friend title often with gifts of vanilla shakes."

"But he didn't try and make you stay? He was okay with you walking away from him?" If she hadn't seen the soft and open expression on his face a few minutes ago, she would be terrified of him right now, because his brows had lowered, and the look on his face was dark and fierce. He looked furious, a muscle in his cheek popping as he ground his teeth.

Still confused about what Mac had to do with anything, she slowly shook her head. "No. I mean, yes, he was okay with us leaving, because he knew I was losing the apartment. But, he didn't try and make us stay. Mac would never do that. Even if he hated losing Sammy more than anything in the world."

"He ain't Sammy's daddy?" She hadn't thought Hoss' face could look any more frightening, but she had been wrong. Terrifying didn't touch the expression he wore now.

Her voice had dropped to a whisper when she answered, "No, Sam's dad is Cal, Calhoun Suiter. I met Mac when I was pregnant, back when I first left—"

Hoss interrupted her, still frowning, "Suiter in the picture?"

What picture is he talking about? She couldn't keep up with the topic changes in this strange conversation and glanced at her purse, where her wallet was, mentally trying to figure out what picture Sam might have shown Hoss.

"I don't...I don't think so. I don't remember any picture with him." Her nervousness not only had her whispering, but nearly had her stuttering, too. She didn't understand this line of questioning at all and was ready to retreat to her bedroom, where Sammy was playing with the few toys he had.

"No, sweetheart, not a picture, *the* picture. Is he in your life? If Mac was okay with you walking away, what did Suiter have to say about you takin' his boy and relocating up north?" Hoss' face had gentled at her obvious confusion, but his focus was still solely on her.

Glancing at Mercy, she saw a sympathetic look she also didn't understand, and then raised her gaze back to Hoss' face. He must be worried she was going to bring trouble down on Mercy, and she needed to reassure him it wasn't the case. Shaking her head, she glanced at the hallway leading to the bedrooms then back at Hoss.

"Cal's not in any pictures, physical or situational. The courts took away his parental rights before Sammy was even born, and his whole life, the man has only ever seen Sammy twice, and not at all in the past six years. Sammy only knows what Cal's mother has told him, and I don't correct any assumptions he's made about his father."

She drew a shaky breath. "Mac owns a diner, and after my parents had kicked me out for being pregnant without a ring on my finger, I landed there. That was the first night I ever had to sleep in my car. Mac traded me a little bit of food for labor. Nearly every night for more than a year, he fed me. We set the tone that first night, because I only had forty dollars to my name and wasn't about to spend it on something to eat, not when I knew I'd need gas, and Mac wasn't a fan of letting me leave his diner hungry."

She swallowed hard, forcing back her tears. "He and his wife have been friends with me ever since, and they love Sammy as if he was their own. I've...I've worked for them off and on since I met them. Sitting in a booth in their diner is where Sammy got the most non-Mommy affection he's ever felt, seeing as how my parents don't care for me, and it trickles down to him most of the time."

She swallowed around the lump in her throat as she saw the look on his face had grown soft again, a concerned expression in his eyes as they stayed fixed on her. "So that's my story, my picture. Sad and crappy, huh?" She tilted her head down to stare at the cushion again, closing her eyes, still holding the tears back with some effort.

She felt the heat before he touched her, and then his fingers were underneath her chin, gently lifting it, and she opened her eyes. He brought her face up, tilting her head so she was looking straight at him. "No, sweetheart. Some shitty things in there, but they reflect on those other people, not on you. Something bad had to have gone down for a judge to strip Suiter of his rights even before the babe was birthed. And, I'm glad you stumbled on Mac and his woman, because young, pregnant, alone, and homeless is a hard way to find yourself, so I'm glad you had something good and sweet in there for you."

He tilted his head, gaze pinning her in place. "Sammy told me I scared you last night. I don't want you to be afraid of me, Hope. I want to be something sweet for you here. Someone you can count on. Someone who believes in you. Let me help you find a job that lets you have sweet, have time to mother your boy, loving on him as much as you want."

His thumb stroked along her jaw, brushing light as a feather across her lips, strength held in check while he touched her, caressed her. "Give me this, honey. Can you do that? All you have to do is say, 'Okay, Hoss,' and we're good." His thumb brushed across her lips again. "What do you think, sweetheart?"

"Okay, Hoss," she whispered, her lips moving against the pad of his thumb, and he smiled.

***

Sam laid on his back on the grass, looking up at the blue sky through the leaves of a tree planted smackdab in the middle of the yard. It wasn't Aunt Mercy's yard, because her apartment didn't really have one. They had come over here so his mom could meet Aunt Mercy's boss, Miss DeeDee, and this was the yard behind her big house. The breeze stirred the leaves, and he had spots all over his vision, because the sun sprinkled down on him in rays like golden droplets, blinding him until he had to shut his eyelids. Even then, the glow remained, shining through the thin flesh. He heard kids' voices and twisted, rolling to his stomach to watch a flood of boys and girls coming from the house into the backyard through the open kitchen door. The kitchen, where he had left the grownups drinking coffee and talking about apartments and furniture.

The littlest kids made a running beeline to the swing set, and the two oldest ones stopped at the picnic table, parking themselves on the top with their feet on the bench seats, pulling phones out to tap away. It looked as if they had been given the task of policing the other kids, and Sam silently snorted. He struggled to a seated position on the grass as two boys about his age walked across the yard to him. When they got closer, he said, "I'm Sam. Your mom said I could be out here." He didn't know what to make of the matching flinches the boys offered him until the shorter one said, "My mom's dead. You talked to Miss DeeDee."

Poop, he thought and shrugged, embarrassed, hiding it by looking down at the grass tickling his bare ankles, where his too-short pants had ridden up his legs. The other boy laughed, the humorless sound a little shrill, and he said, "My mom's dead too. Me and Kane, we're brothers from another mother. Miss DeeDee and Papa Jase take care of us. Sam, you wanna go swing?"

Shaking his head, he kept his gaze fixed on the ground between the soles of his sneakers. There was a fierce tightness around his chest, and he couldn't pull in a deep breath. As he sat there, he tried and failed to imagine how he would feel if his mom died. *If she wasn't around anymore*, he thought, *what would I do?* His ears were buzzing, and that clutch around his chest just wouldn't go away, the lack of air quickly becoming a concern until he pulled in a harsh, hitching breath and the feeling of being in a barrel receded. *She's not sick and we're safe here*, he thought. *Aunt Mercy said so.*

He wasn't stupid. He figured out a long time ago his dad was what the counselor at one of the shelters called a deadbeat. Which meant he wasn't a nice guy, wasn't at all like what Grandmamma had said about him. Sam had paid attention to what the counselor told Mom, even as he had sat there with his head bent over the papers and colored markers intended to keep him busy while the grownups talked. He had heard his mom's hushed attempts to quiet the woman, and seen the tears still welling in her eyes when they walked out into the bunkroom to pick their beds for the night.

After that, he had noted every time his mom talked about his dad her face got tight. Then came his birthday, and when storing the cards in his special box, with a sinking feeling in his belly, he saw that the writing looked the same. Shuffling through all the cards, he found they all had the same handwriting. The same. He knew what that meant, and from that day forward, he decided no matter what he knew, he would never let on he knew. From there forward, he would try to make-believe alongside Mom. Because she still thought his dad was a good guy. Make-believe.

He wished things were different, but like his grandfather said, if wishes were horses, then beggars would ride. He hadn't understood that one at first, but then Mom explained it meant if things were easy to come by, then everyone would have anything they wanted without working. On the surface, it might seem like a good thing, but she said if people didn't have to work for things, then whatever they had, no matter what they had, they would value it less.

Jeans-covered knees dropped into the grass beside him and a hand stretched out, entering his field of vision, accompanied by the boy's voice. "I'm Jonny Morgan."

Clasping his hand around Jonny's, he gripped it firmly and pumped it one time like Mac had taught him, introducing himself, "Sam Collins."

"You aren't from around here, are you?" Jonny gave a little hop with his legs, landing on his butt in the grass and sprawling backwards, elbows to the dirt, careless of his sleeves. Either he didn't care if he got dirty, or maybe he had so many clothes he could change whenever he felt like it.

Sam gave a little sigh, saying, "We're from Birmingham, Alabama. Came up here to visit my aunt." He plucked a piece of grass and, trapping it between his thumbs, put his hands to his mouth and blew, producing a satisfyingly piercing whistle.

"Ohhh, cool. Show me how to do that?" Jonny asked with a grin. "That was awesome."

***

Hope's mind was whirling. Things were happening around her so fast it was hard to keep up. Shaking her head, she decided to put a pause on the conversation. "Wait, please. Hold up. Can we pause for just a minute? I'm not sure I understand what's going on." She held her hand out to the redhead seated across from her at the table. "You manage the club where Mercy dances, but you aren't the manager of this bar, right?"

"Yep," came the cheerful acknowledgment. "I'm manager of Slinky's, nothing to do with the bar except working on the books when they need help."

"So then, how can you offer me a job as a waitress at this other place?" She couldn't remember the name, lost amidst the many ideas tossed across the table between DeeDee and Mercy. "I'd appreciate if you could put in a good word, but I'm more than happy to apply through normal channels. Do they use a temp service or agency?"

Mercy and DeeDee shared a laugh, their glances catching and releasing, then their eyes turned back to her. For her part, she kept her gaze on DeeDee, waiting for a response. When it came, she didn't understand what it meant. "Hoss called."

That was it. The sum total of what DeeDee said, and she left it lying in the air as if it made sense. "Hoss called?" She parroted the words back like an idiot.

"Yep." That cheerful monosyllabic response would quickly get on her nerves, because it was less than helpful to sort out her current state of confusion.

"What does that mean, Ms. Moser?" She laid her hand palm-down on the table and continued, "What does 'Hoss called' mean?"

"Oh, sweetie, call me DeeDee. What it means is Hoss called Slate and asked if we could find a job for you that could support you and your boy. I've got a policy against having family working together, so it puts Slinky's out of the picture for you, but the club owns several other businesses here in town. We'll start with the bar, and then if we need to, we can shuffle you around until we find a fit." Wow. From three letter responses to a much longer one filled with information she didn't wholly know how to process.

"And they'll hire me just like that? What about applying for the job, or interviewing? Background checks?" Furtively, she moved her hand underneath the table and pinched the side of her leg...hard. The immediate sting of tears in her eyes testified to the reality of what was happening around her. She had never been this lucky before, hadn't benefited from anything falling into place in so long she found she didn't trust it and glanced around, waiting for the other shoe to drop.

"Just like that." DeeDee smiled at her and reached out, gripping her hand and giving it a hard squeeze. "Mercy's ours, which means you and Sammy are ours, too."

"I...I don't know what to say," she admitted, feeling tears welling in her eyes again, but for an entirely pain-free reason this time. She had already asked Mercy why Hoss seemed so adamant she work for the club, and hadn't really gotten an answer, and now here was more evidence he was advocating for her, that he was on her side without them even being friends. This was foreign to her; she didn't know what to do with it.

Mercy laughed, bumping her shoulder into Hope's and leaning in close, so the sisters' sides pressed tightly against each other. "To quote Hoss from this morning, all you have to do is say okay."

Hope glanced out the sliding doors into the backyard, seeing Sammy seated on the grass with one of the kids who had rushed through the room earlier, seeking the freedom the backyard represented after whatever they had been doing all day. He and the boy seemed to be in a deep conversation, and then while she watched, her breath caught in her chest when Sammy threw back his head and laughed, the riotous sound reaching her ears even through the closed doors. For once, instead of an intense older-than-his-years facade, he looked like a child, laughing and free. *He needs this*, she thought, feeling Mercy's fingers wrap around her other hand, DeeDee still retaining possession of the one resting on the table. *I need this*.

"Okay," she whispered, watching her son leap to his feet and chase his new friend across the expanse of the yard. The pair headed for a set of playground equipment, and she saw him mimic the other boy and flip upside-down, wrapping his legs over a bar so they hung like bats while still animatedly chattering at each other. Putting aside her questions about this, as well as why Hoss would have called anyone on her behalf, when she had spoken to him exactly twice, she decided to let herself soak up the good luck that seemed to be swinging her way. "Okay."

***

"What's your play here, Hoss?" Deke slipped to a stool beside him at the bar, signaling to the bartender for a beer. He turned, leaned backwards and propped his elbows on the bar, eyeing the girls currently on stage, his posture seemingly relaxed and inattentive.

"Covering for DeeDee, man. Beginning and end, nothing else." Hoss used the mirrors to check the club patrons behind him, affecting a similar nonchalance. "She and Jase went to the doc with Bingo, needed a couple hours. Called and said they needed a couple *more* hours, because it ain't good news." He lowered his voice, "Then Mason called, said there's unrest out west again. Said he wants to make sure we have extra members everywhere it matters for the next few weeks." He shrugged. "So I called you."

Deke sighed, asking, "Is this about Michigan?" All Rebels knew Rogue, blood brother of Demon, a long-dead Michigan biker, was still looking for vengeance on them, and had been since the day his brother died. The fact he was looking in particular towards the Rebels' Fort Wayne chapter was no secret, either.

Several years ago, Demon had been president of the Devil's Sins, an upper peninsula Michigan club. He had arranged a situation and mistreated the woman who would later become Slate's old lady. She dealt with the aftereffects of that abuse for years until Slate made it his mission to woo and win her. Then, after she had finally recovered, and made a leap of faith into Slate's bed, Demon orchestrated a play involving her that went sideways in a bloody way, ending him and nearly killing her. Since then, Rogue, his brother, had refused all attempts by Mason and Slate for a sitdown, and to this day continued to snipe at them from the north.

"No changes there. Motherfuckers are still fucking with our runs and deliveries." Hoss shrugged; the Rebels may have rubbed out the original Devil's Sins, but in the aftermath, Rogue had birthed a new club, calling it Sins of the Brother. Immediately, they had started jacking inventory and fucking with Rebel business on a regular basis, escalating things significantly over the last year. Every Rebel knew it would come to war eventually, and given their history with the people who made up the club, it went without saying that it would be bloody.

Without speaking, Deke lifted his chin in response, and they sat there for a few minutes in silence. It sounded like Deke was going to speak a few times, but then didn't follow through, instead lifting his beer for a drink. Finally, he turned to look at Hoss and tilted his face down, asking as if it didn't matter, "Mercy working right now?"

"Nope," he responded, watching his friend's face fall in disappointment. He let that stretch between them for a moment then took pity on him, continuing with, "She'll be here in about thirty, though. Her set starts at nine, and she is supposed to close, so she'll be here until at least two." Deke didn't look up, but Hoss saw the corner of his mouth tip up in a smile. "You gonna do something about this dance you're doing with her?"

The pleased look fell away and Deke scowled up at him. "What are you talking about?"

"You stupid motherfucker." He laughed. "You ain't fooling anyone but yourself, and doing a shit job of that, if you ask me."

Deke ran his hand through his hair, fingers threading through to the back of his head. "She tell you about her ma?"

Hoss nodded. Mercy had talked to him about her mother and the home life endured in Alabama before leaving as soon as she was legal. When she was recovering from Birdy's beating, she had talked a lot. Some of that due to the painkillers Goose left for her, some of it a need to confide in someone she saw as a friend.

Deke said, "I get why she was the way she was. Looking to wipe out memories of the shit her ma put her through, the grabby-handed boyfriends she'd turn loose in the house with her barely teenaged daughter. The things those fuckers did to her, what they took from her...I get being wild was her way of taking back everything she thought she'd lost."

Deke shook his head, catching Hoss' eyes in the mirror. "I liked her the first time I ever saw her, you know? She wasn't looking for anything like me, though. She didn't want someone to make her think, or be honest about what was going on. She was looking to fuck her mind back straight, but goddamn"—he sucked in a breath—"I liked her. More than you could know by just looking at things from the outside. I liked her. So every fucking time she took a man into her body in the main room, pulled a fucking train, or danced up the stairs with one of our brothers, it tore off another piece of my heart."

Hoss cleared his throat, sensing movement behind them. Ignoring that, he asked, "Why didn't you stay with her after Birdy? When she was hurt? Why'd you stay away?"

"Because him takin' her was on me. I took my assignment, didn't argue with Slate, didn't speak up and tell him to put me on Mercy. If I'd been there, he wouldn't have gotten her. I was on Willa, and I fucked that up, too." Deke lifted a hand, rubbing his fingertips across his brow. "Mercy'd been coking, so Birdy thought she might have something he could use. I listened to the tapes of you talking to her, so I know you got this, but once he figured out she didn't have anything, he cranked her up, tore her up, and tossed her out like trash. Fucking shit, man, I shoulda been there. Kills me I wasn't."

"So why are you angling away from her now? Sounds like you've figured out what you're after, so why the hell aren't you putting that want into effect?" Hoss shook his head. "What are you waiting for? What do you want?"

Deke scowled and said, "I want something with her, but I can't stay straight around her long enough to settle things out, man. She unnerves me and I can't find my balance, can't find my words to say the things I need to say. To apologize to her. To tell her..." His voice trailed off and he glanced down.

"What do you want?" Hoss asked, again boiling things down to the simplest question.

"Everything," Deke whispered, and met his eyes in the mirror.

"Everything?" Both men jumped when the soft voice came from behind them, and Hoss turned around to see Mercy standing there. Her gaze locked on Deke, and Hoss watched as the color leached out of his friend's face. Without turning around, he nodded slowly. She asked him, "What does that mean, Deke? Everything."

Hoss saw the confusion on her face when Deke responded, "It means I want you, woman."

Hoss stood and said, "And that right there's my cue to walk the fuck away," laughing to himself when they ignored him. When he was near the office door, he glanced back to see Mercy standing beside Deke as he slid his arm around her shoulders to pull her closer.

Pausing for a moment, he watched as the man lifted his other hand, using fingers far more used to violence than tenderness to tuck a stray strand of hair behind her ear. Deke leaned into her, tilting his head down as he brushed his lips across hers, and Hoss saw how Mercy, trembling with emotion, lifted on her toes to meet his mouth, giving and taking in one breath. One stanza of their dance had come to a close, and he suspected the next would be even more beautiful to watch.

Smiling, he walked into the office, his thoughts turning to Hope. He hadn't been able to stop thinking of her, and now, standing in front of the desk, he closed his eyes, recalling for the hundredth time how her skin had felt under his hands. How her stunning blue eyes had held him captive for as long as she would meet his gaze. Pulling from his memory, he teased to the surface the heat and softness of her lips...the look on her face when he leaned close and talked to her…the silk of her hair, sliding across her shoulders, thinking about her mass of hair sliding across other places.

Fucking hell, I like her. He liked everything about her, the love she had for her son, how fearless and determined she was to make her own way.

He had put the wheels in motion to get her boy a bed, but according to Myron, there were no three-bedroom apartments free right now, so all the things he wanted would have to wait. He liked her boy, too, and could see he had his job cut out for him to get Sammy on his side, but he would find his in with the boy. He had to go slow, keep to the deep background so the club's enemies wouldn't get a glimpse of what she could mean to him. If they did, then he might never get a chance to find out if they would fit alongside the other like he thought they might…like he hoped and dreamed.

6. Nothing works for long

"Okay," she muttered, maneuvering another plate onto her already heavily laden tray. "You can do this." *Yay, now I'm my own crazy cheering section*, she thought, and then slid the tray onto her flattened palm, tongue tucked into the corner of her mouth as she lifted it to shoulder height with a practiced swing. Five minutes later, she had returned to the kitchen pass-through to load up the next table's lunches. The fast pace continued through most of her shift without slackening, and at just over six hours in, with less than an hour to go, she knew she was visibly flagging.

She had been working here at Marie's, one of the club-owned bars, for about a week. She felt like she was doing a good job, but there was so much to learn: the menu, specials, dishes not on the menu, plus a computerized order entry system that was so complex it boggled the mind. So far, each day still felt as if it were the first, so by the end of her shift, she was mentally and physically exhausted. Even when the shift wasn't as busy, it still felt as if she were being run off her feet, barely any energy left over for Sammy at the end of the day.

She hated feeling like that, about half sick, but wouldn't ask for time off. Not having just started working. She wouldn't be *that* employee, the one everyone knew had problems everyone else had to work around. *I've never given less than one-hundred-percent,* she grumbled internally, *and I'm not going to start now. Just gut through it, woman. You can do it.* Today, even with her mental pep talk, she gritted her teeth in frustration when the hostess waved at her, the signal another group had been seated in her assigned section. She knew it meant Kerry, the relief waitress, would probably have to finish out their service, and the idea of sharing tips was not in that woman's handbook.

Swinging around the corner of the bar, she began her approach of the table with a smile firmly in place. That smile wavered and she felt her step stutter a little when she saw the seats were filled with men wearing black leather. Bikers were the norm here in Marie's, but even at first glance, these men looked different...harder, somehow. Forcing the smile back onto her face, she stepped up between two of them, laying coasters down on the table, bending at the waist and reaching across to set them in front of the men on the opposite side. "Gentlemen," she said pleasantly, frowning when they laughed. "Can I start you off with something to drink?"

"Yeah, baby," the man next to her said, and she felt a hand creep around her hip, a gentle tug pulling her sideways into his body. "Beers all around, and keep 'em coming. Make sure the tab comes to me, yeah?"

The men called out their individual orders and she quickly jotted them down, shifting away from the man without saying anything, moving until his arm fell away. Sometimes it was most effective to simply ignore behavior you didn't want to encourage. "Sure thing," she said. Pointing to the menus on the table with her pen, she told them, "If you are looking for food, the specials are listed in the menus. I'll be right back."

At the waitress station, as she entered them into the computer, she called out the ten beers to Tequila, the Rebel member tending bar today. He was also the bar's business manager, and like most of the

Rebels, he seemed to be a good friend of Mercy's. He was pleasant enough to work for, even if, or maybe especially because, he didn't talk a lot. She finished the entry and moved to the kitchen to collect an order, delivering it and returning to the bar just as Tequila finished. As she loaded up her tray, he paused and frowned, glancing over her shoulder to the occupants of the table, then back to her face. "If those men give you trouble, you give me a yell, okay, sweetheart?"

With a smile, she shook her head. *Nope*, she told herself again. No freakin' way would she become *that* employee either, the one others had to dance around, the one who couldn't handle whatever kind of customers fate threw her way. "Pfffft," she made a dismissive noise. "I *so* got this, Tequila."

Picking up her tray, she turned, setting her shoulders and making her way between the tables and chairs to the group of bikers. As she approached, she saw the symbol on the back of their vests was a one-eyed jackrabbit, the empty orbit filled with what looked like a massive diamond. The word *Diamante* was inscribed on the fabric each had across the top of their shoulders, and there was another piece of fabric sewn to the leather near the hem, but she couldn't read what it said.

"Here you go, guys," she called cheerfully, placing the mugs and bottles of beer in front of the men, referring to her paper a couple of times to make certain she had the beverages and owners paired up correctly. "Y'all wanting to order any food?" She glanced around, catching the eyes of several of the men as they shook their heads, and nodded. "Okay. Let me know if there's anything else. I'll be back to check on you in a few minutes," she told them, turning to walk away.

Her progress halted when the same man as before reached out a hand, gripping her hip, but this time, he pulled her off her feet and down onto his lap. She froze stiff, feeling herself shrinking in on herself, and was about to scream for help, but then she hesitated. Looming over her with a relaxed grin on his face, he didn't look like he intended to cause trouble, so she attempted a laugh, placing her hand on his chest to push away. "Baby," he muttered, "could use some company."

"Sorry," she said with a grin, hoping his feelings wouldn't be hurt by her rejection. "The big guy behind the bar is my boss, and he's kinda particular about having folks actually work for their wages." He released her with a wry twist to his lips, hands to her waist to set her on her feet. Once stable and upright, she patted his cheek, glad she hadn't overreacted and yelled for Tequila. "Thanks for the offer, but I gotta serve the booze."

Glancing around the table, she saw all eyes were on her, and from the looks they were giving her, she wondered if she had offended them after all. Their unapproachably grim-faced stares intimidated her and, gradually, the smile fell from her face. Turning, she muttered, "Just yell if you need anything."

By the third round of drinks, she had figured out how to maneuver around the hands and arms and still get the beers on the table without spilling. All but one of the men had rebounded from their earlier aloofness and now were rowdy and loud, flirting and joking with her at every opportunity. The reserved man sat with his chair slightly pushed back from the table, and she noticed his gaze never stopped attentively sweeping the bar. He had strikingly beautiful red hair and a beard, and she had found herself focusing on him more than once when she served their table. She thought to herself that these men behaved distinctly unlike the Rebel members she had met so far, and she felt a frown wrinkle her brow as she walked back towards the bar.

The Rebels were all consistently pleasant to her, but in comparison to the occupants of this table, she now realized it went further than that, because they weren't just nice, they were too nice. They were friendly, but not one of them flirted with her like these men were. Standing at the waitress station, she waited for Tequila and gave him her remaining orders. Seeing Kerry slipping into the kitchen, she looked at the clock.

"I'm off in five," she said quietly, and he nodded. "Kid gloves," she muttered to herself, looking around the bar, thinking it was how the Rebels treated her. She saw Tequila tilt his head in question at her and she laughed. "You guys all treat me with kid gloves, like I can't handle things." Flinging her hand out behind her, she indicated the table of Diamante members. "These guys, not so much."

"You're ours," he said with a shrug, placing the last bottle of beer on top of her slip. "If they're fucking with you, tell me. I'll sort their shit."

"Whatever that means." She shook her head, turning back to take the men their drinks. Standing next to the man who had first ordered, she told him, "I'm about to take off. Did you want to tab out, or carry over to the new waitress?"

She anticipated the grab from in front of her and dodged to avoid the grip with a laugh, but found herself pulled quickly backwards into the lap of one of the other men, the quiet redhead. With a squeak, she tried pushing off his chest as she had the first man, but his hands held her firmly in place and she could find no purchase to twist free. One of his hands wrapped around her ribs with fingers right underneath the curve of her breast, the other one flattened on top of her thigh, thumb tucked down between her legs, hot even through the fabric of her jeans.

Startled, she stared up at him and sputtered, "I need to—" Her voice trailed off when she caught the intensity of his gaze, his face only inches from hers. He had the deepest blue eyes she had ever seen, his stare filled with strength and power.

"Blondie, you need to calm the fuck down." The redheaded man said this on a growl, as if she had been arguing with him for a while and had finally tested his limits, his hands tightening on her further as she tried to wiggle out of his hold. One of the pieces of fabric on the front of his vest said Fury, and she didn't know if that was his name or some kind of title. She thought it probably was, because it was right underneath one that said President, which was a clear title. The look in his eyes had her

77

so frightened she couldn't have told you what was rolling through her head at that moment, much less why she thought it was probably his name. "Stop squirming around, or I'm gonna smack that ass," he gritted out between clenched teeth, and she froze when she felt the pad of his thumb sweep up along the side of her breast.

"Please," she whispered, still staring into his blue eyes, not certain now what she was asking for. He leaned in, breaking the connection by pressing his face against the side of her neck, and she felt the rough texture of his beard rubbing along her skin. "Let me up." She tried for a laugh, but failed when he didn't release her. "Please, I need to finish my shift."

"What the fuck is going on here?" That rumbling voice came from behind her, and when she tried to twist in his lap to see who it was, the fingers around her thigh tightened down painfully. For an instant, she thought she felt teeth at her neck and stilled her efforts, fear now holding her in place as effectively as the hands of the muscled man. "Fury, you need to get your goddamned hands off her."

"She yours, Hoss?" His name now confirmed, the man who held her pulled his face away from her neck as she sucked in a harsh breath when his words registered. She hadn't seen Hoss since that first day at Mercy's apartment, but knew from the conversation with DeeDee that he was behind her being offered this job. *Please, God, don't let him think this was my fault*, she thought, wiggling again and pushing harder against Fury's chest with the same limited results. Mouth beside her ear, he growled at her again, "Keep the fuck still, Blondie."

"Fuck yeah, you see her working in our fucking bar?" The hard hands holding her down disappeared and she scrambled up, gaining her feet and taking several wobbly steps away from the table.

She sucked in a shaky breath, remembering why she had come to their table to begin with, and said, "I can...I'll just carry your tab over to Kerry. She's coming on, and it's no problem to—"

She didn't get any further before Hoss spoke, interrupting her, "Fury, pay the woman."

"No, no." Holding up one hand palm first, she tried for a smile but knew it probably looked more like a grimace of fear. "No, no. Hey, it's okay," she tried to say, but found herself holding two one-hundred dollar bills.

Fury didn't look at her as he said, "Keep the change, gal." He shoved back his chair, standing in a rush, and she took two more fast steps backwards. At her movement, he glanced her way then back to where she assumed Hoss was standing, shifting to stand in front of her, giving her his back. She hadn't looked at Hoss yet, afraid of what she would see. "Got yourself a little house mouse, Hoss? She's skittish, but pretty enough. Soft in all the places I like my tail to be soft, too. You get tired of the whore, pass her Diamante's way, yeah?"

"Fucking shithead. She ain't no goddamned whore," Hoss said, and his voice sounded strained.

She glanced his direction, but his features were shadowed and indistinct in the bar's lighting. She held her breath, ducking her head for a moment and then straightened, turning to the man in front of her, bringing her chin up with a trembling smile. He turned to her when she spoke, and his blue eyes were absolutely as mesmerizing from five feet away as when only bare inches had separated them moments before. With a hitch in her voice, she said, "Let me get your change. Your tab is about one-thirty; this is too big a tip." She turned to walk to the bar when a light touch on her arm halted her.

Turning, she saw Fury had reached out and was circling her wrist gently with his fingers, this grip so different from how he had held her before. Softly, he told her, "Keep the change, gal. Let's call it amends. I'm having a bad day, but you shouldn't have to put up with my shit without at least some kind of payback." He paused and grinned at her, and the flash of white teeth in that brilliant red beard was startling. In a sweet voice, he said, "You get tired of the Rebels, Blondie, we're in town. Look us up."

"Hope," she heard Tequila call, and Fury turned her loose, dropping her arm with a slow caress of his thumb across the back of her hand. As she turned to look at Tequila, she saw Fury was mouthing her name, his lips moving soundlessly, pursing in a silent puff of air.

The tone Hoss used wasn't soft or sweet; it was cold and angry, and when he spoke to her, the words were final. "Hope, get your fucking ass to the bar and cash out. You're done here. Job's not a fit." Her head bowed and she stood there for a second as it sunk in that he had just fired her in front of the whole bar. She took a deep breath and straightened. Putting one numb foot in front of the other, she walked steadily across the room, head held high and eyes unwaveringly forward while she heard the growling tones of arguing men receding behind her.

***

He stood in the yard and watched her for long minutes, framed as she was within the large window in the kitchen. Seated on a tall stool, the bare toes of one foot alternating between curling and uncurling around one of the legs, and the other resting tucked underneath a rung in the front, her knees were pressed firmly together under the patterned fabric of her skirt.

The swag and drape of the curtains surrounding the opening were cheap, single-colored visual interruptions, blocking part of his view when all he wanted to do was look at her. She had one arm wrapped around her waist, holding herself tightly, as if she needed the pressure to retain her place in the world. Her other arm had her hand lifted to her face, the edge of her thumb pressed against her mouth, teeth worrying anxiously at the skin of her cuticle. As he watched, she shifted her weight and moved slightly, the fingers and thumb of that hand trapping her bottom lip, knuckles pressed against her nose. Even from here, he could see her gaze was lowered, and guessed if he was closer he would be able to see her stare was unfocused, her attention turned inward.

She looked lost and sad, the fear on her face glaring. The bloodless line of her lips twisting at something inside him and he had a sudden, overwhelming desire to see joy on her features instead. As if reacting to his thoughts, she lifted her head, turning and arching her neck to look over her shoulder, gifting him with the vision of blonde curls cascading down her back, like the fall of white and gold wisteria blooming in an overburdened southern arbor.

He sucked in a breath when she moved to stand, watching as the fabric of her skirt swirled around her bare legs, reds and purples of flowers in bloom shifting as if blown by an unfelt breeze. From this angle, he could still see her face and observed with a smile as the corners of her mouth turned up, eyes crinkling when she held out her arms wide, welcoming the approach of the small body bulleting towards her. Scooping Sammy up, she pressed him to her torso and twirled in place, and Hoss watched as the fabric of her skirt again caressed the skin of her legs, and he imagined it continued to move long after she was still again, because it didn't want to give up that touch.

Hoss knew his words had hurt her last night, and wanted to explain, had come by today so he could tell her what had really been going on. When he walked into the bar as had become his routine on the nights she worked, he expected to remain unnoticed as always but was instead greeted with a sight that made his jaw clench. Gaze drawn like a magnet to where she was in the room only to find her perched on Fury's lap, he had wanted to storm over and rip her away, wanted to pull her close and declare she was off limits. It killed him, but he knew with everything going on in the club right now, his protection of her had to be from afar. He had to stay away in order to keep her safe.

Even Tequila told him to cool it, shaking his head from his position behind the bar, because the assholes they were dealing with had a history of taking the fight to family, dragging innocents into the fray. He had been there the night Ruby was pulled from the Devil's Sin's clubhouse, had watched as she died more than once in that fucking basement, Slate losing his mind on his knees beside her still, too-pale body. Hope had enough shit of her own to deal with before having to worry about that kind of trouble coming to roost, and then there was her boy, who might present a different kind of target for a man like Rogue.

However, what he had seen when he walked into the bar was an image he hadn't yet been able to purge from his brain. Every time he closed his eyes, he still saw it, been subject to it all night long. Her jeans-covered legs draped over Fury's lap, his face buried in her neck, the line delineating her hair from his beard hard to see in the artificial twilight of the bar lighting. Fury's hand on her side, fingers spreading from hip to breast, curving possessively around her body, his other hand deep between her legs, exploring the last place Hoss wanted to think about that man, or any man touching her. Then, the spectacle of her fear when she was free. It killed him he still wasn't certain if that fear was of him or Fury. Finally, there was the defeated slant of her shoulders before she walked to the bar, how she had slumped, beaten when he called out to her, careless of his words and audience.

Tequila told him later she had lifted her chin, not speaking, not arguing his edict, simply collecting her tips and turning in her nametag without comment. As if she had expected nothing less, had anticipated it would come sooner or later.

The tableau in the kitchen window shifted, and he saw small arms circling her legs, tightening around the full skirt, and Sammy's face appeared near her hip. Eyes closed at first, he was smiling, seeming happy just to be with his mom. Then, before Hoss could step back and out of sight, Sammy's eyes opened and focused sharply from behind his glasses, brow knitting together in a fierce frown. Hoss could practically feel the anger and disappointment radiating from the boy and knew he would have a much harder road befriending him now, because of how he had hurt the boy's mother again last night. Turning, he stiff-armed the gate, letting it rebound and slam shut behind him from the force of the opening blow as he walked away.

**

Pushing and pulling the vacuum cleaner across the floor with one hand, she used the other to turn up the music on her phone. With Emphatic blasting through her headphones, she smiled softly and tried to force a good mood, dancing up the hallway to *Louder Than Love*. It wasn't that she didn't like the job, because the job was fine. Cleaning offices wasn't hard work, and almost all of it could be done during off hours, which should have made things easier where Sammy was concerned. However, because Mercy worked at a strip club, her work hours always coincided with Hope's, which meant she was often relying on babysitters she didn't really know.

To top things off, her cleaning partner hadn't shown up again tonight, which meant she had the entire complex to take care of by herself. At this point, she was willing to do whatever was necessary to keep this job, because this was number three in the positions she'd had since moving to town. She was a good waitress, and the tips in the bar had been excellent for the few days she worked there, but once Hoss deemed she wasn't fit for the job, Tequila had only shook his head, jerking his chin towards the backdoor. She hadn't argued, had walked out to her car without a word, head held high, even as tears streamed down her cheeks.

The next day, she had gotten a call from a man who introduced himself as PBJ, and he had given her an address and a time. *PBJ, swear to God*. Tequila, Hoss, Slate, PBJ—compared to those names, even Deke sounded normal.

Driving into the lot and parking that first day, she wasn't really surprised at the kind of business it was. She found Down Range Two, one of two club-owned gun ranges, did a brisk business. She was a good receptionist, keeping the reservations organized and making sure everyone had the correct permits. Even now, she wasn't sure what had happened there. One day, she was hard at work organizing the office and getting things entered into the computer, helping out at the sign-in desk as needed, and then the next morning, she got a call from Diablo, the manager, firing her. *Diablo, no joke.* All he would say was to call Prez; they had another job they needed her on more.

Once she figured out Prez was actually Slate, she called the number DeeDee had given her. On the phone, when she tried to ask Slate what happened, what she had done wrong, he laughed softly and told her she hadn't done anything, and some things were better left a mystery.

As she lay sleepless in her bed at night, that laugh didn't help settle any of her fears, though. Which meant she kept going over and over her few interactions with customers at the range, because it had to be a complaint that got her ousted. She couldn't remember making anyone mad, and even though she had initially argued against it, she even wore their uniform in the only size available, changing into the logo-emblazoned too-small shirt at Diablo's direction.

The way he stared at her when she came out of the bathroom after squeezing into the top made her nervous, as did his muttering something about rushing an order of shirts for Hoss. Still, the only real blip on the radar the entire two weeks she worked there was the last day, when Deke came in. He walked in the door and, immediately, she recognized him as the man Hoss had faced down her first night in town. The encounter at the gun range was a blip, because he had been a jerk, again.

She paused, mindlessly running the vacuum over the same spot again. In the quiet, as Emphatic drifted to silence and before Iron & Wine could begin singing *Naked As We Came*, the loud sound of thunder startled her, gaze going to the window to see the rain still coming down in sheets. *Ugh.* If it kept up, it would make the trip home miserable.

Her mind turned back to that day at the gun range, because knowing her sister had begun dating Deke, she hadn't expected his snarky remarks. Cringing, she had whispered a request to Diablo. Permission granted with a head tip, she escaped to the office, closing the door behind her with some relief.

That barrier didn't keep her from hearing Deke talking, though, and her cheeks flooded with color now as she remembered his language about her shirt and the anatomy it failed to cover fully. With that fresh memory, she tugged at the uniform she now wore, pulling the top up in the front, trying to cover her cleavage as she bowed her head, focusing on the cleaning still to do.

It was late when she finally finished, and after putting up all the supplies, she stood in the foyer, watching through the glass as the rain sheeted down. Opening the alarm system, she punched in the code to set the building's alarm, closing the panel with a flat palm before turning to face the door again. Staring out into the darkness for a moment more, she stayed in the shelter of the doorway while she tugged her hoodie up to cover her hair. It wasn't much, but without an umbrella, it would be all the protection she had from the rain. Aware she was eating into the three minutes of grace before things would start to blip and beep, she shrugged and adjusted her hoodie again. Glancing at her phone, she saw it was just after three in the morning, more than four hours later than normal, but at least the job was completed to her satisfaction. Four more hours of babysitting to pay for, but no one would be able to complain, which would mean she could keep the job at least one more day.

She pulled the door closed behind her with a dull thud, the noise barely heard over the combination of rain and her headphones. Bopping to the music, which was now Leela James singing *Tell Me You Love Me*, she didn't notice the shadow that separated itself from the side of the building. Not realizing she wasn't alone until the hand fell on her shoulder, she stumbled when it jerked her around and off balance. When a hand ripped the headphones from her ears, she screamed before she recognized Hoss standing there, hair and shirt soaked from the rain, a furious look on his face. To keep from falling, she had reflexively stretched out a hand, which was now resting against his chest, the rapid thudding of his heart pounding through her palm.

"What the fuck are you doing, Hope?" His voice, raised to be heard over the pounding rain, was so harsh it stole her breath, and she felt her shoulders hunch in protectively. This felt like a bad dream and she glanced around, waiting for Cal to show, because if it was a dream, he would be here, since he usually featured heavily in her nightmares. "Hope, I'm talking to you. Look at me. What the fuck are you doing?" He lifted one of her earbuds to his head and listened briefly, and then frowned and dropped it again.

Nearly in tears, both from the initial fright and now his tone, with a trembling voice, she said, "I just finished. I...I'm headed home." Her clothes already felt heavy with water, and she dreaded the walk back to the apartment, exhausted, and now soaked and cold. Licking her lips, she felt his chest rise and fall with a deep breath and realized her palm still pressed against him.

Stepping back, she was surprised when he followed her by taking a matching step forward, and then he reached up, trapping her hand against him. "Um. I went as fast as I could, and I know the job pays seven to eleven. I'm not looking for anything extra. I just wanted to make it right. I just worked until everything was done." Licking her lips again, blinking the water out of her eyes, she tilted her head to look up at him as he loomed over her.

"Ain't worried about overtime, sweetheart. What I am worried about is you being so stupid as to step into this parking lot at three in the fucking morning in a fucking rainstorm without even looking around. Or being able to hear a goddamned thing over that fucking music you're listening to. That's my main worry." He tipped his head, gaze scouring her face, looking for something, but she didn't know what. He seemed indifferent to the rain and wind, eyes narrowing as she flinched from a flash of lightning. "But since you brought it up, why are you here alone? Because that's a different worry for me."

"Um. Laurie called, said she couldn't make it, so it took a little longer with one person..." Her voice trailed off, because the look on his face was terrifying up this close. It would probably be merely frightening from across a wide room, but because she was only a foot or so away, she caught the full effect of his wrath. She also felt the anger rolling off him, felt the boiling rage filling the air. So all of *that* jacked frightening up to terrifying within seconds. The play of shadows and bright flashes made his face foreign, which added to her weight of fear.

"Are you fucking kidding me? Did you fucking think of calling anyone?" These questions from Hoss were puzzling, and her confusion must have shown on her face, because he took in another deep breath, one she again felt, because her palm was still trapped against his chest. "Did you fucking think of calling me, Hope? Me?"

"Um. No, she said she would take care of notifying Jase. I didn't think I needed to call anyone." Jase was the club's general business manager in Fort Wayne, and for the jobs that didn't need direct day-to-day management, he was the go-to guy. Biting the inside of her cheek hard, she tried to still the trembling of her lips. *I will not cry in front of him,* she thought, and then ducked her head, because, in spite of her best efforts, tears were filling her eyes.

"I'm sorry," she whispered, chin down, tugging her hand out of his grip and gathering up her headphones from where they hung out of her front pocket. She unplugged them, pushing the wires into the back pocket of her jeans, still without looking up, because the tears were entirely too close. "I'm just trying to do the best I can. I need this job."

She squeezed her eyes shut when she felt his fingers under her chin, lifting her face so he could see her. "Oh, sweetheart," he muttered and then reached out, pulling her to his chest in a hug that felt so good and right she could nearly feel the sadness and fear leaving her body, banished by his embrace. The heat and warmth of his body eclipsed the chill from the rain, and she felt a shiver move through her that had nothing to do with being cold. He wrapped her up, one arm pressing against her shoulder blades, and one spanning lower on her back, his hands cupping her side and hip. His body moved as he shook his head back and forth, denying something, his beard scraping across her skin, raising its own crop of goosebumps. He moved again, bending his head down and because her hair was up, she felt his breath against her neck, heated and rapid. "You didn't do anything wrong, Hope. Hush, baby."

He held her for a long time, minutes passing with only a softly muttered, "Hush," when she tried to move. The rain created a silence of sorts, isolating them from noises that would otherwise intrude. Relaxing into him, she wiggled her arms from in front of her and wrapped them around his waist, pressing her palms flat against his back, feeling the slickness of the wet fabric under her hand. She turned her head, laying her cheek against the warmth radiating through his shirt from his chest. Opening her eyes to darkness, she froze for a moment because she had somehow snuggled her way underneath his leather vest. A quick laugh escaped her, causing a matching laugh to rumble under her ear as he asked, "Whatcha laughing at, sweetheart?"

"I think I needed that," she said, making movements to signal her intent to pull away, but his arms tightened around her. "You're the best hugger. Thanks, Hoss."

"I don't think I'm done," he said softly, and she felt his hands gripping her a little tighter, until a few moments later he gave her a little shake before letting her ease back. The rain was beginning to slack off, more of a drizzle now than a true rainfall. "Has this happened before with Laurie?"

"Just a couple of times. It's no big deal," she said with a small grin, but let it fade when he didn't return it.

"And she said she would call Jase?" His tone had firmed again, the humor from a moment ago a memory. She nodded and watched as his face tensed then relaxed. "Let's get you home," he said, turning her while keeping an arm around her shoulders. Walking towards the lot, he stopped in surprise and asked, "Where's your car?"

"It's not far," she said and snorted a laugh when he physically turned them, sweeping the wet, empty asphalt with his gaze before glancing down at her. "I meant the apartment. It's not far."

"You walked," he said, not really a question, but she responded.

"Yeah, it's not far."

"You said that," he said, frowning down at her. "You walk here the other nights you work?"

"Yeah, I'm saving money wherever I can—" She started trying to explain, but stopped when he interrupted her, his frown deepening.

"You can't afford ten dollars gas a week?" He sounded angry at this and she couldn't figure out why, but the tension in his tone shook her as much as the thunder had earlier. "Ten fucking dollars to have your ass safely in a car, instead of exposed on the sidewalk? What about Sammy?"

"I just want—" She spoke, but he interrupted her again with a brusque shake of his head. They stood in silence for a moment as she considered his words, the most important of which were the last three he had uttered, and then she whispered, "You're right, Hoss. I'm sorry. I'll drive tomorrow." Another moment, and when she saw one corner of his mouth curl up, she felt the weight that had settled on her chest at some point during their conversation lighten a little.

"Sweetheart, why don't you get in the truck," he said, seeming to notice the rain for the first time. "You're soaked through." Steering her towards a pickup parked near the building, he muttered, "I'll take you home."

"I have to get Sammy," she said, her hand colliding with his as they both reached for the door handle. With a laugh, she tilted her head up to look at him, expecting to share the humorous moment, but saw a return of the dark look instead, the wet hair curling at his temples a soft contrast to the hard expression on his face.

"Sammy ain't at home?" His brows had drawn together, and the frown combined with the intense look he was giving her made her nervous.

"No, he's at the sitter's."

"Ain't at home in his own bed. You got to go get the boy and wake him up to take him home at," he pulled out his phone and consulted it, "nearly four in the morning? Were you planning on carrying him, or was he gonna have to hoof it, too? How's that going to work when he's in school?"

She lifted one shoulder, imitating an ease she didn't feel. "I'll figure it out."

"You ain't in this alone, Hope." His voice had dropped an octave and sounded full of gravel, resonating in her chest and causing her belly to clench. "You ain't in any of this alone. We're here, waiting. You simply gotta reach out. Ain't in this alone." The look on his face spoke of deep disappointment, and she tensed all over again, because she knew he was important to Mercy and didn't want him to be upset with her.

"No, I know that. I'll figure it out by the time he goes to school. Promise. He's the most important thing in my life. I'll do right by him." She offered him a smile, which again went unreturned. Reaching up, she pushed her wet bangs out of her face. "You don't have to drive me. The sitter lives right across the park, and Sammy isn't heavy. I do this all the time, Hoss."

"Get in the goddamned truck, Hope." Still scowling, he yanked the door open and stepped back, and it was only then that how close he had been standing registered. "I didn't come all the way out here to watch you walk away."

Frowning, she squinted her eyes as she pulled herself into the tall truck, asking, "Why did you come by, Hoss?"

"You weren't home on time," he said, slamming the door and effectively cutting off the conversation.

Silently, he drove to the address she gave him, the frown on his face deepening yet again as they drove down the rutted road and parked. She climbed out of the truck, sidestepping the glistening, rainbow-covered puddles in the driveway behind the sitter's van and skirting around the furiously barking dog chained to one corner of the box-crowded carport. No matter how often she came here, the dog never settled; he always barked and growled. She had the sure knowledge that if she strayed too close, she would come away with a lot more than a nip. She had forbidden Sammy to try to make friends with the animal, which killed him, because he loved dogs.

When she came out of the trailer carrying a sleeping Sammy, Hoss was there to relieve her of the boy's weight, taking him from her arms at the front of the truck and setting him gently into the backseat. She climbed in front and leaned over the seat to buckle him in, arranging his limbs in a way that didn't look too terribly uncomfortable. The truck rocked as Hoss seated himself, and once Sammy was secure, she twisted in the seat, moving from her knees to her butt as she faced forward. She saw Hoss was sitting quietly, leaning his forehead against the steering wheel. "Ready," she said softly, buckling her own seatbelt, feeling guilty she was keeping him from his own bed if he was so tired.

At Mercy's apartment, they reversed the process, with Hoss carrying Sammy into their shared bedroom, laying him on the single bed that had shown up one day. She had come back from job-hunting to find it already assembled and made up with cute hockey-themed bedding. Now she efficiently stripped her sleeping son to his briefs, pulling the covers up over him and leaning in to kiss his forehead.

When she straightened, she saw Hoss was seated on her bed, socked feet outstretched, legs crossed at the ankles, pillows shoved behind his shoulders, which were propped against the headboard. Sitting there motionless for a moment, he watched her, his face impassive. He had taken off his boots and shirt, stripping down to his jeans, and she shivered at seeing the expanse of bare skin across his impressive chest and shoulders. She shivered again, her clothes clammy in the air-conditioned chill of the apartment. At least the expression on his face was far more pleasant than most of the ones she had witnessed so far tonight, and experimentally, she offered him a smile.

Wordlessly, he pointed to a small pile of clothes on the corner of the bed, and she stifled a laugh. It was her standard pajama selection of thrift store sweatpants and baggy shirt. Normally, she left them tucked under the pillow; he must have found them when he shifted things around. She picked them up and nodded, leaving to walk to the bathroom. Changing quickly, she left her wet things draped over the shower rod and returned to the bedroom.

Fiddling with her wet phone, she stopped right inside the door, pausing in surprise, because he was still lounging on the bed. "Hoss, thank you for everything tonight. You're a life saver," she said quietly and smiled broadly when one corner of his mouth rose in that crooked smile she was becoming used to.

"Come here," he responded just as quietly, holding out one arm. "I'm fucking beat. I'll move to the couch before long, but I could use a nap. You look like you're fucking freezing, even in those dry clothes. Why don't we get you warmed up, Hope. Come here, baby."

Not completely sure what this meant, she was too tired to figure it out tonight. Remembering the comfort offered when he held her earlier and Mercy's easy friendship with him, she set aside her questions along with her waterlogged phone and crawled up the bed, settling in next to him, letting his arm wrap around her shoulders. She laid her head on his chest, resting one hand under her cheek. She felt him move, and then his fingers were fumbling at her still-damp hair and the clip holding it back released. He threaded his fingers through her thick locks to her scalp, rubbing lightly. She shifted slightly, burrowing her face into his chest, and heard a drowsy-sounding, "Hush, baby," just before she fell asleep.

Hope woke up early, alone. There was a note for her on the kitchen table and, from the sympathetic looks she received, she was sure Mercy had already read it. Hoss, she assumed it was him, because he was the only Rebel who had been in the house last night, wrote that the cleaning job wasn't a fit. The note said someone would be in touch with another option soon. The salutation of 'sweetheart' didn't work to ease the sting much, and after Mercy left for her set at the club, Hope watched Sammy play video games for a while.

The second time he complained she was distracting him, she moved to sit on the stool by the kitchen window, staring outside at nothing in particular, turning her rapidly diminishing options over in her mind.

7. Anticipation

Frustrated, he crumpled up the paper and tossed it towards the wastebasket. So far, he had been entirely unable to capture any of the things that made Hope...Hope. All of his attempted sketches came up short of ideal, and he wouldn't accept anything less than flawless. Not for this one, not when he saw her perfection every time he closed his eyes. In his mind he could see it, could visualize where the images needed to go, where he could take them, but the communication from brain to fingers wasn't flowing this time.

Hoss closed his eyes and let his mind fill with memories of how it felt to hold her. That morning a week ago, when he stood in the pouring rain, placing his arms protectively around her, still filled with terror of what his brain had been imagining could have happened, and felt her body press trustingly to his. He remembered the swell of emotion in his chest when she curled into his side, innocently resting against him in her bed, her son an unwitting chaperone only ten feet away.

He smiled, because these were the emotions he wanted to capture, that breathless tightening around his chest, the way her body responded to his hand in her hair, respirations increasing as he ran his fingers through her curls. The different satisfaction when she relaxed into sleep and he knew it was because she felt safe with him. He reached out and picked up the pencil, setting his hand to the paper on the desk in front of him.

This time, instead of a solo figure, in long, continuous lines across the surface he drew the outline of a couple. With softer marks, he traced the curves of the woman's ass, and then sketched in the more angular, masculine features of the man's leg.

Several hours later, he leaned back, exhausted but pleased, gazing down at the completed image in front of him. The sweeping strokes and muted pastels used depicted a man on his back with a woman astride him, his hands gripping the curve of her ass where it rested on his thighs, still covered with the coarse denim fabric of his jeans. She was more nearly naked, her posture suggesting she had leaned far in for a kiss, the sweep of her back arching and curving. Bare. The stark color differences were compelling, highlighting the soft, pale, rosy pearl of her skin against the hard, dark, tanned fingers desperately gripping and holding onto the woman as she ground against him.

Hoss felt his cock fattening and hardening as his gaze retraced the lines of the drawing. Shading indicated man's fingers were gripping tightly, creating indentations in the supple skin of her ass, thumb dragging the fabric of her thong to one side, exposing the shadowed cleft between her buttocks. He had captured the couple in an amorous embrace, movement implied in the tension of the muscles working under the skin. There were no identifying characteristics of either the man or woman in the sketch, but Hoss had drawn all he felt for Hope, the sharp edge of his desire. He quickly signed and titled the piece, naming it what it was in truth, *Anticipation*.

***

"I'm sorry," she mouthed, watching as the whirling, plastic dervish descended on the car again, rocking the suspension. She had been washing the front grill of the car when she glanced up and saw the driver staring at her. She had smiled at him, and when the hose became stuck, gave it a yank to pull a little more slack for her use. That was when the car leapt forward, barely missing her as it drove recklessly into the carwash.

Which led them to where they were now, with her and the other workers watching the overhead scrubber as it worked in conjunction with the ones on the side, effectively trapping the driver in the car. With the rear-wheel push on the conveyor track engaged, he couldn't back up, and it seemed his car was confusing the infrared eyes so the scrubber continued to attack the car, over and over.

Looking up, she saw the manager in the viewing window had a phone to his ear. Just as one of the men hit the emergency stop button, she saw the manager wince and his eyes cut to her. Hope sighed, already anticipating the conversation to come.

8. Put tonight behind you

"But I don't know anything about trucking," she said, staring at Slate with wide eyes. Her statement wasn't exactly true, but it had been a job at a trucking company that was the reason she was standing here right now, and this felt…off.

He looked at her kindly, but she saw the muscles of his arms bunching and tightening, the tattoos on his skin dancing across the play of flesh and tendons that testified to the tension he brought into this conversation with her. "Hope, this is about the last thing I have in my back pocket for you. I can reach out to some folks I know here in the Fort, but we're about out of options for club businesses."

Ducking her head, she stared at the pattern of the rug underneath his desk. They were in the office behind the bar of the clubhouse, her first time inside this large, imposing structure. Surrounded by a tall fence, the three-story building sat in the middle of a large, paved lot, but when you went around to the back, there was a huge expanse of grass with picnic tables and playground equipment. For all intents and purposes, it could have been any business, but on the front of the building, above the large porch, was a stark black and white sign that said Rebel Wayfarers, branding the structure as something far different from any of its neighbors.

Once inside, she had been surprised at the large rooms, packed with clusters of chairs and couches, tall tables—all mostly empty right now, but she suspected the space would fill with members as night fell. There was a long bar running down one wall, and at the opposite end of the room were two pool tables. As Slate had escorted her to his office, she had glanced through an open door to find a huge kitchen, with industrial appliances like the ones Mac had in the diner down in Birmingham.

Sighing, she lifted her gaze to see him watching her tolerantly, waiting for her to come to a decision. She licked her lips then rolled her shoulders and lifted her chin. It was time to step away from the club and, once again, take responsibility for herself and her son. "I don't think it would be any better a fit than anything else we've tried, Slate. I'm sorry for wasting your time. I stopped by a couple of the temp agencies while I was out and about this morning, and I've made a couple of calls. I'll…I'll figure something out. Thank you for trying so hard to make this work. I do appreciate everything you've done…everything the club has done."

He stared at her for a long minute, filled with a seemingly immeasurable patience. *Probably waiting to see if I will change my mind*, she thought and broke the contact, glancing back down when he spoke. "Goes against the grain, Hope. I like to fix things, and this isn't a failure I expected. Give me a couple days, and let me see if I can locate something else."

"Temp work comes in kinda seasonal waves, but I doubt they can offer me anything that will get in the way if you find another option for me." She gave him a brief smile, not letting him see how it hurt when he admitted he found her a failure. "I work hard, and I'm willing to do anything, but it feels like I've already let you down with the other jobs.

With this one, for your friend's trucking company? Dispatching drivers? I don't know anything about it. I'm too scared of letting you down again."

"Sweetheart." The familiar voice from behind her caused a tightness in her chest, and she swallowed hard, forcing her injured feelings down. She hadn't seen Hoss since falling asleep in the bed beside him. That had been a week ago, just before he fired her, again. She twisted to see him leaning casually against the doorframe, relaxed, and unlike her, pain free. "You didn't let us down." Knowing it for a lie, she swallowed hard again, and he frowned. He said softly, "We ain't found your fit yet. That's all."

With a quick nod, she stepped to one side, letting him walk into the room as she sidled towards the door, carefully sidestepping so she wouldn't have to touch him. "Thanks again, Slate," she said and lifted her hand. When he didn't return the gesture, she let her hand fall and walked out without speaking to Hoss. Hurrying towards the parking lot, she hadn't made it out of earshot, so she heard Hoss ask in an angry tone, "You piss her off?" She didn't stick around to hear Slate's answer, preferring not to listen to him voice disappointment in her again.

***

Her clearly uncomfortable avoidance of him sliced through him like a broken pane of glass, and Hoss carried the resulting anger into his conversation with Slate. "What the fuck did you do to make her take off like that?"

"Oh, no, brother," Slate sneered, "it ain't me that's the reason for her being pissed today. You tossed her off another fucking job without even giving me a goddamned heads up. The goddamned rules you put into place are fucking you in the ass, man. Keep her safe and off radar but put her in a club joint so you can check the fuck up on her whenever you fucking feel like it? Tall orders, Hoss, especially when you only sweep in every week or so to decide that the latest efforts just don't measure up to your fucking standards."

"We own a fuckton of places she could work that would never get her attention. What the hell's wrong with the used bookstore, or the gas station?" Hoss twisted his neck, glaring out the window, watching Hope climb into her black and white car and he made a mental note to have Gunny look it over, make sure it was running okay. "You keep putting her into places where she's going to catch shit."

Slate sank into his chair with a heavy sigh, looked up at Hoss and pulled at the back of his neck with a rough palm. "She's too fucking smart for her own good. I drop her into the gas station and she's going to balk at the pay you want her to have, brother. This is not a woman who is going to willingly accept handouts. She doesn't know how to let folks do for her, I suspect she ain't never been on the dole." He shook his head. "Spots a lie in a heartbeat, because she's always on the fucking lookout. Don't think I've ever met someone as ready to believe bad about themselves."

"Need to get her in a good place, brother, and soon. Deke says she's worried, asking Mercy all the time about money. She's gotta stay, man. School starts before long and that boy needs to get the help Eddie's offering." Hoss paused, and then admitted, "Fuck, Slate, I need her stable so I have my head on straight. I got a message earlier, suspect you received the same. Mason's fighting shit in Chicago, he's called me back up to Mother for a bit." Hoss took a seat on the sofa across the desk from Slate. "Let's talk what kind of changes this means for the Fort, see who I'm taking, and who you need to stay."

***

Running her bar rag over the counter in front of the man who had just seated himself, she said, "Hi. Thanks for coming in. What can I get you?"

"Beer," he muttered, turning to place his back against the bar.

Rolling her eyes, because the single word didn't give her enough information, she asked, "Got a particular kind you like more than others?"

"Don't fucking roll your eyes at me, girl. Get me a draft, something wet and cold." Looking up, she found him using the mirrors to watch her and she fought against another eye roll.

"Coming right up," she said brightly, turning to pull a chilled mug from the cooler and tipping it underneath the draft spigot, flipping the lever forward with the side of her hand.

She had been surprised when she got the call from the agency about a bartender job at Murphy's Law, but had jumped on the chance for the promised day shift. Working days meant Sammy could stay with Mercy instead of a sitter, which was way more comfortable for both of them.

Mercy's questions when she heard the name of the bar were surprising, because the first thing she asked was if Hoss knew where the job was. She had shaken her head, puzzled, because there was no reason for Hoss to care where she worked unless it was a club business, and thus could reflect badly on him. Finding out Murphy's was a biker bar had given her pause for a moment, but bringing in money was more important than anything else right now. She couldn't keep sponging off her sister, not and be happy.

Today, over the next few hours of her shift, the bar slowly filled up until, by late afternoon, she was hard pressed to keep ahead of the drink demands. Pausing for a breath, she swept the room with her gaze and with a deep sense of disquiet saw she was the only female present. Not that any of the men had given her reason to be uneasy, they might be impatient or flirty by turns, but at no time had she felt threatened. Rolling her shoulders to shrug the feelings away, she grabbed a stack of buckets and half-filled them with ice, trying to anticipate and get ahead of the next round of orders. From behind her, she heard Green's voice, calling out in surprise, "Gator, what the hell you doin' in town, man?"

Green cooked here at Murphy's, and was supposed to be her backup bartender for busy days like this, but she would almost rather he stay in the kitchen, because the big man tended to get in the way.

Glancing up, she saw a new group of men had come in and were approaching the bar. With an internal wince, she recognized the man out in front. He was one of the men from the last table she waited on at Marie's. There was a flash of red from behind him and her breath caught in her throat, because she suspected that color hair could only belong to one man. Gator, as Green had addressed him, stopped short at the sight of her behind the bar, and a broad grin broke across his face. "Blondie," he called, and stepped to one side, revealing Fury behind him. The man's face was tilted down, gaze on the phone in his hand, but at Gator's greeting, it swung up and fixed on her, pinning her in place with an unexpected intensity.

Straightening from where she was crouched by the icemaker, she stood, looking at him. Other than the buzz of noise from the nearly muted TVs scattered around and mounted on the walls, the bar had fallen unnervingly silent, as if they were waiting on something. Even the noise from the pool tables had faded away, and she saw most of the men had turned to face Fury, but their gazes were dancing back and forth between him and her in a way that made her wonder what they were thinking.

Taking the last three steps that brought him to the bar, Fury shoved a stool to one side, leaning against the edge of the counter with his forearms, hands clasped in front of him. He raked her up and down with his gaze, and she saw him begin to smile. As it had before, the expression transformed his face, the well-established lines at the corners of his eyes testifying to the frequency of his smiles and she heard his voice, low but clear, call her name, "Hope."

Taking a breath, she greeted him in the same fashion, letting him know she remembered him, too. "Fury." Schooling herself to stillness, because she desperately wanted to fidget, she asked, "Beer?" At his slow nod, she glanced at the rest of the men now clustered beside him at the bar, the men previously seated there having moved to make room. "All around?" Fury's lips moved slightly, the look on his face slipping into a teasing grin from the pleased smile of before, and he nodded a second time. "Got you," she said, sticking to their laconic exchange. Bending over and placing the ice-filled buckets into the cooler, she racked her brain to remember the kinds of beer each man had ordered before. Quickly pulling out what she hoped were the right selections, placing the final bottle in front of the now-grinning Gator, she asked, "Tab?" Fury nodded again, reaching out to pick up his beer and take a long pull from it.

At his action, the noise in the bar gradually began to build to normal levels, and she shifted, about to step backwards, when he reached out his other hand, gripping her wrist. "When did you start here, gal?"

She shrugged, futilely twisting her arm in an effort to dislodge his hand. "Couple weeks?" She twisted her arm again and he frowned, his hand tightening then releasing her. When he didn't say anything further, she turned and worked her way back up the bar, refilling mugs and setting freshly-opened bottles in front of men. Ignoring the weight of his stare on her, she was making her way back and forth between the patrons and the register, ringing up sales and adding to the many running tabs she had open.

Raising her head when the door opened, she saw several new men walk in, going directly to an empty table near the wall. Grabbing a wet rag, she walked over and wiped the table down before placing coasters in front of the weary-looking men, asking with a smile, "What can I get you?" Her question ended on a gasp as the man to her right looped an arm around her waist, pulling her into his lap, one hand aggressively palming her breast. Held tightly with her back to his front, her efforts to extricate herself were unsuccessful, and he laughed loudly at her furious demand, "Let me go."

His laugh ended abruptly as he was knocked to the right, falling out of the chair and losing his grip on her when she was launched the other direction by a strong hand on her bicep, pulling her to her feet and away from the table. The hand stayed on her arm, but she was shoved behind a broad back bearing a Diamante patch, Fury stepping between her and the table as he said, "Keep your goddamned fucking hands off, Lalo."

The man who had fallen to the floor surged to his feet, and she saw him step forward until he and Fury were nearly chest-to-chest. She shifted her feet, and the hand on her arm tightened until she stilled, and then it loosened, sliding down to bracelet her wrist. Glancing over Fury's shoulder, the Hispanic man scowled at her then tipped his head slightly, transferring the force of his glower to Fury. "You need to keep your tail out of the bar, *brother*." The blatant insolent emphasis on the last word caused Fury's hand to tighten around her wrist, but at her indrawn breath of pain, it loosened again.

"Fuck you, Lalo. What the hell you doin' in the Fort? You're supposed to be in Ocala, tightening down territory there." The energy in the bar changed, lifting, and Hope belatedly realized all the men in the room were on their feet. Those nearest this table had moved away, most giving a cleared space around the two men in front of her. Glancing around, she saw Gator and the men who had walked in with Fury were standing close behind them, just as the men who had walked in with Lalo were likewise gathered at his back.

"Got tired of the beautiful sunshine, thought I'd come visit a different climate." He snorted a laugh, his gaze raking her again. "Wanna explain putting your hands on me?"

"Nope," Fury said, and she saw Lalo's face get tight. "Blondie works our bar; she's ours. I don't know what the fuck you did in New Mexico to lose your old place there, but you ain't even in your new place right now, are you? Neither New Mexico, nor Florida. You've come to my house without even a fucking courtesy call, and I will put my hands on you any fucking time I want." At the movement of a man behind Lalo,

Fury growled, "Go ahead, Chismoso. Go right the fuck ahead. You fucking lost Chicago, and that in a way that came fucking close to putting you out bad. Damned near cut. Now, you want to come to the Fort and start shit with your own fucking patch brothers?" His voice smoothed, becoming cold and slow as he continued, "You wanna dance? Then, bring it the fuck on and let's dance."

The atmosphere in the bar had shifted back to a heavy, suffocating weight and she began to panic, frantically twisting her arm back and forth as she had earlier, wanting desperately to retreat behind the safety of the bar. He didn't clamp back down on her as she expected, but instead, Fury's thumb swept back and forth across the back of her hand, the slow, soft touches dispelling her panic, scattering it and leaving a growing confidence in his ability to protect her in its wake.

They stood there for a minute, and when no one responded, he gave a little tug, pulling her up beside him. His arm flipped over her head, keeping his hold on her wrist so her arm bent double when he tucked her into his side. "Blondie is ours. Hands off, man," he said with a nod, turning them to walk back to the bar, his arm hot across her shoulders. Hope was surprised at the tension she saw in Gator and the other men's faces, because beside her, Fury felt as relaxed and loose as if nothing had happened.

The widening of Gator's eyes was the only warning she had before a shot rang out in the enclosed space. She screamed, flinching, and dropped to her knees on the floor in reaction as one of the neon lights over the bar ahead of them exploded, the flash as blinding as the gunshot was deafening. Fury twisted, his legs straddling her, one foot on either side of her hips as she cowered.

"Oops," she heard as if from far away, and then the bar was filled with movement when the men from the edges of the room flooded in, moving past her position. She focused on the floor in front of her, struggling to bring her breathing under control. She watched as scuffed brown and black leather boots strode and stepped, treading the boards, seeing how the wood bent and warped under their weight, only to rebound, unaffected in any long term way by the treatment received from these men. She hoped she could be the same, but the terror clogging her throat made it impossible to believe.

She screamed again when hands gripped her waist, picking her up off the floor, closing her mouth abruptly and quieting when she saw it was Fury holding her, his arms wrapped around her back. Standing firm as the fight ebbed around them, he was still holding her, staring into her face when, through the buzzing in her ears, she heard Gator say, "What you want us to do with the problems, boss?"

Still flat and cold, his voice threaded through her remaining fear, gathering and ratcheting it up again as he said, "Clubhouse."

"Ya, boss," Gator said, and she turned her head to watch Lalo, Chismoso, and the men who had come in with them escorted out the door, restrained by a variety of utilitarian methods, still struggling against the men holding their arms.

Fury strode forward, lifting her effortlessly and setting her on the bar. He pulled out his phone and glanced down to dial, lifting his gaze back to her face as he waited for a moment, and then said, "Shut the fuck up. Hope's in my bar." The buzzing in her ears grew louder as he paused, and then snorted, saying, "Not jacking with you. She's got her sweet ass on the bar right now, and I'm standing right here, between her fucking knees." He made this truth as he pushed her legs apart with his hips, wedging himself into the space, even as it seemed he retreated from her, sounds other than the buzzing even more muted. There was another pause, and then he said, "I'll walk her out when I see you on the cam."

Without looking down, he pushed a button on the phone and slid it into his pocket. Flicking a glance behind her, he said, "Greenie, get Blondie here some juice." To her, he said, "Gal, you're white as a sheet. Don't you go fainting on me."

There was a noise, and she slowly turned to see a hand holding up a glass of orange juice. "Breathe, Hope. Take a breath, gal," she heard Fury say, and twisted back to look at him, realizing she was lightheaded, the sounds around her receding, even while the lights seemed to dim. From far away, she heard cursing, and then nothing as darkness crashed down on her.

She became aware by slow stages, first of the muted sounds of traffic in the distance, then noises from nearby of birds quietly putting themselves to bed as night came down. There was a fast thud under her cheek, that sound nearly familiar, and she rubbed her face back and forth, thinking she would feel a soft, supple leather against her skin. Instead, she felt the scratching of fabric edges and whispered, "Hoss?"

The arms holding her tightened and she heard a hissed, *"Fuck,"* that drew her eyes open, because she couldn't place who had spoken. Tilting her head back, instead of the familiar and safe features she expected, she found the tense face of Fury hovering over her. That caused her to jerk back, moving away just as a voice she recognized called her name from a little ways away, "Hope?" *He's here.*

She tried to twist away, but as had happened the first time she met him, her efforts were ineffectual until he cooperated. "Please," she whispered, "let me go." She turned her head, trying to find the face she wanted, calling, "Hoss?" Fury's arms loosened and he swung her legs to the ground, his hands at her waist to steady her first faltering steps.

Then she turned and was running, flying over the parking lot pavement, crashing into Hoss. Feeling his arms wrap themselves tightly around her, hearing his voice soft beside her head, asking, "Hope, honey, what's going on?" She shook her head, unable to speak, simply knowing when she heard his voice she had to be with him, needed to be in his arms. Shaking her head again, her hands clutched tightly at the shirt under his leather vest while his hands moved slowly up and down her back.

Projecting his voice, his tone was steady as he asked Fury, "You want to share with me exactly what the *fuck* is going on?"

"Hope was working her shift when we had a little disagreement inside. Things got over and done with, and I called you. Then she passed right the fuck out, so I brought her out here to wait for you." Fury's tone was as quiet as Hoss' had been, and she squeezed her eyes shut, thinking how silly she must look, running from the man who had kept her safe.

"The fuck you mean *working*?" Hoss had tightened under her hands, but he kept moving his palms over her back slowly, soothingly, calming her with his touch.

"She fucking works in my bar," Fury said and laughed gruffly. "I see from your face that's a surprise, and I'm telling you it was a surprise to me, too. I guess Dale hired her while I was in Kentucky taking care of business."

"She don't work for you anymore." At this flat statement, Hope pulled back, looking up at Hoss. She didn't know she was crying until his face softened and he brought a hand up, thumb sweeping her tears from her cheek. "Sweetheart," he said softly, and she shook her head.

"I've been here two weeks, and this is the first problem I've had. Please, I can do this," she said, swallowing hard and wishing it didn't sound like she was asking permission. "I can't lose another job. I can do this."

"No, baby," he muttered, and at his words, she subsided, knowing it was useless to argue with him right now. Hoss lifted his head to look behind her at Fury. "She got shit inside?" There was a noise and one of Hoss' hands left her back, coming in front of her and offering the strap of her purse. Keeping an arm wrapped around her shoulders, without another word, he turned and led her to his truck, parked near the building. He held the door as she climbed inside, waiting until she was settled to close it and walk around the front of the vehicle. She looked out the window at Fury and lifted her hand in farewell as he stood there unmoving, watching them drive away.

At the apartment, Hoss pulled into the lot and parked, sitting with his hands gripping the steering wheel, gaze staring into the darkness. "Hope," he said, and she bowed her head, waiting. "Go on in, baby. Likely you didn't see anything worth mentioning, but just in case, let's keep this quiet. Tell your sister you weren't feeling well. I got some shit to clear, and I probably shoulda called a prospect to bring you home, but I wanted to see you got here okay. Go on in, now. Put tonight behind you."

Through the whole drive home, he hadn't spoken to her, and now, during his entire speech, he hadn't looked at her. It felt as if she didn't exist for him most of the time, with weeks passing between interactions. Then she had to go and throw herself at him tonight, expecting him to catch her simply because she had gotten scared. *He's right*, she thought. *I need to put this behind me. I need to put* everything *behind me. It's time to grow up and put away stupid, childish dreams, Hope.* Silently, she climbed out of his truck, without looking up, not wanting to see if he had bothered to glance her way. She closed the door and walked to the apartment door without looking back.

***

Hoss watched her walk into the apartment and noted everything. How her steps slowed the farther she got from his truck, like she didn't truly want to go. The curve of her neck as her gaze tracked the walkway passing underneath her feet, her head not lifting even when she got to the door. She never looked back, didn't see him watching her, and didn't see the longing he knew was written all over his face.

His mind was running in hundred-mile-an-hour circles, angrily tripping back and forth over the paralyzing knowledge that she hadn't been safe. She had taken a job he didn't know about because he was away, stuck in fucking Chicago for two weeks, dealing with Diamante fallout there, standing alongside Mason. He had rolled into the garage about twenty minutes before Fury made the call tonight, had been in the process of writing up the service his bike needed, when his phone rang. Fucking lucky his truck was still there and he could jump in and go.

He had already known about the shooting in Murphy's Law, the first texts from folks buzzing in about fifteen minutes earlier. He also knew Lalo and Chismoso were in town, because the Rebels had been following and tracking them for the past two months. Keeping an eye on them ever since shit went down with Bones and Watcher, since Mason absorbed their Chicago pain in the form of two other clubs, leaving the Skeptics and Southern Soldiers to deal with their own Diamante problems.

And they definitely had shit to deal with, because the Diamante members formerly from Las Cruces and Chicago were now homeless, wandering the highways and byways of the central and eastern US, each group looking for a home to land on. That was why Fury's move to the Fort with his chapter hadn't pulled any red flags with the national Diamante officers. It was blessed by their leadership because it appeared to move at least one chapter of their club back into Rebel territory, while freeing up Kentucky for displaced members and chapters. Bold moves, they thought. He snorted, thinking, *They don't have any idea what kind of shit is coming.*

The door shut behind Hope and still he watched, expecting to see lights come on, but the apartment stayed dark. She had looked exhausted, dark smudges underneath her eyes, so he suspected she had gone straight to bed. He hoped.

Her bed, where he had laid, her head on his shoulder, cheek against his skin. That hair drifting over his body and stirring him in ways that had him stiffening now at the mere memory. "Fuck," he muttered, shifting into reverse and twisting to look behind him as he backed out of the parking spot. He had to get back to the clubhouse. His brothers would hold his snitch indefinitely, but the longer the banger was out of circulation, the more likely it was someone would note his absence and question him about it.

As he drove, his mind continued to turn over the events from tonight. Seeing her cradled in Fury's lap again, draped across his legs—that shit had taken him straight up to a level of angry he didn't even know he owned. Then, when her name burst out of him, she twisted and got free, leaving Fury without a second look as she ran to him. She had called his name and then run to him like he was the only thing she could think about, like she needed him, needed him to hold her.

Arms around her, he had pressed her close, embracing her tightly. Touching her calmed him, and his voice had been steady as he questioned Fury. His anger had flared again with the knowledge that she had put herself into danger, trying to deal with everything on her own. It wasn't until she said she had already been working there for two weeks that he remembered he hadn't set anything up for her. He had seen her at the clubhouse and talked to Slate, but then he got called out to Chicago, rolling up there with forty brothers. Leaving without setting anything up. Of course, she was going to fucking take care of things; it was all she had known until he tried to help.

He punched hard, his hand thudding off the steering wheel. "Fuck," he hissed, "how the hell can she trust you if you can't keep track of shit?" Her working at the Diamante bar tonight meant she might be on radar for people like Lalo and Chismoso. People he had tried like hell to keep her away from, keep her safe. He had to find out what his snitch had to say, and then he could head back, use the key Mercy gave him, and slip into bed with his Hope. Then tomorrow, they would have a chat.

***

"Obliged you called last night," Hoss said, gaze locked with the red-haired man seated across the table from him. "But I gotta say, I'm not sure why you called this morning." He hadn't been to bed yet, and knowing his lack of sleep was making him irritable, he tried to tamp that shit down so he didn't fuck up this deal with Fury on top of all the other shit rolling around.

"Wanted to see which way the wind was blowing." Fury lifted his cup of coffee. "I told Dale she won't be back. He was pissed off, because he said she's a far better waitress and bartender than anyone else we've had working in the bar since I bought it for the chapter. She was helping in the office, too, straightening out invoices and orders, getting things into a bookkeeping software she was teaching him to use. He's gonna miss her."

"She's good at everything she turns her hand to. Doesn't matter what it is; she's good at it. She works hard, pitches in, figures things out, and makes herself indispensable," Hoss said with a nod. "That's part of the problem, because you combine that attitude with her kind of sweet? The boys all see how she is and want a little for themselves. I've had a hell of a time keeping her safe."

Nodding in response, Fury leaned back in the booth, casually putting one elbow across the back of the seat, stretching out his arm. "You definitely got plans for this one? I heard you weren't a guy to put tail on your bike. You looking to change that?"

"Still working things out, but yeah, leaning hard that direction. Hell, man, you've seen her, talked to her. You gonna try to tell me if I wasn't in the way you wouldn't be headed there yourself? And that's with you only seeing one side of her. You ain't even seen how she is with her boy, yet. Add some breadth and depth onto your image of her and you'd be flat gone like me," Hoss said, then startled, because he had admitted something to this man he hadn't even admitted to himself yet.

With a snort, he said, "She hasn't been in town but a few weeks, and even with the short time I've known her, if it wasn't for the shit we're wading through, I'm real sure I'd have sorted things by now."

"Yeah, I guessed from the accent she hadn't been here long. And, you're dead on, man. I can see why you're keeping her close. There's something about her that makes a man want to put things right for her, want to do for her, no matter what she needs. Didn't know she had a son, man, but you're right about that, too. The thought of her with a kid? Jesus, that just makes the idea of her even sweeter." Fury smiled tightly, looking down at his cup.

"Last night, she ran to you like you held safety in your hands. She couldn't get close enough to you there for a minute." Fury's smile faded and he cut his gaze up to Hoss, his voice low as he asked, "You gonna be able to continue keeping her safe?"

"Yes," he answered immediately and saw a bit of the tension leave Fury's shoulders. "Soon as we get everything sorted out between your Diamante and Rebels, I'll be able to move forward, figure things out with her. Motivates me on your behalf, ya dig?" Fury's teeth flashed in a brief smile, and then he nodded.

Hoss said, "That doesn't mean we've an easy road. As things stand right now, the Rebels have absorbed a lot of clubs in a short time and we are *still* sorting shit in Chicago. Means Mason's dragging his heels a bit at taking in your chapter. It helps you moved them up here, but," he paused, looking at Fury carefully, "you were also a part of Gunny and his woman being snatched up, disappeared. I've heard your side, and I know them showing up at your compound wasn't fronted to you beforehand, but I need to get you and Mason into a room so everyone's clear on how things were, and how they stand now."

"Any time, Hoss. You, Gunny, Mason, and me, I think between the four of us we can settle everything that's needed. With Lalo sniffin' around, I'd like to say sooner rather than later, but the timeline is up to your president." He finished his coffee and looked around the diner. "You own this place, too?"

"Yeah, this is ours." Hoss threaded his fingers around his cup as he glanced around, his mind for a moment on events that transpired in this diner only weeks ago, witnessed from the sidewalk across the street. *A barrel flash and the man's body slumping over in the seat. Gunny standing and walking out.* He shook his head, clearing away the memories. "She starts here tomorrow. Mornings, so she'll only be dealing with the farm crowd."

Fury laughed aloud, tipping his chin up as the sounds of his amusement rang through the room. "Perfect, man."

***

The bell over the door rang and Hope looked up, a ready smile on her face. Out of all the jobs she had worked over the last couple of months, this had to be the best one. Working at this diner evoked warm thoughts of Mac, back in Birmingham, and his struggles to convince her to accept help, to let him feed her. Cleaning and washing dishes had been their compromise and some of her fondest memories of her pregnancy with Sammy were surrounded by the steam- and scent-filled kitchen of his restaurant.

Zane, the farmer who had just walked in the door, was one of her regulars, and she felt the smile already on her face broaden in greeting. Waving a hand to indicate he should seat himself, she watched as he went to his normal table. He tossed down the paper he brought with him, and cupped both big hands around the condiments and jelly on the table to shift them about four inches to the left. Then he sat in the chair and lined the paper up with the edge of the table and, without looking, reached to shift the chair beside him backwards a few inches, out of range of the swing of his elbow. His ritual, conducted every morning at the same time, the movements in the same order. Predictable. Dependable.

Grabbing the coffee pot and a glass of iced water, she walked over as he turned over the mug. "Hey, Zane," she said, pouring him coffee. "Want your usual?"

"Hey back atcha, darlin'," he drawled. "Yep, same old, same old. Where's my boy this morning?" Sammy often came with her. Niko, the diner's owner, had two boys about the same age, and the three kids spent hours in the upstairs apartment, watching cartoons and playing with toys.

"He stayed home with Aunt Mercy today, spouted off something about her offer of a movie and candy being more attractive than a day at work with his mom." She laughed and turned, seeing Zane's normal companions coming in. Consistent. Reliable.

By the end of her shift, she was tired, but like most days, happy. Things were finally going well here in Fort Wayne, and she was comfortable and content. The only area of contention for her was the hurt she sometimes saw cross Mercy's face when one of the men from the club would make a comment about her...past activities.

It had taken nearly three bottles of wine, and Sammy going to bed early, but Hope had finally learned from Mercy exactly how she had first become associated with the club. Mercy's voice had shuddered through the tearful explanations of how she had gone about things, her words carrying true regret and Hope listened as her sister talked about how embarrassed she now was at her actions and choices.

She knew all the things Mercy felt made her unlovable, and loved her anyway. The only thing her sister didn't confess were her feelings for Deke, even if they weren't exactly a secret. Those two had been on again, off again since a week after Hope moved in with her. When they were on, according to Mercy, it was hotter than hot, but Hope had seen the tears when they were off, because neither Mercy nor Deke were happy apart.

MariaLisa deMora

Hope rolled up the apron with her tips inside and shoved it down into her purse, digging in her bag for her keys as she yelled goodbye to the staff and customers she knew. Climbing into her car, she glanced into the backseat, shaking her head as she marveled at the change a bare couple of months could make. From homeless and sleeping with her son in their car, to sharing an apartment with her amazing sister, working a steady job. Life was good.

9. Beautiful

The diner's night manager called Hope in last night when one of the other servers went home sick, and she wound up working more than half of the drunk rush and then all of her more normal, laid-back morning one. Thankfully, one of their neighbors, Willa Shipman, had been available to stay with Sammy in the apartment until Mercy got home from her set at Slinky's, which meant she hadn't been required to wake him and haul him out to a sitter. Now, headed home, she was exhausted and ready to fall into bed for a nap before getting up to run errands with Sammy in tow.

Drained from the not-quite double shift worked on her feet, she nearly didn't notice Hoss waiting in the apartment parking lot, seated on his bike with his feet on the pegs, leaning against the backrest with arms crossed casually over his chest. Her gaze passed right by him when she backed into her accustomed spot, her eyes returning to him only when he moved, pushing his sunglasses up to the top of his head.

Hoss dismounted the bike as she got out of the car, reaching back inside to grab her dirty apron and small bag. From the corner of her eye, she watched him closely, trying to decide what he wanted. This was the first time she had seen him since he dropped her off after the fight at

Murphy's Law, and it all seemed incredibly awkward to her. He walked up one angle of the sidewalk, meeting her at the end of the short cement pad leading to the apartment door. "Mornin'," he said, his voice sounding as raw and tired as she felt.

"Hey, Hoss," she responded quietly, continuing towards the door without fully looking at him. "Mercy's home, but I doubt she's up." She sighed as she tried to fit the key into the lock. So tired her hands were trembling, it took her three attempts to push it home, the tip of the key chattering around the slot for a moment, then just as it fit into place, a large, warm hand covered and steadied hers. She gasped at the touch and tried to jerk away, but Hoss held her hand in place. He assisted her in turning the key, and then plucked the ring from her hands and the door, turning the knob with his other hand and pushing the door open.

Distracted, she stumbled as she stepped over the threshold, and before she could react to correct her misstep, she found herself moving backwards through the air, landing with a soft oof of exhalation. Hoss had wrapped one strong arm around her, pulling her back against his chest, the hard muscles of his forearm pressing tightly against her breasts. "I got you," he muttered in her ear before his arm tightened slightly and then released, settling her feet gently on the floor.

"Thanks," she said a little timidly, not only because she would likely have gone to her knees if he hadn't been there, but also because his touch always left her a little breathless. *Put it behind you*, she thought, mentally reminding herself that even Hoss had told her to push the feelings he aroused in her aside.

Glancing around the apartment, she didn't see anyone. No Sammy and no Mercy, which meant they were probably both still sleeping. "You need me to wake Mercy, Hoss?" Trying for casual, she asked, "What did you need her for?" Looking over her shoulder at him, she stumbled again and he reached out, cupping one hand under her elbow.

"Sweetheart, I'm here for you, not Mercy." His statement didn't make sense, because that would imply...what, exactly? He then confused her further by asking, "What time does Sammy usually roll outta bed?"

She stood and looked at him for a moment, thinking her exhaustion had to be why everything he did or said was bewildering today. Shaking her head, she muttered, "As late as he can manage, most of the time, unless we're going to DeeDee's so he can play with Jonny." Moving farther into the apartment, she dropped her bag on the kitchen counter, turning to squint up at him. "Why? What did you mean you're here for me? Did I screw up again?"

She was so tired her eyes were blinking slower and slower, but even with her blurry vision, she saw the smile curling the corners of his mouth. "Beautiful," he murmured, and she felt the heat of his palm cupping her cheek and closed her eyes, relishing his touch. Nuzzling into it before she could think to pull away, she heard an intake of breath, and then she was swinging through the air, suspended in his arms.

Startled, she opened her eyes to find his only inches away, staring into her face. "I can see you're dead on your feet, baby. Let's get you to bed, and you can get a nap in before you have to be up and doing things. I'll be here if Sammy wakes up." She must have made a noise, because he paused for a moment, then continued, "I'm gonna be right here, sweetheart."

It seemed within moments she was seated on the edge of her bed and he was on one knee in front of her, slipping her shoes off and placing them near the wall. He slid his hands up her calves then paused, one palm on the inside of each knee. "Hope." His voice was hoarse when he said, "I'm going to step out and let you get ready for bed."

She shook her head, and whispered, "I need to get breakfast laid out for Sammy."

"I got it covered, baby," he whispered back, and she slowly turned her head to see the blanket-covered lump that was her son. "Hope, honey, you're falling asleep sitting here. Get ready and lie down. Get a nap in, baby."

Eyelids dipping closed again, she nodded and heard the door close behind him as he left the room. Chin down, she struggled out of her shirt and jeans then unfastened her bra and let it slip down her arms to the floor as she sat on the edge of the bed.

Jerking awake at his hissed, *"Fuck,"* she shook her head again, blinking up at him as he loomed over her. He leaned in close and she watched in fascination as a muscle jumped in his jaw. "Hope," he whispered, the tone of his voice soft as the sound of an owl's wing, and she blinked at him again, realizing she had dozed off between blinks. "Fuck. *Beautiful,*" she heard, and rolled as his hands dictated, her body loose and heavy as she was dragged deeper into sleep.

She sighed and shifted, rolling her shoulders and stretching before sighing again and scrubbing her cheek on the pillow. Her lips curved into a smile because her pillow was firm and smelled good, smelled like Hoss. She brought up one hand and flattened it against the mattress, shoving it underneath the pillow, feeling heat instead of the expected coolness. Her other hand curved over the pillow in front of her face, and she stretched again, covering her mouth with her palm when she yawned hugely. She rolled slightly, reaching her arm over her head, startled when her hand encountered something that wasn't the headboard. A hard hand fit itself around hers, and she realized her head was in Hoss' lap when he laughed softly, saying, "Mornin', baby."

***

As he sat through the morning, propped up against the headboard of her bed and watched her sleep nestled in his arms, Hoss had steadily reminded himself he needed to slow this thing between them down, whatever it was. Being fascinated by her was something he could do, but the insane way his hands had itched to get on her skin today wasn't him. He was the easygoing guy, not an obsessed man who would take advantage of a woman.

When he walked back into her bedroom to find her naked except for her tiny, white panties, he had to dig deep to find that guy. Had to rein himself in, let the good guy take over again, because the man who walked in to see her like that wanted to touch her, taste her, tame her...love her. It was a damn good thing he had already taken off his cut and folded it on her dresser, because if it had taken a moment longer to strip off his shirt and pull it over her head, hiding her form, he didn't know if he could have controlled himself.

Now, watching as she slowly woke, stretching and sighing, twisting sensuously around in the bed right beside him, he was questioning his decision. Because, really, she was too damn appealing, and as he told Fury, the sweet wrapped up in the beautiful was something he found himself wanting more than he would ever have believed possible. He liked every side of Hope he had encountered so far, whether she was awake and sassy, tired and sweet, or brave and defiant, and he suspected he would be willing to take her however he could find her.

Lying beside him, her eyes flew open at his greeting and she stared up at him in confusion, and then her gaze darted to the other bed in the room. *Yeah, I need to call Myron and Jase about a three-bedroom again,* he thought, already beginning to discount the idea of slowing things down. "He's watching cartoons on the DVR, sweetheart." Gaze back on him, her chin dipped until she saw the unfamiliar t-shirt covering her, and those damn eyes came back to him. She lifted one hand to the neckline of the shirt, tugging it out slightly to glance inside, and then he had her wide eyes looking back up at him as she tucked it close to her chest.

"Ask your question, sweetheart," he urged, watching as her eyes traced his bare torso, her gaze pausing on his chest, then his shoulders, then up to his face. He waited patiently, but when it was clear her mouth was not opening anytime soon, he shook his head. "You were sleeping when I came back in, and I didn't want to go digging through your drawers. So I put my shirt on you, baby."

"Oh," she said, lips shaping the sound quietly. She lifted her head, preparatory to moving away from him, and he cupped his hand around her shoulder, holding her in place. Fingertips firmly stroking up and down the back of her neck, he grinned when she rewarded him with a small groan, closing her eyes and stretching her muscles.

"You sore, baby?" He continued the massage, enjoying the play of muscles and heat underneath his hand. He groaned silently when she bowed her neck a little more, the pressure from her head too near his rapidly thickening cock. *Bastard, slow it down, remember?* The thought had barely flashed through his head when he felt the hand she had shoved underneath his leg curl up and around high on the inside of his thigh. *Fucking shit.* Closing his eyes, he blocked out the sight of her lying beside him, covered by his soft, clinging tee. He had to distract himself. "When do you work again?"

"Tomorrow morning," she whispered. "Unless Alyssa is sick again and they need me to cover her shift. Today, I have shopping to do, plus laundry and stuff, and then it'll be back to the diner in the morning at five."

"You were exhausted when you got home," he said quietly. He had watched as she drove into the parking lot last night, her gaze skipping past him as she backed into her parking spot. Dead on her feet, she hadn't even been able to stay awake long enough to change clothes. As far as he knew, she was only working the diner, and he could manage things for her there so she would have more time off if he needed to. He wanted her rested and sweet, and wanted her to have time for him, because the more he saw of her, the more he wanted with her. *Fuck slow.*

"Yeah," she yawned, covering her mouth with one hand. "Thank you for helping me out earlier and with Sammy. Sorry you got saddled with my snorefest. It is probably not what you had planned when you came by to see Mercy. Did you talk to her this morning? Is she up yet?"

"Baby," he said. "You were out of it, weren't you? Told you earlier I didn't come by to see her." He saw the confusion on her face and grinned down at her. "I gotta head out for a little while, take care of a couple of errands, but I'll be back this afternoon. Make sure you're home by three, okay?" He reached down, and lifting her head off his leg, shoved a pillow underneath it and rolled, moving to the edge of the bed. He stood and then bent over, letting his lips brush the top of her head. "See you in a bit, baby."

***

She was standing in the freezer section of the grocery store and knew there was a big smile on her face, and she found, at this moment, she simply didn't care if she had a goofy look on her face. Or who might see her smiling like a loon at the frozen foods arrayed in colorful and tidy rows on shelves behind the glass. She was grocery shopping, because they didn't have much in the way of groceries in the house. Both she and Mercy had been working odd and long hours, which did not leave a lot of time for doing things like shopping. Sleep had been more critical, most days.

She was also grocery shopping alone, which was—while she loved Sammy with every fiber of her being—a joy in and of itself. That was because Sammy did not like shopping and evidenced this with each forced moment by sighing and asking every couple of minutes if they could be done yet. Right now, instead of shopping, he was at the apartment with Mercy, who he had rooked into watching cartoons with him.

Solo shopping was not why she wore the happy expression while standing in the frozen food section, positioned midway down the aisle between the two banks of freezers. That would have to do with what she held in her hand more than anything else did.

She glanced down at the list, and her smile grew. Tacked onto the end of today's list were three items. You could tell they were tacked on, because the handwriting didn't match the rest of the list, where there were already two different samples. Her writing filled most of the space, where neat letters and shorthand notes abounded. She had written things like T.P., and yogo, can g. beans, and bread. The second sample, which was large and uneven, with big, loopy letters, had inserted first the name of a sugary cereal, and then a demand for cookies.

The notes inscribed in the final handwriting sample were sausage pizza, corndogs, and o. rings. Written with strong strokes, the bold, blue ink lay on the paper in fat lines, spelling out sausage pizza, which had been underlined once, corndogs, bearing doubles lines of ink beneath them, and also carrying the extra emphasis of an exclamation mark, but the o. rings was what had pulled the smile to her face. O. rings was not only underlined and marked, but also had four precisely drawn arrows pointing towards it, the arrows of varying lengths so they fit neatly alongside each other.

Someone liked onion rings. A lot. Hope suspected Sammy had enlisted the help of one easy-going Hossman to provide purchasing power for the final three items, because they were some of Sammy's favorite foods. While she had placed cereal in her cart, it was a far different brand from the dessert masquerading as breakfast food he had wanted, and she had bypassed the cookies altogether. This was behavior Sammy could predict, because it was normal for her. She suspected he knew if she thought Hoss wanted these final three things, she would be more likely to buy them.

Glancing down at the list again, she then transferred her gaze to the cart, laden with food. On top of the mounded pile in the basket was proof of Sammy's manipulative success, with two boxes of bake-at-home pizza, a decent sized package of corndogs such as you would buy at the county fair, and an extra-large plastic bag of onion rings.

She glanced at the time on her phone, pushing the cart to the register. It was nearly three, and she still had to make one more stop before heading home.

Forty-five minutes later, she saw Hoss' bike was back in the lot as she parked and, glancing around, noticed Mercy's car was gone. Because of that, she wasn't surprised to find Hoss in the living room when she let herself in, arms laden with bags, the plastic handles cutting into her wrists.

"Sam, let's help your momma bring in the groceries," he said when his gaze landed on her and she smiled. "You help her unload this batch; I'll go see what else she has in the car."

"Mooom." Sammy was clearly annoyed when he turned to see her struggling with the door. "You're supposed to come get me to help." He leapt to his feet, sprinting across the room to take three of the bags from her arm. He was right; it was their normal deal, but she had been distracted by the sight of Hoss' bike sitting there, gleaming chrome pipes and what looked like a fresh wax job on the tank and fenders.

She had squatted next to the last sack of groceries and was tossing canned goods one slow arc at a time to Sammy. He would right the cans and place them on the shelves of the pantry. The doorbell rang and he reached up, grabbing the last can out of the air, and turned to run towards the door, can in hand, yelling, "I'll get it."

From directly behind her, she heard Hoss say, "You and me, Hope? We're going for a ride. That'll be Lucia, the daughter of one of my brothers. I think you've met Bear, yeah?" She twisted her head to look at him, wondering what he meant by going for a ride. Instead of asking him, she nodded, because she had met Bear. His wife was Eddie, the woman who had helped her make huge inroads with the school on Sammy's behalf. She was working alongside Hope to get everything straightened out so he could start school with his age group in a couple of weeks. Citing exigent circumstances and providing testing results to show he would be able to do the appropriate grade-level work, Eddie was confident things were going to be okay. Lucia was Eddie and Bear's adopted daughter, and the girl had recently moved to a spot high on her roster of trusted babysitters. Hearing Sammy's happy shout, she knew Luce must have brought her younger brothers with her, Mickey and Roddy.

"Miguel," she heard Lucia call, and Hope turned to see the three boys race into the living room, throwing themselves on the furniture as Sammy grabbed the TV remote. "*Zapatas del sofas, nino*. Feet on the floor, or shoes off. Miguel, Roderigo, what do you say to Sammy's *mama*?"

"*Hola*, Miss Hope," came in a disjointed chorus from the two boys, and she grinned.

"*Hola, chicos*. How are my favorite boys today?" She walked to the couch and tousled their dark, thick hair, drawing smiles from both boys. "What are you doing here, Luce?"

Lucia looked at her with a frown and Hope turned as she felt a large hand settle on her hip in a clearly possessive hold. Her breath hitched at the warm touch, but she didn't say anything. Looking up at Hoss, who was standing close behind her, she raised an eyebrow questioningly. He laughed and told her, "She's babysitting, so you and me can go for a ride."

"A ride?" Her teeth worried at the inside of her cheek. Did he mean on his motorcycle? She remembered the black and chrome monster she had seen outside and shivered.

"Yeah, it's too pretty a day to spend inside. I wanna show you the world from the back of my bike, baby." His voice was quiet; he had leaned close and was speaking so near her ear the heat from his breath drifted across her skin. "Come on a ride with me, Hope. Let me introduce you to the wind."

"Okay," she whispered, and when he smiled in response, that brittle tightening in her chest happened again, not quite pain, it was more like anticipation. She loved seeing that look on his face, as if she had handed him the world in a word. "I've never ridden on a motorcycle before," she warned him, and her words earned her another smile.

"Was counting on that, baby," he said.

"Have fun," Lucia called from her perch on the living room floor. "I got this under control, Hope. You go and have fun. Hoss will take care of you."

At his recommendation, she grabbed a jacket and met him at the door, turning to see Sammy already so engrossed in the show on the TV he only waved a hand absently when she called goodbye. Outside, Hoss patiently explained the things she needed to know about the bike. Putting her hair up into a tight ponytail, she placed one foot on the peg he folded down for her and swung her leg over the bike behind him. She was attempting to leave a polite distance between them when his hands wrapped around her calves, and with a jerk, pulled her butt forward, tugging her in tightly against him. Feeling the heat of his body through her jeans, she tried to squirm backwards, but his hands held her firmly in place.

His voice held a hint of laughter as he said, "Hope, you gotta be still, baby. Your ass needs to be up here, so you can reach to wrap your arms around me to hold on. Give it a minute; get comfortable." One hand released her leg, but the other continued to stroke slowly up and down her calf. She jerked when the bike started, the roar surprising her nearly as much as the vibration and movement underneath her butt.

This was kind of scary, but also kind of cool, and when he tilted back to talk to her again, his body pressing tight against hers, she thought it was also very sexy. "Lean up, baby. Grab hold of my waist. I'm gonna go slow and easy, but you need to hold on."

Intrigued, she nodded and bent forward at the waist, pressing her chest into his back and tentatively sliding her arms around him. His hand left her leg and she felt his glove-covered palm wrap around her hand and give it a squeeze then both of his hands were on the grips. He did something with one foot, tilting the bike scarily over to the right-hand side for a moment before they began gliding smoothly forward.

Within minutes, they had rounded a half-dozen frightening corners and then were on a county highway, headed out of town. After a few miles, she found the steady thrumming under her butt was calming, and the confident way Hoss handled himself and the bike had her relaxing, leaning into and resting against him in a way she hadn't let herself earlier.

Propping her chin on his shoulder as best she could, she watched the highway in front of them, ducking behind him when the wind began to bite. Looking out at the fields slipping by, the motion mesmerized her, and she was startled when a bike moved up beside them on the left. Hoss tensed for a moment, but then she felt him relax and wave at the other rider. Looking closer, she saw the same kind of patches on his jacket, knowing he must be a member of the Rebel Wayfarers.

She expected Hoss to slow and pull over, maybe stop and have a chat, but instead, the two men rode on nearly side-by-side for about thirty miles. Then the other rider scooted up beside them and gestured. Hoss waved at him again as the man fell behind, changing trajectory to move to a turn lane, pulling onto a smaller country road. Twisting slightly, she watched as the other rider accelerated up that road, the two men separating companionably without ever having spoken a word. Relaxing into Hoss again, she leaned her cheek against his back, once more mindlessly watching the scenery fly by, feeling the ends of her ponytail fluttering and whipping across the back of her neck.

Some time later, she felt a change in the bike's movement and sat up, looking over Hoss' shoulder again to see him pulling into a small park. She grinned, because the sight of the well-kept park confined in the middle of still-tall cornfields was strange. Scanning the lot, she saw they were the only vehicle there. She sat up straight, leaning slightly away from Hoss as he steered towards a cluster of picnic tables near what she hoped was a bathroom. He backed into a parking space and then killed the bike, holding it steady between his legs after he flipped down the kickstand. Reaching back with one hand, he called, "Step off, baby."

She laughed to find her legs unsteady, her throat tightening when he gave her another one of those broad grins. He kept a hand on her arm while he leaned the bike, swinging his leg over and propping his butt on the seat, pushing his sunglasses up on top of his head. Tugging her to stand in between his legs, he asked, "You okay now, Hope?" She nodded and tried to step back, but his hands on her hips held her in place as she shrugged off her jacket, putting it on the small passenger seat. Eyes level with hers, his gaze was searching when he asked, "Did you like the ride, baby?"

She couldn't have stopped the grin that spread across her face if she had wanted to, and when he gave her another one of those smiles in response, she was oh-so glad she hadn't tried. "Yeah," she breathed, her throat feeling tight. "That was incredible, Hoss. I didn't have any idea it would be like that."

He gave a squeeze with his hands then nodded and released her. "I bet you don't even know it yet, but you'll need to hit the washroom." Standing, he turned her and walked with her towards the building. "It's usually pretty clean, but give me a holler if there are any critters inside."

Walking back out, she was wiping her palms dry against the fabric of her jeans when she saw him lounging on top of one of the picnic tables. He had laid back flat, legs dangling over the edge, and seemed to be staring up at the blue sky. When he heard her footsteps, he sat up in one smooth movement, and the heat in his gaze took her breath. She stepped off the walkway towards the table and stopped after a couple of strides, suddenly unsure of herself. Wordlessly, he held out a hand, staring at her, and without giving herself time to think, she took those last few steps to place her hand in his, moving to him when he tugged her forward.

Eyes open, she was staring at his chest, reading the patches on his vest, when his fingers caught under her chin, lifting her face up. She had a moment to feel the sweep of his thumb over her lips before he covered her mouth with his. He wound his other hand around her ponytail, tugging her head backwards and deepening the kiss.

Without conscious thought, she found her hands resting on either side of his waist, fingers digging and twisting into his tee. Her breath was coming in heaving gasps when he pulled back, resting his forehead against hers. She had only a moment to think, *What an amazing kiss*, before he kissed her again, this time his tongue licking along the seam of her lips, probing and teasing. He murmured against her, "Open for me, baby." When she did, granting him access, he groaned and his tongue swept against hers, possessing her.

His arms folded around her, lifting and placing her on his lap, his mouth never leaving hers. The kiss continued on, seeming endless, breaking apart only for a moment so they could gasp at the air, breathing fast, and then crashing back together in a hard, passionate connection. His hand pressed between her legs, fingers rubbing against the seam of her jeans firmly, stroking in time with his tongue delving into her mouth. Licking across the inside of his teeth, she was caught up in the feeling of being owned by this beautiful man, this strong but gentle man, and moved instinctively, pressing her hips forward, pushing against his hand.

Making a noise of denial when his fingers left her, she shivered when she felt them at the waistband of her jeans, working the button and zipper, grazing touches from his calloused fingertips brushing across the skin of her stomach. He deepened the kiss again, distracting her, slanting his mouth across hers hungrily as his hand pushed into the front of her jeans. He slid his rough fingers down and over her clitoris, past that singing bundle of nerves to drive his thick middle finger relentlessly inside her. Her mouth opened wider and he swallowed her moan as he filled her, grinding the heel of his hand against her core while he worked in and out of her.

One arm wrapped around her back, supporting as he leaned her backwards. His hand slipped underneath her shirt, tugging it upwards, his fingertips trailing across her belly. The kiss and his touch had her arching, making needy noises as she chased an orgasm that was building steadily, the pressure and tension growing to unbelievable levels.

He broke the kiss and pressed his face into the crook of her neck, lips moving against her skin as he told her, "Come for me, beautiful. I want to watch you break. I want to know how you look when you come. Give it to me. Hotter than a bonfire, and your pussy feels like satin. Baby, I can't wait to get in there, can't wait to feel you all around me. You feel so right, Hope."

He took in a ragged breath, the heat blistering against her skin as he blew it back out. He moved slightly, and she opened her eyes to find him looking down into her face, the intensity of his expression as arousing as his kiss had been. "Come for me, baby. Let me break you and catch the pieces. I need this, beautiful. Give it to me."

His hand paused a second, and then she felt the fullness she had been experiencing become even more. Two fingers now inside her, moving together and apart, stretching and bringing her closer to the edge of the precipice. The pad of his thumb landed on her clitoris, pressing hard as it moved rapidly side-to-side, and with her eyes wide open, gaze fixed to his face, she called his name urgently, coming harder than she ever had in her life.

His warm whiskey-colored eyes flickered fast, his gaze tracing over her face, down her body to where she knew his arm disappeared into her pants, then back up to her face, that same intensity still present on his features. "Goddamn, you are beautiful, baby. That's it, sweetheart. Give it all to me. Let me see you." The muscles of her stomach jerking, she tried to press her legs together to stop his hand from moving, but he shook his head, denying her, even as his fingers pushed deeper. "I want it all, baby. Give it to me."

At his growled command, she groaned and gave in, letting her head sink backwards over his arm, closing her eyes and relaxing into the sensations ricocheting through her body. His hand continued to play between her legs, stroking languidly in and out, seeming to know exactly what she wanted, even before she did. Fingers running through her folds, spreading the wetness everywhere, gently plucking at her clit to draw a gasp from her, and then soothing with a slow stroke down and inside, again pushing deep.

Gradually, she came back down, and she found she had rolled slightly, curving into his body, cuddling against his chest. He moved his hand to the outside of her panties, pressing the material against her, stroking her a final time through the fabric before he pulled his hand out of her pants. She blinked up at him, watching in amazement as he licked and sucked his fingers, apparently relishing the flavor he found there. His gaze never left her face when, with a grin, he asked her, "Want to taste?"

Embarrassed, she bit her lips, and then gave a small shake of her head. He bent down, still grinning, whispering just before he kissed her, "Liar." His tongue stroked into her mouth and she tasted herself briefly, the faintest tang of bitter covered immediately by something with a darker flavor. "You taste so fucking good, baby," he murmured against her lips.

She felt his hand at her waist and glanced down to see he was tugging her zipper back up, fastening her pants. Surprised, because his erection still pressed firmly against her butt, she looked up at him. The question must have been evident on her face, because his chest rumbled with laughter as he said, "It's all good, sweetheart. I got what I wanted."

With a shake of his head, he leaned down to steal another kiss, the taste of her now much fainter on his lips. "You gave me all of that, baby. I got what I wanted."

***

Hoss held her close, feeling chilled as the breeze dried the sweat on his skin. God, she was so fucking hot, so beautiful, and had absolutely no idea how gorgeous she looked when she broke apart for him just now. He had assumed, because she had a kid, that she probably knew her way around a man, but the way she came, so hard, so...suddenly *there*, he was certain it had been a long time since anyone had touched her like this.

He had seen the insecurity on her face afterward, and now wondered how long it had been for her. This was not a woman who knew the power she held in making herself vulnerable to a man, who knew what it meant when she gave a man what she had given him today. Now, blonde hair glowing in the late afternoon sunshine, she had gone boneless in his arms, muscles loose and relaxed. He suspected if he sat without moving or speaking, she might even go to sleep in his lap. Smiling, he nuzzled the top of her head, arms squeezing tight around her a little.

"Beautiful," he whispered, softly kissing her temple, laughing silently at her wordless sound of inquiry in response. She was so fucking gorgeous, inside and out, fucking stunning. How could she have been with someone who let her walk away, and with his kid in her belly at the time? "Tell me about Sammy's daddy."

He wanted to know, needed to know what he was up against in her memories. Even if he had an idea the man was an asshole, he had still been in her life, in her bed. She had told him the man didn't have any rights to the boy now, but there was a history there, a shared past, because she had fucked him, had kept and carried the man's baby, and he wanted to understand what caused things to fall apart. He wasn't prepared for her reaction, though, because he felt a distinct flinch at his question, saw her lips press together to still a sudden trembling.

"Why?" Her voice was shaky and thin, so different from the rich tone she had used when she called his name, coming hard on his fingers. He suddenly realized the only word she had said since walking away from his bike had been his name. *Fuck, she holds everything close*, he thought, already regretting his question. *Might not have been the best time to bring up this topic.*

"Hope, you have to know I like you. And I think I see the same thing coming back at me from you, so with that between us, this is a conversation you had to know was coming, baby." She needed to learn the safest place for her to ever be was in his arms, and this was a good first lesson.

"I'm not looking to piss on things, mark my spot. I simply want to know whatever you're willing to share." Looking down at her face, he watched as warring emotions rolled across her features. Fear, anger, and what looked like a bone-deep hurt washed over her in waves. She made a noise and moved, so he tightened his arms around her. "Hush, baby. Stay with me. It can't be as bad as all that. Sammy seems to think he's an okay guy."

She barked a harsh laugh. "It's a lie. Everything he knows is a lie."

"How did he get those impressions, then?" He tried to remember exactly what she had said the one other time the man came up. Suiter, his name was Cal Suiter, and he didn't see Sammy. "Suiter, right? You said Sammy hasn't seen him for years."

"Right. Calhoun, but everybody calls him Cal. The last time Cal saw him, Sammy was two years old. Cal came to my apartment on Christmas

Eve and the sitter let him in. I never found out how he even knew where we lived, but she let him in and left. Of course she did; Sammy's dad was there filled with threats and anger, so she left." She shook her head.

"Cal was there about five minutes and bailed, left a note saying he couldn't take 'the brat' crying. He left Sammy alone in the apartment at two years old and walked out. Thank God, the sitter forgot her phone and had to come back, because my blood runs cold at the thought of what could have happened. The little bit Sammy believes he knows about Cal all came from Cal's mother, but we haven't seen her in a long time." She drew in a breath that hitched in the middle, and he gave her another squeeze. "He wasn't the nicest man."

"I'm getting that feelin', baby. He don't have any custody claim on your boy, does he?" What kind of man would do that, leaving a child defenseless like that, his own blood? A fucking stupid one, and the man's lack of intelligence had already been confirmed, because only an idiot asshole wouldn't want to be involved in Sammy's life.

That little kid was fucking amazing, old for his years, and taking on roles most boys wouldn't find room for in their lives until they hit their teens, if then. Like this morning, when he came out to find Hoss watching the news and drinking coffee, he asked a dozen questions all pointing to protecting his mom from heartache. He wondered if Sammy had a better idea about his daddy than Hope knew.

"No, he...it's complicated." She shrugged and tried again to sit up, but he kept her wrapped up so she couldn't move. "Hoss, let me up."

"Nope, Hope." He grinned against the side of her head, pressing a kiss there. "Not a chance, baby. Because you are gonna want to use this moment to pull away from me. This is hard shit. A hard conversation to have, but I need you to trust me. You're safe with me, baby. If I keep you right here and you feel me all around you, that's when you're gonna

135

know you're okay. Me wrapped around you, keepin' you safe." He spoke in a matter of fact tone, and she barked another harsh laugh.

"I've not been safe or okay for a very long time," she blurted, clamping her lips shut after the last word. Her words were telling, because she hadn't meant to say that to him.

"So, it's complicated. What does that mean?" he pushed.

"My parents…growing up was difficult, because the standards were so…rigid. When I got older, all I could think of was getting out, getting away from them. Cal became that option for me. I moved in with him, and my parents basically disowned me, because I was living in sin." She reached up, curling one hand around his wrist, unconsciously seeking a connection. "He got frustrated with me a lot, because I didn't know anything other than how my folks lived. The first couple of times he raised his hand to me, I believed it was because of something I'd done, or hadn't done. I was so naïve, and he was so polished, older."

"But it got worse, didn't it?" He had seen the cycle before. His littlest sister fell into the same kind of relationship with her bastard boyfriend, and it had taken a hospital stay to straighten her shit out. He suspected Hope's story was along the same lines, but knew having a baby thrown in had to make things so much more difficult.

"Yeah," she breathed, rubbing her cheek against his shirt, eyes closed, seeking solace offered in the darkness behind her eyelids. "A lot worse. Then I found out I was pregnant. So I left. There was no way I would subject a child to that." The painful sounding laugh came again, and he fucking hated that noise coming out of her mouth, it seemed torn from her by unspeakable pain. "I didn't have anywhere else to go, so I went home. You can imagine how well my news went over." He gave her another squeeze. "There, something good came of the confrontation, though, because I found out about Mercy. I can't imagine my life without her in it now." She opened her eyes and he saw the glitter of tears before she closed them again, wetness clumping her lashes.

"She's your dad's girl?" He already knew this from talking to Mercy, but giving her something easy to answer would help keep her talking.

"Yeah," she said, the corners of her mouth curling into a short-lived smile. "I wish I'd come to find her sooner."

"You have her now," he said, kissing the side of her face, and she drew a deep breath, letting it out in a slow sigh.

"Yeah." Her hand squeezed his wrist and then relaxed. "I already told you about Mac. He and his wife were my guardian angels, I swear. If it weren't for them, I would have starved, maybe lost the baby. When Cal found me—"

"Found you?" he interrupted, and she nodded.

"Yeah, he found my car one night, dragged me out of it. A security guard saw what was going on and tried to stop him, but they had to use a Taser on him to finally get him...away. There was video footage of the whole thing, so with that and me being nearly eight months pregnant, plus having to stay so long in the hospital, at least I didn't have to testify in court. He was found guilty of attempted manslaughter, and the judge made a ruling based on the physical evidence and testimony from the guard, and that decision means Cal never gets Sammy. Ever."

She dragged in a breath. "The only times he's seen him were ambush moments, not anything I intended to allow. He showed up at Mom and Dad's place at Easter that first year, and Dad wouldn't do anything. I finally called the cops, and they came and made him leave. The other time was the Christmas he found out where I was and showed up, telling the sitter he'd accuse her of kidnapping if she didn't let him see his boy. That's the way he always has talked about Sammy, 'his boy,' like he's a possession. This is my car. This is my boy. Same difference to him."

"He put you in the hospital?" Hoss found he was carefully regulating his breathing, trying not to let on how pissed off he was. The man put his hands on a pregnant woman, beat her so badly she had to be hospitalized. That shit didn't stand, and if he ever got the chance, he would educate the motherfucker within an inch of his life.

"Yeah, wasn't the first time. Was the worst time, though. I nearly lost Sammy. He was born a little early because of it." He felt her small shrug and knew she was pushing her emotions down. "I'll note it was the last time, which is probably the most important takeaway from the experience. For Sammy...things have been hard enough without him learning any of this. When he asks, I tell him his dad's busy, traveling; I make up lies about why he's not around. And the few times I let Cal's mother see him, she filled his head with all the glory and wonder she felt was Calhoun Suiter." A more natural laugh this time, and he caught her gaze when her eyes opened. "It's a lie, but I believe the truth would be too much for him. On top of how he's had to live, it would just be too much."

"How's Sammy handling the move up here?" The boy seemed to be settling in, and Hoss knew from talking to his brothers that Sammy had made fast friends with several Rebel members' kids. He smiled; she was relaxing again and he knew it was because this topic was as natural as breathing for her.

"He's doing amazingly well, given we've had so much change over the past few months. My roommate had left, moving out while still owing back rent, so I was in a hole. Then my paycheck bounced, so I was losing our apartment again. It wasn't the first time we'd lived in the car, but each time I hoped...prayed it would be the last." She made this statement so calmly he didn't know how to respond.

He knew people who had lost their shit, but there were always family or friends around to help prop them up until they got their legs underneath them again. He couldn't think of a single person he knew who was on their own, wholly on their own, like Hope and Sammy seemed to be down in Birmingham.

"Out of nowhere, I decided to come find Mercy. I didn't know if she was aware of me, of our connection. I didn't know if she'd hate me, or my dad, or what she'd be like...or even if she were still in town. I pulled into the lot at Slinky's with eighty dollars left in my wallet, not much better than the first time I walked into Mac's diner. Now, when I look back and think about what I did, I realize it was a pretty stupid lack of a plan, but I was so desperate to not be alone in this anymore."

Her honesty tore something loose in his chest, and he addressed the sudden pain by leaning down and covering her bowed mouth with his own, fiercely possessing her. "You are never going to be alone again, baby," he whispered against her swollen lips as the kiss slowed, and he felt her mouth curve in what he hoped was a smile. "Seems as if Sammy likes it up here. School starts soon, yeah? What happens then?"

"I guess we keep going forward. He gets back on track in school, and I keep working." She shifted, and he let her sit up this time, balancing her on his thighs as he hugged her close.

"What does he like to do?" Hoss was still looking for his in with the boy. Even this morning, as testy as he was at finding Hoss in the apartment, he had been guarded and dodged any questions about himself. "I saw his sheets have hockey stuff on them. Does he like the game?"

"Yeah, he does," she said softly, and now he knew without a doubt, even without looking, she was smiling. That tone said it all. Her boy was her world. "He loves hockey. I was able to put him in lessons and an inner-city league back home, but since we moved up here, it's been too hectic. When I couldn't keep a job at first, no matter what I did, I was afraid all the time we'd be a drag on Mercy, so I didn't want to pay out any money I didn't have to."

Fuck, he thought. He hadn't considered what it might look like when they kept moving her around, but he needed her in a job where she was safe, even when he couldn't be there to watch over her all the time.

She continued, "Things are better now at the diner. It seems like Slate's going to leave me there. I picked up some office work at another place; plus, I'm doing the books for Murphy's Law."

"The fuck you say?" The words were out before he even knew his mouth was open, and he felt her tense up at his brusque, questioning tone.

"Just…hedging my bets. I don't want to be dependent on Mercy's friends in the club, and I can pay my own way, Hoss. She and I have agreed on the split for expenses. But if I got dropped off another job, I wanted…needed to have a backup plan." Her words were carefully spoken, selected so they wouldn't rile him and he didn't like the fact she felt she had to dance around things with him, guarding herself. *Fuck*, he thought again, *I did this to myself*.

"I think the diner is a sure thing, baby," he said gently. "I didn't want you working at Murphy's, because it's a Diamante bar. Is Fury aware you picked up those hours?"

"I'm not in the bar, only in the office, working on the books for Dale. They were a mess, and in the short time I worked there, I'd already started the process of getting them in order. I don't have an accounting degree, but basic knowledge is all they need, and I picked that up from Mac and Nelly. So there's no reason for Fury to be bothered about me helping out." She pushed at his arm, tentatively testing to see if he would let her go, but he tightened his hold around her instead.

"I'll deal with Dale and Fury," he muttered, kissing the side of her head. He couldn't have missed the tension flooding through her, but before he could say anything about her reaction, her phone ringing in her pocket interrupted their conversation. He relaxed his arms slightly and she pulled it out, touching the screen to accept the call.

"Hello?" He couldn't hear the other person clearly, but knew it was female. "Oh, no. Okay. We'll be home as soon as we can get back." She twisted in his arms, looked up at him, and said, "Sammy's not feeling well. How long before we can be home?"

"About forty-five minutes," he responded, noticing some of her hair had escaped her ponytail, so he reached out to tuck it behind her ear, trailing his fingertips down her neck and drawing a shiver from her.

"Tell him I'll be home in less than an hour, Luce. I'm so sorry," she said then listened for a moment before disconnecting and putting her phone into her pocket. "Can we go?"

"Yeah, baby," he said softly, leaning in to kiss her gently, loving the way her face softened when he did so. Tipping her chin up with his fingertips, he kissed her harder, tongue roughly stroking against hers, nipping at her lips. He slanted his head again, eating down her gasp at the hunger he revealed, then shut it down ruthlessly, pulling back to peck a final soft kiss on her lips. "Let's get in the wind."

10. Humor me

As promised, forty-five minutes later, they were walking into the apartment, Hoss' hand wrapped around hers, fingers threaded together. Luce quietly gathered her brothers and shooed them out, telling Hope she had left a pizza warming in the oven and that Sammy had already gone to bed. Hope hurried into the bedroom to check on her son, finding him sleeping on his side, back to the door, covers pulled up to his ears. He didn't seem overly warm to the touch or clammy, so she didn't believe he was running a fever. Maybe it was a short-lived stomach bug, and he would be better in the morning. As she stood, she saw a shadow on the far wall, realizing she had walked away without a word, leaving Hoss standing alone in the living room.

"I'm so sorry," she said, moving across the room towards him.

He looked past her, and one corner of his mouth edged up, but when she turned to look, it was only Sammy lying on the single bed wedged into the room at the foot of hers. "I called the diner, asked them to cover your shift in the morning. I suspect he's going to be okay," he said, reaching out to curl a hand around her waist and draw her out of the room. He left the door open a couple of inches, and then led her into the living room and towards the couch. *Crap*, she thought, hesitating as she wondered how to derail what looked to be an expected petting session.

"Hope, no, baby. I simply want to hold you while we talk some more." He looked back at her, evidently sensing her reluctance. Nodding, she let him thread his fingers between hers again and followed him to the couch, smiling tentatively at him when he guided her down, lying back and positioning her between his body and the back of the sofa.

"What did you want to talk about?" She thought this was probably a safe question, since he already seemed to have an agenda. As long as they didn't talk about her behavior in the park, letting him put his hand down her pants in full view of anyone who could have driven up. Granted, no one had come to the park, but they could have, and she had been so far gone in the experience she didn't know if she would have even recognized an audience.

"The park," he said softly, and she groaned silently. The one topic she didn't want to discuss, and of course, that would be his focus. "I told you...I like you, Hope. I don't want you to be worried about what you think I want, or embarrassed about anything we might do in the future. For me to help you down that road, we have to communicate, so we're going to talk. And then, I have some questions for you, baby."

She swallowed hard and nodded, waiting. When he didn't say anything else, she bit her lip and asked, "What questions?"

His voice was quiet when he asked, "How many men have you been with, Hope?" Oh, God, this was where he decided she wasn't worth it. Not worth his time, because she was stupidly unexperienced and didn't know what she was doing. There had been no one since Cal, and he had been her first.

"One," she said, feeling her lips trembling. Waiting for his dismissal of her, she was surprised when he didn't react.

"How long were you with Suiter?" This question came fast on the heels of the other one, and he hadn't seemed to stumble at the information on the number of lovers...lover. Maybe this didn't have to be as scary as she feared.

"Only a few weeks." The words came out strong, but she ducked her head to avoid his gaze until his fingers lifted her chin.

"Don't do that, baby." Leaning in, he softly kissed her then pulled back with a stern look. "You have nothing to be ashamed of, sweetheart." He said this quietly, and instead of the condescending one she might expect, the gentle expression he offered her was warm and sweet, yet somehow dark, with that darkness causing a flood of heat in her belly. "So one guy and a handful of times got you Sammy?"

"Yeah," she said with a quick nod. "I was lucky." That earned her a full smile and a rumbling laugh, and because of that, she knew he got it, so she continued, "I can't picture my life without Sammy in it. I don't want to imagine what it would be like. So yeah, I got lucky."

"You like waking up in bed with me today?" The question startled her, because they hadn't been in bed, not really. Okay, sure, technically the same bed, because they had been on the same mattress, but she had been under the sheets, and he had been lying on top of them. It had been so...right, waking up next to him. Felt like where she belonged. She wanted to answer him, get it right and make sure he knew how much she had liked it, had liked his hand curling around her shoulder, pulling her close. Making her feel cared for. Wanted.

"Yeah," she said softly. "It was nice." Inwardly she winced, *Lame-o. 'Nice' isn't what a man wants to hear.*

"I thought it was nice, too. Hell, you're sweet all the time, but you were completely...mmmm. Just waking up, all warm and sleepy and sexy as hell. Hell, yeah, you were exactly what I wanted, and I'd like it to be a regular thing between us. For it to be what I think we're both going to want, we need to get you and Mercy into a three-bedroom place. For a couple weeks now, I've had a call into Myron, our money guy in Chicago, but he's not moving fast enough for me, so I'll see what I can find for us." His hand curved around her cheek then threaded through her hair, and she found herself pressing into his touch like a cat seeking affection.

"I get you've got an independent streak, and it seems to me that you and Mercy need some time to get comfortable with this sisterhood thing you've got going on. I'm aware you need that time, or I'd move you into my place right now. I've got plenty of room for you and Sammy, but Mercy stayin' at my house would cause problems elsewhere in my life, and I ain't down for that. This leaves us with finding you girls a bigger place. Which we're going to do." His hand tightened in her hair, angling her head up so she had to look at him. "And, baby, we're going to do it, because I loved what you gave me today. What I said was true; it was what I wanted. Everything I wanted right then."

He paused, his fingers moving through her hair again. When he spoke again, his voice was rough, thick with desire. "I want more, Hope, and I'm going to want privacy from your son when I get that more. When I take you...when you let me take you, and you give that to me like you did today, I'm gonna need it to be just you and me."

The whole time he was talking she was holding her breath, every spoken 'but' making her heart clench. Because until he began articulating it, she didn't know she wanted it, but now she wanted everything he revealed. All of that, she wanted, right alongside him. She wanted to have him look at her like he did today, focused and intent, as if she was the most important and precious thing he had ever held in his arms.

"What would be wrong in having Mercy as a roommate?" she asked. His statement made her wonder about how friendly he had been with her sister in the past. Or if, under the surface niceness, he was like some of the women, shunning Mercy for things she was now sorry she had done.

"Because Deke, who is my brother, wants to get her on his bike permanently, and her stayin' at my place would give her a reason to keep space between them. I ain't gonna be that reason, and I also ain't gonna give her an easy out like that."

He shook his head. "You've met Deke; that man is an open mouth/insert foot kinda guy, and he doesn't have a filter. Especially when he's fucking himself in the head, and he would hugely fuck himself in the head over that. Mercy is a good friend, and he knows we're friends. When she got mixed up in something ugly a few months back, I was here for days, taking care of her. We're *friends*."

There was a slight emphasis on that repeated word. The emphasis underlined what she believed he was about to say, and her stomach rolled with the sure knowledge as his words hit her, hard as punches to the chest, stealing her breath. "We fucked, once, a long time ago, but decided it wasn't the thing for us, because friends are hard to come by."

At his words, she stiffened and when he chuckled at her response, she began pushing at his chest, trying to get away in earnest. *He slept with Mercy. Then, he had his hands in my pants today,* she thought in a panic, pushing harder and trying to twist out of his embrace, her breath coming hard and fast as her throat tightened.

"Baby, hold the fuck still," he growled when she continued to struggle, even after he had tightened his arms around her in what felt like a warning. "Did you not hear what I said?" He paused, and she stilled, but didn't answer. "Answer me, Hope. What did you hear me say?"

"You slept with my sister," she whispered.

After a long pause, he prompted, "What else, Hope?"

"Nothing else. What was there to hear? You slept with my sister, and now you think you want to sleep with me. I don't know why, or how it should make me feel, so I think I'm going to pass on the whole keeping it in the family thing." *Holy crap*, she thought. *Where did that attitude come from? It's going to piss him off for sure.*

Sure enough, his arms tightened around her again, but his voice was soft when he said, "Always so quick to imagine the worst. What I said was yeah, she and I fucked. One time. Only once, baby. It was a long time ago, a lifetime away...more than three years. I didn't sleep with her. I fucked her bent over the back of a chair in the clubhouse, never kissed her. Never touched her in any way that mattered. I got done, got off, threw away the condom, and sat back and watched the next brother take his turn, because that's what she wanted."

She swallowed hard, listening to him, wanting to believe.

"Next day, we had a chat, and I tried to tell her what she was doing would turn around and bite her in the ass, but she wouldn't even hear me out. I told her I wouldn't be part of her self-destruction." He lifted a hand, smoothing her hair back from her face.

"The list of what I did and did not do are very different, Hope. I never held her in the middle of a thunderstorm, feeling shaken to my core, because something that beautiful would come to me for comfort." His hand stroked through her hair again, the pad of his thumb caressing her cheek. "I never had her on the back of my bike, ever. You're the first to be behind me, baby."

Leaning in, he kissed her softly, and then whispered, "I never fingered her, drawing it out for nearly an hour, just so I could watch her face as she broke apart, because I needed to hear my name spoken in passion from her lips. Never felt like I would fall to pieces and lose my shit unless I were near her, touching her, holding her...loving her."

Now she really was sure she couldn't breathe, because things were beginning to look wavy around the edges.

"In all that, I wanna know you're holding onto the fact you feel like something special to me, baby." His fingers found their way underneath her chin, lifting her face to his as he leaned in, pressing his forehead to hers. Lips barely brushing hers, he said, "If I thought it was the best thing for you to move in with me today, we'd already be on our way. You need Mercy, and, whether you've got a handle on it yet or not, she needed you in a desperate way. I think the two of you are saving each other. Make no mistake, I am going to want my time with you, a lot of it, so get used to having my ass around." He kissed her softly, and then rubbed the tip of his nose along hers.

Raising his voice oddly, he said, "And I'm going to want private time with Mommy, so get used to that, too."

There was a noise in the hallway, and she twisted in time to see movement. Jerking her gaze back to Hoss, she hissed, "Was Sammy watching us?"

"Watching and listening to that last little bit." He laughed when she felt the blood leave her face, and she was successful in pushing off the couch this time, rolling over his torso to get to her feet. She stood, frowning down at his smiling face, upturned to her. "He didn't hear anything bad, baby."

Ignoring his words, she trotted to her bedroom and opened the door to find Sammy sitting cross-legged on his bed, staring at her. He was scowling hard, and she flirted with the idea of avoidance before she took a breath, and then pulled the door closed behind her. "How's the tummy, bud?" Reaching out her hand, she ignored his dodging duck, firmly placing her palm against his forehead to find his skin still cool, unfevered. "You need a bucket?"

"What did he mean he wanted us to move in with him? We're living with Aunt Mercy now, and she makes you happy." He had ceased his attempts to get away from her hand and was scowling up at her around her arm. "Why would you want to leave?"

Crap. This was not a topic she would be discussing with her son; it didn't matter what he may have overheard just now. "That's the thing; I don't. Not right now. And, Hoss knows it. He was merely making his wish list. Kinda like you do at Christmas." She sat on the edge of the bed, wrapping her arm around his shoulders and pulling him into a hug. "Talk to me about the tummy."

"I feel fine," he said brusquely, still stiff and unyielding in her arms. "He was here this morning. Then he came back, and now he's here again. Is he moving in with us?"

"No, sweetie," she said softly. "He has his own place. He's enjoying becoming friends, and when you make friends, you want to hang out with those people. Like you do with Jonny and Kane. You enjoy hanging out with them, right?"

He nodded, leaning into her a little. "Why do I have to get used to him?"

"Hmmm?" She made an inquiring noise, not certain how to articulate something she didn't even understand herself.

"He said he was going to want time with you, and I needed to get used to it. Why? Why can't things just stay as they are? Why do they hafta change, Mom?" Was that a tearful quaver in his voice? *Crap.*

"He wants to get to know us a little. It takes time to build a friendship, bud. You know that." He leaned into her a little more and then, with an enormous yawn, suddenly sagged against her, letting go of whatever emotion had him so stiff and upright. She started swaying slightly back and forth. "If your tummy is okay, then you need to head back to sleep, bud. I love you, bunches and oodles."

"Love you too, Mommy," he yawned and sighed, "ice cream and noodles," he finished, sliding out of her arms and under the sheet. "Is he gonna be here in the morning?"

"I don't know," she said honestly, leaning down to tug the covers up to his ears. "Would it be okay if he were?"

"Yeah," he yawned. "But you're my mom, so I gotta take care of you. I'll," he yawned again, "let him know the score. Bring my D-game," he was mumbling now, skidding down the hill into sleep. "Hit the ice hard," he sighed, and she thought he was done, but then he mumbled, "gotta keep my best girl safe. Mac told me so. 'Sponsibilities of the good boys." Another sigh, this one followed by a small snore, then, "No lies."

Standing there for a moment, she traced his features with her fingertips, a caress he would never allow in the light of day. He had told her seriously a few weeks ago he was too old for her to love on him all the time, so she tried to respect that and give him a little space, but she missed holding him like she had done tonight.

Hearing a noise, she twisted to find Hoss had entered the room during her exchange with Sammy and positioned himself on the bed as he had this morning, back to the headboard, legs stretched out over the covers. He was naked from the waist up and had his tee folded, the fabric draped across his ankles. She looked a question at him, and he laughed.

"I liked seeing you in my shirt, baby." He shrugged and his lips moved in that sideways smile that always caught at her breath. "Humor me."

11. **All my waiting**

"Mister Hoss?" The two-word question spoken in a clear tenor voice came from nearby, and Hoss peeled one eye open, even as he shifted Hope in his arms, pulling her soft form closer and rubbing his chin across the top of her head. He didn't see anyone directly in front of him, so he rolled his neck slightly, inwardly sighing as he looked over his shoulder to find Sammy standing beside the bed. The kid looked like he had barely gotten out of bed. His blonde hair was sticking up on top of his head every which way and he was knuckling his eyes fiercely, trying to wake up, glasses still abandoned on the dresser, waiting for their need to be realized.

"Yeah, boy?" He kept his voice down, scarcely above a whisper, not wanting to disturb Hope's sleep.

"Why are you here?" Followed by a jaw-creaking yawn, that question surprised him, because he expected anything except head-on confrontation from the boy.

"What?" Maybe he didn't hear him right.

Instead of repeating himself, using the heel of his hand to rub and scratch at his nose, Sammy finished the yawn with a full-body shake and said, "I'm hungry."

The kid was studiously keeping his eyes off Hope and on Hoss instead, chin turned towards his shoulder and neck wrenched around. Glancing down, Hoss could see nothing amiss, because she was decently covered. He knew she was sleeping in his tee and her panties, but with the comforter pulled up to her shoulders, she could have been dressed in a muumuu for all the kid knew. "Hungry, huh?"

Forty-five minutes later, Hope still hadn't climbed out of bed. He and Sammy had both eaten cereal for breakfast. Then, the boy dragged him into the living room, declaring it was time for his favorite show, and that nothing would do until Hoss agreed to watch it with him. So, Hoss found himself settled on the couch with a little body tucked in next to him, watching early morning cartoons.

They hadn't been seated for more than a minute when Sammy shoved himself upright, pushing up onto his knees on the couch cushion, facing Hoss. His mouth pulled down into a bow and his face was serious, so Hoss held his gaze, waiting for the boy to get whatever was eating at him off his chest. After a couple of minutes of their silent standoff, Sammy finally said, "I don't like it when people talk mean to my mom."

Slowly nodding, Hoss tried to cast his thoughts back to see when he had talked to Hope in a way that would have triggered the kid like this. Coming up blank, he offered a generic, "I wouldn't like it either."

Scrunching up his nose, Sammy scowled and stared at him. "She's a really good mom."

"I can see she is, Sam." He nodded again. "She loves you a whole bunch, and she's probably one of the best moms I've ever known. Except maybe mine."

Tipping his chin down, Sammy's gaze fell to the cushion between them, thinking hard. After a minute, he mumbled, "Yeah, I can see where you'd think your mom was better." Looking up, he said, "Boys love their mothers best."

Hoss frowned. Was the kid parroting something he had heard, or did he actually understand something like that? "Yeah, I guess we do."

Sinking sideways against the couch back, Sammy's gaze cut to the TV then back to Hoss. Clearly torn between enjoying something he wanted to watch, and communicating something important, he chose the hard road, starting with what seemed like a ritual. "No lies." He paused, waiting to see what reaction he would pull from Hoss, and eventually he nodded in silent satisfaction and continued, "You can't be mean to Mom. She's had enough hard. Mac told me she's had enough hard to last a lifetime."

The volume of sound from the TV rose and Sammy glanced that direction, but his gaze never made it that far, instead stopping at a picture in a small frame perched on the table beside the couch. Looking closer, Hoss saw he was staring at a print of the same picture Mercy sent him the first night her sister and nephew stayed with her. Hope's smile was as bright and true as Mercy's, and their shared joy fairly radiated from the image. Whispering, Sammy said, "She hasn't had nearly enough good. Not like it is here, not like since we found Aunt Mercy."

"Do you miss back home?" Hoss asked softly, shocked when the boy shook his head hard.

"Never had a home before now." Sammy's chin had tucked down to his chest, and it looked like he was struggling against tears, his lips trembling.

Fuck. "You like it here best of all, then?" He reached out and patted Sam's skinny leg then threaded his fingers through the boy's hair, offering comfort in an easy caress.

"Mac and Miss Nelly wanted us to stay with them. They didn't want us to leave, wanted us to stay like we did one time." He paused to suck in a hard breath, and Hoss thought he was deciding how much to reveal. Using the side of his hand, Sam swiped hair out of his eyes and looked up at Hoss. "But we don't like to bother people. Mom didn't have a choice that one time. It was when the man hurt her."

"What man?" Hoss' muscles tensed and he knew the boy saw it, because Sam's eyes grew wide, white opening up all around the edges. Hoss growled out, "What man hurt your mom?"

"The roommate we had before Gibson," Sammy whispered, unhelpfully. "Mom calls Gibson a jackhole, because he skated free without paying her rent, but Milner she calls a *really* bad word."

"Y'all had lots of roommates?" Hoss found himself wondering why a single mother would take on men as roommates. Something in this wasn't lining up for him, especially given the confirmation of his suspicions regarding her limited experience with men.

"Not a lot. And, anyways, after Milner, she was way more careful about who it was. Mac told her that where we lived it was best to have it known a man lived there, but after everything with Milner, she talked to them at the diner a bunch of times before giving them a key. He was mean. He talked really mean to her and twisted her arm, hard. He made her cry. A lot. His brother was my hockey coach for about a minute, but Coach was way meaner than his brother, so Mom yanked me fast." His chin was tucked down again, voice thick.

"I wasted a bunch of her money, because Coach wouldn't give her any back. She got mad and said a bad word, so Milner twisted her arm and pushed her down. The ambulance guys let me ride up front, and I got to press the button to blow the horn for red lights. The money is why he got mad." His voice fell to a barely heard whisper, "I told her I was sorry. I tried to stop him. He was mad."

Fuck. She had to be taken to the hospital by ambulance, because some fucking asshole got pissed that she didn't like his attitude with the kid. Hope was probably worried out of her mind about Sammy the whole time. And, the kid was carrying guilt he didn't need, for something that couldn't ever be his responsibility.

"Coach Milner? Was that his name?" Hoss asked. Myron could find the man, and they had a couple of affiliate clubs down that way. Hell, he had family he could reach out to, too. The way he was feeling right now, it was not too late to teach those fucktard brothers a lesson they wouldn't soon forget.

"Yeah, that's Coach." Sammy nodded once, glancing at the TV again then back to Hoss. "Mac told me it wasn't my fault. He said sometimes even good boys weren't able to save the ones we love from bad people. But it's my job." He frowned, opened his mouth and closed it, and then in a gesture Hoss had seen him do once before with Mercy, reached out and cupped his palm around the curve of Hoss' jaw, turning him so they stared into each other's eyes. His lips moved soundlessly and Hoss read, *No lies*, a repeat of what the boy had said at the beginning of this conversation. After a moment, Sammy asked, his voice tight, "Do you like my mom?"

Without hesitation, because this was important, Hoss answered, "Yes, Sammy, I like your mom a lot."

"Then you can't make her sad," the boy answered just as quickly, and Hoss could hear the tears threatening again as Sammy's words fell in a hurried rush from his lips. "You can't be like Milner, or the truck driver, or the man who worked on the car, or anybody else who makes her sad." His hand fell away, the tiny spot of heat on Hoss' face slowly dissipating, but the heat in his chest lingered far longer.

Sammy was hard to follow at times, but Hoss thought he got the gist of it. "A truck driver made her sad?"

"He hit our car when we were on the way here. In Indykanapolis. That was after he made ugly faces at her in his mirror, so I didn't try to get him to blow his horn. Then we got the car fixed, but that man only pretended to be nice. He was really just as bad as the truck driver." Sammy slumped sideways into Hoss' side, turning his head to look at the TV finally. "She didn't even like them, and they made her sad. She likes you. You can't make her sad."

"You guys got in an accident on your way here?" He was incredulous, because he didn't understand why Hope wouldn't have said anything.

"Yeah, the truck bashed the back of the car. The guy who fixed it called it a bang-bang in the gas hole, and Mom got mad when he said that." Sammy cut his gaze up to Hoss' face then back to the TV. "He wanted to like mom kinda like you do, but I did my job."

"What job is that?" This kid was chockfull of information. Hope hadn't said anything to him about her roommates, a wreck, or even a mechanic giving her a hard time. Seems she didn't want to let him carry any of her burdens. He thought, *She's going to have to figure out how to talk to me, get over that reserve.*

"Only the most important one."

Hoss knew the eye roll was implied and he grinned. He guessed, "Keeping your mom safe?"

"Yeah." Sammy moved away slightly and slumped far down on his back, draping his butt over the edge of the cushion, using his legs to keep himself on the couch. "You know. We gotta keep our best girls safe."

"Yeah, we do," he agreed. Maybe this talk was his open door to the boy. "You think I'll be okay for your mom?"

"No." That disappointing answer came without a moment's hesitation, and Hoss rocked back as if from a blow. Then Sammy continued, twisting the knife deeper. "You're not a nice man. My daddy is a nice man. He's got a big car and lots of money. My Grandmamma told me so."

"Is that so?" His tone must have changed, because Sammy looked up at him and warily nodded.

"Yeah. He never gets to help us, because Mom won't ask him. She likes us to make our own way, so we always know where we stand. But, if she'd have ever called him, he'd have jumped in his car and raced to us. He's so rich he probably has a plane. So, he'd jump in his plane, too. He's a nice man." The longer the boy talked, the tighter his face got until it was clear to Hoss that Sammy didn't believe one word of what he was spewing. "My Grandmamma told me Mom never loved Daddy, not like he loved her. He loved her so much he had to go away before I was born. The policemen took him away, because he loved her so much."

Everything in Hoss strained to tell the kid he had it all wrong, to set him straight and let him know he was harboring dangerous delusions, but Hope's words came back to him. She was not encouraging this kind of hero worship, but she wasn't discouraging it, either. She was the mom here, so if she felt that way, then it certainly wasn't his place to set the little turd straight. Instead, he made a noncommittal hum, watching interestedly when Sammy's face tightened even more, obviously wanting a different reaction from Hoss.

"Do you play hockey?" Another conversational one-eighty from Sammy had Hoss shaking his head quickly and then laughing.

"Where did that come from?" Hoss chuckled. "Nope, I don't play. I like to watch it, though. Love the game. I go see the Tridents pretty often. Your mom said you like hockey, right? You want to go with me next time? I can get an extra seat if you want."

"Fort Wayne Tridents? Goons and muckers." He scoffed, which made Hoss laugh again. The kid was a riot. "I'd go see a game with you, though. Mom knows the game; she's not terrible to sit with."

"Was talking about just me and you," Hoss said, letting his statement land in the space between them, watching as Sammy's face changed, becoming wary. That look spoke worlds about what the kid had seen or maybe had done to him, living hard like he and Hope had. Anything good had to be looked upon with suspicion and an eye towards the other person's end goal. *Fuck.*

"Not Mom?" He voiced the question tentatively, unsure of what Hoss wanted.

"Yeah, it'd be a boys' night." He was fishing to see if there was interest, but honestly, Hoss could think of worse ways to spend an evening, especially if it got him a chance to bond with the boy. If things went the way he wanted with Hope, he needed to cement a relationship with Sammy sooner rather than later.

"Boys' night." His voice musing, Sammy cut his gaze over to Hoss then back to the TV. "Just us?"

"If your mom's okay with it, and you want to, yeah. I know from talking to my friends on the team that the Tridents' practice skates will be starting soon, which means games are right around the corner. First home night traditionally has a free skate with the team after the game, if you were interested in that, too." He sat, waiting patiently for a moment, thinking about red and white bobbers on sun-kissed water, and then he yanked the line, trying to set the hook. "If you aren't, that's no big deal, Sam."

Sammy's body jerked upright and he turned to look at Hoss as he blurted, "You're friends with the players?"

"Yeah, a couple of them. A couple of my friends retired last year, but I know some of the guys still playing on the team." He lifted one shoulder in a nonchalant shrug, slowly working the line in, hand-over-hand. *Hell yeah, this is the way to the kid.*

"Who?" That one word was nearly vibrating with anticipation, and he glanced at Sammy to find his eyes fixed on him.

"Who what?" he asked for clarification, because Sammy had been all over the place so far.

"Who do you know? Who was the players?"

"Jason Spencer and Leeland Dugger—" He didn't get to finish his sentence before Sammy was shouting.

"No way! Duke it out Dugger? You know him? And Spencer? He was amazing in Chicago. Fastest forward in the league, and he played in Russia! He's Canadian, but he played in Russia. Did you know he won the cup for the Mallets?" The excited words couldn't tumble out of the kid fast enough, and Hoss grinned to hear it. *Landed.*

"Yeah, I didn't get to see him play in Chicago, but he's talked about the last game often enough. He did well with the Tridents, too." Before he finished, Sammy's head was bobbing enthusiastically.

"Yeah, everybody knows that. You know him? Like…really, really know him?" Brow furrowed, Sammy wordlessly communicated his disbelief.

"So yea or nay on the game?" Hoss was ready to move the conversation past this impasse, because until he could introduce Jase or Lee to the little guy, apparently his friendship with famous athletes would be subject to Sammy's suspicion.

"Yeah!" That was thrown out at him immediately and he nodded.

"Okay, bud. We get your mom's stamp of approval, and we'll be golden."

"Yes. Of course, it's okay." When her voice came from behind him, he twisted to look at her, seeing her eyes were overly bright and wet. Her words had been an almost whisper, but Sammy heard them too, and looking up at Hoss with a wide grin, he bounced on the cushion for a moment before the TV captured his attention again, talk of boys' night and hockey forgotten in the cartoon antics on the screen.

"Baby," he said softly, holding out a hand, wanting her to take those steps to him so he didn't have to get up and leave Sammy. The boy had curled into his side again, and Hoss had curved an arm around him, tugging him in a little tighter. She obliged, walking over and placing her hand in his, threading their fingers together with a squeeze. He tugged and she walked around the end of the sofa, sinking into the cushions by folding her legs underneath her and leaning into his other side.

She eyed Sammy across the expanse of Hoss' chest, softly saying, "Mornin', bud."

Getting a distracted, "Morning," back, she tipped her head to look up at Hoss.

"Hey," she breathed and he bent his neck, bringing his face down, placing his lips firmly over hers in a brief, hard kiss.

"Baby," he repeated, lifting his head to catch Sammy turning back towards the TV, scowl firmly back on his face. "You sleep okay?"

"Mmhmm," she hummed, nuzzling against him with a sigh. "Best sleep in forever."

"Good to hear," he said, giving Sammy a squeeze at the same time he kissed the top of Hope's head. This, he could get used to.

***

Sammy stared at the TV without seeing it. He had tried his best, but it wasn't working. He wasn't going to be able to keep Mom safe from being sad. Jonny had told him to talk up his daddy; they thought it would make Hoss mad—might even make him leave—but he didn't do anything. Didn't act mad or hurt, just stayed on the couch as if it was the only place he ever wanted to be. Watching stupid cartoons.

Then he said he knowed people on the Tridents. Sammy didn't want to believe him, but Hoss hadn't never, ever lied to him, so he probably did know Duke it out Dugger. He sighed and stiffened when he realized he was leaning heavily into Hoss, feeling the arm tighten around his shoulders, hand curved around his bent knees, giving him a squeeze. He liked this. Liked how safe it made him feel, tucked into the big man's side. Liked how his mom's voice sounded when she talked to him or Hoss, because she sounded quiet-happy, which was the best kind of happy he had ever seen from her. Not over-the-top happy, like she could get with Aunt Mercy, but the kind of happy that left a burn in the back of his throat, because he wanted this for her for all the times.

Tentatively, he swallowed, feeling the tight in his throat loosen slightly. He liked Hoss. He didn't trust it, because liking things just meant they could be ganked. Either by another kid or by something else, but he knew from experience happy didn't stay long for him or his mom. He was afraid that eventually, this would be ganked, too.

***

"That much?" She knew her voice was disbelieving, but couldn't help it. The price quoted was too much for hockey lessons. She couldn't pay those fees, not and keep up with expenses, as well as set a little aside.

"Yes, ma'am." The polite woman on the other end of the phone spoke quietly, sympathy thick in her tone. "It covers registration, ice time for practice, as well as games, gear, and staffing. I know it's a lot, but the kiddos get a ton of experience out of the development camp."

"Okay. Thank you. I'll have to think about it." Which was broke-parent speak for 'this ain't gonna happen,' and the woman knew it, because she was quick to interrupt the hanging-up process.

"I do know of another option that might work for you." She paused, and when Hope made an inquisitive noise, continued, "There's a local foundation that does regular lesson sessions year-round, and they have a scholarship program. I can email you a link to their website if you are interested." She heard Hoss call from the living room, having let himself into the apartment. In the past few days, it had become their ritual, and she knew he would seek her out, so she kept her focus on the woman offering her a lifeline.

"Please," Hope breathed, because the one thing Sammy loved more than her was hockey, and if she had to beg this foundation, she would. Rattling off her email address, she waited while the woman read it back, and then thanked her before they hung up, both feeling a little better about the exchange.

Her eyes closed involuntarily when warm hands slipped around her hips to cross low on her belly, a hard body pressing up against her back. His breath was warm on her neck a moment before his lips found skin, and she shivered at the sensation. There was no way she would ever get used to the physical effect he had on her. Everything he did to her felt so good, even if it was only sweeping her hair off her shoulder so he could nibble along the line of her neck. "Who ya talkin' to, baby?" She felt his words in heated gusts of air across her skin, and she shivered again.

"I was calling about something for Sammy. The lady is going to email me some info." She was pleased with the evenness of her voice when she answered him, because it certainly did not reflect the eagerness and terror that had equal space in her head right now. She had made plans without telling him, and hoped...prayed she had gotten things right.

Mouth still working her neck, his hands moved, one roaming upward across her belly, fingers working their way underneath her shirt to cup around her ribs on one side. She felt the sweep of his thumb on the side of her breast and she drew in a quick breath, biting down on the gasp that wanted to escape as his other hand crept downward across her stomach.

He uttered a guttural "Fuck," when she leaned her head back against his shoulder, tilting her head in invitation of more. It was so quiet in the house it seemed a bubble had formed around them, and all she could hear were the soft noises he made deep in his throat as he caressed and kissed her. "Beautiful." More kisses, more scrapes from the edges of his teeth, more hot trails left by his tongue…more. Up to now, they had been limited to heavy makeout sessions similar to what had happened in the park. "Where's Sammy?" He pulled her tight back against him when he asked the question, letting her feel his hard arousal, communicating without using words why he wanted to know.

"He's over at DeeDee's, playing with Jonny." She couldn't control the tremor in her voice, and knew he would understand at her next words. "He's spending the night there. His first sleepover."

"I get all night with you, baby?" Hoss' voice was low and thick, his hand at her breast moving to cover the soft mound, finger and thumb meeting in a brief pinch at her nipple, and then his palm slid across it soothingly as she shivered. He hooked a finger in her bra, slipping it down, baring her breast, trailing his nails over the soft skin. "All night?" His other hand inched between her legs, pressing and lifting, pushing hard until she shifted her hips forward, thrusting against his hand. "*Fuck*," he whispered.

"Hoss," she called softly and he stilled behind her, waiting. "I'm…a little nervous." *Understatement of the year*, she thought with an inward snort. Terrified was more like it.

"I won't hurt you, Hope." His words were more of a promise than she thought he knew, but she must have made a noise of disbelief, because his arms tightened around her. "I won't, baby. Will never hurt you. You're always safe with me." His voice was filled with conviction, and she wanted to believe, but she had never had that before. Never had a safe haven, not really.

His hands were moving again, deftly setting her bra back in place, and she lost the heat of his hand between her legs when he moved both arms to circle her waist instead. She froze, because he was retreating, and she wasn't sure what she had done to stop where they were headed, where—even with the nerves making her legs shake—she knew she wanted to go.

"Hoss?" That quaver was back in her voice as she said his name, this time not in anticipation, but loss.

"Not gonna do anything you aren't ready for, Hope."

He sounded resolved and she didn't know how to shake him, wasn't at all sure how to get things back on track. She had zero experience in this area, and was nowhere near comfortable enough to voice her...desires. *Crap, you can barely say it in your head. How are you going to tell this beautiful man what you want?*

"Want you to trust me, baby."

"Honestly?" She waited for a response from him and he gave her a grunt, finally sounding as frustrated as she was beginning to feel. "I don't know what I'm ready for, and I don't know if I understand what safe means to you. I don't know if it means the same thing to you and me. I'm mostly nervous, because I don't want to disappoint you. You've been so patient with me, all along. I see how you've been there for me since the first night I met you. And you've been patient. Hoss," her voice cracked, so she paused and swallowed hard then repeated his name, "Hoss, I want...this."

Silence, then he gave her a squeeze and nibbled up her neck, pressing a hard kiss behind her ear. "Then it's my place to show you what safe is, baby. Want you to trust me, but I can be patient a little longer." His mouth worked her neck for a moment, hot lips against her skin and his erection pressed against her, still hard and hot behind the zipper of his jeans. "I can be patient, Hope. But you have to trust me, can you do that?"

Immediately, she nodded, not speaking, letting him know that by still being in his arms, she was giving him some of that trust.

"Come for a ride with me," he invited softly, and she nodded again. Without removing his arms, he turned them and then, laughing, walked them with exaggerated strides over to where her jacket lay draped over the back of the couch.

Once on the bike, she snuggled up behind him, wrapping her fingers around his belt in front of his belly, burying them against the heat from his body. Without a word, they rode out of the parking lot and onto the surface streets. Unlike the first time, she wasn't as afraid and tried to lean with him around the corners.

He seemed to have a destination in mind, and knew the route, timing the lights when he could. But, he took every opportunity to caress her, slowly running his hands up and down her calves, threading his fingers through hers, turning his head and demanding a kiss when they had to stop for any reason. Between his constant attention and the vibration of the motorcycle beneath her, she was fairly humming with anticipation for their return to the apartment, surprised when he steered into a large, gated housing complex instead, lifting a familiar hand to the guard as they motored through the entrance.

A few minutes later, he was pulling into a circular drive, and as he passed in front of the garage, the door soundlessly lifted, allowing him to walk the bike backwards into the lighted space. His home. He had brought her to his house, instead of back to Mercy's apartment.

Stifling silence descended when he shut off the motor, and he reached back one hand, wordlessly offering her the stability of his grip as she swung her leg off the bike. Standing beside him, she watched him dismount and take a step towards her.

As he reached out to put his hands on either side of her waist, a voice called from the deepening dusk outside the garage. "Isaiah, I'm glad you're home. I had a question about the contract..." The voice trailed off to silence, and Hope twisted to see a pretty woman in a sleek red shirtdress standing in the pool of light the garage cast on the driveway.

"Evenin', Tamara," he called, turning Hope and pulling her back against his chest. "Hope, this is my neighbor, Tamara Leinstill. Tamara, want you to meet Hope Collins, my girlfriend." There was no mistaking the look of surprise on the woman's face, and Hope immediately disliked her.

"Pleased to meet you," Hope lied, linking her fingers with Hoss' at her waist and leaning into him. *He called me his girlfriend*, she thought with a thrill.

"Yes, you too," Tamara said insincerely, her eyes fixed on a point just over Hope's shoulder, apparently never leaving Hoss' face. "I'll come back later, shall I?"

"Go ahead and ask your question now. I don't know as we'll surface anytime soon," he said softly, his arms tightening around Hope when she made an embarrassed noise.

"Yes, well." She paused and then huffed in what seemed frustration. "The agreement isn't exclusive, Isaiah. I don't know if I can get the gallery to go for these terms." She shrugged one elegant shoulder, and watching the scarlet glide of what was obviously silk moving across her form, Hope suddenly was excruciatingly aware of the coarseness of her own gray shirt rough against her skin. This woman was everything she wasn't, stylish, sophisticated, beautiful. Experienced.

"Then the gallery don't get my shit," he shot back, and Tamara's eyes narrowed, flicking down then up Hope, and then fixing on Hoss' face over her shoulder again. "If that's all you got to say, then I'll end this with goodnight, Tamara. You know the drill. My shit, my terms."

Tamara huffed out a frustrated breath, and then with a brief, smooth wave, she disappeared into the darkness outside the garage without another word. Hoss rested his chin on Hope's shoulder for a moment then muttered, "Fucking woman." Throughout the encounter, he had positioned her in front of him like a barrier and with a sinking feeling in her stomach Hope knew his words had been meant that way, too. A throwaway phrase to make Tamara keep her distance. Hoss didn't like the woman, and Hope understood that tonight she had simply been a convenient line of defense. "Come inside, baby," he said, kissing the side of her head as he turned them.

Reaching the interior door, he opened it with one hand, keeping one around Hope's waist, and then he slapped a button on the doorframe and the garage door slowly closed behind them, shutting out the night, and any further interruptions by his neighbor. "Welcome home," he told her softly, moving her quickly through the kitchen and living room, leading her up a hallway to what was evidently his bedroom. Her steps slowed and he turned to look at her, a questioning quirk to one brow.

"This is your house," she said quietly, and he nodded.

"Yeah, baby," he responded and frowned when she resisted the tug he gave her hand, her feet refusing to move. "Hope, talk to me. What's going on in that head of yours?"

"You called me your girlfriend." She couldn't help herself; keeping eye contact was too hard, so her gaze dipped to the floor. Since she couldn't see his face, the first indication of his reaction was his black motorcycle boots moving, striding firmly towards her. Surprised, she looked up and shrank backwards, because he looked angry.

Pressing her against the wall with his body, his musky scent surrounding her, he caged her head with his forearms, leaning into her, his gaze locked on hers. He didn't speak as his face slowly lowered, and then his mouth was on hers. This wasn't a soft kiss. It wasn't tentative in any way. This was a kiss of possession; he was marking her, owning her. His mouth moved over hers hard and fast, drawing her onto her toes to pursue his lips when he pulled back for a breath, and then crashing back together with bruising force. His teeth clicked with hers and then bit her bottom lip, tugging with a growl that didn't sound playful.

After an interminable time, he slipped his face to one side, panting breaths in her ear evidence he was as affected as she was by the passionate kiss. The scrape of his beard against her cheek made her shiver and raised goosebumps all over her body. His voice was harsh when he said, "Such a tame *fucking* word for what I feel for you, Hope. Because you are all woman, and I do not feel friendly towards you." His tone softened, lowering an octave and turning rich with desire as he ground out, "I want to eat you, fuck you with my fingers, and watch you break for me again. Wanna fuck you hard, so hard the bed leaves marks as it moves across the floor. Want you to ride me, taking yours while I get to watch those pretty titties bounce and shake, play hide and seek in the fall of your hair across your chest, and then see that look on your face of wonder and surprise when you get there on my cock.

"Want to feel your golden hair...all that goddamned, beautiful hair sweep across my legs as you suck me off, taking me deep, letting me fuck that gorgeous mouth. Wanna make love to you slow, your legs wrapped around my ass, pulling me as deep into your body as you want it." He sucked in a breath and laughed humorlessly, his dark chuckle echoing up the hallway. "*Girlfriend.* Tame fucking word for everything I'm feeling, baby."

Listening to him, she had gone still, the evidence of his desire clear in the hardness of his erection pressed against her belly, taut muscles in his arms and shoulders holding him off her. When he spoke about wanting her mouth on him, she sucked in a breath, because the image evoked was so erotic that heat flooded between her legs, arousal making her slick and wet. She wanted that, wanted to give him that. Wanted to be on her knees for him.

As if he knew what was happening, when he finally moved, it was to slide his knee between hers and bring his thigh against her, grinding into her until she gasped his name. "Fuck, yeah, baby," he said with a groan.

"Want you in my bed, no interruptions, no Mercy coming home with a friend, no tummy troubles...no one but me and *you*. And now, here we are, and I have you. All. Night. Long."

He slowly pushed back from the wall, gradually breaking the clinging grasp her fingers had on the sides of his shirt. Wrapping his palm around her wrist, he looked down, watching his fingers move across her skin as he carefully slid his grip to her hand, lacing his fingers between hers. Once he had a firm hold on her, he looked up and she watched as his brown eyes darkened, the tawny ring around his irises becoming small and thin as emotion flooded through him, his gaze tracing her face. "Makes me an asshole," he said quietly and she jerked, but before she could interrupt, he continued, "because I know I'm bringing danger to your door, baby. But right now, knowing you arranged this space of time because you wanted to be with me, all I can think about is your pussy, and burying myself deep inside you, fucking you until you scream." Without explaining...without another word, he turned, leading her up the hallway as if their transit had never been interrupted.

In the bedroom, he didn't give her a chance to do more than glance around before he was pressed against her, mouth back on hers, distracting her as he removed her clothing one piece at a time. Somewhere in there, he lost his own. The only thing she remembered later was him kneeling in front of her, his hands on her legs as, standing, she stepped out of her boots, and then a few minutes later, watching him fold his leather vest across the top of a chair. In between was a cacophony of touch, and passion, and want. Eyes sinking closed when his mouth moved down her neck, heat from his body seared her front, and then her mouth slipped open and she gasped when his hand moved between her legs and his rough fingertips pressed hard against her there.

"Wet, *fuck*. God, baby, you make it hard to—" His fingers pressed deeper, the edge of his hand sliding along the inside of her thigh. "Fucking want you so bad, Hope," he muttered, lips moving against her

169

neck, fingers dragging on an outward slide. "Gonna get you off quick, but then I can't wait any longer, baby. Need you."

She nodded and he spun them, backing her towards the bed. She stumbled when the backs of her knees hit the edge of the mattress, and then was on her back. He put a knee to the bed, stretching out over her, propping himself up on one arm while his other looped around her waist, lifting and tugging her into the middle of the soft surface. Using her heels to push up in the bed, she was surprised when he moved back down, and then called his name like a question when he lifted one of her legs, folding it across the front of his body until he was positioned on his knees between her thighs.

"You on the pill, baby?" His voice was thick with emotion again, face twisted in a beautiful expression of tautly held passion. When she shook her head, he let out an explosive pant of air. "*Fuck.* Hope, you got no reason to trust me on this, so I'm gonna use a rubber this time. But we're going to the clinic tomorrow morning, get some papers to show each other, and then next time, we'll have a different conversation."

Slightly confused, she nodded again, but the question running through her mind must have been written on her face, because he let out another hard breath. "I won't put you at risk, beautiful. Not to make it better for me. And, even after labs are done, if you decide you want me to suit up, then I roll on a rubber. Every time."

Scooting backwards on the bed, he trailed his calloused fingertips down the insides of her thighs, over her calves to her ankles, then back up, the delicate sensation as thrilling as it was exciting. Her chest tightened at his next words, fear threading through her. "That means I eat you now, because latex tastes like fucking garbage. If I fuck you first, I'll have to wait for us to clean up before I can eat you, and I find I'm a selfish, impatient bastard when it comes to you. I want everything, baby. Every-fucking-thing with you."

He framed her core with his hands, eyes to his fingers as they pressed into the crease where her legs joined her body. Thumbs sliding over her flesh, she felt the folds around her entrance tugged open, watched as he blew out a steady stream of air through pursed lips, his gaze fixed on his hands moving over her skin. She looked down his body to see his erection jerking, a bead of liquid slowly making a wet trail down the side of the engorged head.

He locked gazes with her, a pleased smile spreading across his face. "Beautiful," was all he said before shifting, lying on his belly, shoulders between her legs. She felt his breath only a second, and then his mouth was *there*.

"Oh, God," she breathed, her hips twisting and bucking at the immediate and overwhelming sensations assaulting her as his lips and tongue worked in unison in an intimate caress.

***

She was just as sweet as he remembered from the barest taste he had taken at the park. He liked eating pussy, liked it a lot, but he didn't think he ever had better. Couldn't remember better. *Fuck*, he couldn't remember *anything* right now.

Every touch of his mouth on her caused ripples of reaction through her entire body. Teasing her with flicks and licks of his tongue, he used his fingers to separate her lips, tracing up and down, licking along the length of her pussy with the flat of his tongue, alternating that with rapidly flicking the tip against her clit. Her hips were shifting, moving side-to-side in what he knew was an unconscious drive for more.

Gaze focused up towards her face, he saw her mouth open and close with a soundless cry then she called his name again, sounding confused; he watched as she rolled her lips into her mouth and bit down...hard. Her hands wrapped around each other, clenched into a single fist clasped low on her belly, pressing deep into her flesh. Every reaction screamed inexperience to him, but with the way her ass was moving, while it seemed she didn't know what she was seeking, her body knew what it wanted. Running his fingers over her, he trailed his fingertips through the slick wetness as he shifted backwards, lifting his head.

She stilled and raised her head, and he waited until her dazed eyes focused on him before he spoke. "Hope, baby, anybody ever eat you before?" He knew the answer when she squeezed her eyes shut, and found his confirmation when she shook her head, cheeks blushing bright red. "Fuck," he whispered in awe, hands still in motion on her pussy. "Baby, if it feels good, all you gotta do is let me know and I'll do it again. You like my mouth on you?"

Fuck, he had to make this memorable for her, set the bar for all the next times he would have her in his bed. She didn't respond, and he asked the question again, slightly differently, "I like eating pussy. It makes everything better for me. I'll like it a lot more when I know I'm doing it right for you. You enjoying my mouth on you?"

She took a breath and blew it out on a sigh then nodded. In a soft voice, she said, "It's just so intense. It feels like I need to get away, but everything feels so much more *there*, than anything I remember. Good intense, but intense. I'm sorry if I'm doing it wrong." That last was whispered, and he almost missed it as he pulled a gasp from her by spearing a finger deep inside her, rewarding honesty with more pleasure.

He hadn't lied to her, because he very much enjoyed the power the act granted him. A woman handing her body over to him, trusting him to make it pleasurable for her. Fuck yeah, that was a heady rush. It was gratifying in different ways when it was this good, drawing a woman close, feeling her body change and move in reaction to his touch.

He slipped his finger in and out, fucking her slowly, as deep as he could reach, grinding his knuckles into her pussy with each deep thrust, feeling her inner walls tense and clutch at his withdrawal. The muscles in her legs were quivering, stilling only when he seated his finger deep inside, then trembling again when he curved and curled it inside, twisting his hand back and forth to stroke every inch of her pussy.

With Hope, he was finding he loved provoking her raw reactions more than anything. No man in her bed for more than eight goddamned years, no man ever touching her in this intimate way, tasting her, arousing her like this. Her first in so many ways. He would do a lot to keep seeing this look on her face. A fuck of a lot.

Now to address the needless apology. "Nothing you ever do in this bed, or any others we share, could ever be wrong. You feel what you feel, baby. You show that to me. Let me know what's good for you. Let me be good to you, make it sweet between us every time."

He leaned down and nipped at her clit while he ground his finger into her, curling deep inside. Pulling as much of her into his mouth as he could, he flicked her rapidly pulsing nub with his tongue, pushing a second finger deep in her pussy. He slipped his other hand underneath her ass, encouraging her to lift her hips against his mouth. "I want to hear you, Hope," he encouraged her, and received a soft sigh in response. Not quite a moan, but he huffed a laugh, his mouth still working her, thinking, *I can work with that.*

"Yes, baby," he said, pushing deep and curling again, then withdrew his fingers, flicking and licking her opening around his still moving fingertips, caressing her with mouth and hands. Gently using his teeth on her, he heard another sigh. "Fuck, yeah," he murmured, words muffled by her body as he nuzzled into her. Reaching up with his other hand, he found her hands, clenched so tightly together her fingers were ice cold when he unfolded them. Tugging at her, he pulled one hand down to his head, pressing his mouth harder on her when her fingers threaded tentatively through his hair. *Show me, baby*, he thought. *Trust me to do what you want, what you need.*

"Hoss," she whispered and her hand tensed, but he already knew she was close. Her pussy walls were rippling and clenching around his tongue and fingers. Covering her with his mouth, he ate at her using the things she had reacted to, fingers in deep, teeth on her clit, tongue spearing between her lips. "Oh," she said in surprise at his urgent movements, and then breathlessly called, "Hoss."

He kept his gaze fixed on her, watching as the flush of her arousal rose from her chest, up her neck, and across her face. One hand in his hair, the other had flattened on her stomach and he saw her fingertips moving restlessly, tracing circles on her own skin. Her nipples had hardened, sitting on her shifting breasts in pebbled peaks. She gasped, and the muscles in her stomach clenched and jerked in a movement he remembered from the park, so he added a third finger and pushed deep, pressing into her hard. His name rolled off her tongue again, louder this time, that rich tone he loved flowing through the air and caressing his skin. *My baby is so fucking hot*, he thought, watching the play of emotion and reaction across her features.

Eyes closed, she rolled her lips, first the top one tucking between her teeth, and then the bottom, followed by a slow lick of her tongue. He slowed his attack, shifting to long, steady strokes with his fingers and tongue, letting her relax for a moment. Then, right before she bottomed out, he demanded more, using his thumb on her clit while he flicked and licked around his fingers at her entrance.

She called his name again, that gorgeous tone in her voice signifying profound arousal, and then her fingers tightened in his hair, pulling in tentative direction away from her clit. *Fuck, yes,* he thought, shifting so his mouth was lower on her pussy. *Yes, trust me.* He used the fingers of both hands to spread her open wide, pushing her legs out with his shoulders. Pausing a moment, he looked at her, displayed for him, glancing up her body to meet her unfocused gaze.

He froze for a moment, because there was such wonder and surprise in the look on her face it stole his senses. "So fucking beautiful," he said, seeing a smile curl her lips. He would keep telling her those words until she believed them. "Come for me again, baby. Give me this." Her lips parted in a gasp, and he lowered his head, covering her in the heat from his mouth again, thrumming across her clit with the tip of his tongue. He gave her two fingers again, thrusting steadily into her, then he shifted his arm and the new angle had her calling out wordlessly, muscles clenching as she shattered in his hands.

Easing her down with soft and slow caresses, he watched and reveled as her body relaxed, knees falling wide to the side. Head tipped back into the pillow, her mouth worked for a moment then produced a breathy, "Wow." Chuckling, he moved up on the bed beside her, arms wrapping around her and tucking her into his side. Loose and limp, she gave herself over to him, letting him move and arrange her, a heavy, satisfied sigh escaping her when he finally stilled.

"Sleep, baby," he murmured into her hair. "Let's get you a nap." He didn't miss how she froze in place at his words, so he asked her, "What, baby?" There was no response, but she still hadn't moved, and he asked her again, his voice harder, demanding a reply. "What is it, Hope?"

She took two quick breaths, and then asked in a shaky, uncertain voice, "What about you?"

"I'm good," he lied, trying not to grind his teeth in frustration. He wanted to cover her, working his hips as he pounded into her, but she deserved the afterglow from having someone go down on her the first time, and he was trying to let it stretch out for her before demanding more.

"Oh," was all she said, but she still wasn't moving, hadn't relaxed. *Fuck*, he thought.

"Hope, what's wrong?" The edge of his frustration was there in his voice, and he knew she felt it when she tightened further, scooting away the tiniest bit, and he lost the heat of her belly pressed into his side. Scooping her with his arm, he pulled her close again, draping her partly across his chest. "Stop it, baby. No running. Tell me what's bothering you."

175

"You didn't...but now you don't..." Her voice cracked and he squeezed his eyes tight. *Fuck*. Between her and Sammy, he didn't know which one jumped to the worst conclusions fastest.

"Yeah, I do." He grabbed her hand, dragging it under the covers and down his belly, wrapping her palm around his hard length, hissing out her name when her fingers tightened around him. "A fuck of a lot, baby, I do." He jerked his hips up, thrusting through her hand, his fingers threaded with hers, holding hers in place when she would have released him. "I want to fuck you so bad my cock is weeping at the loss." He swept his thumb over the head, flinging back the covers and bringing it to her mouth, hissing *"Fuck"* again as her tongue darted out, capturing the offered sample greedily.

He heard the drawl thick in his voice when he growled out, "You think I don't want you, because I'm trying to give you a little space, knowing that's the first time a man's had his mouth on you, and you telling me it was intense. And that was before you came in my mouth, shattering for me, breaking so powerfully I could nearly see it move through you, waves of passion and pleasure.

"Fuck, Hope, if you're telling me you don't need a minute, then I'll take that space back, baby. Because I want to fuck you so bad that having your soft, little hand on me like this is torture, because as hot as your hand is, I know your pussy is going to be hotter and better. So much better, and I want that for me. Like I told you already, I'm a selfish bastard."

Wedging his fingers underneath her chin, he lifted her face to his, covering her mouth and kissing her so hard and deep that when she moved her hand up his shaft, his balls were throbbing, heavy sac drawing up tight to his body. *Fuck, I'm about to come from a kiss and a two-stroke handjob if I'm not careful.* He rolled them, putting her back to the mattress, rising over her and supporting his weight with one forearm in the bed. "You want me inside you, baby?"

Eyes locked on hers, he saw her lips tremble just before she nodded once, jerkily. "I want to hear it, Hope. Tell me you want me inside you."

Her lips parted on a breath as he waited, and then she whispered, "I want you inside me. Make love to me, Hoss." He kissed her hard, stealing the last whisper of his name from her lips, tongue sweeping deep inside her mouth to tangle with hers. Her palm slid up his arm, fingers curling around his bicep with a squeeze. Stretching out over her, he gave her his weight, wedging his rigid cock between her folds and he pushed, gliding effortlessly through the wetness she gave him. Every thrust brought the head of his cock slipping up past her clit, and he heard the little gasp she gave, felt her hips begin to move against him.

"Condom," he muttered, burying his face in her hair, finding the side of her neck with his teeth, gripping hard as he felt her pulse pounding beneath his lips, and then kissing the sting away. She lifted her hips again and he begin to slide down too far, the head of his cock catching on the edge of her opening and he froze, but she didn't. On the next shift of her hips, his cock slipped inside her a couple of inches and he found himself surrounded by tight, wet heat all around. His ass flexed and he dipped inside farther, and then she lifted and drew him in even deeper. "Hope," he hissed. "Hold the fuck still. I need to get a rubber, baby."

"Hoss," she whimpered, her hands moving up and down his sides to grip his waist, tugging and pulling him urgently. *Fuck*, if this was what she did to Sammy's dad, it was no wonder the man knocked her up, because this kind of raw need, this wanting...demanding, was fucking hard to turn down. Hot. Tight pussy. Willing woman squirming underneath him, her hands scraping and pulling at his control. Bare. *Hot*. Fraying those reins. Tight satin wrapped around his cock. Not caring if he lost her trust or knocked her up. He remembered his thoughts the first time he had seen her, how beautiful he imagined she must have been carrying Sammy. Carrying his baby. Involuntarily, his hips jerked and thrust, his cock plunging in farther. Hot. His.

Fuck.

With a shove and a curse, he pushed up and off her, jackknifing to the edge of the bed, the heat from her body replaced with the chill of the room. With numb fingers he fumbled the wallet from his pants pocket, and cursed again when he saw only one condom. One. All this time waiting and wanting her, and he had one shot. It wasn't any use looking through the house for rubbers, because he never brought women back to his home. He fucked in the clubhouse when he wanted pussy, never here. Hope was the only woman who had been to his house, on his bike, or lying in his bed. All of which meant there were no fucking condoms in the goddamned *fucking* house.

He rolled again, pressing his full length against her, and he took her mouth, her heat wrapping around him once more. Hard, panting breaths, he devoured her and she brought it back to him, her lips plucking at his. Shoving his face into the crook of her neck, he moved, lifting his body so he could bring his hand up to cup her breast. He already knew what she liked there and worked her, plumping the soft mound as he nibbled and licked up the column of her neck. Thumb to forefinger, he pulled and tugged at her nipple, elongating the erect tip, rolling and pinching it gently.

Lifting up again, he kissed her slow and soft, feeling her beginning to twist underneath him, desire moving her and he broke the kiss, shifting to his knees between her legs. Sitting back on his heels, he examined her face and body, loving the reactions she gave him. Breath coming quicker as, eyes locked on his hands, she watched him open the condom, her lips parted in a gasp as he rolled it down his length then slowly stroked himself root to tip, gripping tighter, stroking himself a second time.

With one hand, he reached out and cupped her pussy, curving his fingers over the top of her mound, dragging his thick thumb up, pressing between the folds until he found her entrance. *Fucking wet.* Glancing at her face, he saw the pink of her tongue dart back into her mouth, knowing she had just swiped across her bottom lip, also knowing it was because he was touching her again and she liked it. She didn't have to say anything. He had her tell down; that lip roll and swipe communicated clearly that she was ready.

Stretching out over her, he pressed their lower bodies together, bracketing her upper torso with his forearms, holding his weight off her. Her legs had drawn together, an instinctive protective move, which spoke to pain in bed in her past. Those few weeks she was with Suiter, the man probably didn't take care of her, and tight as she was, anything less than what he had done for her tonight could leave her with painful memories, leave her pussy raw for at least a few days. Right now, however, he was confident he had worked her over enough. He had gotten her there twice already, and *fuck him*, but she was drenched for him. That sureness was in his voice when he told her softly, "Open for me, baby. Spread your legs. Let me in there."

Dipping his head, he traced along her nose with his own, feeling her tentative movements. Giving her a smile and a softly spoken, "Good girl," he kissed her then tipped his hips and started the slow push and glide that would get him deeper every stroke, but without hurting her. Push and glide then pull back, rolling his hips to push and glide again, a little farther each time. "Fuck me back, baby," he murmured against her lips. "Nothing crazy, but I want to feel you move for me." So nervous, she would never try to take hers yet, but he knew she would give it to him if he asked, as long as he made it about him.

Her tentative shifts had him drawing a hard breath, because not only did she shift side-to-side in the bed instead of up against him like he expected, but her core tightened down in a way that made him wonder how long he could hold out if she kept doing that. "Absolute perfection, baby. Just like that. Perfect for me, exactly like that," he urged, rolling his hips again, pushing in farther, letting her make those little circles that dragged him against the walls of her pussy. "Fucking tight, baby. So fucking tight and hot around me. Fucking flawless, you fucking me back like that. Love it. Beautiful."

179

With a surge, he moved forward, penetrating deeper, concentrating on making it good, angling his hips to drive up into her. "Nearly there, baby," he muttered, his lips moving across her jaw to her ear then down her neck, withdrawing to push forward again, deeper. Hot. Tight. His.

"Go ahead," she breathed, tone encouraging, her mouth near his ear, and he chuckled, because he knew she had misunderstood in a way that didn't speak favorably of her previous partner.

"No baby, I got my shit on lockdown. I ain't coming until after you give me at least one more." He rolled his hips, pushing in deeper. "I meant you've nearly got all of me." Rolling his hips, her inner walls stretched tight around him, the snug heat surrounding his cock blunted somewhat by the latex. Grinning silently, distracted at the thought of thanking the condom for added control, he hissed in surprise when she planted her heels in the bed and pushed up on his downstroke, and suddenly his self-control was broken, because he was root deep inside her and it was fucking amazing.

"Aww, fuck. *Fuck*," he ground out, holding deep, feeling her walls fluttering and clenching around his cock. She made a tiny sound of discomfort, but he couldn't pull back, wasn't moving...couldn't move, couldn't suck in air...couldn't even breathe in her scent without losing his fucking mind. Then she moved her hips side-to-side again, and he was no longer in command, his arms shifting unconsciously to pull her close as he thrust hard, holding deep for a split second then plunging quickly six...seven times, sliding deep again for a moment.

"Fuck," he growled, then, "*Fuck*," again as she arched and quivered underneath him, his name rolling off her lips in that goddamned rich tone that touched him in ways he couldn't even begin to understand. "Fuck, baby."

Lifting his torso off her, he propped himself up and stared down at her as he ground down into her pussy. Her face flushed, eyes half-closing because she had come again and was on the way back down.

Come on his cock, no hands on her pussy this time, just him inside her. Moving and shifting, hard and fast, he pounded into her, lunging down for a deep kiss then retreating upward so he could watch her.

"Legs up, baby," he demanded on a hard breath, and her knees came up to rest on his sides, her calves wrapping around his hips. Watching as his cock disappeared into her, he lifted his gaze to her titties. Dipping his head, he captured a nipple between his lips, tugging until she gasped. Drawing it into his mouth, he suckled hard, groaning when her hands came to his head, fingers threading through his hair, tightening when he gave her the edge of his teeth in a hard nip before lifting his upper body off her.

In his mind, he was sketching frantic images, attempting to capture the moments as firmly as he held her in his mouth. The strands of hair caught in the sweat on her cheek, the bow of her lips when she whispered his name, how her throat worked as she swallowed her cries of passion, the movement and tension in the muscles of her forearm when her fingers curled in his hair. Everything about her was deserving of tribute, and even fucking her as wild as he was right now, he tried to impress each moment on his mind so he could bring it back to life later.

Then she called his name as she lifted her hips again, pussy tightening, and he was gone, collapsing on her, cradling her to him while he pushed in deep and held, coming hard. His body jerked with the strength of his climax, locked muscles soothed by the steady pass of her palms across his skin. "Hope," he groaned, "so fucking good for me, baby. Beautiful." Shuddering again, he slowly moved in and out several times before burying himself root-deep again. "I could love on you for days, baby."

Fuck, he was wrung out, shaking and covered in sweat. "Made me lose my shit, baby. So good, sweetheart." He kissed her shoulder, feeling her do the same, loving the soft press of her lips on his skin. "Gotta take care of the condom, baby," he said, moving to slide out, chuckling when her ass lifted up, her pussy chasing his cock. He gave her that, bringing his hips back down and gliding deep one last time. "Baby," he scolded, and then she giggled, and that sound was as rich and full and beautiful as anything he had ever heard. *Fuck*, he thought, his lips parting in a smile. *Beautiful. Mine.*

12. Running

Hope gaped at her phone, reading the scholarship requirements again, staring at them in disbelief. Each criteria, every requirement, few as there were, Sammy fit into as if this program was custom-made for him. Enthusiastic about hockey—uh...*yeah*. Willingness to work hard—yes again. Financial difficulties—duh...single mom. Everything boiled down to those three things, and she gave a little fist-pump.

"What are we celebrating, baby?" Hands slipped around her waist, pulling her back against the hard planes of Hoss' chest. He had left for an errand this morning after making soft, slow love to her, waking her with a deep kiss while his hand moved between her legs. She had been a little tender but had wanted him inside her again, wanted the connection they shared last night, and he made it good for her. He had moved over her, gentle and sweet, strong arms cradling her to his body.

She hadn't heard him return, but liked that he sought her out as soon as he got home, and had developed an appreciation for his hands on her like this. Every time he was near her, he put his hands on her, stroking her skin, trailing his fingertips along her arm, threading his fingers through hers. She liked it. A lot.

"Good news about a hockey program for Sammy," she said, leaning back. She turned her head when he nudged demandingly with his chin, raising her lips to his for a soft touch.

"Yeah? Good deal. Kiddo seems to like the game a little." He chuckled and glanced at her phone. "Spencer's place? That's what you're looking at?"

"The Patterson-Spencer Hockey Foundation? They have a scholarship program that looks like a good fit for us." She grinned up at him, surprised when his face darkened, lips firming into a flat line.

"Scholarship program? What the fuck does that mean?" He asked the question in a brusque tone and she flinched, knew he registered the movement when his arms tightened around her and his mouth found her temple with a soft kiss.

"It means they help out parents like me," she said softly, tipping her head down. For herself, she wouldn't take anything. Even the food Mac pressed on her was for Sammy, nameless bump that he was at the time. She made her own way, always had. But for Sammy? She would beg, borrow, or steal to make his life better, and if asking this foundation for help would get him onto the ice again, then she would, by God, make it happen. Gritting her teeth, she lifted her chin.

"It means Sammy can get back into hockey without him worrying about what it might do to our finances, how it would change things for the two of us." That should lay it out for him, because if there was a chance of them working out as a couple, he had to know it would always be Sammy first. "Because he worries about things like that. I wish he didn't, wish he never had to, but he does. This will make it easier for him to enjoy skating."

"Baby," he said softly, pressing another kiss against the side of her head. "I can make this happen for you."

Okay, maybe she wouldn't do *anything* to make Sammy's life better, because she knew there was no way she would take Hoss' money for anything. Out of nowhere, she remembered his words from the other day about getting her and Mercy a bigger apartment. She hadn't demurred at the time, but there was no way they could afford that, and she thought he probably knew it. She also had the thought now he probably intended to make up the difference, which wouldn't be happening, either.

Shaking her head, she said in a firm voice, "No." She didn't owe him any explanation, no further conversation on this topic, and she hoped he would understand.

"Hope." He gave her a little shake, his arms tightening around her. "Don't do that shit. I've seen you shut down before. Don't do it, baby."

"What did you want to do for lunch?" Maybe changing the topic would make it clear the matter was closed, because she didn't want to mar their time today with an argument.

"Jase Spencer is a member of the Rebels, baby. Our kids go free, as long as they are interested and don't cause shit with the rest of the kids. You're mine, Hope, which means Sammy's mine, too. No need to take up one of the scholarships, when it could go to a kid that needs it. That's how Jase set it up, how he wants it."

A big, warm palm stroked up her arm. "You submit a scholarship application, and the minute he sees your name, he'll call you and tell you the same fucking thing, baby. He's probably going to be pissed at me as it is, because I didn't front him the info first. He is a man that likes large gestures, so get ready for it. He gives, you gotta take it." He snorted a laugh. "And the man gives big. He gave our president a fucking minivan when his twins were born. Your boy will come first with him, ahead of you, so get ready for that, too." His voice had gone tender as he talked, and she relaxed muscles she didn't even know she had tensed.

"Jase Spencer? DeeDee's Jase? He's the Spencer part of the Patterson-Spencer Hockey Foundation?" Now her voice was squeaky and she hated that, since it would tell Hoss exactly how close to tears she was, furious at herself for a misunderstanding that could have bloomed into an argument.

"Yeah. Sammy's a fan of his, too. Got that straight from the source. I'm amazed he don't already know Jase is the super cool hockey star he was fanning over." She could hear the smile in his voice, and relaxed a little more. "Baby, I already planned on calling him. No worries, okay? This is a done deal."

"And it won't cost you anything?" As soon as the words were out of her mouth, she knew they were a mistake, because he tightened in response.

"Hope." He growled her name, sucking in air in what seemed an attempt to calm himself. "Even if it did, if it were something I wanted to do, there'd be no way for you to tell me no, baby." His mouth was near her ear, so he didn't have to raise his voice to get across the fact that he was pissed.

"But no, Sammy going to the foundation ain't gonna cost me a dime." One hand left her hip, digging in his front pocket and pulling out his phone. "I'm thinking you need proof, which pisses me right the fuck off, but here you go." He thumbed the welcome screen open and then pressed a button, putting the call on speaker.

She heard Jase Spencer answer, his tone welcoming and friendly. "Hossman, what can I do you for?"

"You got room for Hope's boy on your ice?" Hoss spoke brusquely and, because of that, she heard the difference when Jase responded, his voice now tight and careful.

"You know it, brother. He skate?"

"Yeah, loves it." Hoss' tone hadn't changed, and Hope squeezed her eyes tightly shut, pressing her lips together to still the trembling that had returned.

"He any good? I'm always looking for someone to help me push Tyler or Jonny, eh?" The barest hint of humor colored Jase's voice when he asked, "Why you keeping secrets, Hoss?"

"I don't know, Captain. Let me see why I'm keeping secrets. Hope, what do you say? Is your boy any good on the ice?" The tone was cutting now, strongly reminiscent of how he had spoken to the woman who came to his garage door last night. The woman he didn't like. Lips still trembling, she nodded, and he gave her a squeeze. "He can't hear your head rattle, Hope. Is Sammy any good on the ice?"

"Yes." She had to work hard to speak. "His co-coaches in Birmingham said he was quick and fe-fearless. He jus...just loves the game." By the time she finished, she was barely capable of being heard; her throat had closed down, choking her words.

"Hope, get Hoss to text me your number. I'll call you later and we can go over available groups and times. If he loves to skate, I want to get him in with Jonny and Kane, especially since that terrible trio is already fast friends. We'll work up to the older boys if we need to. This is exciting, eh?" Jase's voice was soft and encouraging, but they still hadn't covered the cost, and she wouldn't let this chance go by, in case Hoss was wrong.

"The website said there were...were scholarships available?" He didn't answer for a few seconds, and she was unable to still the shudders racking her frame. Fear swept over her, and then a shattering sense of loss. She thought to herself that the woman on the phone was wrong, Hoss was wrong, the website was wrong, but at least she knew now before she said anything to Sammy.

"No, no, no. Hope, honey, you're family, so you get the family rate, eh? And, you are in luck, because, at the moment, that rate is nada.

Zippo, zilch. I don't take money from family. Period. And, if he needs gear, I have a couple of rooms full of donated stuff. What position does he like to play?" His voice had gone even softer, and she shuddered again, biting back a sob, because, for Sammy, this would mean everything.

"He plays defense, but an offensive defense, as opposed to sta...staying at home." She gulped a breath that hitched in the middle, and Hoss' arms tightened around her as she fought to continue. "His la...last coach said he's still settling in and thought he could be a forward, but Sam seems to like playing the D-line." Biting the inside of her cheek hard, she struggled to bring her breathing under control, feeling Hoss' palm slide up and down her arm, calming her.

"Jesus Murphy, he sounds fucking perfect." The pleasure in Jase's voice was too real to be forced, and she felt her lips curve in a watery smile. "Plus, you talk hockey, woman. That's hot. Hoss, you need to bring her to dinner soon, yeah?"

"Fuck you, Captain," Hoss said, and now she heard a smile in his voice, too. "I'll send you her fucking info, but you don't talk to my woman without me there. I'll show you the hot side of my fist, asshole."

"Yeah, yeah. So you say." Jase laughed, then said, "DeeDee's wild gesturing indicates tonight would be good for dinner. You can leave Sammy here until then. I have some interrogating to do anyway, because that kid is closemouthed about the game if he loves it like you say. Jonny's gonna have some 'splainin' to do, too, keepin' secrets. Damn kids, what good are they to me if they won't do my recruitin', eh?"

"See you tonight, brother." Hoss didn't let Jase respond, terminating the call and placing his phone on the countertop. "Hope, you believe me now?" She nodded, and he leaned his head beside hers. They stood like that for a long time, him pressed against every inch of her he could wrap himself around, her taking comfort offered by the possessive hold.

Stirring finally, he said softly, "We're going to talk about expectations, baby. Because we are both going to want things out of this, and I don't want stupid shit to tie us up, or close things off. You get stupid shit in your head, and then don't talk to me? That's when things could go sideways between us. You have to talk to me, baby. No stupid shit between us, okay?" He kissed behind her ear and she sucked in a fast breath, the sensation unexpected and thrilling.

"Right now, though." He worked his mouth down her neck, gripping her shoulder with his teeth and pressing against her butt with his hips. She felt his erection, hard and hot, outlined in his jeans. "I want something else."

***

Hoss smiled, leaning back into the couch cushions, his arm around Hope's shoulders. Dinnertime at Jase and DeeDee's house was wild, loud, chaotic, and entertaining. Bingo was back in the hospital, but his kids were in residence, which meant tonight there were eleven small bodies running around, aged fifteen and down. Nine, a mix of boys and girls, were Bingo's tribe, one boy belonged to Jase and DeeDee, and one was his and Hope's boy. His breath stuck in his chest for a moment, because he liked how that sounded in his head, 'his and Hope's boy.'

When they arrived for dinner, Sammy had raced up and hugged his mother then stepped back. Looking up, he stood in front of Hoss, shifting from foot to foot, staring into his face. His features twisted into something that looked like sadness as he asked, "Did you and Mom have a good day?"

Hoss had frowned, crouching down so he was on Sammy's level when he answered, "Yeah, the best. How about you?" Tentatively, he reached out, cupping his hand around Sammy's shoulder, asking, "Did you have fun with Jonny and Kane?" No way could Hoss miss how the boy leaned into the hold, his shoulders lowering a couple inches as he relaxed.

"Yeah, we had a great time. Coach Spence took us to the rink." He cut his gaze up to his mother, and Hoss twisted so he could see her face, too. "He said he has a Sammy-sized opening on his league team, Mom." That was all he said, and Hoss watched a flash of pain cross Hope's face at his hesitation.

"I talked to him on the phone today, bud. He has this deal for friends and family"—she switched to a poor imitation of a New Jersey accent— "and he made me an offer I couldn't refuse." She grinned, and he caught Sammy's matching smile from the corner of his eye. "I'll sort things out with him tonight, see what kind of schedule we're looking at, and what I can commit to for equipment, okay?"

Hoss felt more of the tension leave the kid's muscles as he told his mother, "Yeah." That single, soft word conveyed an understanding that if she could work it out, she would, and if she couldn't, then the boy wouldn't blame her, because he trusted she would always do her best. These two had a bond that seemed unshakable, having no one else to depend on for so long. In Sammy's case, his whole life.

He was hit yet again by how alone in the world they had been, no one to have their back, no one to give a hand when they hit bottom. Only each other, ever. It was going to be hard for Hope to accept that she had people to lean on now, but he planned on reminding her often enough for it to become second nature. "I'm going to go play outside, 'kay?"

Hope nodded and Hoss tightened his fingers, drawing the boy's attention back to him for a moment, telling him softly, "You need us, you come find us, Sammy." Before Sammy could respond, one of the other kids ran up, slapping him lightly on the arm and yelling, "You're it, Samboni." Sammy whirled, twisted out of Hoss' grip, and raced after the boy, calling back over his shoulder, "Will do, Hossman."

Standing, he took in the perplexed look on Hope's face and laughed. "Every good hockey player gets a nickname. I can think of worse for a boy named Samuel than being called after the Zamboni." Pleased, she giggled, the sound rich and low, just as she had last night, and his cock swelled, beginning to thicken and stand out from his belly. *Fuck*. He had tried all morning to pull one of those from her with no luck, and now here it was, in the middle of his brother's foyer, and he was getting hard because his woman laughed. *Mine*.

Now they were on the couch, listening to Jase talk about the foundation, which outside of the kids, Slate's twins, and his soon-to-be-wife, was maybe his favorite topic. He explained the origin, what was behind the idea, about how he had a coach when he was working towards the pros who had done so much more than the already hard job of coaching. The meaning of the foundation shone from him like a spotlight, the love of giving that had been drilled into him alongside his hockey skills.

Coach Patterson had opened his home to the boys on his juniors team, having them over for meals and movies, checking up on them frequently to make sure their host families were doing right. With every action, he modeled what a good coach did, what a man should be. He mentored them on how to be an honorable man first, a principled sportsman second, and a competitive athlete last.

When his former coach passed away, creating the foundation gave Jase a way to pay homage to the man in a tangible way, and also left him able to keep a foot in his beloved sport of hockey when he retired.

Jase and Hope talked equipment and Hoss was impressed, because as Sammy had told him, she knew her shit pretty well. It sounded like what Jase was offering would be everything needed for the practices and games, and as the discussion wound down, the tension was gradually leaving her body. He hadn't been aware she was holding her worry so close, the fear things wouldn't be as advertised, but when it was all gone, the difference was palpable. She leaned into him, tucking herself into his side and relaxing, resting her arm on his leg, fingers drawing those lazy circles on the knee of his jeans.

Softly kissing the side of her head, he asked her, "You work in the morning, baby?" She nodded distractedly, eyes on DeeDee, who was explaining something about the team mom's responsibilities she was currently taking care of. He shook her then said, "Hope, baby. If you work early, we need to go soon." She looked up at him, smiling, and he captured her mouth with his, kissing her hard and deep, stroking into her mouth possessively, pulling back with a scarcely stifled groan. *Mine.* Turning his head, he called, "Sammy, get your things together, son. We need to get your momma home."

***

Sammy stood in the doorway, watching Hoss kiss his mother. He had talked to Jonny late into the night, far past when Miss DeeDee had told them to be asleep, and they had concluded if Hoss wouldn't go away, then the next thing to try was get close to him. This wouldn't be hard to do, because Hoss seemed to want to be friends. And, Mom liked him. A lot. Plus, Hoss had never been mean to Mom, except that first night, and he didn't want that to count, because from the other man's yelling voice, Sammy thought maybe Hoss had been worried more than anything.

He heard Hoss call his name, caught his gaze across the room and responded with a nod, but that was all he could do, because of what Hoss said. *He called me son*, he thought and his throat got tight like he was going to sick up. The night before last, he hadn't really been sick, so maybe this was his payback for lying to Luce. *My own Daddy didn't want me, but Hoss called me son.*

13. Let me bring you home

"This is perfect," Mercy said with a broad, happy smile, while Hope sat and stared at her in disbelief. "Seriously. Deke is on his way over right now. He wants me to move in with him today, which means we can shift your stuff into my room and give Sammy his own bedroom. His own space."

Hope nodded slowly, mentally tearing up the lists she had made for school supplies and clothes for Sammy. She knew how much this apartment cost, and she could swing it...barely. She also knew if she took on the rent and all the utilities by herself, then once again there would be no room for error.

A panic began to build in her chest and she desperately wanted to talk to Hoss, but he had been gone for nearly two weeks with no word. After the day and night they spent together at his house, she believed they were beginning something...a relationship. But, then he was gone. After dinner at DeeDee and Jase's, he dropped Sam and her at the apartment, barely coming in to say goodbye before walking out. Then, nothing. No calls, no texts. No responses to her attempts at communication. Nothing. Two days in, she had cried herself to sleep, broken at the loss of that promise she thought they had been building together.

All she had gotten from Mercy were sympathetic glances, not even a reassurance her pain would pass, so she hid her tears as best she could. Even now, roughly two weeks out from him walking away, her throat grew tight when she thought about it, because she didn't know what she—

Shutting down those thoughts, she tried to focus on what Mercy was sharing. "School is all lined up for Sammy, and I can still watch him any time at all. Deke's place is actually closer to the diner, and you can drop him off with me before going to work." Mercy looked down at her hands, clasped on her knees, happy promises written in every line of her body. "Everything will work out great."

"You know, with everything going on," Hope said slowly, "I could take this opportunity to reevaluate things. Maybe move, get away from...stuff. I'll probably find a place Sam and I can move to, as long as it won't mess with your lease agreement with the club on this apartment."

Mercy tilted her head and looked at her, sudden uncertainty clouding the joy present on her features. Hope remembered what Hoss had said about Mercy needing her, and rushed to reassure her. "We'd stay in town, Mercy. I can't lose you, not after finally finding you. But that's not today, doll face. Today is happiness and rainbows, because I'm so happy for you. Glad Deke finally figured out what he's been chasing after for so long is you."

With a quick return of her smile, Mercy tucked her chin down and nodded, whispering, "Me, too."

The two sisters were silent for a minute, and then Hope drew a deep breath and clapped her hands. "Packing," she announced with a brisk nod. "We have to pack. He's already on his way and you'll need to take some clothes with you tonight, we can get boxes from the grocery store for the rest of your things." The furniture in the apartment all belonged to the club, which meant it would need to be returned but she wouldn't have to worry about selling or storing it at least. "We'll talk every day, and see each other all the time, right?" Mercy nodded, offering her a happy smile as they rose from the couch.

Twenty short minutes later, Hope pressed her back to the inside of the door, feeling the latch thud implacably into place as it closed. Stunned, she stared blindly into the suddenly empty-feeling apartment. Just like that...just that fast, Mercy was gone. From roommates to gone in less than half an hour. They only had a few weeks of knowing each other, but it felt as if there was an enormous hole in her life already.

Mercy had been so thrilled about how things were working out with Deke that Hope had ruthlessly stuffed her own sadness down. She thought she did a good job of concealing it underneath the real feelings of pleasure gained from knowing her sister was happy and smiling, no longer hiding behind a closed and locked door. She was glad Mercy had found her brand of bliss. Pleased Deke had finally recognized the beauty he held in his hands and decided to make a move to keep it there.

Now, Hope simply had to get a plan together. First up, she had to find an apartment she could afford and do it fast. This one belonged to the club and she had no claim there, not anymore. Not with Hoss pulling away and Mercy moving out. The rent here was also about three hundred dollars more than she could honestly afford. It was nearly the end of the month, which meant she had to start looking immediately, fingers crossed she could find something in the same school district quickly. Otherwise, she and Sammy would be back in the car, and the climate here in northern Indiana was less conducive to that than in Birmingham. She realized that once again, she was back on her own, and the feeling was far more frightening now than it had ever seemed before.

She liked it here, loved the town, and it felt like she was developing ties here, building firm friendships with not only Mercy, but also

DeeDee and Eddie. Thoughts of leaving flitted through her mind and caused her chest to hurt fiercely, the pain nearly doubling her over. The idea of losing these fledgling relationships—something she hadn't known she was missing until she had it, even if Hoss' silence and absence proved he wasn't interested—burned. Mentally rifling through the fake pop can where she kept her cash, she ran the numbers in her head, trying to find a way to stay, at least in town, even if not in the apartment that had begun to feel like home. Her safe haven, torn away.

"Mom?" Sammy called to her from across the room and she winced at the uncertainty in his voice. Deke still frightened her, and she had been so caught up in making sure Mercy would be ready before he showed up in his truck that she hadn't thought about giving Sammy a chance to say goodbye. *Shi—crap. It's not goodbye*, she reminded herself. *I'll find a time when Deke's not home and we can go over and visit Mercy.*

"Good news, boychick," she called gaily, lying through her teeth. "We're on the hunt for new digs, something we can put our own stamp on, make totally our own."

"Mommy? Where did Aunt Mercy go?" Even across the space between them, she could see his bottom lip quivering. "I saw you packing her stuff. Did she leave us?"

"You know how she's been seeing a lot of Mr. Deke, right?" She waited for his head nod. "Well, she's headed over to his place for now. Not so much leaving us, as moving towards her new boyfriend," Hope explained, deflecting his question somewhat.

"She's gone? Just like that? And now we can't stay here? What did we do? Did you talk to Hoss?" Her head came up and, eyes narrowed, she looked at him. Typically, she knew he would offer Cal up as a solution, but now it was Hoss? Hoss, who hadn't called or tried to contact her for weeks? Hoss who had offered her what seemed a lot like love, only to yank it back, brutally forcing her to realize she might never know what real love felt like?

She forced herself to pause before responding, shoving down her pain at Hoss' rejection before answering Sammy. "Bud, we didn't do anything wrong. And you know how I am about things. We always make our own way," she reminded him. "I'll sort things out. Everything's going to be okay. I'm working good, steady jobs. We have this place for at least another couple of days until your Aunt Mercy comes back for the rest of her stuff. And I promise you, I'll have something lined up by then."

"But did you talk to Hoss?" His voice shook with strain when he asked the question this time, and she could see his hands anxiously twisting into the jeans covering his legs. "Did you talk to Hossman?"

Hoss hadn't returned any of her calls or texts, so even if she wanted to, she couldn't talk to him. By avoiding her, he had made it painfully clear she had nothing that interested him, her inexperience and baggage had quickly worn thin any attraction she held for him.

This wouldn't have been a conversation to have over the phone, anyway, even if they were talking. And with how completely he had walked away, she didn't believe that particular conversation would be happening, ever. She didn't know why he had shut the door on them, but when lying alone in bed at night, her brain could think of a dozen different reasons, every one of them pointing straight back to her.

"No, bud. Decisions like this are mine, all mine. You are my responsibility, and I'll sort it out." Her heart clenched when she saw his lips trembling again, and suddenly her head was pounding, the pain swelling to distracting levels within seconds. She reached up and rubbed her thumb and finger across her forehead. Eyes closed tightly against the light, she was glad he had given up the argument, as she heard his footsteps coming towards her and then retreating towards their bedroom. His bedroom for the next couple of nights. All she could think of was finding a horizontal surface, so she felt her way to Mercy's bedroom and lay down on top of the comforter. *God bless, this hurts*, she thought, distractedly hearing Sammy talking.

***

"Mom?" Sammy's voice held the unmistakable watery signature of tears. She was exhausted, but struggled to open her eyes. Within two days of Mercy moving in with Deke, she had found them new living arrangements. Since then, she had packed and moved their boxes, gone shopping for a couple school outfits for Sammy, and kept up with a work schedule that now included four jobs.

This was their fourth night in the new apartment, and she had gone to sleep curled up on the couch, a gift from one of her new neighbors. Sam was speaking from behind her, which meant he was still on his thin mattress on the floor between the back of the sofa and the wall. A narrow, dark space, but it meant she wouldn't trip over his bedding, or worry about stepping on him when she had to go to the bathroom. It also put her firmly between him and the door, the direction from which any threats would come. "Mommy?"

Her voice cracked when she asked, "Yeah, bud?" Licking her dry lips, she squinted into the dark room, trying to discern what would have woken him. Pulling her phone from underneath her head, she saw it was three a.m., still an hour and a half before she had to be up to get ready for her shift at the diner.

"Someone's in the hallway." He was whispering, and alongside those tears was a broad current of fear, something she hadn't heard in his voice for weeks. Something she could have gone an extremely long time before hearing in his voice again. "They knocked."

She sighed and stretched, rolling halfway onto her stomach on the cushions. "It's no one we know, Sammy. They got the number wrong, just a mistake. Back to sleep, my man." She spoke with confidence, because she had not yet updated her employment records with anyone.

Not at the diner, with Dickie at the trucking company, Dale at Murphy's Law, nor Jase at the Foundation, where she was helping organize his office. That last one wasn't a paying job, unless you counted Sammy being able to skate as payment. It made her feel a lot better about accepting the terms Jase had laid down, though, and she thought he understood what it meant for her to give back even a little. *Especially since I'm no longer—*

Cutting off the thought brutally, she refocused on the quiet in the room, and the hallway beyond the locked door. All of that meant, thus far, no one she knew had been told their new address, which further meant no one even knew they had moved. Not relaxing, head cocked towards the door, she softly reassured Sammy again, "Back to sleep. Morning comes early, bud."

Within a few minutes, the slow, quiet breathing from behind her meant Sam had chased his dreams back down, leaving her lying awake, eyes directed towards the door, straining to see in the dark. She heard a soft rattle from the doorknob and frowned. That sounded almost like someone trying to get inside.

When the noise didn't return after several minutes, she relaxed back into the cushions, tugging the blanket up over her jeans, feeling it drag against the fabric covering her legs. She was back to sleeping fully clothed so she could feel ready for anything. Again tonight, she had forced Sammy into pajamas. He had complied, but eyed her jeans and sweatshirt with a scowl, communicating his dislike of the resumption of old habits without saying a word.

She reached up and rubbed her fingertips across her forehead, wishing the constant headache would ease, if only for a moment, but it was unrelenting, even after nearly a week. Hot tears welled in her eyes and she blinked them back, swallowing a sob.

How did we get to this point again so quickly? Her gaze darted around the darkened single-room apartment, memory filling in the details. Water stained ceiling, nicotine-tinted walls, scuffed and chipped tiling on the floor. Everything scrubbed as clean as she could make it, but still tawdry and soiled.

Four walls and a roof, she reminded herself. *Not a shelter. Not the car. Better than the alternatives*. A place she could afford, and still manage to get Sam the things he needed. Her neighbors seemed decent, and a couple of families had boys about Sam's age.

Bikers occupied two apartments on the first floor, and even though it was a different club, she felt a strange sense of ease when she would see those men in black leather vests and their friends in the parking lot. Their eyes always on her and Sammy, intently tracking the two of them as they moved from the car to the building, but not in a threatening way. More curious than anything. Maybe not entirely safe, but not dangerous, either. Friendly as they carried in the sofa, giving her the now-familiar chin lifts in response to her thanks.

It's not the worst place we've lived, she reminded herself, and the thought made tears sting her eyes again. Sammy deserved so much more. In the few weeks they had been with Mercy, he finally had a stable place to call home, and now, no more. *No safe havens*. The thought skittered through her mind as she forced back another sob.

***

Hoss turned a tight circle in the apartment, mouth open in disbelief, tongue pressed firmly into one cheek. Gone. Hope was fucking gone. All the things she had brought up from Birmingham in her car, everything of hers and Sammy's, gone. He blew out an angry huff, eyes flicking across the apartment again. Gone.

Walking in the door the night they got home after dinner with Jase and DeeDee, he had gotten an urgent call telling him he needed to go to the clubhouse in Memphis. Club business. So he revised his plans, kissed her goodbye, turned around, and left. The run was supposed to be a single day, and he thought he would be back before she even knew he had left. That day turned into two, which turned into four, which turned into...too many fucking weeks.

A week ago, Deke texted, told him Mercy was moving in with him, which left Hoss pleased. Not only for his brother, who was finally getting his head out of his fucking ass, but also for him, because it meant there was no reason not to move Hope and Sammy in with him.

For the last few days, he had spent every minute of downtime making plans. He talked to Jase about her work, and got Bear to talk to Eddie about school for Sammy. Asked DeeDee to buy stuff and set up one of the spare rooms on the main floor in his house for Sammy. Through interaction with others, he kept track of her to make sure things were good, asking his questions alongside club business to make it easy, because the Memphis club business was fucked and hard, demanding all of his attention.

He turned in a futile circle, verifying nothing had changed in the past few seconds, taking in the nearly empty state of the rooms, then snorted and said aloud, "Maybe you shoulda shared those plans with your woman, you stupid fucktard. She got stupid shit in her head with you standing right beside her. What the fuck did you think would happen in three weeks with you two goddamned, fucking states away?"

Pulling out his phone, he checked the time. Too late in the morning to find her at the diner, because she would already be off shift there. He found her number and called it, noting the last missed call from her had been more than two weeks ago. He vaguely remembered a text and an unheard voicemail now buried under the ones from club members. *Fuck.*

Putting the phone to his ear, he growled when he got the tones saying her pre-paid piece of shit technology hadn't been paid and couldn't take a message. *Fuck.* Dialing another number, he put the phone to his ear, waiting. "Jase," he greeted, and then hurried on, speaking over the return hello, "Hope said she was working at a couple different places for the club. Do you have a schedule for her?"

"Uh, nope. I trust our employees to keep track of their own work schedules." He heard the humor in Jase's voice when he asked, "You misplace your woman, Hoss? Damn, brother. Haven't you learned you should do a better job keeping track of important things like that? Lost your woman, shit. Sucks for you."

"Captain." The tension in his voice quieted his friend's laughter with the single word, and then he asked, "She talk to you about moving?"

There was noise on the other end of the phone then Jase's voice, tight with sudden concern, questioned, "Moving? No, not a word. What do you mean?"

"I'm back in town, standing in the apartment, and her shit is all gone. Furniture is here, but nothing of hers. Some of Mercy's things are even still here, but nothing belonging to Hope or Sammy. Nothing except the sheets from his bed, clean and folded in a pile atop the bare mattress. Her fucking phone's disconnected."

He walked to the kitchen. "I found bags of canned and boxed groceries on the counter in the kitchen. Did you have a prospect make a food run like I asked?" That was one of the things he had done alongside club business, making sure she knew he would be taking care of her, even if he weren't physically here. There was an affirmative noise on the phone, so he said, "Cut the fucking prospect, then, because it looks like all he did was dump the stuff and leave. Didn't twig to the fact no one fucking lived here."

"Fuck," Jase said softly, and he nodded.

"Fuck, indeed. If you don't have a schedule for her...fuck, Jase. I ain't waiting on tomorrow morning to see if she'll show at the diner." Hoss turned a tight circle again, feeling caged. "Let me know if you hear anything. I gotta find her, man. With everything that went down recently...I can't...she can't be..." He swallowed, unable to continue the path that thought was taking him, and he heard an assenting noise from the phone. Disconnecting the call, he dialed another number and again held the phone to his ear.

"Hoss," he said tightly, identifying himself for the man on the other end of the line.

"My friend," Fury said, warm pleasure threading through his voice.

"Fucking kills me to ask this, but did you know Hope moved?" He clenched his jaw at the shocked suck of air he heard, knowing the answer even before the man spoke.

"No. What the fuck? She moved? When?" The curt questions, barked commandingly, made his hands curl into fists. He pushed his anger down, knowing where Fury was coming from was a place of sincere concern.

"I'm standing in her fucking apartment and all her shit is gone, man. I've been out of town on business for a few weeks, and her shit is gone." Walking over to the kitchen counter, he picked up the objects he found there. "Looks like her keys are here. She ain't coming back; that's clear. Is she still working at Murphy's?"

"Yeah. Give me five." Without saying anything else, the call disconnected, and Hoss stood there, lips pressed into a thin, bloodless line. Shaking his head, he took a jerky step backwards, leaning a hip against the countertop. Thumb moving quickly on his phone, he tapped out a message to Deke, hoping Mercy would know something.

Eyes unfocused, staring at the wall opposite where he stood, he found his gaze tracing the elegant lines of the woodwork that made up the cabinets. The delicate swirls etched into the door swept downward, a dark cherry stain fading to blonde wood where over the years it had been handled countless times by unthinking hands. Beauty waning down to worn and tired through lack of care. The buzzing of the phone in his hand startled him, and he lifted it so he could see the display. A text from Jase read, **_Call_**.

Dialing the number, he waited in silence, and then DeeDee's soft voice filled his ears, soothing him. "Hoss, honey. Jonny knows something. Give me ten minutes, and I'll call you with what I find out. But, they weren't taken, honey. They were _not_ taken." Grunting in response, he disconnected the call, not wanting her to know how deep his fear ran.

The innocents on the fringes of club life were the ones who always paid the highest price when things went sideways, and the Rebels certainly had their fair share of sideways shit in the past few years.

Mercy was a prime example, because only a few months ago, a member gone rogue, exposed as a traitor in their ranks, had turned on her in his anger. He had been dealt with, but not until after he got his hands on her. The motherfucker cranked her up, getting her so high on the potent powder she nearly died from the overdose. Then he took his hands to her, choking and beating her until her features had been unrecognizable on her face for days.

Having confidence Hope had left of her own volition let him take the first free breath since he walked into the apartment.

DeeDee wouldn't have said those words unless she believed them, because she knew the risk a relationship with a one-percenter bought, would know the fear he harbored the instant he knew Hope was gone.

His phone rang, the noise startling him more than the vibration had moments before. Lifting it to his ear, he said, "Talk to me."

"She didn't tell Dale anything about moving, but he said she's been real quiet for the past couple of weeks. Withdrawn, instead of outgoing. Down. Sad." Clipped and curt, Fury's tone reflected the frustration Hoss felt. "He's calling one of the cooks now, gonna see if she said anything to Green. Her fucking phone's out of minutes, too."

Sammy's only request, his only ask was I not make Hope sad. Fuck. "Captain's old lady called; her boy might know something. I'm waiting for a call back." His voice cracked, but he clamped down on that shit. "Seems she didn't tell anyone."

"You didn't catch wind of anything, man? I know you were out of town, but she didn't let on she was leaving or moving or any shit like that?" Fury's question stung, not because he meant it to, but because Hoss had been stupid, thinking she would know what he was planning because of a single statement he made days before he dropped out of contact.

"Didn't talk to her," he responded, voice low and quiet.

"Gone for fucking weeks and you didn't speak to her?" Fury's voice was unbelieving, and Hoss thought he probably deserved that.

"Club business is shit, man. Takes us away when we would least prefer, and for however long the club needs us. You of most should know how this shit works, what it takes to keep things under control and stable." *Fuck him. I'll throw it right back at the man.* "When's the last time you fucking talked to her?"

"Oh, no, brother. You do not get to go there, man. You made it real fucking clear Hope was no business of mine, Hoss. Made it clear to me you felt you already had a patch on that. You're veep of the local chapter of the club I'm looking to fold my men into. I am not going to fuck my entire club in the ass over a woman who runs from me to you, waking on my fucking lap with your name coming from her goddamned perfect mouth. Why the fuck would I go out of my way to talk to her, when all that was clear as a fucking church bell ringing on a Sunday morning?" Hoss frowned at the tone, but he couldn't argue with Fury's words.

"You're right, man," he said quietly as his phone buzzed. Glancing at the display, he said quickly, "Got a call coming in. I'll text if I learn anything." He picked up the incoming call, eyes closed in concentration, brow heavily furrowed. "Yeah?"

Jase cleared his throat, anger clear in his voice. "Seems we have a problem, brother."

"What the fuck?" Opening his eyes, he stared at the worn wood for a moment and then transferred his gaze to the scuffed toes of his boots. Everywhere he looked, things were used...damaged. *Fuck.*

"Well, seems Sammy don't much like you. And, my Jonny? He says he don't like you either, because you made Miss Hope cry. It sounds like you worked hard for about a minute and won her boy over, eh? Gave Sammy an idea you gave a shit about his mom, and him.

Jase scoffed, contempt clear in his tone. "Now? He don't like you. Not at all. You told his mom you wanted them both to live with you, but then you went away, just like his daddy did. You left, and then Mercy left, and Hope somehow got it in her head they had to move. Not your direction either, but into a place that makes Sammy's skin crawl with fear. And now? Now he thinks you *both* walked away, you and Mercy both, brother. A boy like that starting to depend on you, and you fucking walk away? No calls, no nothing? You don't even ask me to talk to her and explain? What the fuck were you thinking?" Jase took a deep breath, blew it out in frustration.

Hoss clamped his lips closed, painfully aware he didn't have any rebuttal, no position of defense, because everything Jase said was true.

After a minute, voice tight, Jase continued, "It sounds like he and Hope are living in some dive of an studio apartment far down on the south-east side. Either it's all she thought she could afford, or she didn't know the area yet, but it's as if she intentionally picked the worst of the worst neighborhoods, man."

He took a breath, and Hoss heard something in the background, and then Jase grunted. "We got a general location, but no address, brother.

I've reached out to Reno. We'll see if he can slap us an assist. He's an officer of the club that owns that part of town. A pretty, golden-haired white woman with a little nub of a boy moving in where she did will have caused waves, and he's our best bet to know where the fuck she is."

He didn't say anything, just disconnected the call. "*Fuck*," he roared, his arm stopping short of sweeping the groceries off the counter and to the floor. He stood, quivering with rage at himself, because he didn't know how to do this, didn't know how to make this right. How to fix it when he found her.

Only vaguely aware of the days as they passed, he had been focused first on the business at hand, which had been ugly and dangerous, potential for fucking up hundreds of lives in the front of his mind every day, and then on arranging things for her in a way that filled him with sweet expectation. Meanwhile, she was back here in the Fort, doggedly making her own way, thinking he had walked out of her life. Walked away from them. Discarded her like her parents had done. Not worth the effort of even a text.

She had no one to count on in her past, no one to take her back ever, and he had been stupid to think she would understand or believe she could rely on him. He fucking knew better, and he still let the days slip through his fingers. Tick tock, winding down, stripping away any expectation of confidence and faith she might have had.

He knew Reno, knew the man was trustworthy. If he had any inkling Hope belonged to the Rebels, he would have issued a no-touch order soon as he knew who she was. That kind of order was only good as long as it was club, though. If there were bangers in her area, all bets would be off. And on the south-east side of town? *Fuck*, he thought, *all bets are off*.

His phone buzzed and he looked at the display to see names and times. Jase had tracked a schedule after all. DRT Transportation, a trucking company owned by Daniel Rupert, a friend of the club. Rupert's brother, Dickie, ran the local office, and that's where she was right now. He copied the text, forwarding it to Fury with a location to meet. Moving fast, he swung around the end of the counter, dropping the apartment keys back where Hope had left them, once again walking away without looking back.

***

"Thanks, Dickie," Hope called, jumping into her car. "I'm sorry, but it sounds like Sammy's not feeling well." Lifting one hand in a brief wave at her boss, her car door gave a groaning creak as she pulled it shut and then buckled in. Focusing on traffic, she didn't pay attention to the vehicles in the lane behind her, not noticing even when they followed her through several turns.

Gliding to a stop when the light ahead turned red, she finally recognized the ringing sounds of motorcycle exhaust pipes nearby, and her breath stopped in her chest when she glanced in her rearview mirror. Fury was there, framed in the small reflective surface, white teeth flashing in his deep red beard when he gained her attention.

He nodded and pointed to the right, so she was already turning that direction just as knuckles tapped firmly on the passenger window. *Tap-tap-tap.* Jumping in her seat, her heart raced fast, beating erratically when she saw Hoss right beside her car. He had ridden his bike up on the line separating the lanes and now sat, staring at her. Jaw set in a hard line, he had pulled his sunglasses off and his gaze traveled across her face, eyes narrowed, brow creased in a hard frown.

With a jerk of his head, he motioned forward, rolling his bike up past, and then roaring ahead of her when the light turned green. She followed him, aware of Fury riding feet from her rear bumper, the two men bracketing her in the heavy, mid-day traffic. When Hoss turned off the road into a shopping plaza parking lot, she drove in behind him, letting him lead her to an empty corner of the lot.

With a practiced gaze, she swept the area, seeing there were two different exits from this section of the lot, noting it would be only dimly lit at night. Hands automatically reaching for her seat belt, she shuddered at where her thoughts had taken her then jumped and cowered away from her door when a sharp rapping sounded next to her head. *Tap-tap-tap.*

Hoss was already off his bike and leaning against her car. Hands bracing him, palms pressed to the metal strip next to the window, his head was lowered so he could look inside the vehicle. Look at her, fierce emotion twisting his features. Through clenched teeth, he demanded, "Hope, open the goddamned *fucking* door." *Crap, he sounds pissed.* "Right the fuck now, Hope."

She reached out and slipped the keys from the ignition, pushing them deep into the pocket of her jeans before unlocking and beginning to open the door. The handle wrenched out of her hands when he jerked the door wide, and then his hands were on her upper arms and she found herself pulled from the vehicle to her feet. Gaze locked on his face, she felt as if there were a vacuum around her, and his voice calling her name came from far away. *He is so mad at me*, she thought. *Why is he so mad? I haven't seen him in weeks and* he's *mad?*

"Shit, Hoss. I've seen that look before. She's gonna faint, brother." Fury's voice was close, but she couldn't pay him any attention, because Hoss' face filled her vision as much as the pain filled her head, and she watched as the anger and hurt on display there dissolved into a sharp, worried fear before fading away entirely.

"Hope?" This came from nearby, the concerned question sounding right above her head. She struggled to open her eyes, lids fluttering for a moment before they opened partway. "Baby, you with me?" Forcing her eyes wide, she saw Hoss' face inches from hers and flinched back in surprise. "Hope, baby...what happened?"

Turning her head, she saw she was on the ground next to her car, lying on the hot pavement. Twisting the other way, she saw Fury squatted down a couple of feet away, concern clear on his face. He lifted two fingers in a brief wave then his hand fell, elbow propped on his knee, the intense blue of his gaze never leaving her.

"I'm okay. Let me up." Struggling against Hoss' hands, he had gotten down on his knees next to her, one strong arm underneath her shoulders. "You startled me; that's all. Let me up," she repeated. "I have to go. Hoss, let me *go*." She heard the tears in her voice. Her eyes dipped closed again as pain bloomed behind her forehead, and she drew in breath with a hiss.

"Baby." She heard Hoss say something to Fury then his hands were moving on her, setting her on his lap, positioned so she was leaning into him. "Where were you headed?" She winced; his voice was so loud, echoing in her head, setting up a painful resonance there.

Squeezing her eyes shut tightly, she gritted out, "The Foundation, they called DRT and said Sammy needed me."

Fury said, "Brother? You think that was Captain?" The pain was ebbing as quickly as it came on, and she squinted, seeing Fury with his phone to his ear. "Captain? It's Fury. I'm with Hoss. Did you call—" He paused, then said, "Gotcha. 'S all good, then? Yeah." With a grin at her, he said, "They were trying to find you. Everything's okay. Your son is fine." Attention back to the phone, he said, "Yeah, we got her." She pulled in a breath then twisted to see Hoss looking down at her.

"Let me up." Even to her ears, her voice sounded thin, reedy and weak, so she wasn't surprised when he shook his head, rejecting her request.

"Not until you get a little color back, baby." His hand lifted to her face, fingers gently pushing the hair out of her eyes. "You're looking better, but you scared the fuck outta me, Hope. I nearly didn't get my arms around you in time to stop your fall." He leaned in, clearly going for a kiss, and then frowned when she turned her head slightly, his lips touching her jaw instead of her lips. "What the fuck, Hope?" His question and tone revealed he was angry again, his worry for her suddenly swept away by returning frustration.

"Brother," she heard Fury mutter, but could only stare at Hoss.

"I get back from taking care of club business and you're fucking packed up and gone, not a fucking word to me. Not a fucking word to your sister, even. No note, no word, no notice. Just packed your shit up and moved on, not giving a good goddamn about what you left behind." His arms tightened around her.

"You remember me telling you I didn't want stupid shit to get between us?" He gave her a little shake, and she quickly nodded her head, not trusting her voice. *Why is he so mad?* "You didn't listen very well, did you? Because this is stupid shit getting between us, Hope. What kind of stupid shit did you let get wrapped around your head, baby?"

His tone softened, and he shifted her on his lap, hand at the nape of her neck, pressing her face into his chest, and she breathed in his familiar and reassuring scent. "I got there and you were gone? Scared the fuck out of me, baby."

She swallowed hard, heard receding footsteps, and knew Fury was attempting to give them privacy. Swallowing again, she said, "Mercy moved in with Deke."

From the perplexed look on his face, she knew he wasn't going to understand until she spelled it out for him. "I've saved a little while I lived with her, but the rent on that apartment was too much for what I make, even with the extra jobs."

Feeling her eyes get wet, she squeezed them tightly shut.

"Hope—" he said, but she talked over him.

"I found a cheaper place for me and Sammy. Something I can afford and still do things like be team mom for the hockey league. Life's not a fairytale where things magically fall into place simply because we want them to. I know I have to work to make things happen, so I did what I had to do. I'd already lost you; I couldn't stand to lose Mercy, too.

Her voice broke and she had to swallow again to push down the tears before continuing, "I wanted us—Sammy and me—to stay in Fort Wayne, near Mercy. So, I tried to find a way for that to happen.

Why is he acting as if I wronged him? He's the one who left us. Tears leaked from the corners of her eyes as she whispered, "You were the one gone without a word, Hoss. You think I left without telling anyone? No, you did. Because, I did try to contact you. I tried. I did. I reached out to you, wanted to find out what had gone wrong at dinner that last night, because I couldn't figure out what I'd done. What I'd done wrong, what was so bad, so wrong, so embarrassing that you walked away without even a breakup text. I tried, but you didn't call me back, didn't return any of my messages.

Shaking her head, she looked into his face, his expression not giving her any idea of his thoughts. "I waited for a long time. But, you didn't get back to me. Zero response. So then, tell me, what was I supposed to think? You walked away without a word, made it seem easy peasy. Good and gone. I got it wrong. Okay, I can deal with being wrong. You were gone, so I went back to what I know, being responsible for myself and my son; making sure I'm putting Sammy first. It's all I know." With a muffled cry, she turned her face away, pushing hard against his body, and his arms tightened around her again, hard bands making her efforts futile. Her sobbing voice rose to a shout as she yelled, "Now would you *please* let me go?"

He had gone still while she spoke, and his voice was soft when he said, "Hope, baby. Not easy, not a chance it was easy. Do you not remember me telling you the only reason I couldn't move you into my house was because I didn't want to fuck up Deke's play for Mercy?" He paused and then gave her a shake until she nodded. "Then why would you think I wouldn't jump on the chance once that play was no longer an issue?

She opened her mouth, but he talked over any words she might have said. "Did you not understand I wanted you there? I've never taken a woman to that house, ever. You seen the inside of my house, baby?" Eyes tightly closed, she nodded and opened her mouth again, but he forged on.

"Fucking right. I told you the first time you walked through my door, 'Welcome home' and I meant it." His fingers stroked her cheek, folding underneath her chin and turning her face up to his. "Look at me, baby." Fingertips stroking across her lips, thumb insistently tugging the bottom one down, he opened her mouth slightly. "Baby, look at me," he pleaded, and she opened her eyes, blinking away the still-flowing tears.

He hovered over her, eyes sweeping back and forth across her features, anguish clear in every deep line etched on his face. "I never tried to do this before, never tried to be someone to anybody. I fucked up. Baby, this is me telling you I'm sorry. I didn't realize you wouldn't understand. Scared the shit outta me, walking into that apartment and everything that was you...gone. Lost my shit, baby. Ain't gonna lose you. I ain't gonna let you run away. No fucking way. I will always find you and bring you home, baby. As long as you love me, I'll bring you home.

She squinted up at him and opened her mouth again, but then closed it as he threw his head back with a groan. "Baby, don't deny it. Don't tell me to let you go. Ain't happening. You named it when you told me you wanted my cock in you. You told me to make love to you. Baby. Let me bring you home."

14. Can't catch me

Fucking killed him, the way Sammy looked at him now. Head down, corner of the eye. Those looks drilled deep and painful, scouring over his skin like barbed wire. Day two of them being moved into his house, and it was crystal the boy trusted nothing from him anymore. Hoss thought he was good at locking his shit down, but Sammy seemed a fucking master. Standing in the kitchen, hip to the counter, he raised a cup of coffee to his lips, sipping cautiously at the hot liquid. His eyes were on Sammy, seated near the bottom of the stairs, elbows to his knees, chin propped in his hands.

Hope had left about an hour ago to drive to Dale's office. She told him she needed to get payroll out the door, unresisting when he lifted her chin with his fingers to take her mouth in a soft, sweet kiss. Unresisting, but not responding as she had before. She may have moved in, but she wasn't with him yet. Not a fucking chance. After everything that had gone on the day before, beyond exhausted when she finally fell into bed, she had been asleep in minutes. He had curled around her, pressing his chest tight to her back, and lain awake listening to her breathing slow and deepen, not needing more than her in his arms to be happy in the moment.

Midway through the night, he heard a thin shout from Sammy. Before he could do anything, she had jerked awake and was up and out of bed, stumbling and nearly running into the wall in her haste. He followed her at a more considered pace and watched as she blindly crawled into bed with Sammy, pulling him into her side with a soft mutter, eyes already closing.

Fuck, she had lost all the easy gained before he ran out on them. He could dress it up all he wanted, but he ran out on them. Sowing distrust and sadness. From what Hope said, it was obvious she felt he left them hanging. He had fucked up hard, seeding doubt and sorrow, and now he would reap that crop.

Tense and nervous even in her sleep, the anxiety bled from her into the boy. As he stood and watched from the doorway, their rest was again disturbed by Sammy's dreams. Both occupants of the bed twisting and moving in their sleep, trying to get away from whatever plagued them in the darkness.

Knee to the bed, he climbed in behind her, answering her startled question with a quiet, "Hush, baby," as he wrapped his arms around them both. Turning her on her side, he tucked himself against her, his bigger spoon to her small one, both cradling the baby spoon. In the morning, when she finally stirred, the sun had edged in around the curtains and his eyes were still open, scratchy and burning from lack of sleep, but Hope and Sam had rested, deep and dreamless under his attentive protection.

Over breakfast, he watched the interactions between mother and son, their bond as strong and pure; impossible as it seemed, maybe even tighter than ever. Hoss had seen how the skin around her eyes grew taut with worry every time Sammy opened his mouth. Hoss knew—would have known, even without Jase's revelations—that Sammy wanted to hate him, and so he braced for the shit that would eventually have to be aired in order to heal.

Time to get things straightened out, he thought and, setting down his cup, called, "Tridents tonight, you and me, Sammy."

Eyes, nearly the same as his mother's, cut to him then away. "No, thank you," came the overly polite, quiet response. Same shit he had been getting since they picked up the boy at the Foundation offices the day before.

"Yep, you and me. Boys' night. I already got the tickets." He turned away, fumbling open the refrigerator door, and stood staring at nothing inside, his mind as empty of comfort as the shelves. "We need some groceries. Grab a jacket."

"I want Mom." The boy's words were spoken so softly if there had been any other sound in the house, he would have missed them. *Yeah, time to clear the air*, he thought, turning to see Sammy staring at the bottom step.

Remembering a previous meaningful conversation with Sammy, he used the same words the boy had thrown at him. "No lies." That got him a frozen kid, stuck in place, staring in front of him with wide eyes, because apparently the phrase held a power he hadn't understood. Not sure what he had bought with the two words, still he forged ahead. "I'm a *fucking* asshole." He stated this firmly, painfully taking in the unspoken agreement in Sammy's gaze when it snapped to him. *Yes, you are.* "I didn't call."

"You didn't call," Sammy agreed, not moving. *Hurt my mom.*

"Fucked your life up for weeks, me not calling and making sure your momma knew what I wanted." Sammy didn't respond, so he nodded in agreement with his own words. Giving the boy both physical and verbal affirmation his anger was acceptable, because it had been earned. "Fucked up your momma's life, too, her thinking she didn't mean anything to me, when she means the world. Caused her to question lots of things, uproot you both to try and keep your hearts safe."

Sammy nodded slowly, still not speaking. *Made her sad.*

"This is me trying to make things right, Sammy. I rolled back into town, and the first place I went was the old apartment, because I wanted to be home. Even without thinking about it, I knew home wasn't this house; it was wherever you and Mama were, so I went where I thought you'd be." He leaned back, crossing his arms over his chest.

"You weren't there, and I lost my fucking mind."

He heard Sammy's gasp at that statement, so he repeated it, leaning forward at the waist and hissing, "I lost my fucking mind. Your shit was gone, and no matter the calls I made, the people I begged for information, you and Mama hadn't shared with anyone. Didn't have anyone she trusted, so she didn't share. Because I'm a fucking asshole and I didn't call."

"You lost your mind?" Back straight, sitting still on the step, Sammy laid his arms on his legs, wiping his hands on the fabric of his jeans nervously. *Fuck.* Remember his daddy lost his mind once, too, nearly killed the boy before he was born. *Easy, I gotta go easy*, he thought.

Nodding, he stood and walked across the room, settling on the step next to Sammy, his longer legs reaching farther down, boots on the step that recently bore the weight of the boy's stare. "Lost my fucking mind, because I didn't know where my Hope had gone. Where my Sammy was. It came to me all of a sudden that neither of you had mindreading in your resume, so I knew I had fucked up big." He lifted his arms, hands far apart, palms facing as he measured the span of his stupidity. "Big."

Another slow nod from Sammy, then a question, "Why didn't you call?"

"Million dollar question, son." He saw the rejecting jolt when he called Sammy that word, a word that meant the world to Hoss, and then he pushed down the hurt, setting the boy's reaction aside for a moment. "I have a thousand excuses, but not a single fucking reason. I can say things like I was busy, or it would get late, or things were good when I left, and while each of those statements are true, not a single fucking one is a reason."

He shook his head, tilting his chin down. "I could have made two minutes time to call and tell her I was thinking of her, because I was, all the time. I could have called at three in the morning and she would have picked up, because she'd know I needed her voice. I know good things don't stay good just because of wishes. Good things need work, and I should have done that work, put in the time to make sure your momma was good. I didn't, because...well, anything I say after 'because' is an excuse, and I've decided I ain't gonna fall back on those. So I didn't call, and that was me fucking up"—he lifted his arms again, stretching his fingertips wider than before—"big."

They sat in silence for a minute, then two, the quiet stretching into comfortable positions, settling around them companionably. Sammy sighed, and then wiped his hands on his jeans again. "It's good you know that."

"Yeah," Hoss agreed. "I know it, so I can put the time in now to fix it. So much harder to fix something than it is to build it in the first place. You'd think I'd be smarter than this. I can tell you one thing, Sammy. If I can fix this with your momma, with my Hope...if I can make her believe and understand how I feel, then you can bet your boots I won't be letting things get broken again. I will hold it close, put in the time, work to make it stay good all the time."

"You really still like her." This wasn't a question, but Hoss answered it anyway.

"Yes, I like her." He hesitated then said, "I like you too, son."

Sammy's chin dropped to his chest, and his face screwed up tight and hard. *Fuck.* His shoulders jerked, and Hoss knew the boy was trying not to cry, trying to clamp down on the feelings overwhelming him. *Fucking shit.*

Reaching out, he wrapped his arms around Sammy, pulling him in close. "I like you too, son," Hoss repeated, and felt Sammy silently jerk again and again, nearly convulsing as he fought to hold in his fears and tears, anger and sorrow. "I ain't going anywhere, boy. You and your momma are stuck with me now."

"I—" Hard, hitching breath. "I lied." This was cried on a wail, the four letters of that word stretching out to fill the air with a swelling pain that ripped through Hoss, flaying him in places he had never felt such agony, and he sensed Sammy's desperate hands clutching at the fabric of his shirt as the boy burrowed closer. "I lied," he wailed again, and Hoss leaned down, pressing his lips to the top of Sammy's head.

"It's okay, Sammy. Whatever it is, we'll sort it out, son." Keeping his voice low, he tried to control the sweep of anger igniting inside, so fucking furious with himself that he hurt the boy this way. He understood Jase's anger more clearly now, because the kid deserved better from the people who loved him.

"I lied, because he's not nice." Still wailing, the words separated by breaths sucked in between raw sounding sobs. *Fuck.*

"Sam. Son, take a breath, we'll sort it out." *Fuck*, how did people do this?

"You can't be like him, because you matter to her." Breathing still uncontrolled, Sammy sobbed against him for a minute, and then he howled again. "You can't tell her I know." What the fuck was the kid talking about?

"Sam—"

"You can't tell her I know he's not nice. She still thinks he's nice, and if she finds out he isn't, then she might not think I'm nice, because I'm his." Fuck. The boy was talking about Suiter, his father. *Fuck.*

"Tell me what you think you know, son," he urged gently.

"I'm not your son." The wail cranked wide open again and Sammy's pain surged around them, carried on the raw sounds coming from his throat. Sammy gripped him tighter, hard hiccups interrupting the boy's nearly futile attempts to breathe.

"Does it count if I want you to be?" *What in the hell am I doing?* This was a promise he wasn't sure he was ready to make. "If I want you and your momma to be my family, does that count for anything?"

"You can't tell her." His voice had dropped to a whisper, but uncertainty had crept in and Hoss pressed the advantage.

"She'll understand better than you think. She knows exactly the kind of man your daddy is, Sammy. Better than most, because she lived with him." It wasn't his place to tell him what had gone down, and rather than confuse him with half-truths, he would just draw the line, urge him to talk to Hope. Then the boy spoke again, crashing things around him like shattering window glass dropping in dangerous shards to the ground.

"Mac told me what he did," Sammy whispered, and at that moment, Hoss hated Mac, a man he had never met. "My Grandmamma visited the diner one time and Mommy didn't know. We went to the park and she told me all these mean stories about Mommy. Tried to tell me my mom was a bad person." He took a deep breath, the stress still thick in his voice, but no longer sobbing aloud. "I told her she was a big, fat liar and she slapped me. Hard. Mommy never hits me. I didn't want Mommy to be mad, so I didn't tell her. Mac knew. Somehow, he just knew."

Hoss listened to him talk, hearing how his speech patterns reverted to the age he had been when this happened. "If Mommy knowed, then we wouldn't go back. Grandmamma lived in the country, like Grandfather and my other Grandmother. Mommy misses the country, and if she knew, then we wouldn't go back, and that would make her sad."

"You need to talk to Mom, son," he urged gently. "It will make her more sorrowful when she eventually learns this, and you know she will, because she's that kind of persistent. Give her a chance to make it right." This drew a half-hitching sob from the boy, and he pressed his lips to the top of Sammy's head.

They sat still for a moment, the hitches in Sammy's breathing coming less and less frequently until they seemed to stop. "You gotta talk to her, Sam. Talk to her and tell her how you know, and how that knowing makes you feel. Let her give you back something, because it will make her better. She might be sad for a moment, but you gotta give her that, son."

He tightened his arms around Sam then leaned down to kiss the top of his head again, closing his eyes at the wash of emotion the scent of soap and skin gave him. That feeling of home he hadn't even known he was missing until he tried to move towards it and found an empty apartment instead. *My boy. Home.*

"Now, let's get you cleaned up, and then we'll go buy groceries. Then I'll call Coach Spence, see if he can get me another ticket so your mom can go to the game with us. Let's go ahead and put your skates in the truck now; we can't forget them. This exhibition game marks the opening of their season, and the Tridents always offer a free skate after the game."

He squeezed him tightly then stood, lifting Sammy with him. "Oh crap, I should put you back down, huh?" That got him a quick, hitching laugh and he grinned. Putting Sammy's feet on the floor, he told him, "Run wash your face, blow your schnozzle, and then let's hit the road, Samboni."

***

He knew he had a big, stupid grin on his face, but he couldn't help it. After talking to Hoss today, hearing him admit he was a bad word—Sammy mentally whispered, *Asshole*—he felt as if nothing could go wrong.

Lifting his hand, he pounded his palm against the glass in front of him, gaining the attention of two Tridents players seated on the bench right in front of him. They grinned and gave him a thumbs-up, one of them mouthing his nickname, Samboni, recognizing him from practice when Coach Spence's friends came to help out. He nodded, and the player raised his hand, putting the knuckles of his glove against the glass. Sammy pressed his fist to his side of the glass, giving him the fist bump, and they both grinned, and then the player turned his attention back to the ice.

He stood, waving both hands over his head when he saw Jonny across the arena, doing the same from his seats right below the press box. Jonny had been the best friend ever, never trying to lie to Sammy and say things would be okay. He only listened and offered ideas of how to be mean to Hoss when he hurt Mom.

He jerked guiltily when Hoss poked his shoulder, suddenly afraid he knew what Sammy was thinking, knew the things he and Jonny had dreamed up. Hoss was directing his attention to the screen hanging from the ceiling, and Sam shouted with laughter when he saw himself up there. Jumping up and down, he waved both arms wildly until play resumed and they put the team back on the screen.

"Holy smokes, Hoss, these are awesome seats," he crowed, bouncing in place then bending over to make sure for the hundredth, millionth time his skates were safely stowed underneath his seat. They were.

"They are good," Mom agreed, and he twisted to see a grin on her face that matched his. "Puts us right here, where we see what the players really think about the game. Will you tell me later which reactions you liked best, and which you liked least?" The game horn blew loud to mark the end of the first period and he saw her face scrunch up, eyes squinting like the sun was shining on her face.

"Mom, you okay?" He heard Hoss moving behind him, talking through the corner of the glass to Coach Spencer, who was working with the team tonight, filling in for their equipment manager. "Mom?"

"Yeah, bud," she said, but he didn't believe the bright she tried to force into her voice. "Let's go find the bathroom during intermission." Standing, she leaned over him, and he turned his head to watch her press her mouth to Hoss'. He liked how Hoss curled his hand around the back of her neck, pulling her forehead down to touch against his, eyes open and staring into hers like he couldn't look at her long enough to satisfy something inside him. She smiled, and Sammy heard her say, "Not going far, love. We'll be right back."

Then he knew she was grinning at him, and saw Hoss' mouth curve upward into a smile, too, because those words meant she was giving back some of the ground she had pulled out from underneath their feet when Hoss was gone. She moved to the aisle and he stood, turning to face Hoss.

Trusting he would understand what it all meant, Sam told him, "Best. Night. Ever." He closed his eyes when Hoss gave him the same hand curl around the neck, pulling him into a tight hug. Wrapping his arms around Hoss' neck, he pushed his face into the rough and scratchy but just so-right-for-Hoss beard and said, "Thank you."

"You got it, Samboni." The words were muffled against the side of his head and he took a deep breath, feeling safe for the first time in forever.

Twisting out of his grip, he skipped to the aisle and then looking up, told his mom, "Race you," before taking off up the steep, cement steps, leaving her shouted laughter behind.

After the game, which the Tridents lost, but he knew it was because the refs weren't playing fair, he was on the ice, skating beside Jonny. Since they moved up here, he and Jonny had become best friends. It felt like they had always known each other, ever since that first day in the Spencers' backyard.

Friends for life, they told each other all the time. *Brothers*, Sammy said in his head. Jonny was talking about something Tyler had done. The oldest of the kids in Coach Spencer's house, Tyler usually felt it was his responsibility to keep everyone in line, and he was pretty good at it, too. Even now, Jonny wasn't complaining, just sounding impressed at how Tyler had managed the tantrums of their twin sisters. With ten kids living underneath one roof, all of them having been through some stuff, it would be more surprising if they all got along all the time.

Caught up in his own thoughts, he didn't notice Jonny had stopped talking until his friend shifted a half-turn, moving to skate backwards in front of him, intently studying his face. "You mad at me?" From the twist of his mouth, he was worried about Sammy's answer.

With a laugh, he shook his head, watching the fear leave Jonny's face. "Never. I'm glad you told." He was glad, mega-glad, because he knew Hoss already knowing what his mom had done made it easier for her to tell him the details. If she had to start by telling him they had moved out, it would have been harder. This way, she only had to talk about the why, which was hard enough. "I'm glad you're my friend." Pushing hard, he skated past Jonny, yelling over his shoulder, "Can't catch me!"

15. You bring danger to my door

"I wanna take you out." He made this announcement after their late dinner, seated at the end of a long table with Hope, watching their friends laughing and talking. Jase and DeeDee hadn't made it back yet from taking all the kids home after the game, with the plan being Tyler and the next oldest, Megan, would watch and get them all to bed. He and Hope would pick Sammy up the next morning, which meant he had her all night long.

From her perch on his knee, she twisted to look at him, her smile sitting uncertainly on her face. He hated it, hated he had done this to her. Like he told Sammy today, he was willing to put in the time, because with her back in his house, Sammy in his house, those walls were suddenly becoming a home, and he liked the feeling. "We are out," she said, tilting her head.

"I mean I wanna take you out on a date." This time he nodded, surer of himself. "Some place nice." Glancing around, he laughed. "Not that this isn't a nice place, but a biker bar isn't where I want you to think of when you remember our first date fifty years from now." There was shouting from the lower bar and he twisted to see. Then, hands to her waist, he lifted and set her on her feet, standing abruptly and turning, finding himself shoulder-to-shoulder with a dozen brothers, their women in a group behind them.

From across the room, he heard Dixie call, "Nuh-uh, motherfuckers. Not in my fucking bar," and knew she had recognized the cuts on the men walking in. Stalking to the end of the bar, the bar manager put both hands on the counter, levering her body up to put a knee on the cooler. Now head-and-shoulders above the crowd, she called again, no-nonsense, "Not in my fucking bar. Get your asses out."

"Shut the fuck up, bitch." This was a snarl from the man in front of the group, Rogue, president of the Sins of the Brothers MC.

"You will not come in here and—" Whatever else she was going to say was lost when her old man came behind the bar and pulled her off the cooler with an arm around her waist. He hustled her to the kitchen door, and then, with her still protesting loudly, pushed her through it, cutting a glance up to where Hoss stood with Slate.

"Prez, what kind of play you want here?" Hoss asked, his eyes fixed on Rogue, who had stopped and was leaning up against the bar.

"Want those motherfuckers out of my goddamned fucking space," Slate bit off the words. "*Fuck me*," he gritted out between clenched teeth. "What the hell are they doing here, Hoss?"

"Women?" Ignoring Slate's question for now, he knew this would not have been his first concern three months ago. He didn't fucking care if he caught shit later about being pussy whipped; he just needed to know Hope was safe, that she would be covered, no matter what went down.

"Prospects. Text Tequila and send them to Marie's." Slate's attention never wavered, still locked on the man whose brother had brought so much pain to his woman.

"Hurley, Worm," Hoss called the names of two prospects, hearing the shuffle of boot leather on the floor as they came up beside him. "Two cages, don't fucking care which, as long as you can take all the old ladies with you. Take 'em to Marie's. I'll let Tequila know you're coming. You fucking text me every time you stop at a light, and you only stop there if you can't avoid a roll. These women are our lives, so treat them as such." Hoss pulled his phone out, sliding the lock screen and texting Tequila, then Jase and Deke, then after some consideration, he gave Goose a heads-up, too.

"Rogue." This was Gunny, growling out a chilling rendition of the man's road name. "The fuck you think you're doing, coming in here with Rebels in the house? I mean, I don't know what the fuck you think you're doing in the Fort at all, but fucking shit, man. You got a death wish?" As he talked, he had walked forward, putting himself between their president and the threat.

Hoss heard Hope asking questions behind him, and then another woman answered her, their voices receding towards the backdoor. Something was off, though, and he quickly counted the men in the lower bar. There were fewer now than before, and he caught sight of another man in a Sins cut working his way towards the outside door down there.

"Fuck," he yelled, turning towards the door and shouting for Hurley just as the door slammed behind the last of the women, pushed so hard from outside the glass cracked, half of it falling to the floor with a crash. Through the broken glass, he saw the women huddled together, a prospect on either side of the group, all of them surrounded by Sins members.

He squeezed his eyes shut for a moment then called, "Gunny, outside," as he twisted back to see Rogue and the other men surging in a group up the short flight of stairs separating the upper and lower bars. Slate rushed past him, headed outside too, and he stood firm, knowing his brothers would have the best chance of keeping their women safe

MariaLisa deMora

out there. With them outside, that meant his job was in here. Reaching under his cut, he pulled out his pistol, calmly leveling it at the rushing men, gratified when they slowed and stopped twenty feet away.

A woman's scream, cut short, echoed from outside, and it was all he could do to hold himself still, to not turn and look. *Fuck.* Feigning calmness, he casually picked up the conversation. "I find myself seconding Gunny's questions, man. What the fuck did you think you'd gain by coming in here like this?" There was a flicker of movement at the end of the bar, and from the corner of his eye, he saw Bear and PBJ, followed by two more Rebel members, prowling through the appreciably thinner crowd. They were moving quickly between those groups of people who were angling for the front exit of the building, bar patrons intelligently trying to put distance between them and whatever the fuck this was going down here tonight.

"Not a club bar. Rebels don't own this shit." Rogue shook his head slowly, tipping his chin towards the shattered door. "Don't you want to know what's going on?" Raised voices came from outside, and another short scream.

Hoss shrugged easily, lifting one shoulder and dropping it, still feigning casual, even while his mind was racing to figure out what play the Sins were making here tonight. He counted five Sins inside, and knew he had seen about fifteen total, which meant there were now ten out back. He ran scenarios through his head, but still wasn't sure why they would have split.

Their entire club could deploy only about a hundred members at any given time, so they had committed a significant percentage of their membership to this run. They would have known how many Rebel members were in the bar based on the bikes in the lot, so they had come inside knowing they were outnumbered. Rogue was president, and he saw two other officer patches on the vests in front of him, so this was their leadership on the line, too.

228

What is their fucking play? "My brothers have it in hand, I'm sure." He saw Bear and PBJ moving up behind the men, but didn't react. "I can't figure something out, though. Maybe you can help clarify something for me."

Chin lifted, Rogue asked, "What's that?"

"How the fuck did your momma raise two sons who turned out to be identical stupid fuckers? She have a gift or somethin'?" Hoss shook his head. "Musta dropped you both, hard. You and your brother, fucked in the head, apparently, if'n you think you can walk in here, threaten our family, and then fucking survive. He found out, hard and bloody, just how fucking wrong he was. Didn't you learn from the mistakes of the past? Ain't that what the name of your fucking SOB club's all about?"

There were more shouts from outside, these male, and in his peripheral vision, he saw Bear offer a reassuring chin lift. Whatever the man could glimpse through the broken door, it wasn't enough to warrant Hoss taking his eyes off Rogue, who hadn't yet risen to the bait. With a chill in his chest, he watched a smile spread across Rogue's face. "You talk to Mason lately?" *Fuck.*

Hoss didn't give him any reaction, didn't have to, because Rogue knew his jab had hit hard. Time to surprise the man. "Bear, wanna wrap this motherfucker up?"

Bear was on him in an instant, hands gripping his arms and pulling him back and away from his men while PBJ stepped between to block their advance. Hoss cleared his throat, drawing eyes back to him, reminding them they were outnumbered and outgunned. Bear didn't take any chances, locking the man down hard, pulling an arm up between his shoulder blades, and then pushing him to his knees. "Done, boss," was all his brother said, and Hoss grinned at him over the kneeling man's head, enjoying the efficiency of movement and language.

From behind him, he heard Gunny say, "All good outside, Veep."

229

With a nod that didn't break the eye contact he continued to hold with Rogue, he said, "Call the clubhouse, brother. Make sure Deke got everything locked down. I'm guessing the women are on their way now, after their...slight delay?"

"Yeah, Tequila's been informed of their progress." There was a pause, and then Gunny said, "Deke, all good, brother?" Another pause, and then, with a tone of humor thick in his voice, he said, "Fucking excellent, brother. Save me a piece of that shit, would ya?" A laugh then a surprised grunt. "Huh. Chicago North, yeah? No shit? Outstanding." A footfall, then another before Gunny spoke softly, words pitched low for him to hear, "All the women are good, Hoss. No worries. You knew we'd have her back."

He nodded, waiting silently.

Louder, Gunny said, "Seems Mason called the clubhouse a little bit ago; our Chicago North chapter happened on an unusual parade happening through our town. Sounds like they efficiently dealt with the shit. Meanwhile, back at the ranch," he laughed, and Hoss shook his head, "Deke dealt with a dozen Sins who wound up in our clubhouse lot looking for directions. Was a cluster for them, man. They shoulda bought a fucking map."

A large hand settled on his shoulder, tugging and gripping the side of his neck, and some of the tension he was carrying fell away. "Deke said he's holding shit for you and Prez. What say we load these fuckers in the cage we dropped their little friends in and take 'em back with us? We'll play a round or two of cat and mouse, have a little bit of game time."

***

Hope stood, cloth rag in hand, looking around at the women gathered near the end of the bar. They had come to Marie's, and once inside the bar, she had quickly and gratefully slipped back into her comfortable role as a waitress. It gave her something to do with her hands, which now only shook when she thought about what had happened tonight. Even as hard as she tried to keep her mind blank, the events kept creeping in around the edges, stealing her composure.

What had *happened?* She shook her head. Everything moved so quickly. It was all so fast she hadn't been able to keep up, couldn't keep things straight. Seated on Hoss' lap one moment, with him talking sweet to her, and then the next they were hustled out the backdoor, only to find themselves confronted by a large group of men.

The front door of Marie's pushed open and she jerked, glancing nervously in that direction, seeing a well-dressed couple pausing before being escorted back outside by Tequila. It seemed the bar was closed to all except the club tonight.

"They won't be here for hours yet, hon." Her gaze flicked to the woman leaning against the bar in front of her. The petite beauty was Coach Spence's sister, Sharon. She had seen her with Gunny earlier and knew the two were a couple. Beauty to his beast, it seemed like, because Gunny was one of the scarier men in the club. Huge, at least six-foot-five, the tender care he had for Sharon and the love in his face when he looked at her went a long way to dispelling the instinctive fear he evoked.

Sharon was the only one of the women who hadn't looked fearful in the back lot of the bar earlier, surrounded by strangers. Even pregnant, her belly softly rounded, she had stepped up beside the two club prospects trying to protect the women, yelling at the other club. Her actions had given them courage, and before long, practically all the women were shouting and gesturing, their attitudes appearing to confuse the men. Then, several Rebel members had come out the shattered door, and the event was effectively over, the rival club members restrained and shoved into a cargo van.

Hope nodded, swiping at the bar top again, twisting to look at the door again anyway. "Seriously, it's okay, Hope. The club has it under control." Sharon's faith appeared unshakable, and then her face went soft. "If you're worried about your boy, don't. I heard from DeeDee earlier there are about twenty members at their house, consuming everything in her refrigerator. The only thing you have to worry about is if he'll have anything to eat for breakfast." She briefly returned the smile Sharon had on her face, and then dropped her gaze to the bar.

"Honey." This was accompanied by a hand covering hers, halting the repetitive movements she was making, cleaning an already spotless bar. "It's okay to be scared, but we were never in any real danger. You're safe, Hope. And, your boy is safe."

Jerking her hand back, Hope drew a deep breath then another. Rolling her lips between her teeth, she bit down hard. Shaking her head, she turned to walk to the back room, only to be stopped by Tequila blocking her way. He stared down at her, a scowl in place on his features. Shaking his head, he sighed then said, "Out with it, girl. It's only going to get bigger and bigger the longer you keep it locked away."

"Where's Hoss?" Her voice was quavering and high-pitched, and she bit her lips again to stop the sound from escaping.

"He's at the clubhouse," Tequila said immediately.

"Why can't I go to Sammy?" Her voice sounded painfully unfamiliar to her ears, and she made a face at the evidence of her fear surfacing so blatantly.

"Orders, sweetheart. No one leaves here until I hear from either Slate or Hoss. Only a president or vice president can lift a lockdown, which is what we're doing here. We have every one of our places locked down, so we know where folks are. It makes it easier to protect everyone, if they aren't moving around or in transit." This answer was also immediate, and his voice was pitched low, just for her ears. Protecting her ignorance, because she was the new kid on the block, and he was telling her things the rest of the women already knew. Mercy already knew all this, too. She had been around the club for years and had probably seen this kind of thing often.

"Does this happen all the time?" *If it does, can I handle it? Do I even want the answer to that question?* Before he could respond, she asked a different question. "Are you sure Sammy's okay?"

"Yes, sweetheart. Sammy is at Jase and DeeDee's, and he's probably sacked out on the living room floor with the rest of the boys. They were all dog-tired after the game and skating, so once they got pizza in them, they were likely out before you even got to the bar. We protect the kids with our lives, sweetheart, from anything, including knowledge that could make them afraid. No one will have told them anything, so he's not sitting there wondering where you are. He's sacked out with his best friends, on an impromptu sleepover, which you approved, hugging and kissing him before he climbed in Jase's SUV." He sounded so certain of everything he said that the quivering in her stomach began to recede slowly. Then, his next answer brought everything swooping back in a rush.

"Listen to me, Hope. This kind of thing doesn't happen all the time, but when you have things others want, then yeah, sometimes people try to come in and take it. We protect our own, protect our family to the death if needed. You're ours twice over, honey, because we owe Mercy. She owns a big fucking marker with the Rebels, but even before that shit happened, she was ours. You're her sister, makes you hers. You've heard this all before, I know, but that makes you ours, too. Now, you're Hoss' old lady, which means any member would die before we let anything happen to you. We got you, pretty lady. Ain't no shit going to get to you, and surely not the kind of shit that rode down from Michigan tonight. You and Sammy, you are club, and we got you."

He leaned a hip against the back counter, gaze on her as his eyes narrowed. "Shit happens around a club, sweetheart. Wouldn't any one of us lie to you about something that important. Shit happens, and sometimes people get hurt. Sometimes people die. Fortunately, that particular brand of shit runs few and far between and, thank God, the way Mason runs the club, it's even farther. You bein' with Hoss means you're going to see the shit when it does happen, because he's one of the men in charge. Your man is our veep, our vice president. That office puts a certain target on his back, and by extension, at times, on yours."

He paused, and sighed again. "My brother is gonna kick my ass, but I'll tell you now—you need to decide if you want him enough to warrant the risk, sweetheart. Because I see from your face this hit you hard tonight, and you're gonna wear yourself out going over it in your head. So figure it the fuck out before he rolls in, so you don't make a mistake based on fear alone." His gaze stayed on her face until she nodded then he lifted his chin with a jerk and moved aside, opening the way to the back room.

***

Hoss tipped his head back, eyes tracking the spray of liquid on the ceiling. Foaming, the amber liquid dripped slowly, froth marking the place the beer had splashed when the bottle exploded against the wall. *Two days. All I got was two fucking days.* His gaze flashed to the doorway to see Hope standing there, mouth agape, drawn there by the shatter of glass and now looking at him with fear in her eyes.

"Baby," he breathed, but stopped when she shook her head and disappeared. "*Fuck,*" he ground out, gaze fixed on the doorway.

She had been quiet when he picked her up in the early morning, quiet but sweet to Sammy when they snagged him from Jase's place, and then just quiet when they got home and Sammy ran to play in his room. Glancing over her shoulder at him when he moved to follow her to their room, her nervousness shown through clearly.

Both Gunny and Tequila had sent him texts earlier, letting him know she was badly shaken by the events. He would have loved to be able to go to her right then, but they had shit to deal with in the basement of the clubhouse, and that was where he had to be. He didn't even bother justifying it, because obligations sucked, but knew in his gut that making sure shit was dealt with would help make her world safer in the long run.

Now they were home and he wanted to bury himself inside her, find that quiet center she brought him, because the night's work had been full of shit and pain, and he wanted to forget it for a while. He felt his lips curling up when he called her name from across the room, but then that smile died as she turned to look at him. Chin up, eyes swimming in tears, she no longer looked nervous; she looked fucking terrified and broken.

Taking the two strides across the room, he wrapped his arms around her unresisting form, pulling her to him. Cradling her head against his chest, he told her, "It's okay, baby. No harm, no foul, everything's okay." Badly shaken, fuck that. She was tore up about it all.

And, who could blame her? It was only the second time she had been exposed to any of the club's fuckery, and the other time had been mild, happening while she had been safely locked in her car. Tonight, she had been unprotected in a dark parking lot, had to watch as men threatened her and the other women, some of them pregnant, carrying precious life inside them. All those lives subjected to the stupidity of the club's enemies.

"Baby," he whispered, arms tightening even as she was pushing at his chest. "Hush, now. It's okay."

"No, it's not okay," she sobbed out, pushing hard at him, twisting in his arms. "Let me go."

"Hope, be still, baby." Carefully, he moved her, steering her towards the bed. Turning to sit on the edge of the mattress, he pulled her into his lap, her still shoving and trying to jerk away. Frustrated at her continued attempts to extricate herself, he barked, "Hope, knock it off."

At his sharp tone, she froze, no longer fighting, but sitting stiff and still, and his arms loosened, because it suddenly felt as if she were fragile, breakable. "Baby," he started, but she shook her head. Changing tactics, he said, "What? Hope, you gotta talk to me. Tell me what's in your head." Her ass shifted; she had created space between their bodies, was as far away from him as she could get, even with him holding her like this. "Hope, what the fuck is going on?"

"I can't do this." The whisper, delicate as a spider's web, fell into the silence between them.

"What?" His heart stuttered until he couldn't pull a breath. Fuck. "What, Hope? What can't you do?"

"I can't do this, Hoss." He watched her trembling mouth form the words, saw a tear track down, resting for a moment on her upper lip then falling to darken her shirt. "I can't."

"What the fuck does that mean?" His voice came from far away, and from her flinch, he knew it was far louder than he intended. Attempting to hold himself in check, he asked again, "Hope, what does that mean?"

"I have to put Sammy first. Ahead of myself. Ahead of what I might want." Now he was confused, because he wasn't sure what Sammy had to do with this. Her face twisted and she brought up her hand, covering her mouth to try and hold in a cry. Her next words were muffled, but clear, and left no confusion behind.

"You told me you brought danger to my door. I saw last night what it really meant. What if it had happened when we were all out? What if Sammy had been there? What if he had gotten hurt? I can't let that happen to us, to him. I've thought and thought, trying to find a way to keep what I want—" Another sob broke free, and she lifted her hand halfway to his face then let it fall, and he saw her lips were pressed tightly together. In a voice clogged with tears, she said, "And I realized what I want doesn't matter."

"No, baby." He didn't even know if he said the words. "No, no." Moving fast, he twisted around, laying her on the bed, leaning into her with his hip, pinning her, even as he bracketed her with his elbows. Hands holding her head still, he looked into her eyes and said again, "No, baby."

"Hoss," she whispered, her eyes tracking up and down his face. "I can't."

"No, no." He leaned down, brushing his lips across her forehead. "No. Give me a minute—"

"I can't," she repeated, and when he pulled back, he saw her eyes were squeezed shut.

"Baby, just give me—"

"I can't, Hoss. Do you think this is easy?" Now her eyes were open again, brilliant blue blazing up at him hotter than fire. "But I can't put Sammy in dang—"

He crashed his mouth down over hers, stopping the flood of her words ripping and tearing his heart out of his chest. Pushing between her lips, he lapped at her tongue, gasps of breath the only noise in the room until he heard himself groan. Eating at her, he poured his feelings into the kiss, feeling her hands beginning to move on him. Dropping his forehead to hers, he listened to her labored breathing for a moment. Sliding his cheek alongside hers, he whispered into her ear, "Don't, baby. Don't take this from me. I need this. I need you, us, so much. Mine. My Hope. My Sammy."

She jerked, and he felt her hands again, but now they were pushing against him, shoving her deeper into the mattress when he didn't move. "Get off," she sobbed, pushing again. "Get off me." He froze, because her voice shredded him, tore through him with the pain it carried. Red and bloody as the floor of the clubhouse basement last night, she flayed him alive. "Get off. Let me up."

Rolling to his side, he pulled her with him, locking his arms around her, hugging her close, tucking her head underneath his chin. "Baby, talk to me. Nothing you say is making any sense. Give me a chance to talk to you." He wrapped a leg over her, holding her to him as she fought to get away, pressing into her.

"It was laid out for me pretty plain last night," she said, her voice muffled against his chest, but no way would he let up on the hold he had on her. He had a terrifying certainty that if he couldn't change her mind here, like this, then when he did let her up, it would be for good, and she would be walking out of his life the first chance she got.

Her voice trembling like her lips had been earlier, she said, "The club is your life, Hoss. And, I understand putting others before yourself, so when things happen like last night, the club has earned your loyalty a thousand times over. I've heard story after story from your friends about how you've always given to the club, and last night they took from you again."

She shivered, and he tightened his arms as she continued, "They are your life, and Sammy is mine. You're the one who told me you were dangerous, and last night, I saw that in truth. Anything could have happened to me, to those women, simply because we were out for dinner and drinks with the men we love."

Every word struck like a blow, because she was right. Last night had been his worst fears brought to life and the reason he had kept his distance from her for weeks, even wanting her as he did. Why he had protected her from afar, because wanting her, being with her, would put her at risk. "I can't do that to Sammy. All he has is me, Hoss. I am all he has, all he's ever known. It's better for me to walk away now before he gets more attached to you than he already is, because I can't do this."

Standing in his kitchen, staring at the doorway where Hope had so briefly appeared, he knew she had gone back to Sammy's room and would have returned to her task of packing. Boxes and tape, suitcases and bags. Things that had made their way into and out of her car too many times over the past few weeks. She was preparing for him to make a call to get his brothers to move her out of his house. Out of his life.

He couldn't be angry, couldn't hate her, because—whether she believed him or not—he got her. Soul deep, he got her. She put Sammy first, which meant even if she could get past what had happened last night, she still had to go, because living with him could place Sammy in the path of shit he didn't need. And, she was right; he was also used to putting others first. Which meant now, he put her first. Ahead of his wants. His needs. Him. No fucking fairytale ending for him. He would put her first and let her go.

16. I will protect you

Hoss sat on a stool in the clubhouse, sliding his half-empty beer bottle back and forth between his palms on the bar. Chin tipped down, staring at nothing, he didn't even register the presence of a body on the stool next to him until a hand reached out, plucking the beer from his grasp. Twisting to see Mason next to him, his body jolted, watching as his friend drained the last of the beer from the bottle. "Fucking warm shit, man," Mason said, thumping the bottle back on the bar and motioning to the prospect manning the liquor bottles and coolers for two more.

"Prez," he said in greeting, eyes still on Mason. "Good to see you, Mason. Didn't know you were coming into town, man. We gonna do it up right, have a barbecue at Captain's place?"

"Maybe," Mason returned, accepting the beer that slid across the bar towards him without removing his gaze from Hoss. "Need to have a chat, brother."

Shit. He had halfway expected something like this, but hadn't thought he would have the office stripped from him so soon. Seventy-five days. *Not that I'm counting*, he thought with a twist to his mouth. Seventy-five days, where all he could do was sleep and drink. Deferring club business to others, not picking up so much as a crayon, sleeping at the clubhouse when he could convince his eyes to close.

That had been his last communication to Hope, a plea for her to stay in his home with Sammy until they knew all danger was dealt with. Safe behind a locked gate and an alarm system even Gunny said was top of the line. Safe from the danger he had laid at her feet, not the legacy he wanted, but the truth. He knew from Jase she was still working, knew from Deke she hadn't left, knew from Mercy that Hope and Sammy were staying in the guest room. Not living in the house, but staying in a single room, as if the rest of the house were filled with nothing but bad memories. *Shit.*

"All right," he ground out between gritted teeth, swinging off the stool and swaying for a moment. Glancing up at the clock, he saw it was not even eleven a.m., far too early to be this wasted. *Fuck.* "Office?" The question gave him a moment to regain his equilibrium, but when Mason answered, he knew his friend understood the delaying tactic for what it was.

"If you can walk that far, fucker." Mason's tone was sad and quiet, jerking Hoss' eyes to him in time to see pain wash across his features.

In the office, Hoss stumbled as he went to sit on the couch, falling sideways into the cushions with a grunt. Sighing, he said, "Give it to me straight, Prez. You takin' my patch, too, or just my office?"

"Ain't taking anything, fucktard," Mason said, shaking his head as he pulled out the chair behind the desk and sat. "Wanted to talk to you and couldn't get you on the phone. Talked to Slate, and he told me what happened after the shit went down with the Sins, man. It's been two and a half months; you didn't think to talk to me about this bullshit?"

"It's only been five months since Utah." He watched Mason's features tighten, but pushed on anyway. "You've been gone on a run out west for most of the last month and a half, Mason. You and her needed a chance to get right, so it ain't like you needed to take time out of the life you're building with her for anyone else's bullshit. I'm not complaining, mind, because if anyone deserved the trip you just took with Willa, it was you. Something you don't deserve is hearing how shit went sideways for me, man. Love you, brother, but it doesn't mean I have to pile my shit on you every fucking time I hit a road bump." Hoss struggled upright, bracing his elbow on the arm of the couch. "You look good, Prez. The run have the effect you wanted?"

Mason pushed his sunglasses on top of his head and grinned, his expression relaxed and open, easy in a way Hoss had never seen it. Nodding slowly, he said, "Yeah. I haven't told anyone else yet, but I married her while we were in California. Place on the coast called the Wayfarers Chapel. Fated, man. I asked her sitting on the prettiest beach I've ever seen, watching kites dance in the fucking wind. Does that sound like me at all? That's the kind of sensitive shit I'd expect from you or Bingo, but damn me if it didn't feel right. Then, sliding my rags on her shoulders for the first time? Putting my stamp on her for everyone to see with that vest? That felt right, too."

Mason laughed. "I suspect she'd talk more about the ring, but putting her on my bike with her wearing my patch? Gave me a fucking hard-on that wouldn't quit. I get it now, understand what would pull a man to mark a woman as his own, understand what drove Slate like it did, why Bear took the shit he did to make Eddie his. I fucking love her, tell her that shit every day, and cannot fucking wait for her to birth our babe growing in her belly."

His face tightened and he frowned at Hoss. "That don't mean I defer an iota of responsibility for the club, man. You having shit and keeping it from me, that's bullshit and you know it. So tell me what's going on and what went wrong. Tell me, and let's see how we can fix it. My brother, my friend. Rebels forever—"

Hoss finished the phrase, "—forever Rebels." He sighed heavily, and then said, "I fucked up."

"You're still breathin'. Still on this side of the sod, so you got a chance to unfuck that if you find yourself so inclined," came Mason's immediate response, and Hoss shook his head.

"I don't think so, Prez. I really fucked up. I went to Memphis, trying to sort the shit there, and I fucked up. I was gone nearly three weeks and didn't call. I thought she would know from what I'd already said I wanted her and the boy in my life, but I didn't..."

He sighed. "I've never had a relationship, Mason. I don't know what one fucking looks like, so when I told her if it weren't for Deke and Mercy I'd have her and Sam in my house, I thought she'd know what that meant to me. I know now she didn't even really fucking know me, because while I'd studied her for weeks, she had been focused on her boy and trying to make sense of things in a new town, with a new sister, new friends.

"I got so twisted up in the beginning, wanting her but forcing myself to stay away because of all the shit rolling around. I didn't want her getting hurt, wanted to protect her, so I watched her, learned her, studied her—but never let her see me. So then I made my play, couldn't wait any longer, wanted...no, needed her. Had her for only a few days when I had to go to Memphis. I fucked up. Lost her. Lost her trust, her faith in me, small as it was to begin with, because she's never had anyone to count on. And, it looked like I proved her right when I didn't call, didn't contact her, didn't come back for nearly three fucking weeks."

Mason made a noise, but Hoss talked over whatever he had been about to say. "I got back, talked her around and got her back, moved them into my home. The second night, we aren't even at home; we're out with the club, when the Sins come calling. Now she gets the full view of what club business looks like, sees the fallout, gets stuck in a lockdown with people she doesn't even know, none of her friends with her, no one she could believe who could tell her things would be okay.

By the time I get her home—" He paused then repeated the word on a scoff, "Home."

Taking a breath, he continued, "She lays it out for me. She's done. Two days, and she's done. I think I can change her mind, and I'm trying everything I know, and then she hits me with the real reason she's done, and fuck me, but I can't see any flaws in her logic."

Tipping his head down, he spoke to the toes of his boots. "She never had anyone to have her back, Prez. Nearly her whole life, she's been on her own. Living hand to mouth, not even paycheck to paycheck, she's kept herself together. She's held her little family together, her and Sammy. Never had anyone to count on, never had a fallback position. As unstable as their lives have been, she's all Sammy knows. When she says she has to put him first, I know she's right. Not bullshitting me, or trying to make a play for some foolish power.

"I've never had a relationship that mattered. I love my Mom and Dad, love my sisters. Love you and my brothers. That pales, man. Pales in comparison. I thought I felt something for DeeDee, but all it took was seeing how Jase was with her to know I didn't feel anything for her like what he did. I've never done that, never knew what it looked like from the inside. Not until Hope."

He sucked in a breath through a throat suddenly tight and burning. "I fucking love her so much it tears me up that she saw me as a big enough danger she needed me gone. She has Sammy, and he depends on her to make the right decisions, trusts her to keep him safe. She's never had a relationship other than that one with him, but she still knew enough to protect him from me."

He drew a breath, hearing it sound as ragged as the ones Sammy hauled in when he cried in his arms. "I got nothing inside me to tell her she's wrong, boss. I look at her and I see everything bad that's happened to Ruby, Eddie, Mercy. I see Willa. I got nothing to hold on to, no reason selfish enough to put her at risk like that. If she's away from me, and safe, at least she's in the world."

His shoulders lifted, and then dropped. "Mason, we found two automatics with big fucking clips in the saddlebags of the Sins. They could have come out with that shit, mowed down every woman standing helpless on the lot, and I couldn't have done anything to stop it. I was inside, taking care of business, not even standing by her side. I miss her so much it's killing me, miss the boy. Fucking hate she's right, and I'm not there, ain't with them. Not having them has leeched all the color from my world, boss. Seventy-five days I've been living a gray existence, and I don't see it getting better anytime soon."

They sat in silence and he watched Mason's gaze flick up to him then back down to the desk. This went on for several minutes, and then Mason sighed. "Go sleep it off then let's get in the wind, brother. Get some road therapy under our wheels."

He grunted and stood then swayed and shook his head. "Fuck, I miss her. Miss my Sammy. My boy. I'll head up, but it's all right. I'm good. You don't have to babysit me, Prez."

"Not babysitting you, Hoss. Just wanting to make sure my friend is gonna be okay. Go on up. I'll be here when you roll outta bed." Mason stood, walked to the door, and opened it. He put a steadying hand on Hoss' shoulder as he walked past, saying, "Like I said, you're breathin', so I still believe you got time to unfuck things."

***

Hope turned the knob and pushed open the door to what had quickly become her favorite room in the house. Hoss' studio. Her furtive pleasure, a way to keep the beauty that he brought to her alive. Joy mixed with guilt, because if she was still in his house, that meant he wasn't in his studio where he obviously spent a lot of time. Walking in, she stood in the center, letting her eyes roam the room. The bright light of late morning filled the space, warming her as it stroked across her skin.

She knew from the conversation with his neighbor Hoss was an artist, but every time she entered this private space, she was stunned. The beauty he created was so spectacular, exquisite, that viewing it took her breath away. Framed pictures crowded the area on two walls, and there were stacks of canvases everywhere. One barren wall was a creamy white, the one that would capture and reflect the most sunlight through the bank of windows. There were four easels lined up in front of those panes of glass, contents covered with white cloths whose silent demand for privacy she respected.

Today, as with most of her visits to the studio, she wandered along the display walls, eyes flicking from picture to picture. Pausing again and again, studying a painting or sketch with great interest, fingers hovering over the surface, she found the details often gave away the true topic matter behind the vision.

There was a grouping of small paintings, done in various media: oil, acrylic, watercolor. In each, the subject was a gray lighthouse. Strong and stable, the lighthouse rested on a solid foundation, a rocky headland or a cliff. Every rendition was slightly different. Reverently, she had taken each from the wall, reading the dates on the back so she knew the sequence of the pictures.

In the first, the lighthouse was solitary, waves bashing against its base, white foam and spray rising in arcs around the building. As the series advanced, other objects appeared. An outbuilding with a multitude of windows, nine in all, the lighthouse sheltering it from the attacking waves. A low, sprawling home, lights flooding through the windows as brightly as the spotlight shone from the lighthouse.

The largest painting was the final one, based on the dates. It was centered in the display, the others satellites circling around. In this picture, the ocean was flat and calm, the color a reassuring blue.

Through dissipating storm clouds shone a brilliant yellow sun raining beams of light onto the lighthouse. The lighthouse looked more worn in this painting, weathered by life and experiences, and she knew in her soul he had painted Bingo.

That beautiful man who held her hand at DeeDee's one day, telling her he wanted to write love songs to her. Sensitive and sweet, wracked by the effects of cancer treatments, but still beaming up at her through his striking, bushy beard as he composed lyrics and stanzas aloud.

Turning, she was about to leave the room, a smile on her face at the love he showed in his paintings for the old man, when she stopped. To the right of the door hung a sketch she hadn't paid attention to before. Not surprising, since there were several hundred pieces in the room. Today, however, this sketch seemed to shout at her. Right above eye level, it was set into a dark, glossy frame, the ivory paper a stark contrast.

One of the more sensual pieces she had seen in the studio, from shoulders to thigh it captured the upper bodies of a couple in a reclining embrace, the man's chest naked, the woman clad in an overlarge shirt. Stretched out on a narrow bed, the sleeping blonde curled trustingly into the man's side.

He was using the fabric of her shirt to pull her to him, and the taut lines of the material stretched tightly across the angles of her back and sides exposed his clutching strength. The tension evident in the muscles of his hand and arm was well drawn; you could see the play of tissue and bone, the desperation in his hold, fingers catching, buried to the knuckle in the cloth gathered into his hand.

Her arm draped across his chest, fingers curved in an easy caress over his shoulder; she was relaxed and sleeping deeply, pressed as close as she could be. Even with her willing participation in the embrace, the man's dread of loss was clear. With the stress in his shoulders and arms, suffusing his posture, you got the sense he didn't sleep, couldn't sleep

MariaLisa deMora

for fear she would be gone when he awoke. When she looked at the back of the framed sketch, she wasn't surprised to find the title was, *Barely Holding On*.

***

Mason stood and watched as Hoss made his stumbling way up the stairs to the room he had been sleeping in for too many fucking weeks. Hated to see his brother hurting like this, but knew from long years of experience there was nothing he could do to assuage his pain. Sighing, he twisted and caught Slate's eye, calling him over with a chin lift. "Talk to me," was all he said, and Slate nodded.

"Fury's sittin' out on the lot. He heard you were here and rolled in a few minutes ago. If you wanna have a sitdown with him right now, he's ready. Gunny's here. Fuck, boss, so is Deke. I saw Hoss headed upstairs, but Deke can sit in for him." Reaching up, Slate pulled at the back of his neck with his palm. "You sure about this, Prez?"

"Yeah. I've not found a single thing that says Fury's playin' us. In fact, all the info we've been able to gather points to him sharing details he didn't need to in order to gain our trust, which tells me he is all in on this thing. Him being patient is just the tip, man. Man's waited for nearly four months for a seat at a table with me, but he has not been idle. He's come in and set-up a backup plan, in case this goes south. He's letting me see he's doing it in a way that will make it easy to fold them in, because every single thing he's done is shit I would have approved had he been asking my opinion. Unselfish, dependable, dedicated to his brothers, and from the looks of things, tired of the bullshit Lalo and Chismoso have been pulling."

Mason reached out, putting his hands on the back of a chair, rolling his palms over the corners, smoothing the fabric with his fingers. Staring down at his hands, he stood for a minute thinking about the things Hoss had said about bringing danger to the threshold of the ones they loved then lifted his head. "We need brothers like that; we need to make sure we can hold what we have, Slate. Bring him in, and let's get this party started. Then I'll have some things to share with you. I suspect Bear's gonna be in before long, and I want to do a run with Hoss once he sleeps off his drunk."

Two hours later, he had found that not only did he respect Fury, he liked the motherfucker a lot. Every suggestion the man had was good, thoughtful in ways he needed his members and officers to be. Scoffing at himself for already thinking the officer route, he shook his head then laughed at the prospect who, startled at his physical reaction to the internal conversation, began pulling back the beer bottle he had held out. "Gimme the fucking beer, Pros," he said with a grin, accepting the again offered beer.

It would be tomorrow before they officially folded the Fort Wayne Diamante chapter into the Rebels, because Fury wouldn't do it without Hoss there. With a serious look that told Mason he wasn't entirely sure his suggestion wasn't going to piss off the national president, he still laid it out there that Hoss deserved to be part of it. He had put in the time, working the deal for months, and Fury wouldn't snub his backing in bringing them to where they were today.

Dedication. Commitment. Patience. Tipping the bottle to his lips, he was taking a long drink when raised voices at the door drew his attention.

Looking around, he saw several Fort Wayne members headed that way, including Slate, so he stayed where he was. When he saw it was Tyler, Bingo's oldest nephew, he straightened, thinking this could be bad news. With wild eyes, Tyler was glancing around the room and, upon spotting Jase, gave a shout, "I got it!"

Still unsure what that meant, Mason had just started walking towards the door when Jase returned the shout, "Told you, eh? You're good, boyo. Jesus Murphy, Ty, tourney team captain. Nicely done, son."

With a huff, Mason let out a breath he hadn't even been aware he was holding and gave Jase an easy smile, hearing Fury come up behind him.

There were three boys behind Tyler, two of which he knew, and one of those had eyes the same color as ones he saw in the mirror every day. With a grin, he greeted the boys, "Jonny, Kane, come on over here. Tyler, little man, congrats on the leadership role. Now you just have to earn it every day, yeah?" He heard Tyler's laughing response as he moved around Mason to Jase, chattering a mile a minute about all his plans for his team.

Putting one knee to the floor, he waited with outstretched arms for the two boys to come to him, surprised when they hung back. "No hugs for Uncle Mason?" That got them kickstarted and Kane nearly tackled him with the force of his attack, arms wrapping around Mason's neck. Jonny was only a little behind him, and as he often had in the past, stood a little back, giving Mason a chin lift before offering a wide grin and barreling into him. Grunting, Mason took the hit, wrapping one arm around each boy and lifting them as he stood.

Shifting his hold, he positioned them against his hips as if they were sacks of feed, securely cradling them to his sides. "Got me some boys," he roared, feeling as well as hearing the giggles from the two kids. Shaking them in place, he gave a half-spin, whirling in place until he saw the last boy again. With a chin lift, he told the little guy, "I'm Mason."

"You aren't going to hurt my friends, are you?" The blond kid had taken a step forward when he asked the question, eyes focused hard on Mason. "I can't let you hurt my friends."

"I ain't gonna hurt these taters," he said with a laugh, letting the still giggling boys slide down until their feet were again on the floor. "They're my best buds." He looked at the boy again, surprised at the tension carried in his shoulders and arms. *He's honestly afraid I'm gonna hurt the boys*, he thought with a start, and that took him to one knee again, putting himself at the boy's level.

"I ain't gonna hurt them. And, I won't hurt you. Won't let anyone hurt you, if I can stop it from happening." Glancing around, he saw most of the members had gathered around Jase and Tyler, but Deke was standing behind the boy, an uncertain expression on his face. "Who's kid is this?" *Shit.* He didn't mean the question to come out like that and hated seeing the boy recoil away as he did.

Deke stepped forward, resting a hand on the boy's shoulder and, surprising Mason, the boy didn't attempt to shift away, accepting the weight without flinching. Deke was familiar enough to the boy that he recognized him without looking. "This is Hope's boy, boss." Deke swallowed hard. "Mercy's sister, Hope. This is Sammy." *Fuck.* Hoss' boy.

Eyes darting around the room now, Sammy asked in an almost offhanded way, "Why would you care?" Then the boy's gaze came to rest on Mason, and he sucked in a breath at the burden of sorrow to be found there. This was a kid who had been hurt time and again until all he expected was pain and disappointment. *Fuck.* Hoss' boy.

"I care, because you belong to Hope, so you belong to us, 'cause she's ours, boy. But you already know this, dontcha? She's ours, makes you ours, too. Won't let anybody hurt you or your mom." Mason said this steadily, confidence in his words. "Like you were ready to protect your friends just now? These taters?" He reached out and ruffled Kane's hair, cupping a hand around Jonny's shoulder. "I will protect you."

At his words, the boy whirled and, without a sound, ran up the hallway to the outer door, hitting it hard enough on his way out that it rebounded shut with a loud crash. He stared at Deke, shaking his head, watching as Jonny and Kane wordlessly ran up the hallway and out of the building behind him.

17. I need beauty in my life

Mercy huffed, the sound of her frustration plain in his ear when she said, "No, Hossman. I love you, and you know it, but I am not going to talk to you about Hope."

Squeezing his eyes shut, he knew his tone was near to a growl when he said, "Just tell me she's fucking okay, Mercy. Jesus *fuck*, woman. It's not as if I'm asking you to rob a fucking bank."

"No, you're asking me to help you extend your pain, and I will not." Her words were quiet but hit the mark, and he dropped his head.

Pressing the phone tightly to his ear, he whispered, "Mercy, please. I just...please."

"Hoss, baby," she whispered back. "You gotta move on, sweetheart. The two of you agreed it wasn't good to continue, and you have to give her that now. You gotta move on, Hoss. She is—"

He interrupted her, his voice tight with strain, "What the fuck do you mean she's moving on?"

"Hoss." Her voice had become tentative, faltering, and he waited for her to continue.

When she didn't, he again said, "The fuck. You mean. She's moving on?" Silence from the phone. "Mercy. You telling me she's dating?" More silence. "Is that what you mean? She moving on with someone in particular? Are you fucking kidding me?"

"Hoss."

Now her repetition of his name was pissing him off, and he roared, "I fucking know my own name, Mercy. What I don't know is the fucking name of the fucking moron she's moving on with." Nothing. "Fuck this, and fuck you. Fuck Deke, too, if he knew this and didn't tell me." He was about to disconnect the call when he heard a whispered word, and he barked, "What?"

"Dickie Rupert. They're going to that steak place near the mall." Without another word, she disconnected the call, and he stared at the wall in front of him for a moment.

Dickie Rupert was a brother to Daniel, the man who married Mica. Mason's first love, who had gone to a citizen, because he didn't think she could handle a life in the club. Mason had drifted for a long time afterwards, riding the currents back and forth aimlessly, his sole focus the club. Then he met Willa, a woman he latched onto in a way that made it impossible to think of him before her without knowing it was needful, all his pain, all his loneliness—needful, because it brought him to her.

"I ain't Mason." He made this statement to the calm air in his room at the clubhouse. Ninety days. She was still living in his home, and he was here. Waiting, but for what? Waiting for her to remember she wanted him? Or... *No. Waiting for me to wake the fuck up and fight for what I want.* "I ain't Mason, and I ain't gonna let that fucking citizen waltz in and take what's mine. She ain't fucking moving on; she's fucking moved in, and I'm too fucking stupid to realize she's waiting for me to figure it out."

Taking a deep breath, he grabbed his jacket and slipped it on then strode out of the room and down the stairs, flipping a finger at the prospect behind the bar when he heard his name called hesitantly. "Ain't got time for shit. It's important, they can fucking find me."

Minutes later, he was sitting astraddle his bike's seat in the parking lot of the steakhouse, looking at the sea of cars. Pulling out his phone, he dialed, and then said, "No time for bullshit, Myron. Get me the make and number of Dickie Rupert's ride here in the Fort." At the club treasurer's question, he barked, "I said I didn't have time for fucking questions, man. Look the shit up. I know you got access to the BMV database."

It got quiet on the phone, and he said, "No time for bullshit, man. You can't help me, or won't help me? Tell me, and I'll move on my fucking way." A moment later, Myron was reciting information in his ear and he grunted his thanks, already scanning the lot to find the truck he was looking for parked on the edge of the lot. *Fuck*, he thought, *she's in there with him right now.*

Dismounting the bike, he walked to the door and opened it, ignoring the hostess when she squeaked a question at him. There Hope sat at the bar, back to him, but the golden fall of her hair was unmistakable, even in the low light of the restaurant. He stepped over to the bar and slid onto the empty stool next to her, seeing Dickie's eyes fixed on the TV in the corner, where a football game was on. The man wasn't paying attention to Hope, who wasn't paying attention to his lack of attention. Chin tucked down, she was talking to her wineglass, fingers twiddling with the stem as she spoke quietly, oblivious to her new audience.

"—day, I've regretted the things I said to him. Sammy looks at me and asks every morning, even now, three months down the road, asks me when Hoss is coming home. Calls it that, 'home,' not Hoss' house, but home, as if we belong there. I should have already moved out, but I can't bear the thought."

This couldn't be her first glass of wine; in fact, he suspected she was tipsy enough he would worry about putting her on the back of his bike right now. Pulling out his phone, he texted Hurley and told him to bring a cage, instructing him to park it in the lot near his bike and leave the keys behind the overhead visor. Slipping the phone back in his pocket, he dialed back in on Hope's conversation with herself.

"—to my door, and he was right, but I don't care anymore. I just...miss him." Picking up her glass, she drained it, nearly missing the bar when she went to set it down. "I love him."

Dickie looked over then reached out and patted her hand absently before glancing around the bar. His gaze locked on Hoss, and all the color fled his face when Hoss grinned at him, knowing his teeth showed in more of a snarl than a smile. Snatching his hand back, the man visibly swallowed then started to speak, "Hope—"

With a quick shake of his head, Hoss interrupted him and then tipped his head to the door. Dickie nodded and slipped off his stool, but before he walked away, he leaned close to say, "I'm sorry." Hoss wasn't sure if the words were directed at him or Hope, or what the sentiment was supposed to cover, but he gave the man a chin lift anyway.

Hope never blinked; lost in her thoughts, she kept staring at the now empty glass. Watching her closely, he flinched when she brutally bit her lips and then shook her head slightly, reaching out to turn the wineglass in random movements, back and forth. Pulling his wallet out, he threw some bills on the bar then turned to see a familiar car pulling into the lot as he shoved the wallet back into his pocket.

Taking a steadying breath, because he wasn't certain how she would react to him being there, Hoss leaned close, putting his lips near her ear to softly say, "Hope, baby." She jolted, but didn't look at him. Didn't raise her eyes from her fingers on the stem of the glass, but her lips parted and she breathed out his name like a wish, "Hoss."

"Baby. Let's get you home, yeah?" Holding his breath, he reached out and covered her hand with his, turning it so they rested palm-to-palm, and then he threaded his fingers through hers. "Home, baby." Standing, he tugged, and she came off the stool and on her feet, weaving in place for a moment, eyes still fixed on the glass.

"Hope," he called, and when her eyes finally lifted to his, he sucked in a breath at the dullness he saw there. Her chin quivered and her eyes filled with wet before she closed them, shutting off the sight of what he had done to her. "Baby," he said softly, cupping her cheek with one palm, thumb tracing across her lips. "I can't live without you, Hope. I need you, baby. Let me take you home, okay?"

She nodded and lifted her chin, eyes fluttering open as she looked at him again. Her mouth worked for a minute, but nothing came out, not until he leaned close, fingers sliding up into her hair and cradling her head into his neck. Then, mouth moving on his skin, he felt her lips pressing into him just before she said, "Please, don't wake me up. Please, oh, God. Please. Don't wake me."

"Hush, baby," he whispered, lifting their joined hands between them, resting them against his chest. "Home."

Helping her into her coat, they stood like that for a minute, and he wondered what was going through her mind, wondered if she was too drunk for this to be real. Wondered as she did, for a moment, if this was a dream. Taking in a breath when she softly said, "Not a dream," realizing he had spoken aloud.

Pulling her into his side, he slipped an arm around her waist, prepared to hold her up if needed, but she walked steadily towards the door. He saw Hurley climbing on the back of Tequila's bike and laughed silently, wondering why the prospect agreed to ride bitch, but glad he at least thought of getting a ride back to the clubhouse, because he would have driven away and left the man standing in the lot before putting him in the car with Hope.

She started angling towards his bike and he steered her to the car, lifting a hand in a brief wave at Tequila. He saw his brother had a broad grin on his face as he rode away, Hurley leaning as far away from him as was possible on the small seat without falling off the bike, scarf over his nose and mouth, gloved hands tightly clutching the back of the seat for dear life.

"Here, baby," he said, opening the car door and holding her hand as she settled into the seat. He leaned in, pulling her seatbelt across and latching it, turning to see her face only inches away, a look of amazement on her features. "Hope," he breathed, and then her mouth hit his, hungry and hot, her tongue sliding across his bottom lip. "Goddamn, baby," he murmured against her lips. "You want me, Mama?"

"Mmhmm." She made a noise deep in her throat and he let go the control he was holding a little bit, kissing her back, taking over, working at her mouth until their breath came hard and ragged, loud in the silence of the car. Pulling away, he saw a small smile on her face and leaned in, brushing her lips with his a final time.

"Let's get you home, baby," he whispered, straightening and closing her door to walk around and climb inside. Once he did, he shifted to look at her, asking, "Hope, where's Sammy?"

"Home," she said softly, turning her head to lean it against the back of the car seat, her gaze trained on him.

"Sam is at home?" *Thank fuck*, he thought, *I don't have to stop somewhere and pick him up.*

"Yep, he's at home. Hoss' house, but our home." The corners of her mouth tipped up and he smiled at her, working the gearshift and clutch to move through traffic quickly.

She reached out and laid a hand on his leg, fingers curling around the inner curve of his muscled thigh as he operated the pedals. *Fuck.* She was drunk, had to be, and there wasn't any way he would do anything to fuck up this second chance, not even if she pushed him.

"Hope, honey, how much did you have to drink?" She made a humming noise as he worked the clutch again, powering through a turn. *Nearly home*, he thought, and then her hand was sliding up his leg, heat burning him through the fabric of his jeans. "Hope, no. Wait, baby." *Goddammit.* "Hope." Fingernails scraped across his zipper, trailing along the ridges of his already stiff cock, and he reached down, moving her hand back down to his knee. *Fuck.* "No, baby. Wait."

Turning into the gate, he rolled down his window and lifted a hand at the guard on duty tonight. Seeing a car he didn't know parked in front of his house, he asked, "Hope, who's with Sammy?"

"Luce," she said and smiled wide. "I like Lucia; she's sweet. She's sweet on Benny, too. Luce and Benny. Bear will have him in a full-body cast if he tries anything, though. I heard Benny say so the other day. Luce's been babysitting Sasha since Eddie went back to work. Bear'd have that darlin' little girl in a papoose and carry her everywhere if Eddie let him." She giggled, her voice low and rich, and he groaned at the sound.

Her head lolled a little when he turned the car into his drive, and she grinned at him again. "Deke wants Mercy to go off the pill. Isn't that sweet? Mercy and Deke having a cute, little, baby Deke? Sweet."

Setting the emergency brake as he killed the engine, he told her, "Sit tight, baby. Let me come around and help you out."

"All right," she sang, her voice lilting sweetly. Turning, she looked at the house then up at Hoss when he opened her door. "Where's my car?"

"In the garage, ain't it?" He pulled her from the vehicle, tucking her against his side as she wavered.

"Not unless you're magic." She giggled, her voice again dipping into that rich tone of pleasure that raised every hair on his body in response. "Poof. Magic Hossman." She giggled again. "I didn't plan on drinking, so I drove tonight."

"Dickie rode with you?" Now he was confused, because he had seen the douchecanoe's truck in the lot.

"No, silly. He met me there. I wanted to have…" Her voice trailed off, and her face lost the look of humor it wore, the smile sliding away as her lips pressed together. "Since…" She sighed. "I didn't want to have to depend on…so my car, my out." Shrugging, she stumbled, and he tightened his arm around her as they walked to the front door.

The instant the boy caught sight of him with his arm around Hope, Hoss realized he hadn't begun to prepare for this, and the pained and frightened look on Sam's face underscored his devastating lack of foresight. Up to that point, he had only been glad Sammy was already safe at home, that he was taking Hope home, a sweet and tipsy Hope, who had not only forgiven him and confessed to herself she loved him, but had initiated a hot, deep kiss, hinting at the night to come.

Now, seeing the color blanch from Sam's features, his mind began turning in futile circles, looking for something to say that wouldn't come across as calloused or make him out to be a bigger asshole than he already knew himself to be, making and breaking promises with only days between. Without a word, the boy's chin slowly rose until he was looking at Hoss over his cheekbones, glass lenses glinting in the overhead lighting. Sam's hands involuntarily clenched into balls, shoulders thrust back—preparing for a hit or a fight, it was hard to tell. Whatever Hoss could have found to say was derailed by Hope, however, as she called, "Bud, look who found me! Hossman is home, baby."

Her fingers tightened on his and he wondered if some of the buzz from her wine was falling away, because she seemed much steadier on her feet. A little of the tension left Sammy's frame, and when Hoss knelt, even more bled away as Hope began leaning into him, fingers idly trailing through his hair. "Hey, Sam," he said quietly, flicking his gaze to Lucia sitting, a silent witness on the couch, and then back to the boy.

"You promised." The whisper was so soft he read the boy's lips as much as heard the words, and his emotions at that moment had him silent and frozen in place. "You promised, and then you lied. You said the words, said you'd work." Drawing in a rough, hitching breath, Sammy sighed and then repeated, "You promised no lies." On a whisper he repeated, "No lies."

"And this is me keeping that promise." Hoss' voice was low and surprise at his words twisted Hope's fingers in his hair. "Love you, boy. Love your mom. Love Mama." He paused, because there was a painful slipping feeling in his chest, like his bones had suddenly gotten three sizes too small, clenching down on his heart. "This is me telling you I didn't lie, and this is me showing you and Mama I'm here for the long run. Putting in the time, doing the work, making things right. Because I love you both. Can't live without you, son. Love you both."

As he spoke, the pain flashing across the small boy's face nearly killed him, but by the time his words finished echoing through the room, Sammy had already flung himself at Hoss. The boy's last steps a flight through the air, landing against Hoss' chest with a heavy thud. Launched himself, because he knew Hoss would catch him.

Trust and belief like nothing he had ever experienced, and Hoss found himself happily knocked on his ass in the living room of his home, one arm holding the small boy who had just let him in, and one arm around the hips of the woman who had delivered them both into life.

***

Several hours later, a definitely un-tipsy Hope was curled up beside him in his bed dressed in one of his tees. Feet towards the headboard and eyes on his face, she was resting her cheek on his stomach, barely north of his hips, her hair draping across his thighs.

Hoss was trying studiously to ignore his hard-on, clearly visible beyond her head as a developing bulge in the sheet covering him to the waist, and painfully present in the throbbing in his cock and balls. Holding her hand in his, he slowly stroked across and down the back of each finger, up over the knuckle and then down the back of the next, methodically moving from pinky to pointer, then back again. He would never again take for granted the ability to touch her, to hold her, to love her.

He paused for a moment on her ring finger, thinking about Mason's words to him from a couple of weeks back. 'I get it now, understand what would pull a man to mark a woman as his own.' *I get it too*, he thought, and then dragged his attention back to what Hope was saying.

Not meeting his eyes, she was trying to explain everything that went through her head over the past three months and more. From her side of the fence, she had struggled with her emotions being all tangled up by having him pay attention to her a few times, and liking that notice from him, wanting to please him, but finding everything broken and torn down by periods of absence in between. No time for trust to build, because he seemed to run so hot and cold.

Then things had become intense for a few days, with their bike ride and first encounter in the park. The time they spent in his home, making love...then that attention reverting again to nothing at all for weeks, a silence during which she convinced herself that she could never be what he needed. Then he reappeared, and she and Sammy both were installed in his life and house not even forty-eight hours before that door suddenly slammed again. Everything she said pointed at self-doubt and a twisted belief that she wasn't worthy. At nearly every turn, she was trying to pull the blame blanket high on her shoulders, taking it on herself when he knew the real score.

"Hope...hush, baby," he said gently, giving her hand a shake. Clamping her lips closed, she lifted her gaze to meet his, eyes swimming behind unshed tears. *Fuck.* "You. Did. Nothing. Wrong." Arching his eyebrows for emphasis, he repeated his words, "Seriously, baby. You didn't do anything wrong. Nothing." The look on her face as she turned away ripped through him, and he could see she wasn't hearing him, couldn't believe him…so he decided to try a different tact.

"You love me?" He kept his fingers moving slow and steady over the back of her hand, eyes to her face, so when she cut her gaze up to look at him, he caught and held it. "Hope, baby, do you love me?" She pulled in a quick sobbing breath, and then like silk, her hair moved across his skin as she nodded. "I love you, too." When she opened her mouth to speak, he cut her off, shaking his head. "That's the truth, baby." Gripping her hand a little tighter, he told her, "No lies."

I need to let her in, he thought, and found the place in their joined past where, for him, everything began. "I ever tell you what I thought about the first time I saw you with Sammy?" Tilting his head, he grinned at the puzzled look on her face.

"I don't think so. Do you mean that first night when I came to Slinky's? When I was looking for Mercy?"

He was glad to hear her voice was low but steady. "Yeah. Mercy had to run back inside, and you squatted down to talk to Sammy about what was happening next." He gave her hand a squeeze and then jackknifed to a sitting position, pulling a pillow from behind his back to push under her head. Laughing at the confused look on her face, now beyond puzzled, he kissed her cheek and said, "Back in a sec, baby."

A few minutes later, he walked into the room to find she had rolled to her back and was staring up at the ceiling. Lifting her arm, she pointed to a section of ceiling over the window. "Every few seconds there's a rainbow reflected up there. How is that possible at night? I can't figure out where it comes from."

He carefully set the canvas he was carrying by the wall and lay down next to her, reaching into the space between them to capture her hand in his. "Crystals," he said softly.

"I thought those needed sunlight to cast a rainbow."

"I have several hanging from the rafter ends outside. Some are positioned for sunshine, so when there aren't any clouds, the room fairly lights up with the reflections." The rainbow flashed again and he grinned. "Some are set-up for the security lights, so I can have the rainbows even at night. When the wind blows, even at night sometimes you can catch a dozen or more flashing across the room."

"Why would you do that? You said you didn't bring women back to your house."

Twisting his neck, he looked at her. Now he was the one puzzled, because visitors and beauty didn't line up in his book. "I don't. So?"

"Who did you do this for then?"

Turning to look back up at the ceiling, he waited for another flash before softly telling her, "Me. I need beauty in my life, need enough of it to balance out all the darkness and pain I see. This is a small thing, but it pleases me to see it before I go to sleep."

Twisting to lay on his side facing her, he reached out his hand and swept the hair back from her face. "Like it pleases me to see you, baby." Tracing the bridge of her nose with his fingertip, he said, "The first time I ever saw you, my initial impression was of beauty and light...endless golden beauty and brilliant light. Then you squatted down next to Sammy and pulled him into your arms, holding him so tightly, engulfing him with your love. I thought you looked like a momma chickadee on a branch, her wings out to cover her chicks and keep them from harm."

Sitting on the edge of the bed, he reached out to the nightstand and picked up the framed picture of Hope between Mercy and Sammy from that first night. Lying back down, he held it up so they both could see it. "Then Mercy sent me this, and it reinforced those feelings. Seeing you sandwiched between them, covering both of them with your love. Momma chickadee."

He handed her the frame and levered himself off the bed. "It took me a month, but I finally captured that essence. I called it *Mama*. Just *Mama*, because the caring and sweetness shone through, as it does with you." Picking up the canvas from where it leaned against the wall, he turned it around and looked at the painting again, feeling a strong satisfaction in his chest from the goodness and light the work brought into the world.

Turning the picture, he wasn't prepared for her reaction. Instead of commenting on his use of light or shading, or even the composition of the piece, after looking at the painting for several quiet moments, she burst into tears. Carelessly, he dropped the stretched canvas on the floor and lowered himself to the bed, pulling her into his arms. "Baby," he crooned. "Oh, sweetheart, what's wrong?"

"Is that how you see me?" Her question was muffled, her face pressed deeply into the crook of his neck.

"Strong and beautiful, protective? Yes, baby. I see you exactly like that. Momma chickadee on a branch, daring the world to come and threaten her chick." He stroked her hair then, twining his fingers at the back of her head, he used his hold to tilt her face up, kissing her lips softly. "Yes, baby."

"It's so beautiful." She sighed, moving to bury her face in his neck. "How can you see me like that, when all I do is let people down?"

"You see the face of that boy you tucked into bed an hour ago? Did he look like you've let him down, ever?" He started to move, and she made a complaining noise, shoving her face deeper into the crook of his neck so he wrapped his arms around her, holding her tighter. "You didn't. You haven't, baby. You've done the best you know how, every step along the way. Putting him first, like a good momma would, even when it meant you and I were miserable." When she gave a hitching sob at his words, he stroked her back, whispering, "Hush, Hope. We're going to figure this out. Me and you, baby."

He continued to run his hands up and down her back, soothing her with touch and words, repeating his confidence in her, faith in her love, trust in the truth of their relationship. As he fell asleep, hours after she did, the last coherent thought he had was a soft pleasure his family was home in time for Christmas.

18. Responsibilities weigh heavy

"But school's on a two-week break," Sam spoke into the phone, his tone aggravated. "Why can't you come over to play?"

"DeeDee said there's a party at the clubhouse this weekend and we all have to go, so I'll see you then." Jonny's tone was no less aggravated and Sam grinned. Going to the same school had cemented their fast friendship, and having parents and caregivers who were friends meant they normally spent part of nearly every day in the other's company. "Bingo's going back to the hospital, so they have a bunch of stuff to take care of, and Kane don't want to leave him right now."

Oh crap, he thought, remembering how sick Uncle Bingo looked the last time he saw him. "He's going to be okay, right?"

Jonny took in a heavy breath, blowing it back out before responding in a soft voice, "I don't think so, Sam. Jase talked to me and Tyler and Megan yesterday about helping the kids. It sounds bad." He took another breath before saying seriously, "I saw Mason today, too."

Sam sucked in a breath. They were convinced that when Mason came to town for days and days things were fine, but if he only came back to town to stay for a day, that's when things were going wrong.

Something he and Jonny had noticed months ago, so they had started using the man's presence as a barometer of sorts for trouble. It made the first day of Mason's visit nerve-racking every time as they waited to see if he would stay or go. "Don't mean anything. Maybe he's staying. Don't gotta be a fast trip."

"I hope so. I hope he's stayin'. DeeDee said he and Miss Willa made a baby. He's going to want to be the dad, you know it." Jonny sounded hopeful.

Sammy cleared his throat from the sudden thick feeling that settled there and said, "It's holidays. He could be here to see Miss Willa 'cause it's holidays and 'cause they made a baby. That would mean he'd stay a long time. The longest."

"True, but Bingo looks bad."

They sat in silence for a minute and Sam could hear the background noise on the other end of the phone. Jonny's house never seemed quiet, not like it was here at Hoss' home. "Let me talk to Mom, see if she can call Aunt DeeDee. Maybe you can come over, and we can have a sleepover after the party." He tilted his head, looking down at his toes scrunching in the carpet. "You and Tyler both. He's going to have a harder time than even Kane if something's wrong with Uncle Bingo. It wasn't long ago he was talkin' and rememberin' about being sick himself."

"Yeah, okay." Jonny made a noise and Sam laughed. Jonny asked, "What?"

"Sounded like you were trying to fart and whistle. A fartistle." Both boys laughed hard for a minute, the sounds of their humor slowly trailing off until Sam said, "Best fartistle I ever heard," driving them both into additional peals of laughter.

"Sam," he heard Mom calling him from the kitchen, so he told his bestest best friend, "I gotta go, Jon boy. Mom's callin' me."

"All right." He heard the goodbye in the tone, so his finger was already moving towards the disconnect button when he heard Jonny say, voice tinny through the speaker now that it wasn't against his ear, "Sam?"

Knowing Jonny wouldn't be extending the call for grins, he put the phone back to his head and said, "Yeah?"

"I wish we was brothers."

"Me, too, Jonny," he said softly, and then grinned. "If you want, I can loan you my mom anytime. She's awesome."

He shrieked as he was lifted into the air, an arm around his middle holding him then turning him upside down. Scrambling to hold onto the phone, he giggled hard as he heard his mom ask, laughter light in her voice, "Who are you renting me out to this time, boychild?"

"I gotta go, Jonny," he called, finger tapping all around the red button as he wiggled to get out of her grip, hearing the laughter on the other end of the phone even over his own.

***

"Go get in the car, Sam." *Oh, poop*, he knew that tone. It was the 'holy crap I can't believe you just did that' tone, but this time it wasn't directed at him, but at Aunt DeeDee. *Aunt DeeDee.*

"Yes, ma'am," he said quietly then paused. "Can Jonny and Tyler still—"

"I said to go ahead and get in the car, Samuel. I'll be there in a minute." Her tone hadn't changed. If anything, it sounded more like that skim of ice frozen on top of puddles in early winter up here, crackling noisily underfoot as it broke into brittle, ruined splinters. *Poop, poop, poop.*

"Yes, ma'am," he repeated, cutting his gaze up at Aunt DeeDee, seeing how white her face had gone. She knew Mom was mad, too, but didn't seem to know what to say. *Poop.* As he walked out of the room, he saw Mom's hand was on Aunt Mercy's wrist, fingers clamped tightly, holding her in place behind Mom's body, saw the tears in Aunt Mercy's eyes.

Poop. He had to do something. Walking up the hallway, he muttered to himself, "I am going to the car, just not straight." Unsuccessfully trying to convince himself this wasn't disobeying, he turned and zigged quickly into the kitchen, zagging out the backdoor to where the men were gathered around a big bonfire, hats tugged low against the cold. *Poop.*

Scanning the area, he saw Hoss standing, beer in hand, talking to Mason—*Bringer of Trouble*—and Uncle Deke. Hearing the voices now raised in the building behind him, he sprang into a full run, calling loudly, "Hoss. Hossman!"

Strong arms gripped his waist and swung him up, letting him rest his legs on either side of Hoss' hip. "Hey there, Sammy. What's up, little man?" Hoss asked, and without thinking twice, Sam reached out and cupped his palm over Hoss' cheek.

"No lies," he whispered, and his gut lurched when Hoss suddenly stilled and focused entirely on him. "Mommy's doing something bad."

"What do you mean, Sam. What's Mama doin'?" Hoss' voice rumbled in his chest, and the tone was still soft, but he sensed a tension that hadn't been present before.

"She's mad at Aunt DeeDee, and Aunt Mercy is cryin'," he whispered. "Mommy told me to go to the car."

"Fuck," he heard Uncle Deke say, and then Hoss was setting him back on his feet, telling him, "Go do what Mama said. Go on to the car, son. We'll be there in a bit."

***

Hoss walked into the clubhouse, not knowing exactly what he would find, but given Sam's warning, not entirely surprised Hope was on her feet, facing down nearly every old lady in the room. He had come in quickly and so caught the tail of what she was saying. "—and if you think you can sit there and talk to my sister like she's trash, then you have another think coming, because I won't stand for it.

"If any of you has never made mistakes, have never looked back on any past actions with dismay or even disgust, then fine; you can throw stones. But you need to have a care where you toss them, because it could be your own glass house destroyed." She sucked in a breath, paused when she saw him, and then shook her head and continued as Deke pushed past, pulling a sobbing Mercy into his arms.

"Has Mercy done things she's sorry for? Yes." She nodded, swinging her head to look around the room. "Has she paid for her behavior, has she changed things, made restitution where she could? Also, yes. Are there things she did for which there is no excuse? Sadly, yes. But, she does not deserve to have it all thrown in her face again and again." She pointed at Ruby then at DeeDee. "I might expect this kind of condemnation from women who've had charmed lives, but not one of us in this room has come through life unscathed. Some of us," she gestured at herself, "more damaged than others.

"I would never look down on you for decisions you make, not when I don't have any kind of window into your heads. When I have no way of assessing the pieces and parts that went into the choices with which you've been presented. When I don't know your families, or any past shame anchoring you on paths that, a year or two down the road, you will soundly regret. I. Would. Never. But, yet, you do, and you are. Shame on you."

She swung to look at DeeDee again. "You asked me once why she didn't come to your house? This"—she flung a hand out at the hen's party along the wall—"is why. This kind of painful and raw raking over the coals, again, and again, and again."

She looked at Eddie. "You made me feel safe enough to tell you the things I did to ensure Sammy and I stayed together. Was I wrong?" Hoss took the last step to place himself behind her, telling everyone in the room—her, the women, and the men piling in the door—that he had her back. Putting his hand on her hip, he pulled her back into his chest, securing her there with an arm around her waist.

Without turning, she said, "Hoss, can you take me home? I think I've outstayed my welcome."

Before he could move a muscle, he heard Mason say, humor threaded through his voice, "Fuck no. You ain't going anywhere, woman."

Fuck.

Hope tensed in his arms and, voice pitched low, Hoss carefully said, "Prez, now might not be—"

"Hope Annabelle Collins." Humor gone, Mason called loudly, ignoring him, and Hope jolted at his use of her full name. "You know what being on the back of Hoss' bike means? Do you understand the full ramifications of that act? He's my veep here in the Fort. You get what it means to be his woman?"

"I...I..." she stuttered self-consciously, and he saw Mason shake his head.

"Didn't think so," Hoss heard, and immediately expected to be verbally blasted. Because her behavior reflected on him, his failure to make sure she understood the place granted to her in the club based on their relationship could be huge.

Mason shocked him by saying gently, "Not surprised, hon. Things have been so unsettled since before you even got into town I'm surprised Hoss has had time to talk you into stayin' with his rank ass, instead of haulin' it back south as fast as you can to escape. That's my fault, more than anything, because I depend on this man. More than he knows, I depend on him.

"Let me explain a bit. You with me? You listenin' to me, Hope?" Mason was staring at her, and he waited patiently until she gave a quick nod. "You bein' with Hoss means you have a right to have your voice heard. Veep's old lady's voice carries weight, and that weight means responsibility. Means you have an obligation to protect everyone owned by the club. Like my old lady"—he reached out a hand to the side, but didn't pause his words—"or your sister, or any woman who cleans the bar or strip joint.

"No matter from what, or who, whether it's internal or external pressures or danger. This is your burden, woman. Your charge. Means you have the back of every woman in this room, including if having her back means pitching that weight against other old ladies to get shit sorted out. To keep families strong, making it so brothers don't have to square off against brothers."

Willa's hand met Mason's, and he pulled her into him. "Looks to me like you're doing fine, Hope. You'll find your place, and I expect no less of an effort than I saw tonight, you hear?"

He watched as Mason's gaze raked the group, settling on someone behind where Hoss stood, near the outer door. "Come here, Sam."

Letting go of Hope's hip, Hoss reached out his hand, not surprised at all when a small, warm one grabbed hold. Tilting to look down, he saw Sam's attention was firmly on Mason. With a squeeze, he let Sam know he had him, no matter what, pleased when he got a glance upwards and a small smile. Then Sam's attention was back on Mason, even as he gave Hoss a return squeeze.

"Good enough," Mason said, laughter once again evident in his tone. Hoss looked back up to see Willa tight against Mason's side, her arm around his waist. Lights glinted off the rings on her finger, her other hand moved to protectively cover the rounded belly protruding from below her breasts.

A quick vision of Hope's naked finger flashed, and then he focused on his president, who had started speaking again. "I'm not going to tolerate any kind of shit towards any old lady, or anyone owned by this club. Not a whit of it's allowed. Everyone under this roof, and under my patch, is under my protection."

Winking at Sam, he said, "Ain't that so, Sam?"

Hoss looked down to find Sam nodding slowly then was surprised when the boy spoke up, agreeing with Mason. "It's the right thing to do, protecting the ones we love."

"That's right," Mason agreed readily, turning to look at every member and their families gathered in the main room. "We protect the ones we love. Our old ladies"—He gave Willa a squeeze and she grinned up at him until he swooped down to kiss her hard. Lifting his head, he continued—"Our club, our families, and our brothers. Rebels forever—"

"—forever Rebels." The shout came from every corner of the room. Before the echoes faded away, Hoss met Mason's gaze, giving him a chin lift of thanks that was returned before Prez lowered his face to his woman again.

19. Gone

Distractedly, Hope pushed the hair out of her face with the back of her wrist and then answered the phone, "Hello?" She was seated on the floor of the bathroom, leaning against the wall, one shaking hand holding the toilet lid open while the other held the phone.

"Issues, honey?" Hope frowned at Jase's question, because it didn't make sense. She thought to herself, *How would he know I have the flu?*

"Huh?" Head pounding, more complicated words were beyond her right now. Throw in the way her stomach was roiling, threatening to toss back the ham and cheese omelet she had eaten this morning, and she was not going to hold up her end of any conversation very well.

"I gots an empty spot in my lineup today where there should be a small, but mighty Samboni. Did you need one of us to pick Sammy up for practice? Tyler is standing in the doorway with keys in hand, totally itching for a reason to drive again today." His tone was gently joking, but she knew behind that was a disappointment, because one of his boys had deked out of practice.

"Did the bus not drop him off? It's Thursday, right? I didn't get my days mixed up?" That was the regular routine on Tuesdays and

Thursdays, when he had practice after school. On Wednesdays, he rode the bus to the Foundation offices too, but it was because she was working, and he would ride home with her from there. Mondays and Fridays she picked him up outside the elementary school building, and they would go shopping, or head to the library for a homework session. If the weather cooperated, sometimes they would hit up a park before going home. *Home*, she thought with a smile before her stomach rolled again. Tipping her head back against the wall, she blew out a steady stream of air and closed her eyes.

"Yeppers, Thursday all day, unless it's snowing, in which case it's Snowy Thursday. We thought maybe he was sick. Hoss said you had a stomach thing yesterday, so DeeDee and I were watching the kiddos to see if they'd come down with it, too." Sick kids meant no visiting Bingo in hospice, so she was glad Hoss thought to mention it to them. Jase couldn't see her, so he didn't know how his next words hit her, striking like a blow. "Jonny said Sam wasn't on the bus. Said he hadn't seen him since lunchtime."

The two boys had nearly every class together. In their grade, they didn't actually change classrooms, except for non-academic things like band and art. Thursday was art, which Sam had, but Jonny didn't, but that was before lunch. Her voice came out as a broken wheeze as her stomach rolled again, "Since lunchtime?"

His tone now cautious, Jase asked, "Hope, did you pick Sammy up from school today?"

Shaking her head, she struggled up off the floor onto her knees, and immediately tossed the phone to the floor as her stomach decided movement was the worst thing ever and she bent double over the toilet bowl, retching again and again.

By the time she was spent, the call had disconnected and she didn't blame him, because noisy vomiting wasn't high on her list of things to listen to, either. Then, with a sense of panic, she remembered his question, the cause of her movement. She had scooped up the phone and was attempting to stagger to her feet just as Hoss called from the front of the house, "Hope, baby? Jase called, said you were pukin'. You okay?"

Did you pick Sammy up from school today? Shaking her head, she ran water and bent over to slurp up a big mouthful, swished and spit it into the toilet, flushing it again. "Hoss, did you pick Sammy up today?" she called, thinking to herself if he had and hadn't told her beforehand, if she could summon the energy, she might need to be pissed.

He was in the doorway when she straightened, shaking his head. "Baby, you know I'd clear that with you first." And she did, he was that kind of thoughtful. Her gaze locked on his and she whispered, "Jonny told Jase he hasn't seen Sammy since lunchtime."

"Call the school," Hoss said straightaway, and then repeated himself, "Call the school, baby."

***

"I don't know," she half yelled, half groaned, twisting in Hoss' arms and lunging back to where she had set the small trashcan down, heaving again.

"Think, Hope," Gunny urged, ignoring her illness, thumbs beating out an irritatingly loud rhythm on the edge of the table, even as she gagged miserably. "You drove him to school and dropped him off at the end of the block?"

Hoss had called him as soon as Hope was off the phone with the school. They were still waiting for a call back from the district superintendent, but records indicated someone had signed Sammy out of school at lunchtime. She hadn't been able to get ahold of Mercy, but she and DeeDee had called everyone else they could think of. They were expecting to find Mercy had picked him up for something, but Hoss wanted to make sure they covered all their bases, just in case.

man like he was with Sharon and their daughter. Gunny continued, "Hoss, man. Any chance she's caught?"

Shaking his head, Hoss tried to decipher Gunny's southern Louisiana saying, but failed. "Caught what? The flu? Yeah, she's been puking for a couple days."

"No, brother. Caught pregnant."

Hoss scoffed, but then realized Gunny wasn't kidding. "Unlikely, man. I'm religious about wrapping my shit up. Especially given her history of running as soon as things roll off dicey. You heard her call it in there; Sammy's our son. Love that boy like he is my own, but I'm not looking to add to our little family."

Even as he said the words, he knew it was a lie. Bald-faced and painful, and a lie. Since nearly the first time he saw her, he had wanted Hope carrying his baby, their baby. But, when he broached the subject with her over the past two months they had been back together, she had shut him down. Every time, shut him down. That hurt too badly to admit, even to these men.

"Brother—" Gunny started, but Mason cut him off.

"I'm seeing the same thing he is, brother. Is there any chance she's expecting?"

Hoss stared at Mason like he had lost his mind. "One time. In September. Back five fucking months ago, I rode her bare. Woke her up with my mouth and hands; hot, willing…wanting. Softest, sweetest, tightest…best. Been denyin' myself since, so, yeah…I'm pretty sure, Prez." He shook his head, fighting down the urge to lash out. "Now, anyone want to tell me why you think we ain't found anything yet?"

20. Spider monkey

Sam sat in the rear seat of the big car, staring at the back of the head of the man driving. Several times he had tried to come up with something to say, but the words kept running out of his head before he could open his mouth. Lifting his hand, he gingerly used the fingertips to poke and prod at his right cheek and the bone above his eye. He had seen the bruise in the mirror of the motel bathroom this morning, and knew why the man made him sit on this side of the car today, so no one would notice his huge raccoon black eye. *I'm half a bandit*, he thought bleakly.

The music snapped off and he tensed, leaning slightly to the right in order to use the mirror on the windshield to see the man's face. Sam had seen the sign for Alabama about an hour ago, and had begun to wonder obsessively about what would happen when they reached Birmingham. *Maybe I'm gonna find out. Maybe he's gonna tell me*, he thought, and then grimaced when the man's voice filled the car.

"Nearly home, son," Calhoun Suiter said, looking at him in the mirror with a grin. Sam didn't like his smiles, because they were frighteningly fake, his stiff upper lip barely lifting to show part of his teeth, but the rest of his mouth never moved. His eyes never smiled, either, but he had found yesterday that when his father frowned, when he was displeased, then everything about the man got involved. When he scowled, it was as if the anger was pushing out from inside him, drawing everything tight in its wake.

Without meaning to, Sam responded, heard his voice ringing in the car and immediately wanted to take it back, but was also really glad he said the words. That he told the man he didn't matter. With everything he and Jonny had talked through about Hoss, the thing Sammy held on to was how good Hoss was. Sam wanted to be good, too. "I'm not your son," he yelled again, and then was dodging back against the seat and the door when the man's large hand swung blindly backwards, thrashing back and forth, mindlessly seeking to connect with a target frantically on the move.

With grunts accompanying his exertion, Suiter ground out, "My fucking kid." He swung back, missing Sam's face by bare inches, the breeze from the force of the blow the only thing to touch his skin. Knuckles cracked hard against the window, the sound loud and shocking in the enclosed space.

"My boy." Another grunt and a swing, this one finding its mark, snapping Sam's head to the side as the knuckles on the back of Suiter's open hand connected right over the existing bruise. Sammy cried out, clapping his hand to his face and pressing back into the seat harder. "Took you." Swing and another hit, this one on his forearm, less painful, but still enough to knock him sideways into the door, where his head hit the window hard. "My own mother won't talk to me, because"—swing and miss—"my boy's mother fucking took him out of"—swing and hit—"state."

Dazed, Sammy didn't register Suiter had gone quiet, that he had stopped reaching to hit him, didn't know the car was slowing until he heard Suiter's disbelieving voice asking the silent interior of the car, "What the fuck is this shit?"

Looking out the window, Sam's eyes widened when his gaze caught on the mass of bikers who were surrounding the car on the highway, pressing close to the side of the vehicle, the rumble of the bikes suddenly loud, wrapping around him with familiar comfort. Eyes darting back and forth, relief sprang to life inside him, even when he didn't recognize any faces. These bikers didn't hold any fear for him. After living with Hoss for so long—*Hoss is my home,* his brain supplied—these men didn't frighten him like Suiter did.

A big man with long hair pulled back into a ponytail gave him a thumbs up, mouthing the words, *You okay?* Sam nodded and reflexively touched his cheek. The man stared and then scowled, turning his head and yelling something at the men riding around him. Heart racing as he looked around, Sam saw there were bikes on only three sides of the car. They had left the passenger side open and were forcing them onto the shoulder, the bikes in front steadily slowing down, making Suiter stop the car.

Before the car even came to a halt, the door beside Sam was yanked open, and the man with the ponytail leaned in, a long necklace dropping out of his vest as he bent forward, and his hands unclipped Sam's seatbelt. As he worked the latch, Sam looked up, catching Suiter's eyes in the mirror for a final time. His mouth, again moving without conscious volition, yelled, "I'm not your son. I belong to Hoss. *Hoss* and *Mommy.* I belong to Hoss!"

"Kiddo, cool it," the man muttered, hands shoving under Sam's armpits and pulling him from the car. "I heard ya, man. Chill. Right in my fucking ear, I heard ya. You belong to Hossman. I get you. Fam, dig it." Swinging him high, the man said, "Arms around my neck, kiddo."

There was a shout from beside them, and Sam turned to see a bunch of the men had gotten Suiter out of the car. He was yelling, his face red and ugly, angry-looking as he shoved at the chest of one of the men surrounding him, only managing to propel himself backwards when the man didn't move. Suiter nearly lost his footing, stumbling into the grass at the side of the road.

"Kiddo, eyes on me, dig? I'm Retro, and I guess you already get I'm a friend of Hossman's. He called, asked me to pick you up. Said you might be needing a ride."

Turning to look up at the man, Retro, Sam nodded. He wasn't afraid, not exactly. Certainly not as afraid as he had been for the past two days, but these men were strangers—*stranger danger,* his brain hissed—so hearing Hoss' name helped to settle the bit of fear he did have. "Is my mommy okay?" His throat had tightened so much he could hardly force the words out. "He said..." He pulled in a breath then another. "He said he would hurt her."

"Your mom's fine, Sam. I was told to make sure you knew she was fine. Your mom said you have a word, right? I'm supposed to say 'Samboni.' Now I don't understand what the hell it means," he grinned at Sam, and then winced along with Sam when the answering grin hurt his face, "but clearly you do, and that's good. Samboni, got it?"

Sam nodded, eyes fixed on Retro's face, thinking he looked like someone he knew. "See, your mom and Hoss, they figured out it had to be something like that. Something like that kind of lie would be the only reason you'd go with this ballsac. Lemme see that face, kiddo." Retro sounded angry at the end, and Sam obediently lifted his chin, letting the man scrutinize his cheek. "Fuck, little man, you need some ice. Little dude, that's not cool, him hitting you like that."

Sam shook his head, and then said, "His mommy hit me once. I bet she hit him a lot."

"Fuck," Retro hissed then continued walking towards a group of parked bikes, still carrying Sam. "I ain't got a lid for you, Sam, so we're going to have to ride super safe to get you home to your mommy. I bet she never hits you, does she?" Sammy shook his head, and then looked down at the necklace Retro wore. The necklace had a heavy silver ring threaded onto the chain, which swung back and forth as he walked, keeping time like a heartbeat.

He tipped sideways so far Sammy clutched at the shirt under his vest. Then Retro straddled one of the bikes that had really tall handlebars, turning Sam in front of him so he was sitting on the tank, but facing away from the car, where—

"Tell me what else hurts, little dude."

There was a high, wavering scream from by the car, but when Sam tried to turn and look, Retro held him in place and told him, "Eyes on me, yeah? Remember that."

Retro's mouth moved sideways when there was another scream, this one cut short and he muttered, "Change of plans. We're gonna assess at the clubhouse. Right. Okay, kiddo." He reached down and pulled a jacket from one of the bags hanging down beside the back wheel. "Put this one on." Retro helped him into the jacket and pushed the sleeves up until he could see Sam's hands, and then he turned Sam to face him, pulling his legs up around Retro's waist. "Pretend I'm the monkeybars at the playground, hold on like the ground's pouring red hot lava and you can't drop or you'll burn right up. Hold on tight."

Sam blinked at him a couple of times, because it actually sounded like a fun game, and he made mental notes to talk to Jonny about it when he got home. *Home*, he thought, and saw Hoss and Mom's faces.

"Yes, sir. Okay. I can do that," he said softly, knowing Retro couldn't hear him over the sound of the motorcycle. As they pulled out onto the road, followed by a dozen of the men on bikes, he wrapped his arms around the man's neck and held on tight, the chain of the necklace pressing a pattern into the skin on the unbruised side of Sam's face.

As they rode, Retro sang songs, off-key and with no regard for rhythm, but the singing was fun and easy, and Sam gradually relaxed into him, falling into a deep sleep, soothed by the rumble of the bike and the pleasure heard in the man's voice.

"Little dude's a spider monkey," he heard Retro say, and then there were other voices dancing at the edges of his senses. Voices he knew and should be able to recognize. "Wrapped around and held on tight, even after he fell asleep. He's been snoozing since we pulled in, probably 'bout four hours, Hoss. I had Mudd's old lady ice his cheek. It's already lookin' a lot better."

Hoss. Sam sat straight up and looked around the room, frantic to see if it was real, but scared to death it was a dream. Retro was standing by the doorway of what looked like a bedroom, and Hoss and Mom were walk-running to where he was on the bed. He watched their faces as they got close, Mommy dissolving into tears, and Sam knew when Hoss cataloged the damage done to his face by the way his features tightened. *Home.*

21. My song for you

"No. You don't fucking understand, *brother*." Hoss put slight emphasis on the last word, making sure Slate knew he was serious. "I either deal with him here, or I bring him home. Ain't gonna be no waiting around to make sure the fucking law is gonna do their shit." He pulled in a hard breath then blew it out slowly, trying to calm himself. "Slate, man. You don't know wha—"

"Oh, yes, I fucking do, brother. Yeah, I do fucking know." Slate cut him off hard. "You misplace the knowledge of what you saw in the Sins clubhouse two years past, Hoss? She fucking died there, but before she died there and was brought back to life by Goose, she was taken from my fucking side. My goddamned, *fucking* side." Hoss heard a noise and knew Slate had just thrown something in the office. *Fuck.*

"My goddammed. Fucking. Side. Taken. For hours, I didn't know who. Then I knew who, but I didn't know where. Then I did know fucking where, but had to wait. Couldn't go off halfcocked, because that wouldn't do anyone any fucking good. That's where you are right now, brother. But you're a fucking step ahead of me, because you got your boy back already and he's still breathin' air. He ain't laid out in no hospital bed, with you wondering for fucking hours if he's gonna remember you when he wakes the fuck up. He's upright, able to tell you if he's fucking hungry, or hurting, or scared, because you got him the fuck back."

Slate was silent on the phone for a moment then huffed out a breath. "You got him back, and we, by God, got Suiter's shit on lockdown there. We give Deke's brother a day to sort shit with LEO up here, and if he can't, then you talk to me. I hear you wanting to clear your trash there. Retro said the Bastards'd assist with removal, so you will give it one fucking day. One day, knowing if that fuckstick goes downstate for interstate kidnapping then he's doing some hard time, in a hard place, walking side-by-fucking-side with people who we can convince to be incredibly unhappy with the shit he's pulled on your boy and your woman.

"His life is done, brother. Today, tomorrow, a year from now...his life is done. You got Sam back. You got Hope with you. Do you fucking get how fucking precious that is, brother? You got them both, man. Fucking amazing shit right there. So you will get your shit under fucking control and you will lock your own shit down until I give you the fucking green light to go one goddamned direction or the other. You get me?"

Hoss tilted his head, not answering, just looking down at the scuffed toes of his boots and listening to the laughter of his woman and boy in the next room as they argued over who was the best goalie in the league, of all absurd things. Fucking hockey, but it made Sam laugh, so his Hope was all over that, using it to bring laughter back to their boy.

Every time either of them looked at Sam's face, it brought the harm suffered at his father's hands back home. The black and blue echoes of that man's touch on their son was a lasting reminder of how fragile their world was, when hands could reach six hundred miles and spread their hate underneath the skin of a child so precious and good.

Every time Sam tracked Hope moving across the room with his gaze, face tight, a sense of panic hiding right below the surface, they knew he was remembering the cruel promises Suiter had given him as surety against his behavior. The conceited bastard uncaring of the soul scarring and fear left behind on someone he saw as a thing. Nothing more than a pawn. The boy a moving piece in a scheme to regain a legacy he had been cut out of.

Now, as the silence on the phone stretched for minutes, Hoss listened to a quiet beyond the miles separating them, a stillness telling of shared experiences, and a belief in the other to do what was right. Some people would have been put off by that space of time empty of words, but both he and Slate were comfortable within it until it passed. Once it had, Hoss sighed and said, "I got you, brother," because he did.

Disconnecting the call a few minutes later, he stepped into the doorway separating the two hotel rooms, seeing Hope sitting on the small loveseat with Sam. He was leaning across her lap, twisted into pretzel knots, seeming to try and touch her with as much of his body as he could and still see the screen. Hope, for her part, was also staring at the TV with an arm tucked underneath him, holding him tight against her, elbow bent, hand cupping his side across his belly, her other hand threading through his hair again and again, tracing the features of his face and then returning to thread through his hair, pushing it back off his forehead.

Hoss glanced to the TV set, and then did a double-take, staring. He saw Retro front and center on the steps of what looked like the county courthouse, a microphone held to his face by a petite brunette news reporter. The segment title on screen gave his name as Jeremiah Rogers, and Jerry, better known as Retro and president of the Bama Bastards, was talking about how great it felt to rescue what amounted to his eight-year-old nephew from danger.

He took a picture of the TV with his phone and texted it to Slate, saying only, **Lookit this shit**. In a couple minutes, he received, **Clinched it 4 ya. Damn ur brother's a fucktard**. Knowing Jerry's little stunt would mean the courts would now be fully invested in nailing this fucker, as he walked over to slide behind Hope and Sammy, pulling them both against him on the loveseat, he found he agreed with his president's assessment.

Next morning, he woke from sleep to the buzz of an incoming text on his phone, laid to one side on the nightstand. Hope was curled into him, and Sammy had wormed under the covers on his other side, plastering himself over Hoss' chest, his hand laying softly on his mother's cheek in his sleep. When they went to bed the night before, it was with silent acknowledgement of their need to be together, even if they had three beds total between the two rooms, they all piled into the king and started the night with his big spoon wrapped around her smaller one, both of them again cradling their baby spoon.

Groggily, Hoss reached out and picked up the phone, angling his head so he could see the screen. "Oh, fuck," he said softly. Typing a two-word response of, **Got it**, he placed the phone back on the table, tightening his arms around his family, letting their warm bodies and the sounds of them softly breathing soothe him. In his mind, he repeatedly returned to the message, the pain not yet fading of reading the words, **Bingo passed**.

***

Sammy's interview with his caseworker and the assigned officer went well. They honestly didn't need anything from him, because not only did Suiter have a history of violence against Hope, but had also rather eagerly confessed to kidnapping and then beating the boy. Hoss had every expectation his cooperation tied tightly to the discussion the Bama Bastards had with him the previous day.

Standing outside the Bastards' clubhouse next to Jerry, Hoss held out his hand, unresisting when his brother grabbed it to pull him into a tight hold. "Love you, brother," he heard the rough whisper.

With a grin, he responded, "Love you too, man." Stepping backwards, he looked up into his brother's face. "No words, man. I called and, without me even putting words to it, you fucking dropped everything to answer that ask. Gave me my boy back, safe. Let his momma keep her place on this side of sane. Which is sayin' somethin', because in the time he was gone, it was a near thing, Jerry. Fucking appreciate what you did for me."

"Isaiah." With a headshake, his brother moved in again, wrapping him up in a hard hug. "Family, yeah? It's what we do." Hoss heard the whisper and nodded. "Your woman's a beauty, brother. Gorgeous gooey goodness, inside and out." He released him and stepped backwards again, asking Hoss, "You paint her yet, brother?"

"I have a...few...pieces with her influence," he said with a wry grin.

"I bet," came the quick rejoinder. "I just fucking bet. Y'all look good together, and look good with that pogo stick you call a boy. Fucking spider monkey on speed, he's unstoppable." He glanced around, asking, "Hope still pukin'?"

Hoss frowned. "She sick again?"

"Mudd's old lady said she puked on and off all morning. She gave her some crackers to settle her stomach. Said it worked great when she was carrying her kids." Jerry twisted to look into the kitchen area of the open main floor.

"Where's she at?" Hoss asked, closing his eyes for a moment. Clenching his teeth, he was trying not to react to what Jerry had said.

"Bathroom, pukin', I'd guess." Jerry laughed.

"Fucktard. Mudd's woman...where is she?" He opened one eye, squinting at his brother. "Mudd's woman got a name?"

"Name's Rhonda, and she's right here," he heard an amused voice from behind him.

Swinging around, he looked down at the rounded woman grinning up at him. "Need you to make a quick run, Rhonda. If you don't mind," he said, and she nodded.

***

"Baby, open up," he called through the closed door, hearing the toilet flush and then water splashing in the sink. A second later, the handle moved, and Hope pulled the door open, a wan smile on her features, hair scraped back from her pale face into a tight ponytail.

"I'm sorry I'm still sick," she said quietly, wincing when a shout came from downstairs in the clubhouse. Sounded like Jerry's kids were hitting it off with Sammy, if the happy yelling was any indication.

He reached out a hand, curling his palm around her waist, pushing her gently back into the bathroom, and kicking the door closed behind him. Bringing his other hand out in front of him, he showed her the box he held. Keeping his eyes on her face, he watched as she cut her gaze from the pregnancy test box back to his face, back to the box.

"It's not a stomach bug, baby. Let's see if we can rule in one of the better options." At his wording, her eyes grew large and her head gave an involuntary shake. "Oh, Hope. Don't do that. Don't be afraid, baby. This time? If you are, things will be so different for you this time around. But let's first see if we can rule it in"—he gave the box a shake—"or if we have to rule it out, for now." Her eyes widened even more at his plainly spoken expectation, but she stretched out her hand and took the box from him.

Five minutes later, he held her as she sobbed against his chest, and filled with wonder, his eyes kept going to the screen on the test, where the large pink plus sign showed. Now they had to figure out how far along she was, because while she was a little thicker around her hips and belly, he didn't have any idea about what to expect. If it was a failed condom, could have been anytime over the last three months.

293

Hands smoothing up and down her back, he said, "Tell me what you're afraid of, baby. Share those fears. Let's shine some lights on them and tame 'em back, yeah? Let me help you carry that worry."

"Hoss," she breathed his name, and he bent his head to nip at her neck, hearing her suck in a quick breath. "Babies change things."

"Yes, they do," he agreed immediately. "Diapers, all the flippin' time. Clothing sizes, frequently. Hearts and emotions, most definitely."

"I mean in a relationship." She pushed at his chest, and he helped her sit up, noting how pale she still was.

"Not to be harsh, but were you in a relationship when you were pregnant before?" Gazing at her steadily, he watched her lids dip closed then open, giving him the full, potent force of her scrutiny.

"Well, no. But—"

He interrupted, "State secret? I've never been in a relationship with a woman who's pregnant, either. Good news? We'll figure it out, because we're both committed to making this work. We're committed to Sammy and each other." Leaning in, he brushed his lips across hers. "I love you, Hope. This doesn't mean I love you less. If anything, baby, my heart is so fucking full right now I could crow from the rooftop that you're mine. Signed, sealed, soon to be delivered...mine."

"We didn't plan on this." Twisting her neck, she looked down at the floor. "You didn't...I didn't expect..."

"Didn't plan on a lot of things. Don't mean they're gonna turn out to be crap, sweetheart." He nudged her face up with his chin, and kissed her again. "You've had all of three minutes to adjust. Give yourself a little more time, baby. We'll sort a doc soon as we get back, see if we can set something up after Bingo's service."

At his mention of the old man's name, her eyes filled with tears again. "He was so sweet," she said, collapsing against his chest. "So sweet and kind. He read me a bunch of his poetry at Christmas. Some of it I even understood. He tried to explain it to me, how he used something called tercet rhymes in his ballads, but unrhymed in most of his other work. He was good, won some cowboy poet awards, and when he told me that, he laughed and laughed, because he wasn't a cowboy."

He nodded. "Bingo was the best." Mind filled with memories of the old man, he sorted them, shuffling through to find his favorite. Not surprising, it was one of Bingo with the kids. Reclining in a glider swing Jase and DeeDee put in the backyard for him, so he could watch his tribe run and play.

In this memory, for which Hoss was already selecting a palette in his mind, Bingo sat in the middle of the seat, arms around Jonny and Sammy, who were leaning into his sides, bracketing him like bookends. Add-ons to his tribe. Kane and his little sisters and brother sprawled in a pile on the grass in front of the swing, faces upturned to their uncle, engrossed in the story he was telling. Tyler and Megan, framed in the background, sat on the picnic table, as was their habit, but were near enough you could tell they were listening as Bingo spun a tale for the little ones. This would be Bingo's legacy, the sheer capacity of love he had and gave so freely to everyone. A legacy of love.

"Gonna wait until we're closer to home to tell Sammy? Or, want to give him time to wrap his head around things, maybe call Jonny and Kane early on, make sure they're doing okay? He's that kinda kid. He's gonna be worried about his friends."

"Let's wait until we're in the car; this way his reaction can be private, but it gives him time to adjust. And yeah, call his friends if he wants. Thank you." She whispered this, lips against his neck, arching into him, and at the touch, he felt a tightening in his groin.

"Baby, if you don't want me to fuck you in the bathroom, you need to behave," he warned her, and then grinned when he felt the brush of her lips again, followed by a sharp nip and scrape of her teeth. "Oh-ho. I see." He laughed, turning his head to capture her mouth, fingers working to release her hair from the tie binding it back. "It's like that, is it?"

* * *

As they both expected, Sam's tears fell hot and fast for the man he proudly claimed as family, calling him Uncle Bingo. No surprise, because when Sam loved, he did it with every fiber of his being. Losing someone he loved would draw lines of pain across his heart as deep as that love.

They had also anticipated his need to make sure his friends were okay, and at his tentative question, Hoss had immediately handed his phone over the seat of the truck to Sam. He told him to call away, telling him they were about six hours out and would be stopping by the Spencers' house tonight so he could see his friends, and reassure himself things were good with them.

What was a surprise was his fluent recitation of some of Bingo's poetry. Hoss found himself having to clear his throat several times over the half-hour that was Sammy whispering the lines and phrases to himself. Looking in the mirror, he saw the wet shining on his boy's cheeks, face turned to the window, staring out at the passing scenery, but clearly without seeing anything other than what was in his head. One phrase stuck out, because Sam whispered it several times, intensity broken by moments of silence.

"Sam," he started, and his voice broke, so he cleared his throat and began again. "Sammy, do you know what the name of that one was?"

"Yes, sir. He said it was for Aunt DeeDee, called it 'My Song For You.' I think it was a favorite," Sam said, face not turning from the window. Repeating the phrase again, quietly, he said, "Finding your joy in living, Love too full to hold within." He sighed. "Was he alone? That was a thing he was afraid of, I think, that he would be alone." He turned his head, gaze catching on Hoss' in the mirror. "He never came right out and said so, but you could tell. He wanted to be with family when he got bad."

"He was not alone," Hoss said, trying to infuse certainty in his tone. He knew this for a fact, because he, Jase, and Gunny had all noted the same fear, and before Suiter snatched Sammy, Hoss had worked with Sharon to get a rotation set up for staying with Bingo in hospice. Even if DeeDee and Jase were there with the kids, Bingo's friends wanted as many folks as they could round up to get a chance to sit with him. There had been offers from a dozen different clubs in the area, because that many people knew and loved the old man. "He was surrounded by people who loved him, and who he loved."

"I wish I'd have been there." His voice was thin and sad, and Hoss glanced in the mirror to see Sam was crying again. "I hate him."

At his words, Hope sucked in a shocked breath, because you could mistake and think he was angry at Bingo for dying, but Hoss knew better. He understood who Sam was talking about. "I know, son. I hate him too." Now Hope was looking at him, and the anger bubbling just under her skin was clear as day. "He made it so neither of us could be there for Bingo. I hate Suiter, too."

The way her body jerked meant Hope had finally recognized who they were talking about, and now the emotion simmering under her skin was fear. He wondered what was going through her mind, if she would try and rethink this thing between them, use the baby as a reason to pull away like she had before. What had happened once could happen again, and even if the source this time was from her past, she knew at any time there could be danger from his associations.

His jaw worked back and forth, teeth clenching so tightly at the thought of losing her again that he knew the muscles would be popping, and then her hand was on his leg, heat and pressure anchoring him. Glancing over, he saw she had twisted to face him, leaning forward. He caught and held her gaze for a moment, and then she said, "I love you. Stop it, Hoss. I'm not going anywhere. What did you tell me this morning? We'll figure it out?" She gave his thigh a squeeze. "Back atcha."

22. Both hands

Hoss stood straight and still in a chill that said winter was not totally over, looking out at a sea of color. He was on a slight rise, affording him a view few had borne witness to: several hundred bikers in full club regalia, surrounding a tiny tent with a dozen chairs set next to a yawning hole in the ground. As the preacher spoke words aimed at comforting the family, the only sounds in the field were the creaking of leather and the shuffling of feet on ground still mostly frozen.

Under the tent were the kids, along with Mason, Jase, and DeeDee, which was to be expected. Also, there were Bingo's last surviving family members, and that familial connection looked to have surprised practically everyone except Mason and Gunny. Delaying the funeral by two days gave Bingo's brother, Harddrive, time to ride in from Wyoming, and the shock on Slate's face when the man walked into the clubhouse had been interesting to see. Hoss knew there was a story in that association, especially the way Mason grinned when the old man asked Slate if he still owned the Indian he had sold him decades before.

Another surprise surrounded Harddrive's kids, because his son rode in with him and had folded into the crowd of Rebels as if he had been born there. That ease was bolstered by him knowing far more members from the different chapters represented than many of their own members did. Even Gunny had sought out the man, and Hoss watched bemused as they stood and talked for nearly two hours, ignoring the push and swirl of people around them.

The last shocker was Harddrive's daughter, Bingo's niece, who lived right here in the Fort. Dixie, the bar manager at one of their favorite hangouts, had come to the clubhouse with her old man not long after Harddrive walked in last night.

Today, the seven adults and nine kids sat under the tent together, younger kids held in comforting laps while Tyler and Megan wedged into seats between Jase and DeeDee.

Standing stoically, he didn't turn when he heard footsteps come up beside him. Waiting for the echoes of the twenty-one-gun salute to fade away, he watched attentively as the flag covering the casket was removed, carefully folded, and then presented to DeeDee. Hoss clenched his teeth as he watched her accept it, one arm firmly on either side of tiny Gilda's body, the little girl sleeping in her lap, exhausted from the confusing emotions of the past few days. Preacher stepped close, leaning in and speaking first to Mason, and then Harddrive, before turning to walk a few steps away.

Glancing over, Hoss wasn't surprised to see the red-bearded man standing beside him. "Fury," he acknowledged the man who was now his brother. "How's life treating you these days?" Holding out his hand, he clasped wrists with him, noting the reserve in his face. "You got shit, man?"

Shaking his head, Fury said, "Nothing that can't wait, Hoss. Today's for remembering, and my shit can definitely hold off a day or two to give the men and women who knew Bingo time to grieve."

Hoss nodded, turning to look down the hill again. The club's women had come in cages, driven by prospects from the eight different chapters represented today. As they always did, his eyes locked on

Hope, where she stood next to Mercy, Sammy between them, his hands reaching up to clasp theirs, the boy acting as the bridge between the two sisters. He knew Hope was still struggling with the idea of being pregnant, especially after seeing the obstetrician yesterday.

After poking and prodding her belly, using a measuring tape on her skin as if they were in a tailor's shop, the doctor had rolled in a machine.

Hope clearly knew what to expect, but when Hoss heard their child's heartbeat swelling in the room, the wonder of it nearly took his legs out from under him. The doc laughed as the nurse pushed a chair over towards him. With a shake of his head, he rejected it, bending over Hope from the top of the bed and kissing her lips with bruising force. "That's our baby," he whispered, and she nodded, gripping his hand tightly.

Then the doc started asking questions rapid-fire and Hoss straightened, seeing a panicked look on Hope's face. Flipping the machine around, the doc pointed one long finger at the screen. Hoss looked on, confused, as images appeared and disappeared before he could make sense of them, black and white flowing across the screen, as fluid as waves on the ocean.

The moments where he could recognize anything were fleeting, and then the image settled with a dark void in the middle of the screen. Slowly, gradually, a form came into focus, and he saw a tiny profile—forehead, nose, chin—all come clear to him. Once he had that image as a point of reference, he began seeing things like an arm, moving slowly then tucking down to the baby's chest. "The heart looks good," he heard the doctor say, and he saw the fluttering movement deep inside the baby's body.

Then the image changed, the form going away, and the doc laughed. "We have a runner."

Hoss watched as the process was repeated, the void he now understood was Hope's uterus gradually framing the child's limbs, head, and torso. There were several times when the doctor froze the screen and took measurements.

Then he turned to look at Hoss and Hope, asking, "Mom and Dad, it's not one-hundred percent, but unless this little one is hiding something, I'm pretty confident I could tell you the gender."

Hoss looked down at Hope, nodding, and with a tender expression, she nodded too, turning back to the doctor, who grinned. "She's not cooperating very well, because I'm pretty sure she's already a princess."

Bending down, he whispered against Hope's lips, "We're having a little girl." Pushing the doc's hand out of the way, careless of where he still held the machine's wand, he covered her gel-coated belly with his palm. "That's Sammy's little sister in there, inside you." Kissing her again, softly he said, "I fucking love you, Hope Collins."

"I love you too, Hossman," she whispered.

"So let's talk due dates," the doc said, and Hoss looked up at him, annoyed, because he wanted another minute to soak it in. "Hope, I think your dates might not be quite right. Based on what I'm seeing, the pregnancy is about twenty-four weeks along."

She sucked in a breath, clamping down on Hoss' hand as the doctor continued, "It's not uncommon for a pregnancy to be undetected for several weeks or even a few months, but this means we have to get our ducks in a row fairly quickly. We're going to need to do some blood work, and I'll have the girls up front call Alabama, see if we can get a copy of the charts from your OB there. The good news, from your perspective, is you only have about four months to go. Everything I've seen today looks great; the baby is active, and you're healthy. No concerns from my end of things."

Fury pulled him out of his reverie with a brief, humorless laugh. Hoss looked up and said, "What?"

"I've asked you three times if you guys needed anything picked up before my boys head back to the clubhouse, but you were staring off into space." Fury slapped at his chaps, knocking dust off his leathers. "Where were you, Hoss?"

"Our boys," he said, eyes trained steadily on Fury's face. This kind of shit had to be nipped in the bud fast and hard, or they would wind up with a division in the chapter. "Every member is ours, so you sayin' you got some special boys ain't gonna fly."

"Noted," Fury said briefly, frowning. "You didn't answer my question."

He grinned, twisting to look back down at the mass of people moving to the bikes and cars parked on the roads surrounding the area of cemetery they were in, easily dialing back in on Hope. She was standing, looking back towards the tent, having stepped aside to let the rest of the women flow around her. He saw Sammy trotting back towards her, Jonny and Kane in tow. Breathing deep, he said, "Hope's pregnant."

After a few moments, when the other man still hadn't said anything, he glanced over to see Fury's eyes on her, his body posture tense as he watched her walk out to the cars, herding the boys along in front of her. "We found out yesterday morning the doc thinks it's a girl."

Fury drew a noisy breath through his nose and stood, still not saying anything for another minute or two. Then, slowly, as if he were considering the nuance of every syllable, he said, "Both hands. You find sweet and good like that, you hold onto it with both hands. Tight as you can. That is a fucking magnificent woman, and now," he shifted in place, and then continued, "she's carrying your babe. Both." Turning his head, he glared at Hoss. "Hands." Turning stiffly, he walked away.

"*Fuck*," Hoss breathed, not having expected that kind of reaction, shocked at the depth of anger Fury held for being on the losing end in their long ago concluded tug-of-war with Hope.

***

"Mom, can I see if Jonny and Kane want to come back to our house?" Sam looked up, squeezing the hands that held his securely, looking between Mom and Aunt Mercy. It had been like this since they got back to Fort Wayne, someone always within reach, making him know he was safe and loved.

"Sure, bud. Ask Miss DeeDee first. Don't get Kane riled up in case it's a no, okay?" Mom reached over and ruffled a hand through his hair, scratching gently in that way he loved.

"Yes, ma'am," he responded, squeezing her hand before he dropped his hold and ran back towards the tent. Aunt DeeDee was talking to one of the men he didn't know, and Sam hung back for a minute until she noticed him. "Aunt DeeDee, can Jonny and Kane—"

She didn't even let him finish the question before nodding and answering, "Sure thing, Samboni. I'll call your mom later. We'll organize the transfer of kids."

With a grin, he darted away, his gaze scanning the crowd for his friends. Kane was standing next to Tyler, digging in the grass with the toe of one shoe. He turned his head, looking around again to find Jonny was standing on the pile of dirt next to the box that Uncle Bingo was in, that box looking precariously balanced on top of the yawning hole in the ground.

His heart lurched for a moment, because he thought Jonny might fall in, but watched him smoothly step up onto the device that held the box, metal and straps holding it in midair. *Suspended*, Sam thought, kind of like the past couple of days had felt, where everything moved slowly enough you nearly couldn't see the change.

He walked over slowly, trying to make a bunch of noises so he didn't sneak up on Jonny. It looked like he was talking, and Sam knew from his own pain that whatever Jonny was saying to Uncle Bingo had to be important. Too important to interrupt or listen in on. Jonny looked up at him and nodded, tilting his head to call Sam over.

He stepped up on the metal bars beside Jonny and stared down at the top of the box. There was a wadded pile of wilted yellow flowers in the middle, the dandelions lying right next to the white flowers arranged in the shape of the Rebel emblem. Without missing a beat, Jonny said, "Sammy's here, Uncle Bingo. So many people came today to tell you goodbye. You'd be laughing your butt off at all the bikes. I saw a whole bunch of Indians. So pretty."

Sam sucked in a breath at Jonny's words, because this was how they talked to Uncle Bingo all the time. It was like Jonny was having a normal conversation with him, just kinda one-sided.

Jonny said, "I'm tryin' not to be sad. You know, like you told me?" His voice lowered, imitating Uncle Bingo's gruffness, "'No tears, John boy. Don't need no salt spread upon my path.'" Pausing for a moment, Jonny swallowed and said in his normal voice, "I want to think of you in a better place, without hurtin' all the time. I promise to help take care of the tribe. Any way I can, I'm going to be there for Tyler and Kane and Simon, and even all the girls." He paused and took a breath, and then said softly, "Pinky promise."

"Me, too," Sam said, stretching out his hand and waiting for Jonny to reach out. They crooked their little fingers together, holding the grip for a minute, somberly sealing the promise. Sam rested his hand on the box, one fingertip moving across the smooth surface, mentally tracing the lines and whirls making up Uncle Bingo's name.

"Remember when you talked about how beauty was everywhere we looked? We just had to keep lookin' for it? I liked that poem you told me last week, and I asked Aunt DeeDee to write it out for me." Jonny dug into his pocket, coming up with a few more crushed flower heads, which he carefully placed on the pile. "Got you some flowers, too." He patted them into place. "They were pretty." He reached back into his pocket, pulling out a piece of paper, carefully folded, but wrinkled and smudged. He reverently unfolded it, smoothing the paper across the top of the box.

Sam caught a glimpse of movement behind them and glanced back, seeing some of the Rebels were standing close as Jonny began to read.

Beauty lies
They say
In the eyes
Where what we see becomes truth
Where what we know becomes twisted
That twist bursting seams with joy wasted
Bringing down our towers of unused youth

Beauty lies
They say
In the mouth
Where what we state can hurt or heal
Where what we hear can give us peace
True peace reaching through passionate release
Giving the courage to look within and feel

There was a noise, and he looked behind them again, seeing Uncle Bingo's brother had pulled out a red bandana and was wiping his eyes. He watched as Mason settled a hand on Uncle Harddrive's shoulder, pulling him close. Aunt DeeDee walked up on the other side of him and wrapped an arm around his waist, her mouth twisting with sadness as she leaned her head on Uncle Harddrive's shoulder. Sam turned back to look at Jonny and swallowed hard at the tears he saw in his best friend's eyes.

Beauty lies
They say
In the heart
Where what we hold turns faith to certainty
Where what we endure imbues our dreaming
Filling private passion with rich meaning
Eager ardor wholly worthy of raw clarity

Beauty lies
They say
In the soul
Where what we consume feeds our brightness
Where what we absorb can nourish good
Enthralling brilliance blinding as it should
Our tribe surrounded free in captive rightness

They stood in silence for a moment when Jonny finished reading, not even the shuffle of boots breaking the quiet. "Love you, Uncle Bingo," Jonny whispered, his fingers occupied with working the paper back into a neat square, creasing already established folds before shoving it into his pocket. Lifting his head, it looked like he finally became aware of their expanded audience and ducked his chin in embarrassment, using the back of one hand to wipe across his eyes. With resolution, Jonny sucked air in through his nose, releasing it slowly as he firmly said, "No tears."

His throat was thick and tight, that sick feeling seeming stuck there for the past two days, and Sam pushed past it to say, "You and Kane want to come over? Mom and Aunt DeeDee already said it's okay with them."

Jonny nodded, jumping off the metal bar, pushing off with both feet to land well away from the hole. Sam followed suit, and they ran over to where Kane stood, gathering him before they all went running back to where Mom waited.

23. You want me, you got me

Hoss lay in bed beside her, head pillowed on his arm, watching her sleep. He trailed his fingertips down her body, between her breasts, then onto her stomach, finally settling his palm over her belly. Now that they knew she was pregnant, he couldn't imagine how they had missed it, how he had missed the changes to her body. On their last bi-monthly visit, the doc had confirmed it was a girl, reassuring them all the blood work had come back normal.

He shifted in bed, turning to put his head on Hope's thighs, nuzzling into her pussy. She still preferred to sleep in one of his tees, and he reached out to drag the soft fabric up, exposing her belly. Using his teeth and lips, he plucked at her underwear then nuzzled her through them again before lying still, laughing quietly at her groaning protest in her sleep. Turning his attention back to her belly, he stroked her skin with his palm, softly grazing the roundness developing between her hipbones.

Closing his eyes, he let his hand rest there, breathing in her scent, feeling the heat from her body where he was curled around and over her. There was a light but solid thump against his hand, and his eyes shot open. She had been trying to get him to feel the baby kick for two weeks now, but he had not yet been graced with this...*thump*...miracle. "Our child," he whispered, letting his eyelids sink closed again. *Thump.*

***

"How's Hope?" Jase asked from his position on the ice, leaning up against the boards, where Hoss stood watching the boys' practice. "She get over the pukey-face antithesis to fun?"

With a grin, Hoss nodded. "Yeah, she's hungry all the time now. Eats like every two hours, seems like. Love watching her. So fucking beautiful, I can't even express what I feel, man. I think it's fair to say she's over the pukey-face."

Jase laughed. "Did you hear Slate preening the other night? Twins again, man. I think I'm gonna get him a shirt that says *Slate's Super Swimmers.*"

"Yeah, Ruby and DeeDee were at the house yesterday, planning baby showers and shit. I got the full rundown, as Ruby put it, on pushing not one but two watermelons out of a lemon-sized hooha." Both men laughed, gazes on the kids gliding across the ice.

"DeeDee's over the moon again. All these babies, she's been in baby heaven." He shifted his feet, blades sliding back and forth. "Got our tribe, too. Fucking miss Bingo, man."

They stood quietly for a few minutes, Jase frequently calling out drill commands to the kids, eyes following their swoops and curving lines across the ice. Hoss broke the silence between them, asking, "How are the boys doing?"

"Kane's a fuckton better than Jonny," he answered immediately, the quick response communicating this was something wearing on his mind. "I have the twins in another skate group, and they're doing well." He tensed, watching something the kids were doing and then leaned back, relaxing. "Tyler and Megan, the two oldest, they're hit hardest, which is only natural. Lost their mom to cancer, then Tyler's own battle with it, and now Bingo. They remember their mom, you know? Gilda, she was barely born when her mom passed, so she doesn't have memories other than the ones family members have planted with stories, cultivated with repetition." He shook his head. "Jonny, though. He's tore up. Loved that old man like he was blood."

"Sammy gets in the way of them healing, you let me know." The three boys had been inseparable since the funeral, and it seemed if Sam wasn't staying at Coach Spence's house, the other two were at Hope and Hoss' place, heads together, talking about everything and anything.

"He's a helpful cuss, eh?" Jase glanced his way, and then focused back on the kids. "Gotta go. Time for some competitive play. Kinda sorta needs an adult." He glanced over again and grinned. "I've looked for one of those around here for a while now, but can't seem to find an adultier adult than me, so I guess I'm all we've got."

Grinning, Hoss lifted a hand in a casual wave, watching Jase glide out to where the boys were gathering at center ice.

***

Sam focused on what Coach Spence was telling them. It was to be a quick set of drills, two players taking the puck up ice to the goalie, trying to score, wave after wave of attacks on the lone defender. This was one of his favorite exercises, because it was offensive, not defensive, so no hooking or slashing as they moved up the sheet of ice, just the control and finesse brought to the maneuvers with your own puck handling and ability to work as a team.

Jonny skated up, trying a new backwards stop they were learning, nearly taking a tumble when his hips turned far beyond the ninety-degree position. Sam frowned and told him, "Your back foot wasn't right. Get the back of the blade out beyond your shoulders, past your helmet." Jonny nodded, pushing off to skate a circle, turning backwards and coming in again, this time performing the maneuver correctly. Sam grinned, looking down at the skim of shaved ice dotting his pants and socks. "Nice dusting. Are we on the same practice line?"

"Yeah," Jonny responded as they watched two different lines run through the drill, neither of them scoring on the goalie. "You dump to me," Jonny told him, turning to face Sam, who nodded. They worked well together, and the play could go either way, but he was fine with Jonny's plan. Tentatively, Jonny asked, "How'd the video thing go today?"

"Fine." Sam had to go to the courthouse today. Again. It meant he didn't have time to skate this morning, which made him mad, and he hadn't wanted to go. He had pitched a fit, making his mom mad, because the whole thing reminded her that his dad—*not your dad, Hoss is your dad,* his brain said—had kidnapped him. That's what the lawyer called it. Kidnapping. *I'm a kid,* he thought, remembering their first day in town, when Aunt Mercy turned him upside down. He burst out laughing, and Jonny looked at him with a grin when he stuck out his tongue and bleated like a goat.

"You're weird," Jonny said with a laugh as they skated up, Sam scooping the puck up on the blade of his stick and bouncing it in the air twice before he began moving forward.

"Ain't it great?" he yelled, barreling towards the goalie then dropping the puck back and to the side. He skated across the area in front of the net, careful to stay outside the blue ice, screening for Jonny. There was a ringing clank as the puck hit a post, and then he heard the goalie groan, knowing from his response it had gone in. Raising his arms high, he shook his stick over his head, skating back towards center ice. He and Jonny were a great team.

***

"Hoss," he said, watching the mirror to see his reaction. "Can I ask you something?" They had left practice a few minutes ago, headed home, the stinky scent that was hockey equipment permeating the inside of the truck.

"Sure thing, Sam," Hoss responded easily, glancing into his side mirror before changing lanes.

He wished they were already home, wished he could touch Hoss' face in the way Mom did when it was important. But, if Hoss didn't agree, and he lost it, he didn't want Mom to see him upset, so it had to be now, when it was just him and Hoss. With his sister coming, it was way too easy to make her cry, and he hated to see that look on her face. Like when he woke up yelling from his dreams, the ones where his dad—*not your dad, Hoss is your dad*—took him, and he couldn't get home. In the dream, he ran and ran until he was so tired he could lie down on the rocks in the road and sleep, but he never got home. Even if he could see Mom in the dream, he couldn't ever make it to where she was, and he would wake up yelling, mad and sad and scared all at once, and it made Mom unhappy.

"What is it, son?" Hoss asked, and that did it; that word was the trigger he needed. Because Hoss used that word real often, and Sam had to know if it meant what he thought it meant. Had to know for sure, even with the things Hoss had said in the past. Even with Hoss and Mom having a sister, who would be theirs in a way he wasn't, knew he wasn't, because his dad—*not your dad, Hoss is your dad*—wasn't Hoss.

"Do you love me?" His throat was tight, and he knew he was making a face, so he turned to look out the window as if this didn't matter. As if nothing mattered. Because if Hoss didn't agree, he had to have a way to hide what it would do to him.

"You know I do, Sam," Hoss said easily, turning on the blinker before pulling into the parking lot of the grocery store. They were running a few errands before heading home, and grocery shopping was one of them.

"I love you, too," he said, hating how small his voice sounded, but when he glanced over, he saw Hoss nodding, eyes on the cars in front of them. "Can I call you Dad?" He swallowed. "I don't have a dad," he said, and then rushed to add, "and it's okay if you don't want me to. I don't have to. I just thought with the baby it would be less confusing for her if we both called you Daddy." Biting his lip hard, he tried to still the quivering taking over his chin, making it jerk up and down like a yo-yo.

The truck abruptly stopped, and was still rocking in place when he felt hands at his seatbelt. He barely had enough time to take a breath before he found himself hauled over the seat and tucked between Hoss' body and the steering wheel. Hard arms folded around him, holding him safe and close, and he heard the thick in Hoss' voice when he said, "You do have a daddy, son. Me. You want to call me Dad? You wantin' to give this thing between us a name? Fuck, yeah, call me Daddy. Makes my fucking day you want that. I've waited a long time for you to ask, son."

Sam started crying in earnest, wrapping his arms around Hoss' neck and burying his face in that strong, solid, *safe* shoulder. Harsh and hoarse with what sounded like joy, Hoss said, "Love you so much, boy. You want me, you got me, warts and all. This baby coming doesn't have a fucking thing to do with it, either. You've been my boy for a long time now."

They sat like that for a while, Sam's sobs finally trailing off to silence, Hoss seeming content to sit and hold him as long as he needed. "Can we change my name to Rogers?" This was the second question he wanted to ask, because if Hoss was going to be his daddy, then he wanted the world to know where he belonged.

"You want that, son?" The thick was back in Hoss' voice and Sam pulled back, looking up to see tears standing in his eyes. Wordlessly, he nodded, and Hoss' arms pulled him back into another tight embrace. "I'll see what we can do, boy. Gotta get Mama on board with this one, but I have an idea that will pave the way." He sighed, his breath ruffling the hair on top of Sam's head. "Can you keep a secret?"

Sam scoffed, because of course he could keep secrets when it was important. "Yeah," he said, his tone indicating it was a silly question, and Hoss laughed. He moved, one arm leaving Sam's shoulders, and he dug in the inside pocket of his jacket, pulling out a box. Plucking the offering from the flattened palm, Sam opened the box and stared. There was a beautiful ring inside. He had seen enough movies to know this was important, the kind of ring a man gave a woman when he asked her to the wedding. "You want to marry Mom?"

"Yep," Hoss said. "In the worst way, or the best, depending on how you look at it. I'm hoping she says yes." He paused. "Would you be okay with that, Sam?"

"Yep," he replied, mimicking Hoss' tone and drawing a laugh from him. "So we'd all be Rogers?"

"Yep," Hoss said again, and they both laughed this time.

***

Hoss watched her moving between the kitchen and the table, hair wild around her head, mouth moving faster than her feet as she carried plates and silverware to the sink. *God, she's beautiful*, he thought, remembering back when they had first met and he knew in his gut she would have been gorgeous carrying Sammy. *I was so right*, he thought, smirking a little to himself.

Sammy had surprised him today with his questions, shocking the shit out of him and blowing him away with the ask. Hoss knew a bit about the adoption routine. He had worked with the club's lawyers when Bear was going through the process to adopt four kids who had lost their daddy due to club business. Granted, the bastard had died because of his own fucking choices, but the club took care of their own, and Bear had stepped into the void to take on the kids. Reluctantly at first, but then fully embracing the role pressed on him.

Gradually, he realized Hope had stopped talking. She was leaning against the countertop looking at him. With an apologetic smile, he moved to her, putting his hands on either side of her waist. Leaning down, he pressed his lips to her forehead. "I'm sorry, baby. I was a million miles away. What did you say?"

"I asked if you'd considered the names I texted you." She smiled up at him. It wouldn't be long now and they would be holding their daughter. All the more reason to move forward with what he intended, making her and Sammy his legally, not just in the eyes of the club.

"I love you," he said, and she tilted her head.

Nodding, she said, "I know you do, Hoss. And, I love you, too. Is this your way of telling me you didn't like the names?"

He dropped one hand from her waist, pulling his phone from his pocket and thumbing the screen to life. He pressed buttons, pulling up the text application, and grinned at her. "Peony Ann?" Looking down at her, he barked a laugh. "Seriously, woman?" She made a face, and he looked back at his phone. "Zinnia Emily?" Leaning down, he pressed his lips to her forehead again, laughing openly. "Were you doing the wrong kind of nursery shopping today?"

She was supposed to have been picking up sheets and blankets for the baby's room. He hadn't noticed any bags when he was in there earlier, putting the last pieces together for the bassinette that went with the crib they purchased.

"Shut up," she said, pressing her cheek to his chest. Her words were muffled when she said, "I admit I might have been at the kind of nursery that needs soil and water to nurture life. But Peony is a great name."

"Huh-uh. Nope. Baby, say it slow. Pee On Knee. She'd never survive junior high. You gotta predict the nicknames, make sure you pull only good options into the mix." He laughed again, putting his phone back into his pocket. "Does your middle name have significance?" he asked.

"Not that I know of," she said, sighing and leaning into him a little deeper. "I hate Annabelle, anyway."

"We'll find the right one, baby," he said, sliding his hand up her back, rubbing her neck and the back of her head. "Six more weeks, and she's going to be right here with us." There was a rumble of thunder in the distance and he glanced over at the windows, seeing clouds were scudding across the sky, blocking out the evening sun, reminding him of their first sweet, soaked embrace. *Six weeks*, he thought. Time to get moving; time for the biggest ask he had ever considered. Adjusting his stance, he leaned against the edge of the counter, arms locking her into place.

"When did you know you loved me?" he asked.

"What?" Her tone was startled, and she tried to pull back, but he tightened his arms.

"When did you know you loved me?" Repeating the question, he scanned through the snapshots in his head to find the one he wanted. "I think I knew when I walked into Mercy's apartment that first day and you were sittin' on the couch, back to the door. I'd spent the morning with Sammy, loved his ass already, because he was so protective of you. He didn't take no shit. The kid drew a hard line with me. Loved that about him, hated what it said about what you'd been through together. Then, that afternoon, I walked in, heard you talking about piecing things together to make your way, and knew I had to make things better for you. Couldn't think straight for trying to find a solution I could live with."

"What does that mean, something you could live with?" Her voice was small, and he reckoned she was thinking about the first few jobs she held, working for the club.

"Your job had to have three things going for it. First, it had to be able to support you and Sammy in a way that would take the worry off your face. That was important to you. It was clear just in our short chat you needed to understand you were covered, that you had shit in hand, so it became important to me, too." He squeezed her, and then kissed the side of her head.

"Second, it had to be safe for you. And, by safe, I don't mean not juggling chainsaws, but safe around the kind of men the club life attracts. Safe in ways you weren't even aware you needed to be safe. That was by far the hardest, because everywhere we put you, like bees to honey, you drew in the men. Without even trying, you drew them in. And because of the club shit at the time, I had to keep my distance, couldn't lay claim to you like I needed, wanted to."

He stopped talking for a minute, content simply to hold her. She prompted him, "That's only two. You said there were three?"

"Yeah, the third was I had to be able to see you whenever I wanted. Needed to know where you were. Fucking obsessed, it seemed like. That was me with you." He rested his chin on her head. "Lots of times I'd keep track of you and you wouldn't even know. My head was fucking stalker central for a while."

He laughed. "The back gate at Mercy's apartment complex got a lot of use. I'd stake out the common yard and watch you through the window, just to be close to you. Trying my hardest to give you and Mercy time to figure out the sister shit you had going on, so I didn't want to be in your space all the time, but had to see you. Had to know you were okay."

She made a noise and he shook his head, tightening his arms again. "Let me finish, baby, yeah?" She nodded and sighed. "The night I picked you up at the offices, when you were cleaning? I'd stood in the backyard for two hours, waiting on the lights to come on, letting me know you were home. I was crazy with worry, and then you come bopping out of that building, not even looking around. I couldn't stay away. Held you." His voice lowered. "Touched you."

She nodded. "First time we slept in the same bed."

317

"Yeah, hardest fucking thing I ever did, letting you cover up with your shirt and sweats then watching you sleep, my hands on your body, forcing myself to let you sleep without waking you with my head between your legs. Thank God, Sammy was in the same fucking room. Helped keep me honest, yeah?" He shook his head, and then pressed another kiss to her temple. "So, when did you know?"

"The day you took me for my first bike ride," she said softly, and he sucked in a breath. "I've never been possessed by a man the way I am with you. I've never wanted to give myself to anyone the way you seem to need...demand from me. But that day, you organized everything, just for me. In order for us to have a little time away, time to be grownups, time to get to know each other. Then, when your plans fell apart because Sammy faked a tummy ache, you didn't get mad or anything. Took it in stride, you simply accepted things had changed and went with it. I felt safe, and cherished. I felt loved, and loved you in return."

"I want to marry you," he said and felt her freeze in place in his arms. "Soon, Hope. As soon as we can work it. I want to marry you. Want to give you my name, give Sammy my name. I love you and, God knows, the two of you are mine forever. This would just make it official." He paused, but she didn't say anything, so he asked, "Hope, would you marry me?" Reaching into his pocket, he pulled out the ring box, turning them so he had room to move.

Putting one knee to the floor, he looked up into the face of the woman he loved. The only person who filled in all the places that, before her, he didn't even know were empty. He opened the box and removed the ring, gripping her hand and sliding it halfway onto her finger. "Marry me, Hope."

She stared at him for a moment and then squeezed her eyes shut, and his heart began to pound. *Fuck*, he thought then sucked in a hard, relieved breath when she said, "Yes."

24. Our family

"I'm right then, guardianship is not an option? Way to go is adoption?" Tipping his head back, he stared at the ceiling in the clubhouse office. On the phone with Myron, he wasn't being provided with the answers he wanted, but would take what he could get.

"Yeah, guardianship is a tough road, plus it doesn't give you the name change you're asking about. It'll be a fuckton easier to get stepparent adoption, especially since you're marrying his mom," Myron told him. "We can get the ball kicked off for the adoption; I already know most of the steps. There'll be the home study, background check, interviews and shit. Sammy is too young to have to sign consent, and I'm assuming you have his mom's go-ahead on this. That leaves the dad."

"Not a concern," Hoss said brusquely, his voice low and angry at the mention of Suiter. "Parental rights were terminated before Sammy was even born, and after the sick fuck kidnapped him, ain't no judge giving him the time of day where this boy's concerned."

"Sammy in counseling?" With this question, Myron's voice had softened, gone musing, like he was thinking hard.

"Yeah, he sees the counselor once a week just to deal with the fallout from the whole fucking ordeal. When he had to do the depositions, we even set him up twice a week for a while. With their questions forcing him to relive the shit, we did it to make sure we stayed out ahead of anything brewing in his head." Hoss' jaw clenched, because every time he thought about Suiter still breathing air, he was struck with the wrongness of it all. He needed to call Jerry, see how that fuck's life was shaping up for misery and pain.

"Dude or chick?" Myron's question was out of left field and Hoss had to adjust his thinking for a second.

"Uh, the counselor? Woman. Why?"

"Get the counselor on board. That kind of psych write up will absolutely grease the runners on this thing." His voice was firm, confident. "You're marrying Hope on Saturday, right?"

"Yeah, God willing," he said. This was Monday, and he was working hard to make sure everything was ready by the end of the week.

"Hang up with me; call his counselor. Tell her what he asked you, tell her what you and Hope are doing, and then tell her you'd like to give him his wish on the same day you give his mom your last name. She's going to suck that emotional romantic shit right the fuck up, and then she'll feed it to the judge." Myron laughed. "Am I invited? I'd like to see this shindig."

"Of course, Myron. And if you get this for me? I'll kiss you full on the lips, brother." Hoss grinned, a clear path in front of him, and the confident words of his friend gave him hope things would work out like he wanted.

"Pass on that, man, but I'll be there Saturday. Text me the deets, yeah?"

***

"I, Hope Annabelle Collins, take you, Isaiah Jude Rogers, to be my lawfully wedded husband." Hoss heard the words, but couldn't focus on them. Knew they were important, but all he could do was look at the woman who was marrying him today. Right here, right now, becoming his.

They were in Jase and DeeDee's backyard, and he was standing in front of their friends, holding both of Hope's hands in his. Glancing down, he saw Sammy's smiling face staring up at him from beside Preacher, the Rebel member officiating at the ceremony.

Everything had fallen into place with shocking speed. Not only had their marriage license come through, but also Myron had ridden in today and handed Hoss a thick manila envelope, standing there with a broad grin on his face. Thumping Hoss on the back, he had leaned close and whispered, "Judge came through. Signed papers are in there. He's yours as of about two hours ago."

"Hoss," he heard Hope whisper, and he blinked. She was smiling and tipping her head towards Preacher, so he looked over and saw a grin on the old man's face. "Your turn, baby," she said softly, and he looked down at her.

"You are my life," he said without preamble. "I'll do anything to make you happy, anything to keep you safe. Anything that is mine, is yours, but you"—his voice lowered to a growl—"are all mine." He reached out a hand and rested his palm on top of Sammy's head. "You and Sammy are my family, and Hope, baby, you own me. Anything I can fucking do, anything you need from me, I'll make it happen. I will…I do." He paused and angled his body in, resting his forehead against hers. "I love you, Hope Annabelle Rogers." He shifted and dropped a kiss on her lips then said, "Got something to deal with. Gimme a sec."

With her laughter ringing through the air, he knelt in front of her, leaned in and pressed a quick kiss to her belly, and then reached to his back pocket to pull out the folded envelope. "Sammy, come out here, son." Reaching out a hand, he gripped the back of Sammy's neck, pulling him into an embrace, ending with his forehead against his boy's.

"Samuel, you were not given a middle name at birth. You're my boy, my son, and you know I love you, right?" Sam nodded, gaze fixed to his. "Not long ago, you asked me if I could give you my last name, same as I did Mama today, yeah?" Sam nodded again, and appeared to be holding his breath.

With a laugh, Hoss leaned back and told him, "Breathe, son." He held up the envelope and said, "These papers do two things. One, they say you are my son, from now to forever. My name's on your birth certificate, telling everyone you belong to me. Two, they change your name from Samuel Collins, to Samuel Isaiah Rogers, so you carry a part of me with you beginning today."

***

Sam didn't even notice he was holding his breath until Hoss reminded him to suck in air. *He adopted me*, he thought, gaze stuck on Hoss' face. Hoss asked, "Does that sound all right to you, son?"

Reaching out his hand, he cupped Hoss' jaw in his palm, and then invoked the most solemn words he knew. "No lies." Hoss shook his head, staring at Sam. "I love you." He looked up at Mom, reaching up his other hand to grip hers, fingers wrapping tight around her hand. "I love Mom." He looked back down to Hoss and swallowed, ready to say the words he could never take back, would never want to. "Daddy," his voice cracked and he swallowed again, and then he saw the wet in Daddy's eyes and sniffed. "I love you and Mommy."

Turning, he was still fighting back his tears when he looked up at the preacher. "Can you say the wedding words, but about us?"

"I sure can, boy," the man agreed, and Sam turned back to stare at his dad as they both listened to the man. "I now pronounce you a family."

Turning to look at Preacher, he made a face, "Did I mess it up?"

"No, Sammy," the man said, "you did real good."

25. Love, tripled

Hope lay in bed, propped all around with pillows. From them not knowing she was pregnant for months, this baby had definitely made her presence known over the past few weeks. She groaned and reached back to rub her tailbone. Between the headache that had settled behind her eyes and this back pain, she couldn't find a comfortable position. The OB said her blood pressure was up a little, not really anything to worry about, but Hoss grabbed the recommendation she spend more time resting and ran with it until she was virtually on bedrest as far as he was concerned. As he promised, nothing about this pregnancy was like her first, because she had him.

Two more weeks, she thought, closing her eyes and listening. There were voices in the distance; it sounded like Sam and Jonny were in the living room. Because she was listening so closely, she heard the sound of someone quietly moving up the carpeted hallway, jeans brushing together, the light creak of leather. Without opening her eyes, as soon as the bed shifted, she said, "Hey there."

His palm skimmed up from her knee, over her thigh, up to her hip, and slipped behind her, taking over the rubbing motion on her low back. His voice low and loving, Hoss asked, "How's the head, baby?" Sighing, she made a face and he grunted. "Back hurting still?" With a nod, she arched and curved her spine, rocking her hips forward, tilting her pelvis to stretch out the muscles that were tight and painful. "Yeah, I see it is," he said, crawling across her, pausing in a hover to kiss her temple then settling behind her, using the heel of his hand, as well as his fingertips.

Twisting her shoulders, she leaned back into him, loving how he supported her without a word of complaint. Looking up at him with a smile, catching first her top then her bottom lip between her teeth, she tilted her chin up, silently asking for a kiss. His hands on her always caused the same reaction, and he laughed when he saw the wanting look on her face.

"Baby," he said with a headshake, leaning in to kiss the tip of her nose. "That belly's too big, and you know it." His voice softened, causing her to shiver when he said, "I love you." He slipped his hand up her side, fingertips trailing over her ribs to cup her breast, gently tweaking the sensitive nipple and drawing a gasp from her. He slid his hand down, palm flat over her swollen belly, slowly and softly rubbing small circles as he went. "I can make you better, though," he said, his voice now rough with a swell of matching desire, and she felt his erection when he pushed his hips against her.

His fingertips inched her nightgown up and he pressed his hand down between her thighs, clearly surprised at what he found there. Rising on one elbow, he looked down at her with affection and humor in his eyes. "It's like that, is it?" She nodded with a grin, knowing he had discovered she wasn't wearing panties.

"Lock the door," she whispered, running her tongue over her bottom lip. "But, kiss me first."

Leaning in, he grazed his lips across hers, but she knew this was only his opening move, as it so often was. His kisses came in stages, from the initial, seemingly tentative advances, to breath-stealingly passionate, and then finally ending back at soft and sweet.

Nibbling on her bottom lip, he dragged her mouth open, and then his hand was on her jaw, holding her in place as he angled his mouth across hers, possessing her, driving into her mouth and tangling his tongue with hers. His fingers were softly caressing her cheek, and when he pulled back so their lips were barely touching, she opened her eyes to find him staring down at her.

"I love you, Hoss," she whispered, and as he always did, he took in a surprised and pleased breath that stirred emotions she had never known until this man walked into her life. "Now go lock the door, because while my belly's big, nothing's changed from where you are right now, so I want my husband to snuggle up behind me and love me slow and sweet." She reached down, pulling her nightgown up and over her head.

"That I can do, baby," he whispered, pressing another kiss to her lips. When he returned to bed, he had divested himself of his clothes, so slipping in behind her was a delicious slide of skin on skin. Pressing his thigh between her legs, he ran one palm from knee to hip and back down again, then curved his arm, trailing his fingertips up along the inside of her thigh. She knew what he would encounter, so was ready for his whispered, "Fuck, baby. Drenched."

Twisting her neck, she offered him her lips and he took them, fingers working between her legs, tongue working in her mouth. Kissing her deep and hard, he showed her the edge of his ardent desire, avid, finely honed. All hers.

Tipping her hips to press back into his erection, she reached down and wrapped her hand around his, dragging his palm up her body to her breast. "Mama's demanding today," he chuckled, obligingly wrapping his fingers around the soft mound, plumping and caressing her.

She tipped her hips again, and he slipped between her legs, the head catching and dragging against her there. His mouth moved to her neck, and she felt the sting of his teeth followed by a harsh intake of breath when she tipped her hips again, accepting him into her body.

"Fuck, Hope," he ground out, "feels so fucking good."

They moved together, apart, then back together, Hope reaching up to cup the back of Hoss' neck, holding his mouth to her neck and shoulder. She lifted her leg, rocking backwards slightly, draping her knee across his hip, and he groaned as he slid deeper inside. "Love you," he said, the words muffled against her neck.

"I love you," she responded, and he grunted, sliding slowly in and out. "So much, Hoss. You've made my life so full of love, of living. Filled it right up, full to the top. Can't imagine my life without you, baby. It's like I was sleepwalking and you woke me up, shook me up."

She cupped her hand over his again, slowly sliding it down her body, pausing when both their palms were over their daughter inside her belly. "You gave me this, which I didn't know I wanted, needed, but I did. You made me fall in love with you, and I'm so glad, baby."

His mouth pressed against her neck, he said, "Gray. That was all I could see most of the time, before you. Precious few splashes of color, and I'd try so fucking hard to capture those moments and hold onto them, because they were so rare. Now, everything is in color. My whole life is shaded in brilliance, because of you."

Pushing his hand farther down, threading her fingers through his as she placed their hands between her legs, she said, "Faith Inez."

He stilled, pressed deep inside her, and she felt his body shake, knowing it was with laughter. She lost the heat of his mouth and he asked, "Mama, you just name our little girl?"

She nodded, twisting her head and opening her eyes to look up at him, smiling because, even with his laughter, he had wet in his. "Faith, because...well, I think that one is self-explanatory. Inez means pure, and she is the product of a love so pure and right it fills me up every day, Isaiah. Faith Inez Rogers."

***

"Hoss, hold up, man," he heard and swung around to look back into the clubhouse main room. Mason stood in the office doorway. Frustrated, because he was about to head home, he blew out a hard breath and then moved back towards his friend.

"Yeah, boss?" Eyes fixed on Mason, he didn't care if his restlessness to be gone from here was evident. He wanted to get home to Hope, check on her, and make sure everything was okay. They were only four days from her due date, and with every hour ticking past, his anxiety ratcheted higher.

"Give me fifteen. Put a timer on it if you need to, but give me fifteen." Mason moved back, and Hoss jerked to see the men gathered in the room.

"The fuck did these guys come from?" he asked with a grin, walking in and clasping wrists and hands with each man in turn. "Seriously," he turned to look at Mason, pulling free from Duck's hug, "I pissed for like a minute. Did you have them stashed underneath the fucking desk when we were in here talking inventory?"

Fury, Watcher, and Bones all laughed at that, and a low rumble came from Duck. Lifting his chin, he greeted the other man in the room a little less enthusiastically. "Pike, how you doin'?"

Mason interrupted, "Talk to us about Memphis."

"Fuck, boss," he groaned. "If you want a recount of that shit storm, it'll take a lot longer than fifteen minutes."

Mason looked grim as he said, "High points, brother. Just hit the high points."

He nodded and, looking around, selected a seat at the end of the desk, leaning his elbows on the flat surface. Palms scrubbing at his face, he took a minute to compose his thoughts, hearing the men in the room settling into chairs and on sofas, recognized the snick of the latch in the frame as the door shut. Without opening his eyes, he cleared his throat and began.

"Memphis has been a problem since day one. My opinion, I still think we should close the fucking chapter, rolling the boys into Little Rock. Mob and bangers have a chokehold on that city in a way what makes it hard to keep our shit straight from theirs. Corruption as old as the south breeds in the streets and alleyways there." Opening his eyes, he gazed down at the desktop for a moment.

"We found Lalo had been circling our house there, taking over territory until he literally started to choke us out." He gestured towards Fury, standing in a casual lean on the opposite side of the room. "Our brother gave us the info; Mason sent me on a hunting trip. In the time between gaining the knowledge and my run, things had gone to hell in a hand basket. So much worse than expected, it took three weeks to sort that shit.

"Sitdown after fucking sitdown, I listened to the gripes and complaints of clubs from Arkansas, Mississippi, Tennessee—even fucking Texas clubs came to the table. Respect paid on both sides, I laid the foundation for further friendly negotiations with several clubs. Meanwhile"—he lifted his head and gazed around the room—"Lalo was having his own meetings." His eyes stopped on Slate and noted the expected jerking response when he continued, "Ling was his primary contact, biggest dealer in town, ran shit straight out of his place on Beale."

Slate spoke up, "I've had dealings with Ling. He's a brutal motherfucker. He and Lalo should have made good bedfellows."

Nodding, Hoss said, "Yeah, you'd think, right?" Shaking his head, he said, "You'd be wrong. Ling was too hard even for Lalo to stomach, and they had a...disagreement." Pike made a noise, and Hoss swung his gaze that direction with a nod. "Yeah, Pike. You know about this part, don'tcha."

With a sigh, Pike strode forward a single step. "Is this about Memphis, or St. Louis?"

Mason growled, "Memphis, motherfucker. Now shut the fuck up. Ain't everything about you." Chastened, Pike stepped backwards, putting his shoulders to the wall.

Hoss shook his head, looking around the table again. "I'm guessing since Watch and Bones are both here, this is about Diamante's recent losses. Lalo gave up Memphis, but he left a fucking void. He vacated, pulled out within about twelve hours of giving the order. Fucking imbalance of power, we couldn't let it tip to Ling or he would've fucking owned the town."

He scrubbed at his face, hearing the screaming, pleading voices of men already dead for months. With those memories, it wasn't hard to imagine the wails of children for their fathers, women for their men. "We partnered with the reformed Outriders in Lexington, Freed Riders of Texas, and a dozen other clubs. Then, with their help, and our intel, we burned Ling's empire to the ground."

"So Lalo pulled up stakes and walked away? No blowback?" Fury's voice was soft, curious.

"Yeah. Found out later he headed towards Virginia first, but then not two weeks later, we heard grapevine reports he got picked up by DEA in Florida. Nothing confirmed, and you boys all know if it could be found in a national database, Myron would find out the shit.

He shook his head and twisted to look at Mason. "We sharing everything, boss?" At his nod, he shifted in his seat then said, "Last thing we truly know about Lalo was an intercepted email to Deacon acknowledging receipt of a package sent from Cali. We don't know what the package was, who it was...but the assumption is Lalo was given someone to mentor.

"And that's it. There are details Myron or I can provide about the numbers and businesses in Memphis, but those inter-club interactions are the most important parts. We now have good relations with a dozen clubs where there was no personal knowledge before, people we can call on in a pinch. We fucked Lalo's play with Ling and rid the beautiful town of Memphis of a blight that was poisoning it for decades." He stood, pushing back from the table, getting a nod of thanks from Mason for his willingness to stay and participate in this brief meeting. He shook his head. "What we don't know...can't know is what the fallout will be with Diamante."

***

"One more push, Hope," he repeated the doctor's words to her, softly encouraging his exhausted woman. "One more, baby. Time to bring it home. Faith is ready to meet her momma, one more push." He swept her sweaty hair back from her temples for the thousandth time, willing to do it a thousand more.

Since she woke him last night, calling him from the bathroom where her water had broken—sweet-smelling fluid staining her nightgown and making her thighs slick, flooding the tile floor—he had been taking snapshots in his mind. Holding the moments to bring out later, for the rest of his life, to remember what this looked like, what it felt like. It was like falling in love all over again, his stomach twisting with fear and giddiness.

"One more push, baby," he said, seeing the look of determination edging into her features, knowing another contraction was making its presence known. He shifted, gripping her hand and wrist, giving her a strong anchor to lever her body up with.

Their eyes caught, gazes locking as she pulled her torso up off the bed, shoulders bending and curling. She nodded and then took a deep breath, bearing down as he and the labor nurse started counting. Halfway through he saw the look on her face change, her eyes rounded in surprise at the different sensation, and he heard the doctor say, "Stop pushing, Hope. Relax a second. Let's get her shoulders out slow and easy."

Glancing back towards the doc, he couldn't see anything around the man's head and shoulders wedged high between his woman's thighs, so he turned back to look at Hope. She had slumped back to the bed, trying hard to blink back tears, and then he saw her eyes go round again. Her head lifted and jerked to look down her body at the sound that started small, squeaking and hitching after every tiny breath, and then grew to fill the room. She looked up at him and he smiled. "Sounds like love," he said, and she threw one arm around his neck, pulling him down for a sobbing, open-mouthed kiss.

***

"Prez," he said with a grin, swinging his legs off Hope's bed to stand, reaching out to pull Mason into a one-armed clinch. "Welcome, brother." He had been stretched out beside her, watching her doze in and out, resting in between feedings as best she could.

"Brother," Mason greeted him with a grin, thumping him on the back.

Hoss looked past his friend and, seeing he was alone, asked, "No Willa today?"

"Naw," he stepped back, "she's home with Garrett. Boy's got colic in the worst way. Hasn't stopped crying for nearly three weeks." He grimaced. "She's handling it better'n me. I told her this morning I needed a run and she laughed, holding my boy close to her shoulder, him squallin' hard and loud. Told me go on, let the wind blow my head straight."

"Shit, brother," he said, wincing in sympathy. "That sucks."

"Yeah, but he'll settle out and we'll get on with things." Mason shrugged, stepping around Hoss towards the bed. Softly he asked, "Little Momma, how you doin'?" He held out his hand and Hope reached up, gripping tightly as she smiled.

"Good, really good," she said, and then sniffed. "Interesting cologne choice, Mason," she remarked with a laugh, and he frowned and then shook his head. She asked, a proud smile on her face, "Did you see Faith?" He shook his head again, and she turned to look at Hoss. "Honey, walk him down. Get out of here for a few minutes; go show off our daughter."

"What's your girl's name?" Mason asked, leaning down to brush his lips in a tender kiss across Hope's forehead.

"Faith Inez," Hoss said with a grin.

"Good name," Mason agreed. "Come on and show me my boy's potential old lady." That dragged a loud laugh from Hope, who shook her head. "What?" Mason feigned surprise then laughed softly. "Can't fault me for wanting to keep my family together, can you? I'm just looking ahead, makin' plans."

Shaking her head again, she shifted to her side, putting one hand under her cheek. "Goofballs, the both of you."

Walking down the hallway, Hoss was surprised to see there was a large gathering of men near the nursery windows. Shaking his head, he asked, "You bring the whole club, Prez?"

"Naw," Mason said with a chuckle as they reached the group and Hoss was surrounded by their brothers, their family, congratulations ringing through the air as friendly hands pounded his shoulders and back. "There's another hundred at the clubhouse impatiently waiting their turn."

26. What she showed me

"Ready for a stroll, baby?" he asked, leaning down to kiss her forehead. "Doc said walking is good. Let's have a slow stroll, go gather up our daughter, and bring her back to the room for the night."

She sighed and stretched, winding her arms around his neck and pulling him down for a kiss, pressing her lips firmly against his for a moment. "Sammy's still coming later, right? Mercy and Deke are going to bring him?" She swung her legs to the side, sliding out of bed and standing next to him, swaying for a moment as she laughed, grabbing at the rail on the bed.

"Yeah, Sam will be here in an hour or so. When he called, Deke said they're feeding him first." Hoss reached out to steady her, hand on her hip, while she shrugged on her robe, tying it loosely in front.

Looping her arm through his, she said, "I could use a bottle of water. I hate the smell of the city water." She flicked her finger against the pitcher standing on the rolling table. "Weirdest thing, I've been smelling oranges all day, but the water here still stinks."

Hoss grinned, wrapping his fingers around her hand, pulling her close for a quick kiss. "Love you, Mama," he said softly as they moved into the hallway.

"Love you so much, Isaiah," she told him. "Love of my life. I don't know what I did that deserved to find you at the end of my trip from Alabama, but I've thanked my lucky stars every day that I did. Me and Sammy, we needed love like you've shown us." Her voice sounded thick and, because he knew she hated for him to see her cry, he kept his eyes fixed on the window at the end of the hallway.

"Do you smell that?" She asked this loudly, finally drawing his attention down to her face, and sudden fear clenched hard in his chest, his heart stuttering to a halt as he saw one of her eyes was almost entirely black. "Oranges," she slurred. Her suddenly rigid grip was dragging at his arm, and as if in slow motion, he saw her knees beginning to buckle.

He reached out, grabbing and holding her upright as her body sagged backwards over his arms. He remembered the first time he got her back, the day she fainted and he was barely able to stop her from falling. This felt different; her body was loose and lax in a way that wasn't natural. This wasn't a faint.

Shouting came from behind him, the pounding of running feet, but all he could do was stare at her face as her eyelids closed, covering the sight of both eyes now black, pupils fully blown. Her form had gone limp, hanging heavy from his arms, trying to slide from his grasp, mouth open and unbreathing. Sinking to the floor with her in his arms, he saw the boots of his brothers surrounding them, felt their hands trying to take her from him. Then, as if from a distance, felt the sobs racking his body when they succeeded, his arms suddenly as brutally empty as his chest.

Kneeling on the hard floor of the hospital hallway, he rocked backwards over his heels, tilting his face to the ceiling as he gave voice to the grief ripping through him, because he knew what had happened. Felt the difference in her body when she left him. He flashed to a remembered image of Ruby, pale and still on a basement floor and knew, unlike Slate and his woman, there would be no miraculous intervention for him and Hope. From the pain in his chest, the shaking of his hands, and the rawness in his throat...he knew she was gone.

***

Gaze fixed on the floor between his boots, he felt numb, removed from everything happening around him. They had seated Hope's doc in a chair across from him and the man was leaning forward, head in his hands and not trying to hide his own grief behind a professional face. Hoss felt a hard hand grip his shoulder, pulling him sideways into a body, strong arm around his shoulders holding on tight. Eyes still streaming tears, he looked up at Mason, seeing the anguish twisting his friend's face and knew it reflected the pain on his own. He turned his head, burying his face into Mason's stomach, wrapping his arms around him.

The medical phrases circled around in his head, but he didn't give a shit about knowing the why. Knowing the words like cerebral cavernous malformation didn't change the fact Hope was gone. Understanding this wasn't anything they could have foreseen, or even likely fixed if the docs had known about it, didn't matter. None of it mattered, not really. He had noted the part about genetics, knew it was something he would have to revisit at some point, but that wouldn't be today. Today he was just trying to keep sucking in air, one anguish-filled breath at a time.

Muffled and small, he heard himself ask, "What the fuck am I supposed to do now, brother?"

Wordlessly, Mason's grip tightened, holding on, holding him in place, holding him together. He heard the doc get up and leave, heard other footsteps come into the room. He felt other arms circling his shoulders, hands resting on his head as he sobbed, unashamed of his grief, because—as fierce as it was—it didn't hold a candle to the love he had for Hope. That's what he held onto, the idea that his love for her was bigger than anything else; it had to be. Her last words to him came back, and he wasn't aware he was repeating them aloud until he heard Mason's tortured voice say, "*Brother.*"

Hoss pulled back, looking up, finding it hard to focus through his tears. "She said I was the love of her life. Said she didn't know what she'd done to deserve my love, said she needed me. Sammy needed me. Mason," his voice broke again, "what the fuck am I supposed to do?"

He watched as Mason fought for control over his emotions, the struggle playing out across his face. Before he could speak, however, Hoss heard an unexpected voice, one he hadn't heard in far too long, and he turned to look at Tugboat walking into the room, the sea of black leather-clad men moving out of his way. "You go on."

Tug and Bear's mother, Maggie, had been away for months on a trip to California, and Hoss' breath caught at the knowledge they would never get to meet Hope. *Fuck*, he thought, as awareness ripped through him that his parents never met her. "You go on, son. You figure it out every day when you set your feet on the floor beside your bed, and you thank God for it every night when your knees hit that same floor."

Tug kept speaking as Hoss pushed to his feet, the hands of his brothers still touching him, supporting him, wordlessly telling him they were there, they had his back, and they would do anything he needed. All he had to do was put words to anything, and they would break their backs for him. "You make a life for your boy and your baby girl. One that honors the life of their mother. One that honors the love she had for you. That gift she gave you. Let that love take root inside you and grow until it's all anyone can see. That love you shared with her? You gotta let it shine, brother. Her love will tell you what you need; just let it talk to you."

Behind Tug, he saw the hallway door open and the doc walked back in. From the tender care in his posture, Hoss didn't have to ask to know he had brought Faith back with him. Being in the same room with her made the air electric, and he stared at Tug. That energy filled him up, and he suddenly got it. He understood what Tug was telling him, speaking with the wisdom of loss, and love.

Soft and quiet, Hoss said, "Love them like she'd want to be loved, like she would love them." He paused for a moment, the drying tears on his face making his skin feel uncomfortable, too tight. Smiling used muscles he felt would break before stretching, but instead shattered the feeling, freeing a bit of joy in its place. He said, conviction rich in his voice, "Like she loved me."

Tug nodded, turned and took Hoss' baby from the doc, cradled her to his chest, and looked down at her. He gently pushed the blanket back from her face and whispered soft words, making sweet nonsense noises to the child in his arms. Precious. *Loved*. Watching his friend with his infant daughter, Hoss' heart swelled with emotion. His voice stronger now, more certain, he said, "With every fiber of my being. Love them."

Stepping over beside Tug, he reached out a hand, cupping the back of Faith's head, conscious of the delicateness of her skull, of how tiny she was. Newly born, fragile and precious. He found himself overwhelmed by the terrifying knowledge she was totally dependent on him. Just him. She was his.

"She's gorgeous, Hoss. Most beautiful little girl I've ever seen," Tug said, lifting her and placing her in Hoss' arms so he had to take her. He had held her earlier, walked her to and from the nursery, rocked her to sleep after Hope fed her. This was different, felt different because this time it was with the knowledge that Faith needed him to take on both roles. He accepted the burden, feeling the weight on his shoulders ease minutely as he held her close, protectively.

Nodding, he didn't raise his gaze from his daughter's face as he fell in love all over again.

27. Inspired

Seated in the hospital chapel, Hoss told Sammy, hand on his bowed head, "Son, sometimes we have to accept we won't ever know. This is one of those times. We can't know, won't know, so you gotta let that question go. Everything happens for a reason, and I believe meeting Mama was fated for me. Because it brought me you, and now Faith."

He smiled through his own tears, cupping his palm behind Sammy's neck and giving him a squeeze. "I got Hope, and then I got you. And, in all of that beauty that is our family, I got Faith, and I got love. Why don't we head up those stairs and go see your sister, yeah? Let's go say hello."

Sam lurched sideways, plastering himself to Hoss' side, and he wrapped his arms around his boy. Sam hadn't spoken beyond asking what had happened and why, and Hoss didn't know what was going through his head. With a sense of déjà vu, he thought, *How in the fuck do people do this? How do they parent through something this profound and damaging? When the potential for screwing things up is so high, how do I make sure he comes out the other end safe and sane, whole and good?*

"She loves you so much, Sammy," he whispered, pressing his lips to the boy's head. "You know one of the things about you I respected from one of the very first times I saw you? We were in Aunt Mercy's kitchen and you got up in my face, because you said I made Mama cry. Told me if I wanted to be her friend, then I had to mend my ways. I had to work for it."

He swallowed hard and then said, "You were right, every time you told me how to be with Mama. From that first day until here, when you told me something, I listened to it, because most often, you were right. And you were right, because you love. With everything inside you, you love. Love her, love your Aunt Mercy, love Jonny and Kane, and love Bingo. Then you loved me, and I realized being inside that love was a hundred million times better than seeing it from the outside, and I knew what kept the smile on her face all the time. Your love."

Sam's body jolted and jerked as the sobs tore out of him, and all Hoss could do was hold him, trying to give him back one tenth of what this boy had given him. "I ain't going anywhere, son. You take all the time you need. We'll go only when you're ready."

"And if"—Sam sobbed, breaths sounding painful—"I'm not ever..." He couldn't continue, hard hiccups racking him, and Hoss was reminded of times past when Sam cried himself to sleep in Mercy's lap or when he cried until he was exhausted sitting beside Hoss. *Love that deep*, he thought, *brings risk, but look at the reward when you find the ones worth it all, worth everything.*

"Teaching me another lesson sitting right here, Sammy," he shared. "You're hurting, son. I know it; I hear it. Son, I feel it in every line of your little body. Your love is huge, so big. Only a love that big could hurt like this. Your momma knew how you loved, knew you loved her huge." He paused, sorting his words out before he let them loose. "Knew you'd love Faith like that, do your job."

"My job?" Sam's voice was still breaking, but he got this out, the question clear.

"Only the most important one." He repeated Sam's words from nearly a year ago back to him, and knew he recognized the phrase, because he went still under Hoss' hands. "You remember what you told me?"

Sam nodded, and then pulled back, looking up into his face, eyes bruised with sorrow, cheeks shining with the wet still streaming down them. "We gotta keep our best girls safe."

He brushed those tears from Sam's cheeks. "Faith is our best girl." Sam nodded again, sniffing hard. Hoss pulled a wad of tissues from the box nearby and handed them to the boy. "Blow your schnozzle, son." He took a deep breath, desperately wishing Hope were beside him, trying not to imagine she would be there when they went up the hallway. "Let me know when you're ready." Leaning back, he looped one arm around Sam's shoulders, tipping his head up to stare at the ceiling, trying to hold his own shit together so he could help his son.

***

Two weeks, he thought with a sigh.

Coming home from the hospital to find all the places she had made her mark in their home were still there, bittersweet with equal measures of pain and joy. Two weeks of continually stumbling over things that tore the wound in his chest wide open again. "Miss you, baby," he whispered into the air of the nursery, careful to keep his voice soft so Faith didn't wake.

Mercy had stayed with them the first couple of days, until after the service. She, Sharon, and Willa had made sure they came home from the hospital to a house filled with friends and the things a brand new baby needed. Hoss had watched the revolving door of keepers, everyone giving, no one demanding anything from him or Sammy that they couldn't offer. Not conversation or time. Just being there in case they were needed, giving the two of them space to mourn, space to come to terms with what had happened...was happening.

Jerry had driven up with his wife and kids, Mom and Pop flying in the next day. Seeing his mother holding Faith had torn him up. He had to excuse himself from the room more than once when she talked about how the baby looked like him, because he saw only Hope in their baby girl's face. Wanted more than anything for her to look like her momma, prayed her blonde hair never darkened, that it would look like Hope's, shining white and yellow in the sun.

Moments like that were the hardest, because he couldn't even find the words to tell what he was thinking, just kept everything locked up inside, trying to make sense of it all in his head. *Gray.*

He and his mother had words more than once. Because, as loving as she was, she didn't know Hope, didn't know what she would want for her daughter. Sure didn't know what Hope would want for her son, so when his mother tried to convince him to let Sammy see Hope in the casket the night before the memorial service, he nearly lost his shit.

Thank God, Jerry stepped in when he did, guiding their mother over to sit on the couch across the room. There was no fucking way he would let that be Sammy's last memory of his mother. If Hoss could have erased the vision from his own memory, he would gladly have done so, because the shell that lay in that fucking box was as far from Hope as white was from black.

His Hope overflowed with light and beauty. Seeing her body lying in the satin-lined casket, hands carefully folded, tamed hair braided and drawn over one shoulder, he knew without a doubt she was gone; he had indeed seen her light go out that day in the hospital hallway. After that, he had no dreams she was coming back, that she would walk back in through the front door. She was gone.

Preacher, the same Rebel who had married them, buried Hope. When the old man's voice gave out partway through, Tug stepped up beside him, hand on his shoulder, steadying him and taking over until Preach could continue.

The day after the service, his family returned to Alabama, and he nicely but firmly put Mercy out, too. It was time for him and his kids to figure out what kind of family they were now, in their little unit of three. That was also the day he went back into his studio for the first time, standing in the large room.

Turning in a circle, staring at the tables and easels, he felt as if he didn't know what they were anymore. Saw no place for them in his life. Painting was synonymous with love and happiness for him, and at that moment, he couldn't see his way back to those emotions again.

Up every two hours with Faith, he gained admiration for Hope with every feeding, every diaper change, because she had done this with Sammy. He wasn't arrogant enough to think it was the same, because as he had told her about the pregnancy, everything was different when you had people to count on. Before him, before she met Mercy, she had no one to lean on, and he knew he had a thousand brothers he could call. So different, but as he looked down at his daughter sleeping in his arms, it still felt the same. Because Hope was gone.

Closing his eyes, he called up the memory of them laying crossways on their bed, him showing her the first painting she inspired and her stunned reaction that anyone, even him, would see beauty like that inside her.

"I love you, baby," he whispered, and his mind supplied her voice telling him, *I love you, too. I love our daughter, Isaiah. Make sure she knows that.* He felt the ghost of a touch on his arm, looked down to see the skin raised in gooseflesh.

He took a breath, finding it a little easier than yesterday, and leaned in to kiss Faith's head. "Mama loves you, baby girl," he whispered, filing the memory of his blue-eyed daughter's pink cupid bow lips away like a snapshot.

***

Crawling up into Mom's lap, he laid his head on her shoulder, feeling her warm arms wrap securely around him. "You so got this, Sammy," she whispered, her lips pressed against the side of his head. Safe. Loved.

"I love you, Mommy," he said, his eight-year-old voice steady and sure. "I take care of our best girl and love her, too. Pinky promise."

"You love Hossman, too, right?" She squeezed him tight. Loved.

"Hossman…Dadman." He grinned when she giggled happily, filling the space around them with bubbles of hilarity and joy.

Thirteen-year-old Sammy woke slowly, letting himself stay wrapped in the warm feelings from the dream as long as possible. *Loved.* Hearing someone in the hallway, his eyes popped open while he waited. After what seemed like an hours-long hesitation, knuckles rapped softly on his door as his father called, "Sammy, you up, son?"

"Yeah, Dad. I'm awake," he responded, feeling a swell of pleasure at their simple exchange. "Faynez up yet? She got the first day of preschool jitters?" He grinned, waiting for the reaction to his favorite nickname for his little sister, combining her two names into something that sounded so southern it could be a real name, Faith Inez…Faynez.

The door opened and his dad's head stuck in, a broad grin on his face. "She's going to hate you if the kids call her that, you know."

"I know," he said with an answering grin. As his dad started to turn and walk away, he called, "Dad?"

"Yeah?" Pausing in the action of closing the door, Dad turned his head, looking back at him.

"I dreamed about her again," he said softly and saw the gentle smile break across his father's face. "It was good."

"I'm glad, Sam. You hold onto that, son. Both hands, you hold onto that." He walked into the room, sitting on the edge of the bed. "She loves you so much, you know?"

"I know she does," he said, loving the fact his dad always talked about his mother's love in the present tense, keeping her alive for him. "She told me I had this."

With a laugh, Dad reached out and pulled him into a hug. "She's right; you *so* do."

Loved.

Epilogue

"You'll get it, Samboni," he heard and grinned, looking at Jonny through the visor on his close-fitting helmet. Gliding to his position, he watched as Jonny bent over, head angled up, eyes focused intently on his opponent across the circle. "Don't matter you're my brother, Sugar Kane," Jonny said, shifting on his blades to get a better purchase. "You're going down."

Kane silently glared at him then twisted to look at Sam, giving him a nod of greeting. Then his gaze flicked back to center as the linesman spoke, giving them their instructions. Neither man changed position nor acknowledged the words from the official, their focus entirely on the referee's hand, waiting for the movement that would signal the start of the game.

Just before the puck dropped, Sam's eyes went to the box across from the pressroom. There, hands on the rail, bodies bent in identical postures of attention, he saw his father and his sister, here to watch Kane's first professional start in a hockey game.

As Dad had taught him, he shuffled rapidly through the slices of memories his father called snapshots, finding the one he wanted and bringing it to the front of his mind.

Five years ago, wearing a suit jacket he knew needed to have the shoulders let out again, because he was growing that fast, he stood against a wall in a gallery, watching his father receive the accolades earned through hard work and dedication.

In his first showing since before Sam came into his life, Isaiah Rogers' artwork was on display, but not for sale. He had made that clear to the agent, ignoring her arguments about the value of the paintings, because he didn't care about the money. Dad had talked to him about this for weeks before signing the contracts for the showing. Worked to make sure Sam was okay and understood why he wanted these paintings to remain privately owned. Because they were his memories of Hope, and precious to them both.

Faith had been eight and overwhelmed, plucking at seams on the dress Aunt Mercy and Aunt DeeDee helped her buy. First, overwhelmed by the dress itself, because it was far more girly than the jeans and sweats she most often wore. Then, even more overwhelmed when Dad put one of Mom's necklaces around her neck, shifting her long blonde hair out of the way and wordlessly kissing the side of her head when she reached up to stroke the cameo pendant.

Leaning against the gallery wall beside him, surrounded by the images documenting the love their father had for their mother, he knew her eyes were still on him instead of the paintings when she asked softly, "Tell me the story again?"

Pressing his bottom lip tight against his teeth, he made a face at her and then nodded with a grin. He loved this story as much as she did, and telling it was a way to keep it fresh in his mind. A way to ensure he didn't lose any part of Mom.

"We were on our way up here from Birmingham, and when we pulled into the parking lot of the place Aunt Mercy worked, Mom was laughing at something I said. She got out of the car and stood there for a second, then turned around and bent down, looking back into the car. She smiled

and told me, "Come on, Sammy boy. I got a really good feeling about this. Hop out, bud. Welcome home. Let's go meet our future."

Faith spoke up, because she had heard the story so many times she could have told it as well as he did, but she never tried to take over where Mom was speaking, because she didn't have any memories of their mother other than the ones he and Dad had tried to instill. She knew him inside and out, though, so she spoke over his voice, saying his words along with him, asking the question, "Are we home now, Mommy?"

He grinned, pointed over to where Dad stood talking to Uncle Mason, and said, "And then Daddy talked for the first time, and she said he sounded like home. So, I knew we were."

"That's a lovely story." The soft voice came from beside them and Sam turned to see a woman looking at Faith and him with a gentle smile. She made a small gesture with her hand, indicating the gallery and said, "Your mother is the inspiration for all this beauty?" He nodded and she looked away, her gaze glancing across the pictures before her eyes settled on the piece next to him, one showing a couple standing in a rainstorm, clothes plastered to their bodies, foreheads pressed together, in their close embrace oblivious to the tumult going on around them. An island of stillness and love. The nameplate on the wall beneath it giving the title as, Hush, baby. "Your father's a lucky man."

Faith's voice was small when she said, "Mom died."

The woman sucked in a painful sounding breath, but then after a moment, instead of the normal platitudes the kids had heard over the years, she said, "That had to be a profound loss for all of you. But, he had this for a time. Look at all the love." She repeated, "Your father's a lucky man."

Focus snapping back to the ice when he heard the shouts and grunts from the battle over the puck, he narrowed his eyes, watching the action closely. Seeing the pass, and then accepting the snap of the puck right on the sweet spot, where the tape covered the blade of his stick, he took off, legs powering through the first strides, stick working the puck back and forth easily, skating into the future.

The End (of this story)

MariaLisa deMora

THANK YOU FOR READING *HOSS*!

Thank you for reading *Hoss*, book #7 in the **Rebel Wayfarers MC** series. This book, more than any other, was a struggle to get onto the page in a way that made sense to the characters. The main female character has lived in poverty with her young son for years, separated from the support of her family by circumstances, desperate and in need. Alone. Like many single parents, she works hard to make certain her little family of two stays sheltered, fed, and most importantly, together.

Homelessness is a real issue in the U.S., as well as other countries around the globe. In the U.S., families make up about thirty-five percent of the total sheltered homeless population. Most are single-parent families headed by women, making up more than eighty percent of all sheltered homeless families. At least sixty percent of sheltered homeless women have children, but only sixty-five percent live with at least one of them. Families broken.

Please note the use of the word *"sheltered"* in those statistics, because these are the ones we know about. The ones who are lucky enough to find safe beds, warm meals, and helping hands. These figures do not count the most vulnerable families, the ones separated from society, subject to predators, and living in tent cities, automobiles, motels, or on the street.

More than four million single parent families in America were homeless in 2013. All studies indicate that figure has only grown in the intervening years. In large urban areas the evidence is painfully present on the street and asleep on park benches or in doorways every day, but even small rural towns are not exempt as families struggle with finances, health issues, job loss, or any combination of the three. In one place in this book, Hoss tells Mason that Hope had been living hand-to-mouth, not even paycheck-to-paycheck, and for too many families this is true. Homelessness can be just one financial misstep away. Their real life.

Resources can be difficult to track down when you don't have stable housing, which opens the door, giving us all a chance to help, even if we cannot afford to assist monetarily. Simply being familiar with the opportunities in your area can allow you to become that desperately needed alternative resource.

For someone struggling to keep their family together, to lift themselves up and keep from drowning under the weight of it all, seeing your outstretched giving, helping hand can mean so much. Take a moment and become that supportive shoulder, give yourself a chance to hold out that caring hand. It can matter more than you might ever know. We're all in this together, trying to make our way as best we can. Help make that process a little easier for someone. Become the brother, sister, or friend they didn't know they had.

For more information about homelessness in your region of the U.S., and to find resources to help combat it, please check out the following resources:

Child Care Aware
800-424-2246
www.childcareaware.org

Health Care for the Homeless Clinics
www.bphc.hrsa.gov/hchirc/directory/

Homelessness Resource Center
Email: HomelessPrograms@samhsa.hhs.gov
www.homeless.samhsa.gov

The National Center of Family Homelessness
Email: info@familyhomelessness.org
www.familyhomelessness.org

National Center for Homeless Education
www.serve.org/nche

United States Interagency Council on Homelessness
202-708-4663
www.usich.gov

United Way's First Call for Help
Dial 211 from any phone
www.211.org

HOSS' PLAYLIST

I put together YouTube playlists of music both mentioned in the book, and used during writing and editing. Want a peek into the mind of me? Be sure of your decision, it's not always normal here!

Hoss' playlist: bit.ly/hoss-playlist

ABOUT THE AUTHOR

Raised in the south, MariaLisa learned about the magic of books at an early age. Every summer, she would spend hours in the local library, devouring books of every genre. Self-described as a book-a-holic, she says "I've always loved to read, but then I discovered writing, and found I adored that, too. For reading...if nothing else is available, I've been known to read the back of the cereal box."

Also by MariaLisa deMora

Alace Sweets

A dark thriller, this book is not a light read. Filled with edge-of-your-seat suspense, this intense story commands the reader's attention as it drives towards the explosive ending. Alace Sweets is a vigilante serial killer, with everything that implies and is sure to trip all your triggers. Be ready.

At seventeen, Alace Sweets turned a corner in her life, taking the wrong shortcut home from school.

Resisting the harsh knowledge her attackers will never be made to pay for their actions, Alace takes a stand. Justice must be served, and if fate's scales are out of balance, she's determined to set things right as best she can.

When the laws of men fail, the rules of Alace prevail.

5-Star Reviews for Alace Sweets

"deMora has a superb story-line and exceptional character development. All of her characters have such depth that will intrigue the reader..."
~Turning Another Page

"Hot, sweet, dark thriller."
~Beth D

"It will keep you on the edge of your seat and give you chills."
~Escape Reality Book Blog

"Disturbing, haunting, sickly; yet hot, sexy and heart racing!"
~Amanda L

"From the first page [deMora] pulls you into the world she has created and you do not even try to escape..."
~Little Shop of Readers Blog

"A must read for all those dark, gritty romance fans out there."
~Sweet & Spicy Reads

"You will find yourself so drawn into the story that the outside world is blocked out and your locking the doors and turning on all the lights."
~Danena F

"Don't judge me for bonding with a vigilante serial killer, she's more than what she does."
~iScream Books

"Thrilling...chilling...full of suspense, nail biting edge of your seat excitement."
~Tracey H

"Every time MariaLisa deMora picks up her pen (or opens her computer), she creates characters you want to believe in."
~Gail S

"Intriguing dark storyline, beautiful love story and nail-biting conclusion, what more could a reader ask for?"
~Manda M

"This book takes you a dark and twisted ride that is gripping..."
~Renee Entress' Blog

"This book is dark and gritty and I literally had to take a day off from reading it because it's that intense."
~My Girlfriend's Couch

"This is my favourite book so far from this author ... I recommend this book if you enjoy dark romantic thrillers."
~Cheekypee Reads and Reviews

"There's not enough stars to give this book and 5 just doesn't really do it justice!"
~DeLane C

"I couldn't put this book down from page one! Tried to stop & go to bed but couldn't sleep thinking about Alace and got up & finished the book."
~Debbie M

"MariaLisa DeMora, wordsmith that she is, made this a story of the enlightenment of a woman and finding love in a life where she has had none."
~Kat W

"Whatever deep dark trench [deMora] pulled a character like Alace from should be revisited again and often."
~Confessions of a Serial Reader

ADDITIONAL SERIES AND BOOKS

Please note that books in a series frequently feature characters from additional books within that series. If series books are read out of order, readers will twig to spoilers for the other books, so going back to read the skipped titles won't have the same angsty reveals.

Rebel Wayfarers MC series:

Mica, #1
A Sweet & Merry Christmas, short story #1.5
Slate, #2
Bear, #3
Jase, #4
Gunny, #5
Mason, #6
Hoss, #7
Harddrive Holidays, short story #7.5
Duck, #8
Biker Chick Campout, short story #8.5
Watcher, #9

A Kiss to Keep You, novella #9.25
Gun Totin' Annie, short story #9.5
Secret Santa, short story #9.75
Bones, #10
Gunny's Pups, novella #10.25
Never Settle, short story #10.5
Not Even A Mouse, short story #10.75
Fury, #11
Christmas Doings, #11.25
Gypsy's Lady, #11.5
Cassie, #12
Road Runner's Ride, novella #12.5

Occupy Yourself band series:

Born Into Trouble, #1
Grace In Motion, #2 (TBD)
What They Say, #3 (TBD)

Neither This, Nor That series:

This Is the Route Of Twisted Pain, #1
Treading the Traitor's Path: Out Bad, #2
Trapped by Fate on Reckless Roads, #3 (TBD)

Other Books:

With My Whole Heart
Alace Sweets
Hard Focus

More information available at mldemora.com.